An ass kicking...

Could one actually smell it when it was upon them? Cuz her nose was twitching with the scent of one.

The thick, acrid smell of a can of whoop ass being popped open

Yup, she was in for a licking. A serious tongue-lashing, and there was no escape. The predator was loose and on the prowl, just waiting to pounce on her with freshly polished nails and hair that shone so bright it made your eyes tear up looking at it.

The hunter?

Kelsey Little.

The hunted?

Tara Douglas.

Tara fought the onslaught of fear and panic that settled in her gut as the pack of Junior Miss America wannabes gathered around behind her in the girl's locker room. The scent of her own perspiration lingered in her nose and her hands trembled as she fought to open her locker, trying to pretend that Kelsey and her crowd of perfectly flawless, rah-rah compadres weren't cackling at her. She tucked the towel tightly between her breasts and popped open her gym locker with a jerk, keeping her back to them and her flushed cheeks hidden in the cool recesses of her locker.

Breathe ... they're just a bunch of stupid girls. That didn't soothe her much. That "bunch of girls" were prettily disguised barracudas, looking to chew up her well-rounded flesh and spit it back out.

Whose Bride Is She Anyway?

By

Dakota Cassidy

Liquid Silver Books
Indianapolis, Indiana

Published By:
Liquid Silver Books
10509 Sedgegrass Dr.
Indianapolis, IN 46235

Liquid Silver Books publishes books online and in trade paperback. Visit our site at http://www.liquidsilverbooks.com

Manufactured in the United States of America

ISBN: 1-59578-238-9

Cover: April Martinez

Whose Bride Is She Anyway?

Dedication

With heartfelt gratitude, this is for Linda and Mike of Liquid Silver Books. Two people who gave me my first shot out of the gate and welcomed me back with open arms after my life had taken one of those crazy turns called disaster. Also, to R. A one-liner snark king, the other half of my brain and the whole of my heart.

Prologue

Evanston High 1992--You want a piece a this?

An ass kicking...

Could one actually smell it when it was upon them? Cuz her nose was twitching with the scent of one.

The thick, acrid smell of a can of whoop ass being popped open

Yup, she was in for a licking. A serious tongue-lashing, and there was no escape. The predator was loose and on the prowl, just waiting to pounce on her with freshly polished nails and hair that shone so bright it made your eyes tear up looking at it.

The hunter?

Kelsey Little.

The hunted?

Tara Douglas.

Tara fought the onslaught of fear and panic that settled in her gut as the pack of Junior Miss America wannabes gathered around behind her in the girl's locker room. The scent of her own perspiration lingered in her nose and her hands trembled as she fought to open her locker, trying to pretend that Kelsey and her crowd of perfectly flawless, rah-rah compadres weren't cackling at her. She tucked the towel tightly between her breasts and popped open her gym locker with a jerk, keeping her back to them and her flushed cheeks hidden in the cool recesses of her locker.

Breathe ... they're just a bunch of stupid girls. That didn't soothe her much. That "bunch of girls" were prettily disguised barracudas, looking to chew up her well-rounded flesh and spit it back out.

"Well, well, look at Tara Douglas, girls. What are you looking for in that locker? More condoms so you can help Jordon *study*?" Kelsey crowed, sarcasm dripping like a melting ice cream cone in the hot summer sun with each venomous word she spat.

Ah, the ever popular Kelsey Little, Tara winced. Captain of the cheerleading squad and head bitch on wheels at Evanston High, doing what she did best ... reign supreme.

She clenched her eyes shut as the small crowd of pom-pom queens twittered at Kelsey's reference to Jordon Sanders, Kelsey's boyfriend, and Tara's *supposed* squeeze.

Yeah, like Jordon Sanders could squeeze anything more than his biceps while admiring himself in a full-length mirror.

Like Tara Douglas could *squeeze* anything that belonged to Kelsey.

She ignored Kelsey's hot breath on her neck and continued to root around in the locker for her underwear and bra. The palm of Kelsey's hand slapped her locker shut with a sharp bang, just missing her fingers. She leaned forward into Tara with imposing menace, so close she almost choked on the smell of Love's Baby Soft perfume. Tara jumped, cringing at the confrontation she knew was about to happen and was helpless to avoid. Her heart raced as impending doom lurked.

Kelsey loved a good show, especially if she had her fellow, brain-sharing goons to egg her on and participate in a little dork bashing.

Feeling none too brave, but just shy of chicken shit, Tara turned to face Kelsey, refusing to give in to the overwhelming need to push her way past the humiliation patrol and run. Kelsey had been belittling her at every turn since she'd began tutoring her stupid jock boyfriend, and she was sick and tired of being the butt of her jokes.

Not to mention--she was sick of her butt being made into a joke.

It was big.

So?

Tara didn't need anyone to openly share that for her in large groups. She had a mirror. It came in double wide, thank you.

Yes, she was overweight--as if it wasn't obvious. Clearly Kelsey didn't opt for the startlingly original when it came to taking potshots. And wait, big surprise, she couldn't wear short skirts or tight jeans. Not if she didn't want rolls of doughy flesh bulging from every available outlet, anyway. Her mother told her she'd grow out of it, but she was almost eighteen and at five foot four, six foot two was looking less and less likely. Growing a foot or so was the only thing that would put her in proportion to her current weight.

Her options were becoming sorely limited according to her tape measure.

And finally, to seal the geek deal, she didn't wield pom-poms and a flaming baton.

Sometimes, for the sheer joy of making Kelsey's brain cells flutter, she just wanted to walk up and stick her face in Kelsey's perfect one and yell, "I'm fat--fat, okay!"

Big deal. What was so special about being skinny anyway?

Tight jeans in a size four... A date every Saturday night ... underwear that didn't look like they belonged to Omar the tentmaker... Being on the cheerleading squad.

Whatever.

Tara tightened her towel and pulled it self consciously over her butt. Kelsey's teeth flashed in a wicked smile of absolute power, knowing she had Tara where she wanted her and reveling in it. Her long blonde hair jiggled as her head bobbed on her neck and she spat, "Tell me something Tara, does Jordon make you swallow?"

A profusion of color swept over Tara's face and the heat of embarrassment lingered on her cheeks, pricking at her flesh.

Swallow what? She bit her lip. Wait, scratch that. Whatever was supposedly being ingested, it couldn't be anything nearly as enjoyable as a plate of fries smothered in ketchup.

She didn't have a clue what in all of hell Kelsey was talking about, but she knew it *had* to be sexual by the gasp of the forbidden everyone made. Fear continued to pulse through her veins, rushing in waves that left her knees weak. Her stomach was doing the Highland fling, and her teeth weren't far from clacking their way out of her mouth, but she fought the fight of the meek anyway. "Get away from me, Kelsey. There's nothing going on between me and Jordon. I tutor him, that's all," managed between tightly clenched teeth.

Oh, God, please don't let me freak out now. Be calm, stay cool, and try not to notice that Kelsey's face is so close to yours you could count the blackheads on her pert, upturned nose.

Kelsey had blackheads? The horror...

They might be mingled with a smattering of freckles, but they were there. Interesting. Popular girls got blackheads too. Maybe not as many as Tara, but a blackhead sighting had occurred and she wasn't feeling nearly as inferior as she and her tube of Clearasil had a minute ago.

Kelsey flicked a stray piece of Tara's hair with her fingers. "Yeah? That's not the rumor I'm hearing. I hear you begged Jordon to screw you and he felt so sorry for you he mercy fucked you for helping him. Jordon told us all just last night at Candice Walker's party, didn't he girls?" A sea of shiny, Pert Plus heads nodded affirmatively, just as Tara expected they would. What else could they do? They were the Stepford cheerleaders, and no cheerleader worth her weight in cartwheels ignored Kelsey when a group opportunity to taunt a defenseless nerd became available.

Well, if what Kelsey said were true, and it wouldn't shock Tara, it only went to show what a dipshit Jordon really was. Who bragged about a mercy fuck to a bunch of girls, *especially* his own girlfriend? In front of *his girlfriends' friends* no less?

Duh.

Jordon was a moron. A waste of perfectly good, functioning grey matter. Sure he was cute, but somehow, frighteningly simple.

Tara stiffened at the implication she'd had anything more than a tutoring session with him. Her response reflected her astonishment, squeaking on its way out, "I did *not* have sex with Jordon. He's not even my type." *He would need to at least have a higher grade point average than my pet rock collection.*

Tara gripped the towel tighter as her legs trembled and Kelsey's green eyes narrowed, boring into hers.

"Your type?" Kelsey screeched her grin of malice widening. "What is your *type*? Do they have types for slobs like you? You slut! Why would he lie about something like that? I guess *fat girls* get off too, huh, Tara? Do you really think Jordon is going to actually take you somewhere in public if you screw him? Like maybe you'll actually get to go to a party with us?"

"We--are--not--*screwing*!" Tara half screamed, panic rising in her throat. "We just study, that's *it.* Now go away. Don't you have to practice pyramid building or something?" Kelsey's pretty face turned ugly at Tara's rebuttal.

Oh, oh, oh ... maybe that might have been a wee bit overboard in the slam department. She swallowed hard, waiting for retribution. *No one* dared crack wise at a cheerleader, especially if the cheerleading wonder of the world was Kelsey Little.

Kelsey suddenly laughed and it wasn't because she found Tara amusing. It rang with the sound of evil. "I'm not going away until you tell the girls and me what you do while you're with Jordon. Admit it, you *fucked* him." The word *fuck* came out of her mouth like sludge from a sewer.

The group of perfect faces that made up the "in crowd" at Evanston High became a blur over Kelsey's shoulder, as Tara's eyes zeroed in on Kelsey's face, only inches from hers. "I--I told you," her voice quivered, to her embarrassment, "We study ... that's all. Jordon ju--just needs help in Trig."

Kelsey twisted a finger around a stray black strand from Tara's ponytail and yanked it. "Do you help him jerk off while he does his algebra?"

Tara might have rolled her eyes if her scalp wasn't pulled so tight any movement at all was impossible. She might even giggle if Kelsey didn't yank it harder, so hard tears came to her eyes. *Algebra had nothing to do with trigonometry, you waste of good oxygen.* Like Kelsey would know anything but the formula for mixing moisturizing creams.

Shit, she wished she had the guts to actually say that. Instead, she opted for the very-effective-thus-far, "Go away, Kelsey! Jordon needs to pass Trig if he wants to graduate. I'm just helping him. Don't you want him to be able take you to the prom?" God, she hated Kelsey Little and she hated her even more because Kelsey was quicker than she was. She hated that she even had to waste time defending herself over something so ridiculous. As Kelsey delivered slam after slam, the side of Tara that shoved those dateless Saturdays and cruel words off into the far recesses of her brain began to emerge like an evil twin who'd been put up for adoption at birth.

Kelsey snorted hard, her nostrils flaring. "I don't want him, not after he's screwed with a porker like *you.*" The pom-pom sextuplets all snickered their agreement. Tara briefly wondered if they all shared the same brain, occasionally renting it out to a cheerleader in need.

Her face was now flaming as everyone laughed over Kelsey's stab at a complete sentence that involved more than "go team, go!" Jerking her head up, she ignored the sting of her scalp and the strands of hair Kelsey lost her grip on as the tendrils pulled free. Her gut burned and for a nanosecond, she saw red. The color represented her last frayed nerve. For every cruel joke Kelsey had made, for each time she walked down a hallway and had to hide behind a corner to avoid her nemesis, it spilled to overflowing and for a mere moment, overwhelmed her. Suddenly, nothing mattered but striking back as hatefully as she could. It didn't matter that she would pay later, at the moment she could see nothing but the person responsible for keeping her from being free to do as she pleased.

Kelsey Little...

Tara's thick tongue finally found movement and a sneer came out of her mouth before she could stop its rapidly gaining momentum. "I guess I can't be *that* much of a porker, can I, Kelsey? Jordon sure didn't scream out *your* name when he was doing *me.*"

The locker room became deadly silent, seething anger permeated the sweaty stench, and for a mere moment Tara was horrified at her words, seeing their faces change from evil glee to mortification. Her gut heaved as the implication of what she'd just spewed sunk in. She wanted to take it back--sort of--and then, as her courage outweighed sanity ... she didn't want to take it back. Not even *sort of.*

Wham! Take that, Barbie!

Ooooh, that was good! Tara silently congratulated her efforts. Whew, where had that kind of rare form of venom come from?

It came from Kelsey taunting her, day-in and day-out, over this stupid tutoring thing with Jordon. Jordon Sanders couldn't sharpen his pencil without studying for it and most sessions he spent talking about how many inches around his thighs were. Doing anything more with Jordon than imagining how hard it must be to have his tiny brain helplessly floating adrift in his head, was just ... well, it just left Tara utterly confounded. Why in the world would Kelsey think she wanted to have sex with Jordon when he couldn't even *think* without breaking into a mental sweat? Tara liked her boys complete with IQs, please.

Why would Jordon say he had sex with her? It was absurd and most likely a lie Kelsey made up so she had a reason to terrorize someone. Did she really need a reason?

The opportunity to find out never presented itself because Kelsey jammed her fingers into the top of the towel wrapped around Tara as her face turned crimson too. The ugly mottled color crept over her neck and her green eyes turned dark emerald. Tara's hands were numb from clinging to keep the flimsy towel in place. Kelsey jerked her forward and she began to lose her desperate grip. Her fingers clenched tighter as she dug her nails into the thin terry cloth; they began to bend painfully while she clung harder. “Listen up, you fat, ugly pig! You better shut up, or you’ll regret it.”

Wow, that was insightful--a huge revelation. As if Tara didn’t regret it already. Her ears burned as Kelsey’s words rang in her ears and her picture perfect friends began to chant, “Fight, fight!”

Tara’s stomach heaved. Kelsey wouldn’t physically fight with her, would she? Nah, she might break a nail or worse still, lose the bounce and behave in her flaxen curls.

But Tara would live to regret how wrong she was as Kelsey dragged her forward, and pairs of hateful hands tore at her towel, twisting and turning her until it was yanked rudely away from her body. Naked, she shivered as the cool air hit her clammy, fear-soaked skin and the towel was left in a puddle at her feet.

The throng of girls half-pulled, half-shoved Tara toward the locker room’s double doors. Hands gripped her roughly, digging into the flesh of her arms and ramming into her back. The heels of Tara’s shoeless feet dug into the concrete flooring as she fought to keep from being thrown out into the hall. It loomed in front of her and she struggled violently to stop the shoving. Screaming until she was hoarse, she begged them to stop as the noise around her became a muted roar and in a matter of seconds, she found herself in the outer hallway, confronted by a gawking bunch of Evanston basketball players.

Completely naked... As in buck...

Tara whirled around, her cheek pressed flush against the door, and began to pound furiously on it. She didn’t know what to do first. Cover her exposed flesh, or try to push her way back in. Shrieks of laughter echoed from behind the firmly shut door, as tears flowed down her face in salty bubbles, falling to her bare feet and splashing on the tiled floor.

Tara pounded harder with her fists against the heavy metal, but to no avail. Rivulets of blood began to seep between her knuckles and her hands throbbed, but she kept hammering on the door, begging.

Vaguely she heard the comments from the crowd of boys as they swirled above her frantic wailing.

"Look at that fat ass," someone yelled with disgust in his tone. "Maybe she's hungry, is it feeding time at the zoo? Hey, want a cheeseburger? Mooooo!"

Tara's world narrowed to the small point of escape the door had become as she hit it repeatedly with her fists. "Please," she sobbed, her mantra hoarse and dry, "please, let me in!"

The shrill sound of a metal whistle pierced the catcalls and taunting. Heavy footsteps scattered, assaulting her ears as they thundered through her head.

The door finally gave way with a deafening creak as Tara fell into it and collapsed on the floor, sobbing. Soothing hands helped her up and guided her to the gym teacher's office, covering her naked body with towels.

Tara couldn't remember much after that but her swollen hands and the clucking concern of her mother as she drove her home and tucked her into her bed. She only remembered staring at her ceiling and praying for death. Her mother assured her only angst riddled teens did that and this too would pass...

She never told a soul who pushed her out of that locker door, because telling would make her not only a bigger geek, but a snitch too. Nor did she give it up when the video tape of her degradation was played at graduation rehearsal. If she thought she'd suffered before the locker room incident, she could never have fully prepared for that video tape to be shown to the whole senior class of Evanston High. She'd forgotten about the video camera in the hall used to monitor any hanky panky between locker rooms. The remainder of her senior days were spent with her head hung low, zipping in and out of classes as fast as she could, repeating the words over and over in her head as she was taunted endlessly. *It doesn't matter, I'll never have to see them again in six months ... four months ... three...*

Thankfully, no mention was made in the yearbook via strict instructions from Principal Clark, but the few who dared labeled it covertly as the "moo incident" in their class memories under their photos.

There were no dates, no size-four jeans, only Tara, her books and her wish to see Kelsey Little vanish from the face of her planet.

Or at the very least be really uncomfortable.

But she vowed that one day she'd exact some skinny revenge on Kelsey Little. Someday she'd show her what Tara Douglas was all about. She'd be successful and more importantly, thin. She'd walk right up to Kelsey and say, "How do you like me now?"

She'd show Kelsey...

Senior class bitch, cheerleader from hell and homecoming queen of Evanston High.

Chapter One

Do I look fat in this?

"Whose Bride Is She Anyway?"

Hell's bells, Tara couldn't believe she'd made it this far in the auditions for, of all things, the reality television show her old high school nemesis was the star of. Here she was in California, sitting in a crowded reception area after twelve rounds of interviews, smiling until her lips stuck to her teeth to get on the most popular reality show this side of planet earth. This was *it.* The last interview--the big showdown for the top spot as jury foreman on "Whose Bride Is She Anyway?"

She took a deep breath and watched as people came and went from the ominous mahogany door labeled "Producer". As in the man who would call all the shots and held the key to Tara successfully pulling off the payback of the century.

A woman to her left whispered something about the "contestants", making Tara turn to see if they too were stuffed in that office, but she hadn't seen too many hunks come out.

Water, she needed water. Her throat was dry and scratchy and she'd been at this interview crap all damn day.

Tara clung to the number in her hand. It labeled her as potential jury member number two-twenty-three and it held her place in line. They were only on interview two-hundred or so ... it was going to be a long wait with each interview at fifteen minutes apiece, so she could afford the time to go find some water. She clung to her number as she went in search of a water fountain.

Slipping out the door, she headed down the hall and saw a man bent over at the waist drinking from a fountain in long gulps.

Tight buns in faded blue jeans--damn, they got hotter and tighter as she closed the gap between herself and the fountain. Lord, that was the last thing she should be thinking of at a moment like this. Every bun from here to Beverly Hills was tight. So what?

Tara cleared her throat and a head popped up ... the head that eventually led to those tight buns.

A ruffle of shaggy blond hair fell over his forehead, streaked from the sun, thick and shiny. His blue eyes locked with Tara's and his mouth was slightly ajar. A bead of water trickled down lips that were firm, but full. "Um, I'm sorry, I was hogging wasn't I?" His deep voice was like a waterfall of chocolate, trickling down over Tara in a cascade of shivers. She stared back at him, simply because words failed to produce much more than a caveman-like grunt under her breath.

He grinned, a flash of perfectly aligned white teeth and stood up. Fully erect, he was ... well fully erect... Tall and solid, thickly muscled, but not plastic like she'd seen so much of since she'd come to California for this audition. Tara blinked and took a long, slow breath. "It's okay--ta..."she cleared her throat again because she sounded like an armadillo in mating season. “Take your time. I--well, I--can wait. I mean they’re only on number two-hundred, so I have loads of time. Really, drink all you want. It’s okay, you look thirsty and I don’t blame you. I mean it’s hot here, right? The sun is...”

“No, I’m done, you go ahead,” he interrupted, backing away from the fountain and offering her his spot with his hand. His *big hand...* He looked confused and who could blame him? She was running off at the mouth, something she did often when she was nervous.

Tara forgot she was thirsty, forgot everything but this big man’s chest, staring her in the face. “Th--tanks,” *Oh, God...* “I mean, *th*ank you.” Accent on the letters t-h.

Jesus!

He smiled back at her, but continued to stand his ground, unmoving, unblinking. His blue eyes just wouldn’t let go of hers. Was he an actor? Was this eye contact thing like a technique you were supposed to practice on complete strangers? Cuz it was workin’.

She was *not* bending over in front of this man to drink from the fountain. He would see her ass.

And?

What the hell was wrong with her? Who cared if he saw her ass? As asses went, hers would pass. She wasn’t sure what it was passing, some silent test she’d made up in her head, but nonetheless, it would fare all right. She stomped over to the fountain and pushed the button to make the water come out. Nothing ... she pushed again ... still nothing.

“Here, let me help. You have to push slowly if you want a steady stream.”

Magically the water sprayed up and out and Tara took small sips, quickly, standing back up and using her thumb to wipe the excess water from the side of her lips. “Tank...” *argh!* “*Th*ank you,” she said slowly, avoiding his gaze.

"My pleasure," his scratchy grumble pierced the quiet of the hall.

Finally raising her eyes, they appraised one another

Then, silence and nothing but the pounding of her heart in her ears, yet they continued to stare at one another, his eyes holding hers until someone yelled in their direction.

"August!" A thin man came running down the hall, waving his hands and heading in their direction. "August, I told you--you have to use the fountain in Hall *B*."

August? What kind of name was August? He *was* an actor, Tara decided. They all had names that were far fetched and hid something awful, like their real names. His was probably Bubba or Cletus.

August wasn't apologetic as he looked over his shoulder one last time at Tara, his eyes lingering for a moment on her face before he turned to the thin man. "If you're going to keep us holed up in there like that the least you can do is give us water. How was I supposed to know where Hall B was? I just found the water. I didn't care what hall it was in."

The man put his hand on August's back and directed him back down the hall as he spoke in a rush. "I know, I know. I'm sorry, we're on overload here and I should have been more careful..." Their voices faded as they took the turn at the end of the corridor.

He must be on an audition, hence the eye thing, Tara figured. But he didn't look as fake as most of the men she'd run into since she'd come to California. He was vivid in the way most actors--she supposed--should be, yet raw and edgy with all that silent eye contact. Definitely had presence...

A shiver like spider's legs skittered up her spine. It was all technique, or whatever actors called it, designed to make women's libidos go "whoa", and hers had responded in typical teeny bopper fashion.

As Tara walked back down the hall she wondered about his name. He really should think about changing it.

August? Well, it was ... a month, for crap's sake.

* ~ *

Now that she was back in the waiting room, watching interviewees for the jury come and go from her corner chair, she gave some thought to Kelsey Little while trying to set aside her encounter with that August person who was much more like an Adonis than a man named after a month.

Out of the blue a thought occurred to her, one in a long string of paranoid thoughts that made her squirm with discomfort. Was there a lie detector test on this show? Because if so, she was doomed.

She fidgeted and refused to acknowledge the very idea that she'd been lying boldly about knowing Kelsey. It wasn't a lie. She *did* know her. Sorta...

Hookay, so she'd told a wee white lie to get *this far*.

Oh, all right, she conceded mentally, she'd lied *a lot*. Yep, she'd told a really *big* white lie, but the end justified the means, she reasoned with herself. So Tara Douglas and Kelsey Little weren't really *friends,* per se, in high school. The producers of "Whose Bride Is She Anyway?" didn't need to know that. All the rules on the show's website said was that the potential jury foreman had to be a friend from high school.

Define friends.

Tara sighed. Okay, so she and Kelsey weren't even *acquaintances*.

Jeez, so they came from two *completely* different worlds if she allowed brutal honesty to reign supreme.

What of it?

"I did know Kelsey Littman in high school!" a woman's voice protested loudly as it was ejected from the producer's door.

Tara almost laughed aloud from her corner of the room. *Littman?*

The nice secretary smiled serenely at a woman as she motioned her out the door of the producer's office. "That's lovely, but not according to our records, dear." The disgruntled woman stomped out of the waiting area with a flounce of hair.

Oh hell. They were checking records? Guilt chomped at Tara's intestines like a round of Pac Man. She glanced around the room nervously as if at any moment someone from her past might out her. She hunkered further down in her chair and grabbed a magazine from the table beside her, covering her face with it so she could get in touch with the vibe that had brought her here in the first place.

Some much overdue payback for Kelsey Little.

Kelsey Little didn't know Tara had existed in high school. Not in the way you acknowledged someone friend-to-friend, anyway. Kelsey instead had taunted and tormented her all through high school and then, she'd been responsible for the most humiliating event in Tara Douglas's life.

Bar none.

Tara was Kelsey's *complete* polar opposite. Short and overweight, president of the trigonometry club, debate team captain and home every Saturday night her *entire* high school career.

Alone. As in just Tara and her bag of pork rinds.

Definitely not a candidate for the illustrious Evanston cheerleading squad.

She wondered if Kelsey was as evil now as she'd been in high school. Evil like Kelsey's was inherent, inbred, a defective mean gene.

Tara shook off the bad karma that attacked every time she thought of high school. All she wanted to do was get on this stupid show as Kelsey's jury foreman, but as the waiting room continued to fill up rather than empty out, she was becoming skeptical.

"I think I did it!" a large man with a thick moustache touted as he left the interviewing room. "I think I'm going to be a jury member!" He cracked his knuckles confidently and smiled at the whispering crowd gathered on the far side of the room.

The jury members were comprised of people responsible for choosing Kelsey's eventual groom-to-be. Kelsey would pick from two of the men the jury offered her, based on their month-long assessment of chemistry with Kelsey and willingness to win her heart via videotaped dates. The jury was in charge of grilling these helpless contestants to be sure Kelsey ended up with the right guy.

Hah! That was exactly where she wanted to be, at the helm of this choice made in Kelsey's honor. She'd get a paid vacation at a tropical resort *and* the ability to revel in the payback of the millennium. Because she was going to help all of America see just what a selfish, conceited, backstabber Kelsey was.

Another potential jury member sat beside Tara, a chair away, making her peek out over the top of her Time Life. Thumbing the pages, Tara pretended to read while noting it wasn't anyone she knew.

"Interviewee number two-hundred and twenty," the secretary called from the office door. A short, round woman with red hair jumped up and waved her number.

Tara's stomach heaved again. Only three numbers away from a shot at nabbing the jury foreman spot and possibly on her way to big time payback.

Revenge on national TV--exposing Kelsey for the bitch she was--was Tara's ultimate goal. She'd also take the opportunity to show off her new bikini, if her balls got just a little bigger and half-naked suddenly became life-affirming rather than a traumatic battle of flesh over mind. Maybe she'd prance around in front of Kelsey in a thong just because she could. Flash her some newly sculpted Tara booty or something.

Look, Kelsey! It's me, Tara Douglas. See this ass, you rotten bitch? It ain't the one you threw out of the locker room door anymore. Wanna see my thong, thong, thong?

Well, okay, no thong, just some cute shorts or something.

If her self-esteem would quit freakin' on her she'd do just that, because Tara Douglas was no longer the fat geek. She wasn't sure that was ever going to be possible, but she wasn't the meek girl Kelsey remembered. Tara was still just as organized, maybe compulsively so, still just as smart, she just looked better for it. Speaking of organized, had she brought her lip gloss?

A guy wandered in from the outer door and nodded at her with a wink as he drifted toward the secretary's desk. The attention she garnered from men still surprised Tara.

"I think he likes you," the girl two seats away giggled.

Even now she had trouble reconciling herself with the new and improved Tara. The Tara men now eyeballed with lust in their hearts and hard-ons in their shorts. She'd come a helluva long way since high school and she was proud of that, but the old Tara, insecure, her self esteem jar half empty--reared her ugly head from time to time. Sometimes it was harder for her to be pretty than it ever had been being what polite society called unattractive.

It was pressure. Lipstick and mascara and cellulite cream and all sorts of crap to keep her body flab free. If she had just one more round with the "thigh-master," she'd bust or her thighs would explode, whichever came first.

She fought a sigh when the girl to her right asked what number she was. "Two-twenty-three," she mumbled from behind her magazine, hoping to avoid conversation.

"God," the girl said, "I feel like I've been waiting forever for this moment."

Tara nodded, understanding fully what that was like. Everything she'd done in the name of perfection was all for this moment.

A moment Tara didn't consciously know she'd craved anymore, but found once she'd had a sampling of, left her wanting *more.*

Kinda like opening a bag of revenge potato chips. You couldn't have just one.

It was a moment that cropped up out of the blue, and not in the way of your typical high school reunion. Tara hadn't realized how much she still despised Kelsey until she got wind of the fact that she was going to be on this reality show and then, it all came back in a rush of clarity. Crystal clear and rife with a vengeance she could taste.

But even now, newly sculpted as she was, as improved as she'd like to think she'd become, when she looked in the mirror she still saw the ghost of the same old Tara Douglas from the class of nineteen-ninety-two.

Chubby and ugly. Nary a date in all of her high school history and just a little freaked out about how much she loathed Kelsey for making her senior year miserable. And making her the Evanston senior class joke.

Hate however, was indeed a powerful motivator.

Kelsey Little deserved to rot in flawless hell for Tara's humiliation, and she couldn't wait to be the one who blew the air that fanned the flames licking at Kelsey's perfect cheerleader behind.

"I'm up next!" a far-too-enthusiastic contestant said as he held up his number.

A sharp pang of fire ripped through Tara's already upset stomach; reaching for her purse she dug around for her bottle of antacids. Popping it open, she threw a handful in her mouth and crunched them in an attempt to repress her burning intestines.

James Bond she was not.

Shoot, she wasn't even a very good liar. All of this cloak and dagger crap seemed far better suited to a Charlie's Angel, because she was an undercover Kelsey hater, masquerading as a former high school *friend*.

Crunching harder on the antacids, she hoped to fend off the guilt eating her guts up and spitting them back out like a Fear Factor contestant for just a while longer.

Looking around, she tried to focus on the other people who were looking to cash in on her ticket to walloping Kelsey. The room was packed. What if someone from high school was here and recognized her? She eyed the short chubby red-head in the corner of the reception area. She looked familiar, Tara thought as her stomach took a nose dive.

Oh, hell ... it was *Candice Walker*. Not a cheerleader in high school but a wannabe, always trailing behind Kelsey like some damn dog cleaning up her path of leftovers. She'd hand Mr. Perfect over to Kelsey and ask if she could cook dinner for the happy couple too. Suck up. Suddenly, Candice looked up and directly at Tara. Well, she could say hello... "Hey, Candice, long time no see. I'm here to fuck with Kelsey. Wanna play?" Instead she lifted her chin and pretended she didn't know who Candice was.

Not that it mattered, because Candice didn't seem to know who she was either. Fine, it was just as well. She didn't need anyone horning in on her op to weave a web of deceit.

She'd waited a long time for this opportunity.

Okay, maybe not exactly this particular *kind* of opportunity. Honestly, Tara really thought she and Kelsey would run into one another in like the local grocery store and Tara would wander up to her, look her in the eye, and ask, "How do you like me now? Not such a fat ass, am I?" Neener, neener, neener.

This op was a just a smidge bigger in epic "look at me now" proportions.

Tara gnawed on the inside of her cheek. She sounded like every scorned geek looking for revenge from here to eternity. It was like a bad episode of "when geeks attacked".

Another candidate plopped down in the seat next to her. "It's packed in here," he commented.

Tara nodded again and ignored him. He was intruding on a good internal battle and she couldn't focus with endless personal chatter. She blew out a long breath. God, what she was planning to do was cruel, but then again, so was Kelsey and she had to cling to that if she was going to go through with this.

Rushes of guilt assaulted her as she continued to wait to be called for her interview, watching as people wandered in and out of that door that led to the interviewing. Remnants of the girl she used to be, no doubt.

A good girl--a good *fat* girl.

The mahogany door popped open and a young woman in low-slung jeans wandered out and she wasn't looking too happy. Another girl similarly dressed flew up to her and asked, "How did it go?"

The young woman shook her head, but Tara couldn't hear what she was saying.

Tara's stomach sank. Oh shit, who was she kidding? This was awful. She was an awful person to want to go through with this. Maybe she should just forget it. Who gave a damn if Tara Douglas spent her senior year hiding in her bedroom because Kelsey had video of her naked butt in the hallway outside the locker room?

While a bunch of sweaty jocks roared with laughter and made cow noises. No, that incident was something Tara would live with forever.

No one cared. Only Tara did.

Her face burned again as if she were right back in high school, pounding on that damn door for all she was worth. Her hands clenched tightly in her lap and wrapped around the bottle of antacids. She could still remember the sharp throb in them as she begged to be let back into that locker room.

Bitch. Kelsey Little was a selfish, overblown, egotistical big mouth who needed a good dose of her own meds. Tara would happily pry her mouth open and pour them directly down her throat.

Tara Douglas wasn't timid and mild mannered anymore and she wasn't a fat ass either.

She reminded herself--again--that revenge was sweet and Kelsey Little deserved this in sticky, cavity like portions. She needed to toughen up if she was going to be a bigger bitch than Kelsey. She'd waited a long time to see the likes of Ms. Little squirm in humiliation. Tightening her jaw, she regained her focus.

Her Mission Impossible, if you will.

Duh, duh, da da, duh, duh da da. The theme from the movie played in her head. Her mission: pick a freak of nature for Kelsey so she'd at least have to spend a year in hell with him to win the million dollar cash prize. Taunt her, remind her that Tara Douglas, Evanston High nobody, was the Captain of the humiliation squad now.

Yeah...

So screw the girl she used to be and screw guilt with a capital "S".

The man next to Tara left and another girl took his place, svelte and sleek in tight fitting clothing. She smiled absently at Tara. "Hi," she murmured.

Tara smiled back and ran her hands over her own tight jeans, feeling self conscious. Tugging at the area where her phantom belly used to be, Tara unconsciously sought to tent her shirt, covering the roll of flesh that she fully expected to seep out from underneath her T-shirt, between the top of her jeans and ooze from just below her breasts. Of course, that didn't happen, because there was no roll of *anything* anymore, but old habits died hard. Her habits kept stalking her from the grave.

Who could fluff this damn shirt out anyway? It was like a second skin, as sleek and as supple as her midriff had become.

Tara squirmed in her seat, shifting positions and crossing her legs. No one from her past would ever recognize her, not now, and she wanted to keep it that way. The shows producers would only choose one high school *friend* to be on the jury and Tara planned for that *friend* to be her.

No matter what.

The secretary popped her head out of the door again and called into the crowd, "Contestant two-hundred and twenty *three...*"

Chapter Two

The Contenders

Bah ba bah, ba ba ba ba,h ba bah (work with me here). Can you hear the Rocky theme song?

Tara squirmed in her seat as Henry Abernathy, the producer of "Whose Bride Is She Anyway?" flipped through his clipboard of applications. She ran her tongue over her bottom lip slowly, waiting to see if good old Henry reacted. His eyes certainly were *not* glazing over with untamed lust.

Maybe she still didn't have the seduction thing down pat? The heavens above knew she'd practiced enough in front of the mirror.

A vixen you ain't, honey. Well, Hell. Okay, one more shot at this.

Thrusting her breasts forward, Tara pretended she was disinterested and bored. Henry's eyeballs were not responding with the usual pop. He never once looked up from those damn papers.

He was gay.

Okay, scratch the big seduction scene. No amount of cleavage and booty was going to catch this guy's attention. She'd have to rely on her brain, not something that was foreign to Tara. Not by a long shot, but to a degree, she rather took personal pleasure in her newly acquired looks, and wasn't above using them for personal gain. She remembered a time when she'd scorned the pretty girls for using their looks to get what they wanted. If she'd only known the benefits she would reap as a result. Tara took a quick peek at her thighs to make sure they weren't splitting the seams of the jeans she'd poured herself into.

No, she reminded herself, that didn't happen anymore. She could wear her clothes as tight as she liked and it made no difference, nothing was ever going to bulge on her body again if she could help it.

By all things Richard Simmons, I do solemnly swear.

Henry Abernathy's chair creaked as he tilted it back and fired his first words since she'd entered the room. The hum of the video camera droned in the background. "You do know the show requires the jury foreman to know Kelsey Little, right?"

Tara nodded and took in his gaze solemnly. *Oy*

"So, Tara, tell me how well you know Kelsey Little."

Well enough to know I hate her guts, how's that? "We didn't talk on the phone every night, but we hung out in school." Not a total lie, Tara soothed herself. They did *hang* out. At least in the same science class when they'd passed papers to one another. She sat behind Kelsey every day for a year, that *sort of* constituted hanging out, right?

"Were you on the cheerleading squad with her?" Henry tapped his pen on the desk in front of him.

Click, click, click.

Tara tried to keep from visibly cringing. The cheerleading squad...

Hah! Yeah, that was me on the top of that pyramid, all thighs and cellulite.

"No, I wasn't a cheerleader."

Remember, less is more. Just say as little as possible about your relationship with Kelsey and you might skate through this unscathed.

"So, exactly what was your relationship with Kelsey?" *Did Henry seem a bit skeptical here? Well, shit. How did you define their relationship?*

Tormentor and the tormented? Hunter and the hunted?

Tara battled another cringe as a bead of sweat popped out on her forehead.

Play it cool. It wouldn't look good to have sweat marks under her armpits. "We hung out together, went to a party or two. Did the girl-thing." 'Nuff said.

"Hung out together?" Henry drawled. "Were you a close personal friend?"

Define close. "We were friendly enough for me to know what she likes in a guy." Tara followed that statement up with a smile, a slow, upward tilt of her freshly glossed lips. It was, after all, the truth. She *did* know what Kelsey liked in a man. It wasn't a difficult task. Low on brain fuel, big on six-pack abs; hold the grammatically complete sentences, if you don't mind.

"What makes you think you're qualified to pick a potential husband for Kelsey?"

Tara almost snorted. She wasn't qualified to pick her nose, let alone a husband for Kelsey. That's what would make this fun. She tried to keep her expression composed.

She cocked her head in thought and pondered how to answer. "Well, Kelsey and I had very similar tastes in high school, in guys anyway. We liked a lot of the same things. I want the best for her. I want her to have the man of her dreams."

And a good dose of universal, televised humiliation. Her stomach lurched. Damn, there was that pang of guilt again, sucking up all of her revenge energy.

Henry didn't look too impressed with her answer. His blank stare mirrored her own. Okay, she was tired of this stupid, inane crap and her mind kept wandering to the guy in the damn hall. It was time to show Henry that she wasn't the least bit interested in his lame show because her focus was drifting.

Reverse psychology and all.

Tara leaned forward, letting her breasts rest against his desk because it was unlikely it would make the slightest difference to him. She eyed Henry closely, making him noticeably shift in his big producer chair. "It's like this, Henry--I'd love to be on your show, who wouldn't want a free tropical vacation for a month? But, I'm not going to try to sell you anything here. I'm smart enough to know there's a line of salivating wannabes a country mile long just looking to be on this show. Everyone has their own personal reasons, I'm sure. I think mine are clear. I knew Kelsey in high school, even if we didn't socialize in the same circles very often. I'm hoping to help her choose a husband because she obviously wants one and we had similar tastes in beefcake. So either you want me or you don't. It's as simple as that. I'm probably the only one with an IQ higher than a tomato plant and I'd say that makes for interesting television, wouldn't you?"

Her ears burned at her rather bold answer. It sounded so vain. Conceited even. A bit too confident?

Henry narrowed his eyes. Tara watched his mental wheels spin. "Thank you, Ms. Douglas. We'll be in touch."

You are officially dismissed. Vamonos. Scram.

Tara rose slowly and ran her hands over her legs. Maybe her thighs didn't look as good as she thought they did after all. Sticking out her hand, she offered it to Henry Abernathy, behaving as though it didn't matter one way or the other if she was chosen for his stinking show. "It was nice meeting you, Mr. Abernathy."

Henry offered her a limp shake and looked back down at the pad on his desk. He was scribbling away as Tara made her exit.

As she stood outside the door of the audition room, her legs felt weak. She'd screwed it up and now she'd never have the chance to toy with Kelsey the way Kelsey had toyed with her.

She slowly headed down the long hallway that led back out to the parking lot and caught sight of the large blond guy with the name of a calendar month leaning against the wall in all his hunkiness. He was so damn hot, Tara thought, and he'd have to be to still catch her attention after a whooping like the one she'd just taken from Henry Abernathy.

Catching a glimpse of herself in the windows that lined the corridor, Tara decided today was a "fat day". It must have been, because all of a sudden, she was seventeen again and Kelsey was taunting her because she couldn't even make the cut for a brainless reality TV show.

Another evil plan foiled again...

* ~ *

As Henry Abernathy watched the broad, well-muscled back of August Guthrie disappear out of his office door, he flipped through his application one last time. This piece of mouth-watering hunk was perfect, short on words and an even shorter fuse. To sweeten the pot, he knew Kelsey from high school. A scorned boyfriend maybe? That always made for exciting television. Maybe August could be the secret bomb he dropped on Kelsey's picture perfect world, smashing it to smithereens and checking the selfish bitch's attitude with a big black mark. What a diva that one was.

Henry had been against her as the final choice all along, but he was out-voted in the end. Everyone on staff thought she was vain enough to make America spend every Tuesday night at ten p.m. glued to their television sets, just waiting to see what she would do next. There was nothing Henry would like more than to see Kelsey Little wallow in her own load of crap.

Ruffling a feather or two kept things very interesting, add to the mix that August Guthrie was hot and you had the makings of a hit. All shaggy blonde hair and flaring nostrils, a hard line to the set of his mouth and biceps like bowling balls.

Hot, hot, hot.

Then there was the very pretty Tara... Tara Douglas didn't know Kelsey Little from a hole in the wall, Henry mused, as his callous producer's mind raced to make something sordid of this opportunity. Of course, he'd have his people check to be sure they'd at the very least graduated in the same class. He could do that in minutes. It was a requirement to be a jury foreman on the show, but no one said they had to be best buddies.

Just friends. Sort of. And Tara was the *perfect* jury foreman. She was more than just great looking. Fans of the show would eat up her wholesome yet sultry looks. You could strike a match on those cheekbones of hers.

Henry scribbled *bikini* on his notepad by her name. Tara should definitely wear one on camera. The male viewing audience would be hard pressed to keep from having their flags waving at full staff while watching her. She was better looking than Kelsey--that was for sure. He was going to wet his knickers just waiting to see if the contestants liked Tara better than Kelsey. Though he couldn't afford any more controversy after the last season. Unless he used the hullabaloo to his advantage...

Something about Tara Douglas made Henry's heart go pitter-pat and it wasn't her ass. Though he supposed from a heterosexual point of view, her ass was rather pleasing to the eye. She was up to something and that was A-okay with Henry. He could smell controversy like little boys could smell cookies baking in the oven.

It meant payola.

This season was going to be a hit for Henry Abernathy, bigger than last year's ever was. He swiped at the drool forming in the corner of his mouth. Life was going to be very sweet if he could pull this baby off. Tara rather reminded him of the volatile August Guthrie. Quiet and introspective one minute, then whaling him with this aura of insecurity he couldn't quite put his chubby finger on. Henry buzzed his secretary, grinning smugly at his sheer brilliance. He checked August off as one of the twenty men who'd better hold onto their hats, because he was one of the final twenty contestants and he'd better be prepared to hit the friendly skies ASAP. Leaning back in his chair, Henry chuckled and thought, *let the games begin...*

Chapter Three

What was I thinkin'?

As Tara headed out to the parking lot to grab her rental car and spend the night sulking in her hotel room before she had to go back home and live with the agony of defeat, she heard her name called from across the studio's big parking lot. Turning, she cupped a hand over her eyes to block the sun and scan the surrounding area.

"Ms. Douglas! Wait!"

Tara caught a glimpse of Henry Abernathy's secretary running in heels, waving a big manila envelope.

What now? She just wanted to go home and forget she'd ever considered this. More paperwork maybe? Did you need to fill out "loser" paperwork? *Sorry, Tara Douglas, you just didn't make the cut, but could we trouble you to sign on the dotted line, sealing your loser deal?*

"Oh, Ms. Douglas!" Henry's secretary gasped, fanning her face with the envelope. "I'm so glad I caught up with you. Mr. Abernathy would have my head if I didn't."

Tara smiled vaguely and furrowed her brow. "I'm sorry. I missed your name when I was waiting to be interviewed."

"Oh," she chuckled, "I'm Linda. It's a pleasure to meet you. I have some exciting news!"

You too can be excited about being a loser... "Um, I'm not sure what you mean. Did I forget something? Did I miss a disclaimer?"

"Oh, no it's *nothing* like that. Guess what?"

Okay, she'd play. "What?"

Linda bobbed her pretty head in disgust and stomped her foot. "No! You have to guess!"

Guess? What was this, trivial pursuit? "Guess?"

Linda shook the envelope she held in exasperation. "Yes! Guess!"

Tara was tired and plumb not interested. Maybe if she answered the "guess" correctly, she'd get a nice parting gift. "Oh, I couldn't even venture to. If it's not more paperwork, then I'm plain stumped. I'm all guessed out," she said flatly.

Linda looked disappointed that Tara didn't want to play. "I know, all those interviews and tests and stuff are grueling, huh? Okay, so I'll just tell you."

At this stage of the game, that might be a right fine idea. Tara leaned against her rental car and folded her arms over her breasts. "Okay."

"See this?" Linda waved the envelope under Tara's nose.

"Uh-huh." She nodded.

"Know what it is?"

Her loser certificate? Ah, yes to make it all official and all. She could frame it. "I have no idea and no, I can't guess." Tara smiled.

Linda thrust it at her. "Well, silly, open it."

She threw her purse through the open car window and tore open the envelope, peeking inside she pulled out the official

"Whose Bride Is She Anyway?" letterhead and began to read it.

Tara's expression went from wary to shocked. A grin spread over her lips in astonishment, then a frown, then another grin. *Holy Shit!*

Linda put her hand under Tara's chin, clapping her mouth shut. "Cool, huh?"

Indeed. She nodded wordlessly.

Hell's bells ... they'd chosen her as the jury foreman.

Tara's knees began to shake as her eyes blurred from the long day and an end to her goal in sight.

"Did you read the small print?" Linda shook Tara's shoulder.

She squinted and looked to the spot where Linda's finger pointed, reading the smaller print below her acceptance letter.

Oh...

Well, that was just silly. Who could possibly leave at this very moment to go to Hawaii? I mean, really, she thought as her head spun. Who could just up and leave with no notice whatsoever to anyone? She had a job and an apartment. A fern that needed watering...

Bills to pay ... a more definitive blueprint for "Kelsey Little disaster" to design.

But the letter said if she wasn't prepared to board a plane tonight, then she would be excluded from the competition.

Well crap. If she didn't sign this now and go, she wasn't ever going. What a friggin' crappy thing to pull. All this high-and-low emotional stuff was going to be the death of her. How could she possibly prepare mentally for this if she didn't have *time*? Humiliation was a craft best given one's single-minded efforts.

Linda leaned over her shoulder and asked, "So what are you going to do?"

Tara ran a hand through her hair and started putting her brain into neatly filed compartments of organization. Call mom, call work, return rental car, go to hotel, pack bags... Clothes, she didn't have any clothes but what she'd brought with her for a couple of days. They couldn't make her go without clothes. That settled that.

"But I have nothing to wear. I can't just jump on a plane for a month and have no clean underwear with me. I mean when I watched all of the other shows the jury talked about how they had weeks to plan to leave. How can I go without clean underwear..."

"We take you shopping. You have two hours to buy what you'll need and a budget the size of two of your paychecks. This is a new twist they added, sort of a catch-you-off-guard thing. It's happening to the contestants too."

"Well, the contestants don't need anything to wear but a Speedo! I mean all it is--is some suntan lotion and a thong."

Linda laughed at her obvious anxieties. "Those are the rules and," she looked at her watch, "you have five more minutes to give me an answer. Your flight leaves tonight."

"But my stuff at the hotel..."

"We'll send someone to get it. Four minutes..."

"And my rental car..."

"Staff will take it back for you. Three and a half minutes."

"My fern..." Tara said weakly.

"Can't help ya there. Two minutes."

She grabbed Linda's arm and covered her wrist watch in frustration. "Oh, all right! I'll go!" Tara grabbed the pen Linda held out and signed the release, scribbling her name quickly before she freaked out. "There," she said with a matter-of-fact tone, "now what?"

Linda smiled. "Now you get whatever you have in this car and come with me."

She lost her focus on Linda for a moment as she caught the large body of that August guy weaving between cars in the parking lot. Damn, he was hot.

Tara popped open the back door and began digging around for her spare pair of shoes. Her thoughts were jumbled and her head ached. How the hell was she going to put this all together in her head in one plane ride to Hawaii?

Could one *plan* in enough time--on a flight to Hawaii--to destroy someone?

~

August Guthrie swaggered in and out of the cars in the studio parking lot and paused, trying to remember where the hell he'd left his rental twelve hours ago.

Damn, he felt stupid. Well, his best friend Greg couldn't say he didn't take him up on his dare. Greg had triple-dog dared him to try out for the show when he'd found out from his cousin that Kelsey Little was on it. August couldn't help it if the people responsible for helping him make this dare happen didn't want to play.

Henry Abernathy had grilled him like a piece of shrimp on the barbee. What kind of question was *what makes your heart sing?*

Yes, he'd known Kelsey in high school. Lying about that would have sunk him like the Titanic because it was easily checked. Yes, he was a competitive man. No, he didn't need the money the show offered.

Locating his rental car, August ignored the replay of his interview with Henry in his head and took a few more weary steps toward it. Maybe he'd just go back to the hotel, sleep and drive back home. He hated to fly. He needed time to think about this newest rejection in a long list of them where Kelsey Little was concerned.

Some guy was leaning on the trunk of his car, legs crossed, dressed perfectly and eyeballing him as August went to the driver's side and ignored him.

"August Guthrie?"

August turned to stare at him. "Yep."

Tall, dark and Hollywood held out his hand. "I'm Darren, Mr. Abernathy's assistant."

August's face registered recognition. "Sorry, I didn't recognize you at first. It's all kind of hazy, ya know?" *Like coming off a two-day bender.*

Darren chuckled, "Yeah, I do know. It's a long couple of days going through all of the tests and interviews, but I think you're going to find it's paying off for you."

August cocked his head. "Huh?"

Darren stuck out his hand and slapped the other across August's back. "You're in."

He was in? In as in--in the *final* cut in?

Darren read his mind. "Yeah, you're a contestant on 'Whose Bride Is She Anyway?'."

August's eyes flew open. "Wait a second. I thought they weren't choosing anyone for weeks?"

Darren's dark eyes smiled. "It's a new twist we kept close to our chests and here's the real catch, you have to leave *today*."

"What?"

"Watch my lips," Darren said and pointed to his mouth, his pinky ring glistening in the sun. "If you want to be a contestant on the show, you have to leave *today*."

"Today?"

"Today."

August began pacing the length of the small parking space, his head filling with a "to do list". How could he friggin' leave today? He had a business to run and a goldfish to feed. He didn't have enough clothes with him for a month. Or a plan to win Kelsey. How could he practice winning her if he didn't have time to do anything but get on a plane? You couldn't win a woman without a plan--he had to get his head into the game first.

He stuttered, "But..."

"It's now or never," Darren assured him.

"My rental..."

"The staff will get it."

"Um, clothes?"

"Bought and paid for by the show. You don't need much, a few bathing suits, some T-shirts, sandals."

"My goldfish, Jerry..."

"He has water."

August finally laughed. "Can I call home? I'd have to make some arrangements."

"Yep, one call."

"Like jail?"

Now Darren laughed, "Yeah, like jail."

Well shit. If he didn't do it, Greg would call him a chicken-shit bastard. If he did, he could well be on his way to getting married in front of a live audience. He gulped for the first time since he began this crazy venture, his throat was tight.

Marriage to Kelsey Little. Holy hell. And there was no backing out either. If you signed you couldn't leave unless you were voted off by the jury. There were clauses and crap in that contract.

August saw the value of the show catching them off guard. It made you make snap decisions you might not if you had more time to rationalize. That was what the show was all about, wasn't it? Making a life-altering choice in a month. What was the worst that could happen? He'd lose and go home.

No big deal. Losing wouldn't be as bad as backing out on Greg's *triple-dog dare.*

"You have like five minutes, August," Darren warned, "and then I need you to sign this contract. The one you reviewed before the final interviews." He pulled it out of his back pocket and slapped it in the palm of his hand.

Five flippin' minutes? Who decided to leave town in five minutes? For a month, no less? Didn't these people care that he had a life--a company to run? And most importantly, a goldfish to feed? Of course they didn't. They cared about putting you on the spot and dangling the Kelsey carrot in front of your interview-weary eyes.

August walked toward the front of the car and sighed, absently watching a woman in tight jeans, three rows ahead of him, ass end out of the trunk of her car.

Nice ass...

He straightened immediately. What kind of thought was that to have when he was pondering boarding a plane to compete in a reality show for the woman of his high school dreams? Jesus...

August Guthrie, you are swine, even if she does have a nice ass.

"So ... we on?"

He turned back to Darren, determination all over his face. "Yeah, you're *on.*"

Chapter Four

Is it hot in here, or is it just me?

Tara wobbled her way out of the airport and into the hot noonday sun, fighting the nausea that assailed her with each step. Cloying heat and humid, oppressive air assaulted her, bathing her clammy skin in a rush of warmth. Surely, the jaws of hell had opened and exhaled hard. It was like a frickin' furnace here.

"Aloha!" a beautiful Polynesian woman greeted her with way too much going on in the perky department, perfect olive skin, and a big flower necklace. Screw her for being so damn perfect when it was so damn hot. Tara winced. She felt bitchy and whiny, and it was because she was setting out to do something so unlike her she wanted to spew. Why couldn't she just do this and enjoy it?

Someone chuckled from behind her, "You've been laid, so to speak."

She turned and gave the male voice a weak smile, *yes laid. If only...* Oh, shit! Her eyes opened wide and her stomach did the jitterbug. The guy from the water fountain loomed in all his God-like blondness was right behind her, smiling. The guy with the name of a month on the calendar. August ... was August still looking for water? Was the water in Hawaii better than in California? What right did he have to be here, when she looked like this? What kind of a name was that, anyway? Who named their kid after a *month*? Maybe it was the new "in" Hollywood name and all the hunky guys wanted it.

He appeared as shocked as she was. "So, we meet again. What brings you to Hawaii?" he asked, piercing her with his blue gaze, sending her heart rhythms into valve replacement inducing beats.

Tara was fumbling for an answer when someone yelled sharply, "August! Could you please stop taking it upon yourself to just go wandering? You're not supposed to be here!"

He leaned in close to Tara, making her throat clog up and whispered, "I think I'm in trouble again...," then smiled devilishly before turning and following the voice that had scolded him back into the crowd.

Tara dropped her luggage and reached for the back of a steel chair provided for airport patrons and dug in her purse for her bottle of water. Although a cold shower might be more appropriate due to the heat and the hunk. Who was he and what was he doing in Hawaii? This was too much of a coincidence.

A thunderbolt of brilliance hit her just then. Was he a contestant? Oh, that would so suck if he hooked up with Kelsey and she had to watch.

One of the male jury members she recognized from the plane sidled up beside her and said cheerfully, "Hi, I'm Andy Jacobs."

"Nice to meet you," she smiled weakly, still distracted by June, er, August. "I'm Tara Douglas. I wonder where we go from here?" Jury members were gathering around with their luggage and anxiously awaiting the next step. She'd spent much of her time on the flight alone while the others chatted excitedly, nursing her guilt and her fear of the Barbie plane crashing at any moment.

"I think over there." Andy pointed in the direction of the rows of vans. "C'mon, you don't look so good. I'll help you." He put his hand under her elbow, dragging some of her luggage behind him and guided her toward a van where a chubby island man, dressed in a typical Hawaiian shirt and khaki shorts stood with a sign that said, "Whose Bride Is She Anyway?" on it. She followed Andy, dragging the rest of her month's worth of luggage. Her silk shirt clung to her damp skin and her mouth was dry.

Beads of perspiration gathered on her upper lip. Lord, it was hot here.

"Welcome to 'Whose Bride Is She Anyway?'! I'm Konani, and I'll be taking you to the island." He bowed majestically before them. His thick black hair gleamed in the sun, casting an almost blue tint to it. His accent might have been charming if she wasn't ready to hurl.

After checking their IDs and marking them off as "arrived," they all piled into the cool interior of the van and sped off to destinations unknown.

Ko-whatshisface chattered excitedly about the sights they passed, keeping his banter friendly and light.

Much vegetation, lush surroundings, bright sun, was the most she could gather from his rambling. Yada, yada, yada.

Yay Hawaii! Tara made a face. *Thanks, Julie the Cruise Director. Now could we get to where we're going so I can sit in one place without moving?* she wanted to scream at him. Her stomach lurched violently as the van took a sharp turn. "Will we be there soon?" she squeaked, gulping to fend off nausea.

Andy leaned forward from the seat behind her and whispered reassuringly, "We'll be there soon."

She really wanted to enjoy the scenery but she couldn't stop the roller coaster ride her stomach was on.

Konani looked in the rear view mirror, his brow wrinkled in concern as he glanced at Tara. "Whatsamatter with the pretty lady?"

She clenched the seat in front of her in the grip of death with one hand, and motioned for Andy to do the talking with the other.

"She's not feeling so good," Andy said. "I think it was the flight. She'll be just fine now that we're on land."

"We not done yet, lady." Konani's tone was cheerful.

"Done what?" Tara croaked through parched lips.

"Done flying..." He trailed off as they approached yet another landing field.

Groaning, she wondered where the hell this damn place was. Remote was remote, but c'mon already, even Gilligan's island wasn't *this* secluded. They'd only lost him for a couple of prime-time seasons.

Andy thumped her on the back. "Don't worry, you can hold my hand."

~

Tara bit her lip and tried to focus on what Henry Abernathy was saying, but she couldn't stop the room from spinning. Man, they weren't kidding when they said a remote island. Another van had picked them up and deposited the group at the first of many rows of large huts, where they all joined in an informal gathering room. Tara was still recuperating from her flight on the aircraft that Lego built when Henry Abernathy and crew showed up to give them each details for their stay on the island. God, she hated to fly.

Some of the people from the plane traipsed in. An elderly woman with a knitting bag plopped down in a chair a few feet away. She looked tired and grumpy. Three more people filed in, each wearing the same weary look as the next. She vaguely heard Henry introduce her as jury foreman and she obliged him by absently waving to everyone while she fought the need to blow her cookies.

Henry's voice droned on and on about the shows rules... No contact with the outside world until the show was over, unless it was a monitored phone call or an extreme emergency. Like *death*. Never tell a soul anything other than you were going to be on the show "Whose Bride Is She Anyway?", because of course, that was good promo. If you'd signed the contract it meant you were in it for the long haul. No backing out, no quitting from this point on, or lawsuits up the wazoo would make you miserable for the next lifetime.

No this, no that... Yada, yada, yada. She'd signed away nearly everything but her internal organs to get on this show.

When Henry paused to address some technical issues the crew was having, Tara breathed a sigh of relief.

She was disoriented, tired and overwhelmed. Long past panicked, she was working with full on freaked out. Yeah, she was on sensory overload, yet found herself ever compulsive, mentally ticking off a list of things she'd accomplished in the few hours since she'd made it on the show.

Called Mom, asked her to water her fern. Calmed Mom down and told her it was all going to be fine. No, she'd assured her mother, she wasn't getting married. Someone else was...

Check.

Called work, threatened to quit if they didn't let her have the vacation she'd stock-piled for five freakin' years. It was perfume, *not* the cure for cancer.

Check.

Breathe.

Check.

Tara closed her eyes and leaned her head back on the cushioned chair.

"Excuse me..." A male voice interrupted her train of thought from the chair beside her. "You okay?" Andy again ... he was so sweet. He leaned in closer to check on her.

She took a deep breath and wiped beads of perspiration from her upper lip. Christ, you couldn't breathe in here. Didn't they have air conditioning in Hawaii? "I'm fine, Andy, thank you." *Pass the oxygen, please.*

"You don't look fine." He was taking quick peeks between the people milling about at her face. A face she was sure was not doing its job hiding her utter terror.

No shit, Columbo. *Calm, slow breaths, Tara.* "Really, I'm okay, thanks for asking. I just hate to fly and I'm relieved it's finally over."

"You're sweating."

Observant too. "Yeah, I'm always bit shaky after getting off a plane. But it passes. I managed to fight the urge to run down the aisles of the plane screaming, 'we're going down!'" she joked.

Andy blanched and leaned into her, his round face concerned.

God, she hated small talk; worse, she hated sitting so closely to someone you could count the hairs in their nostrils.

"So it's been quite a day, hasn't it?" He observed, way too damn cheerfully if you asked her.

Tara gulped and smiled weakly. "Well, if you take into account that I've been up since three this morning and it's now, seven in the evening, waited forever to be interviewed, left said interview thinking I was a loser, found out I wasn't, shopped until the show's credit card bled, then landed here, all in one jam-packed, emotionally charged day, then yes," she giggled, "it's been quite a day."

He laughed, "You looked pretty beat on the plane. We didn't want to disturb you."

"I'm sorry. I hate to fly and coupled with the long day ... I was just fried. I'm sorry I didn't get to know everyone." She shrugged her shoulders and smiled. "So you're a jury member..." he certainly wasn't one of the contestants ... he wasn't exactly the cover boy for body beautiful.

That was catty wasn't it? Since when had she begun to judge anyone on their appearances alone? It was that evil Kelsey Little's warped way of thinking, teaching her bad manners. It wasn't so long ago that Tara was anything but perfect. She couldn't claim perfection even now. No one could. *Shutting up...*

"Yeah," he smiled back. "I'm a juror."

"Like Henry said, I'm your foreman." She tipped an imaginary hat at him.

His blue gaze steadied on her. "Man this was something, throwing us together like that without any warning. Cool, that you're foreman. Think they have enough rules? I'm beginning to wonder if we'll even actually *see* the contestants, they're so closed mouthed about where they are on the island."

Ah, yes. The rules were aplenty. No fraternizing with the contestants, as if that would happen. They were all big-on-brawn, short-on-brain-cell reproduction. Right now, she cared little about anything but some peace and quiet. She didn't want to talk, but she didn't want to alienate anyone with a loner attitude either.

"Well, we're jury members. We'll be together a lot, so I imagine we'll know where they are soon enough." *Now, go away and leave me alone. Let me contemplate death by yarking.*

"Are you nervous about being on the show? I mean, the cameras on us all the time and stuff?"

Gab, gab, gab. Tara sighed under her breath and fought off her crankiness. This was going to be a long night, filled with meaningless conversation that she wasn't up to, but it had to be done. She pinched the bridge of her nose to ward off a headache because it didn't sound like Andy was going to shut up anytime soon and she was feeling bitchy because she was tired. It wasn't his fault.

Be nice to your fellow jury member, she chided herself. Make friends.

Friends, yes, she would make friends, because she was going to need them. "Nervous? Not really. I'm *more* worried about picking the right man for Kelsey." Yeah, right, good one. Remember to keep a straight face at all times while lying through your set of newly capped pearly whites. God, she was becoming deft at lying and she hated it.

But Kelsey's demise will justify your means, her evil twin reminded her. Straightening her shoulders she smiled at Andy and waited for him to respond with something deep, thereby making her feel as shallow as a baby pool.

Andy shrugged. "I'm just here for the vacation. I really need it. A month in paradise is more than this average Joe can afford and I'm a big fan of the show. Plus, we get paid to do it. Good food, the occasional cool waitress chick in a bikini poolside." His bushy eyebrows rose as he wiggled them at her.

Yes, the ever-popular cool chicks in bikinis , was too tempting to deny oneself. "I can promise you the cool chicks in bikinis wasn't the clincher for me, Andy. I really want to see Kelsey find a mate. We went to high school together." Tara fought to contain herself from adding, *She called me fat ass my entire senior year and then showed half the school said ass on a big screen TV. Of course I want her to have a mate ... a primate. A knuckle dragging Neanderthal.*

"Cool. What was she like?" Now he was interested.

Tara almost snorted, but caught herself in time by covering her mouth with her hand. *Tell me, Andy, can you spell* horrifying bitch? "She was okay, I guess. We didn't move in the same circles, but we passed each other at parties, talked here and there." *Like ships passing in the night...* "She probably won't even remember me." Tara felt another twinge in her intestines. They were boycotting her lies by tying themselves in knots that only a seafaring ship's captain could unravel.

"I think it's really nice that you want to help find the love of Kelsey's life. She's probably going to be really happy to see you again after all these years." Andy grinned at her.

Yeah, if only you knew *how* happy.

Silly Andy.

If only she could tell him of the treachery and deceit Kelsey spread with such glee throughout the land--better known as Kelsey's Kingdom. How happy would she be when she was the focus of some of her own bad karma, doled by none other than Tara Douglas? She wanted to snicker out loud, but that would be a dead give-away, no?

Okay, ix-nay on the aughing-lay at the misguided man who hasn't a clue to your evil motives. Kelsey would be about as happy to see Tara as she would if her favorite brand of nail polish stopped production. She needed to answer Andy, and she needed to do it fast. "We're not allowed to communicate with Kelsey, isn't that what Henry just said? So we won't be spending too much time reminiscing unfortunately. My plan is to enjoy myself. It's not that I'll mind the vacation though. It'll be good to catch a ray or two."

Andy cocked his head, his eyes growing serious. "You know what I want to know? How can you marry someone you hardly know and let a jury pick the guy? Plus, do it in front of a live studio audience?"

She wanted to laugh maniacally. Because Kelsey had about as many brain cells as a group of Weight Watchers clients at McDonalds, eyeing up the fry lady. She oughta know, she'd been a part of that group for a long time. Lost fifty pounds to prove it.

"Kelsey is looking for something she apparently hasn't found elsewhere."

He made a face. "And she thinks she'll find it on *national television?*"

Tara gulped. "Who can say what motivates a person to expose their deepest desires on national television? I'm sure Kelsey has a reason, just like you and I have our reasons." *Oh, that was fabulous. Ten for execution...*

Andy looked bewildered. Like because she didn't share his love of a good bikini, her purpose for living would cease to exist. "I know what my reasons are," Andy smiled, "what are yours?"

Okay, so she'd practiced this in her head a lot in the several hours since being accepted, reminding herself each time guilt assaulted her conscience that payback was the proverbial *bitch* and Kelsey was a bigger one. Here goes. "Well, of course, like I said, there's the vacation, but also a sense of satisfaction in sending two people off into the sunset with a lifetime of happiness under their belts. If I can help make that happen, then why not?" Tara slapped her practiced smile on, the slow curve upward of her glossy lips, adding just a hint of come hither for mystery. Then she scrunched her eyes shut. Not just because she was such a liar, and she'd fry in hell to infinity and beyond for this charade, but because she was coming closer to seeing Kelsey again and her stomach was on fire.

She felt like she was going to *die.*

"So what do you do for a living?"

"I'm a chemist in a perfume factory." Tara watched and waited for the yawn that usually accompanied that statement. No one on the planet found chemistry interesting but her and Bill Nye the Science Guy.

There it was... A big disinterested yawn, exposing every filling Andy owned. "Cool," he winked at her, "I write commercial jingles."

Tara's stomach rolled with a vengeance. "That's fascinating." Not really, but if it would shut him up so she could focus on her funeral arrangements she'd be grateful.

Roses; she'd like to be buried with roses; a sea of them in fact ... maybe her best friend Louise would read a heartfelt eulogy about her life.

Tara Douglas, high school geek turned sometime Sports Illustrated cover model/ chemist/avenger of all things dork-like--died today as she planned the demise of her high school nemesis Kelsey Little.

She'd snort at that thought if she could summon up the energy to suck in some H2O. Tara clenched the arms of her chair, digging her nails into the plastic, fighting the next wave of nausea. The room began to clear as the jurors waited for the golf carts to take them to their huts. Each sat quietly, absorbing the day's events.

"I said, get--off--of--me!" someone screeched into the weary, lulled silence outside the hut. "I'll go where I want to go, you buffoon!"

"This is *not* your final destination," a distinguished, yet calm voice cut into the stunned quiet that had all of the jurors, including Tara, sitting up in their seats. "Now come with me and I'll show you to your hut."

"Fuck my hut, Tattoo! I'm hot and sweaty and I'm sick of you chinky island guys already. I've been dragged around

Fantasy Island and back again. Take me to my hut and get it right!"

"It's been a busy day, *Ms. Little*. We apologize for the mix-up. If you'll follow me..."

The voices faded into the late afternoon and the elderly woman with the knitting bag, Mary if Tara recalled correctly, began to snicker.

The rest of the jury sat wide eyed and astonished. No one moved as they all looked at one another with shocked expressions.

Tara was the first to recover, her stomach oddly taking a turn for the better.

Kelsey Little, she thought, meet your jury...

Chapter Five

Ain't life grand?

Yep, this was paradise all right. Palm trees swaying in the warm tropical breeze, mother-of-pearl-white stretches of beach and a turquoise ocean. The sun was just beginning to set on the horizon as the jury left the small golf cart that brought them here, streaks of purple mingled with the orange ball slipping away in the sky.

Tara lifted her face to the breeze, letting it wash over her. Her stomach was somewhere back in the large meeting hut, having lurched and rolled its way to this fine destination, but she was feeling better.

Andy whistled. "Man, this is some place, huh?" He nudged her.

"It's fabulous," she agreed. The perfect place to exact revenge on a stuck-up bitch. A bitch who'd just shown the whole jury what the meaning of the word was.

Men dressed in white uniforms swarmed the dock as they relieved them of their luggage. Tara strolled behind them, luxuriating in the beginning of the end for Kelsey Little.

Meow. That isn't nice. No gloating, miss.

Right, no gloating. Tara sobered, shaking off the urge to do a cartwheel right there on the dock. Somehow, she figured it might not be appropriate behavior for the foreman of the jury to form a conga line over Kelsey's pending humiliation on *live* television. Or at least the audience would be live. Guilt tweaked at her gut for like the two thousandth time. She shoved it aside in favor of the warm fuzzy she was getting from successfully making it this far without being caught. Slipping off her shoes, she let them dangle from her fingers and smiled.

"What are you smiling about?" Andy intruded upon her mental pat on the back.

"What's not to be happy about? We're in Utopia for a month. Can't beat that."

"Whaddaya think about the other jury members?"

God willing, they're easy to manipulate. "I didn't really get to know them well on the flight. Again, I apologize. I was feeling pretty awful, but I hope they're all as nice as you."

His beefy cheeks flushed with color.

They followed the bellhops to rows of thatched huts lining the far end of the beach. Tara wiggled her toes in the silky sand as they made their way across the beach. Each hut sported a label with the names of the members of the jury. A twinge of satisfaction rippled up her spine when Tara saw hers clearly marked as foreman. It was set apart from everyone else's by at least a half mile of beach, affording her privacy and she guessed, recognizing she was the foreman.

Foreman, as in the head honcho, the big Kahuna, in charge of the whole darn shebang. It didn't say captain of the cheerleading squad, but it was close enough.

Oh, Hell, this was a mistake wasn't it?

No, no it wasn't. Kelsey deserved every last moment of sheer torture for what she'd done to her.

Man up, girlie and stop being a big baby.

Squaring her shoulders, Tara absently waved a goodbye to Andy and opened the door to her room.

She caught her breath, forgetting round two thousand and one with her misgivings for a moment.

Whoa, this was some gig. Trailing behind the bellhop, she flopped down on the edge of the enormous bed. A canopy of white, filmy gauze surrounded it, tied in decorative rosettes on the four posters.

Holy shit! Tara grinned as she sat at the edge and bounced. It was like landing on a soft white cloud. Her fingers ran lightly over the puffy comforter as she dropped her shoes and dug in her purse for some singles to tip the bellhop. He bowed respectfully, but shook his head at her offer of money. Smiling, he left her to revel in her new surroundings, closing the door quietly behind him.

Silence filled the cool air, hushed and filled with the voice of chickening out.

No, dammit! Kelsey was going to get what she deserved if it was the last thing Tara did. She opted to focus instead on her ultra-cool surroundings.

A huge basket of fruit sat on the corner table by the sliding glass doors, but her stomach rebelled at the thought of food just yet. Instead, she went to take a peek outside. A vista of blue-green ocean greeted her, as the soft swell of water rolled in and out on the tide.

Jeez, this was sweet indeed! She did a little dance. Woo hoo Hawaii!

The cool air turned her body temperature to just below fried, reminding her how sticky she was from the humidity. A shower was definitely in order.

As Tara began to unbutton her shirt, she hesitated. Was this the show where hidden cameras were in the rooms? No, that was big sister or somebody's cousin, if all her research was correct.

Her hut phone rang, shrill and sharp. Tara jumped. *They knew...* They'd done more background checks on her and they knew about her evil plan...

She picked up the phone cautiously and answered with a gulp, "Hello?"

"Good evening Miss Douglas, this is housekeeping."

Oh, God, even *housekeeping* knew... Tara shook her head and swallowed. "Hello. What can I do for you?" *Do you want me to pay you off to keep your clean little mouths shut?*

"No, ma'am," the accented voice said cheerfully. "I'm calling to see what I can do for *you*."

Aha! They did want a pay off! "Do for me?" she asked hesitantly.

"Yes, ma'am. Any special requirements? A particular brand of soap, maybe shampoo?"

Tara's hand went to her stomach. Did they have soap that washed away guilt? "Oh, thank you, but no. I'm sure whatever's here is just fine."

"Wonderful! But please, don't hesitate to call us if you need anything at all. Just dial two-one-one."

Tara rolled her eyes in relief. "Thank you again," she hung up as if the phone was a loaded gun.

She groaned and padded to the bathroom, staring in awe at the creamy surface of the sunken tub and adjoining shower. The gleam from the shiny, gold fixtures almost hurt her eyes. An arched window above the bath gave her yet another glorious view of the ocean. Tara peeked out and caught sight of a very large blond man in the distance, wandering up the beach. Squinting against the sun, she looked closer as he gapped the distance to her hut; his large body muscled and tan against the setting sun.

Wow. Nothing like something yummylicious to take your mind off your troubles.

He lifted his head and cupped his hand over his eyes. Tara ducked. She would not get caught eyeing up the hunks, assuming that's who he was. He looked lost, which was probably par for the course when your biceps were bigger than your brain.

God, she was jaded.

She perused the bathtub again. Oh, yeah, baby, nothing like a good soak after humiliating the crap out of Kelsey.

Tara caught herself. She was gloating again.

Whatever.

Stripping the remainder of her clothes off, she opened her carry-on bag and located some shower gel and shampoo. The hard spray relaxed her achy muscles as she soaped up and gave some more serious thought to what she was about to do as the time drew closer to the show beginning.

Guilt flushed her cheeks again and a tremor of fear swept over her. What if she were caught? Would Kelsey tell the shows producer that they weren't exactly buds in high school? Nah, she wanted the limelight more than she cared about Tara and she certainly wouldn't credit Tara with being able to one-up her, nor would she want them to know what she'd done to Tara. Like she'd told Andy, Kelsey probably wouldn't even remember her. Humiliating Tara in high school was a blip on her screen of life. She'd done it so often that it had to be a blur. All part and parcel of a day in the perfect life of perfect Kelsey. Besides, Tara looked different now. If worse came to worst,

Tara would gush over her and tell Kelsey how profoundly fabulous she was. That was always what worked in school.

The show must have done their research, they'd run a background check that rivaled the CIA before she was chosen to interview. Surely, they knew *who* Tara was, and either cared very little, or they were looking to cash in on it. Either way, it hadn't raised an eyebrow and she wasn't about to complain as long as she could quit looking over her shoulder.

Toweling off, Tara went to unpack and find something cute to wear. Maybe that little black evening dress that everyone was always talking about and she wasn't able to claim bragging rights to until she'd lost all that weight. She smoothed a hand over her belly. She was by no means what one would call "skinny", but she was rounded in all the right places and firm thanks to the many hours she'd spent on a treadmill with a little tofu on the side. Looking down at her thighs she squinted, examining them. She always expected to see pockets of cellulite taunting her. Maybe she should have done more leg lifts? Another round of sit-ups...

Okay, she needed to stop this.

Like now.

It wasn't enough that she'd worked like a dog to lose the weight, now she was going to critique herself just because Kelsey was within a five-mile radius? It was vain and shallow and ... well, just *too* Kelsey like. As if she wasn't already subscribing to the Kelsey school of the shitty by setting out to humiliate her on national television. Tara didn't lose the weight because she wanted to impress anyone. She'd lost it because she needed to.

Enough!

Securely wrapping the towel around her, she went in search of her luggage and something slinky.

Slinky was good. Crossing the room, she grabbed her suitcase and hauled it to the bed, sifting through it until she found her little black dress purchased in some Beverly Hills shop Linda had taken her to. Tara fingered the label, running her thumb over the tag. Size eight... It still felt wrong sometimes, even if it really was true. Linda had gushed over it. “Oh, Tara, you are gorgeous! God, what I wouldn’t give to have a body like yours. It’s killer,” Linda had sighed and Tara had blushed.

Laying the dress out, Tara sat at the edge of the puffy bed and took some head clearing breaths.

A turquoise blue envelope caught her eye on the floor by the door. Her gut clenched, they’d found her out and they were going to kick her off the show. Oh, damn ... that couldn’t be, could it? Crap, now she was screwed, they’d caught the geek in action and it was over. The show was going to boot her ass outta here, quicker than she could say, “eat my thong, Kelsey Little”. Then, she’d be splashed all over the front of the rag mags, wearing dark sunglasses and hanging her head in shame to avoid the paparazzi.

Dramatic indeed.

Ugh, the guilt... Shaking her shoulders, Tara thrust aside the gnawing stab in her belly and exhaled sharply, focusing only on *evil.*

Crouching, Tara grabbed it and ripped it open with a shaky finger. What next? The show was infamous for catching folks off guard.

Tara scanned the note. Ah, the ever popular getting to know you luau. Tara had watched tape after tape of the past three seasons of “Whose Bride Is She Anyway?” This was where the fun began and the gloves came off. Jury members would assemble to meet one another and eat a roast pig or something. Glancing at her watch, Tara realized she had plenty of time to primp and fuss and war with her guilt. After all, this was national television, a girl needed to look her best.

* ~ *

Jesus Christ in a mini skirt, this was some place to land in. Jet lag and the pukes were long forgotten as Tara sauntered into the 'getting to know you' soiree. Island music played on the gentle breeze from the band assembled along the pool. A long table with a feast fit for a small country lay on festively decorated platters. Floral arrangements flanked the arched entryway and along the gazebo at the other end of the patio. Twinkling white lights hung from the palm trees, draping along the gleaming, mahogany bar. Straightening her flowered sarong, Tara tucked the tie between her breasts and made her way over to the dining area.

Her stomach growled. The scent of roast pork and pineapple wafted under her nose.

Yum.

No pork. It was high in calories and had like a bazillion fat grams that her thighs just couldn't accommodate if she wished to retain her size eight status.

She'd have to be very careful she didn't eat her way through this damn show. It all looked good and it all looked like it could cost her extra sit-ups, giving Kelsey something else to quite possibly taunt her with.

Ick! Nothing like sit-ups to make her rethink that pork butt.

Or having a *porker's butt...*

Grabbing a flower from one of the many arrangements, Tara tucked it behind her ear. Her long dark curls caressed her bare back, supple and sleek from working out. Tara felt good, yet her hands shook as she smoothed them over her hips.

Pre-show jitters, no doubt.

Andy waved her over from the far end of the long table. He was sipping from a coconut shell and bobbing his head up and down as the elderly woman from the jury chatted with him.

"Tara! Pull up a chair." Andy slid down the bench and offered a seat to her between the two of them.

"Hey, Andy."

"How do you feel?" Andy's smile was sympathetic. "Better, I hope. You look great."

Tara curtsied her 'thank you' to Andy. "And who's this you're over in the corner charming to pieces?"

"Tara Douglas, this is Mrs. Mary DeWitt."

Tara offered her hand to the thin, grey haired woman.

"Aren't you pretty? Do you feel better?" Mrs. DeWitt commented, smiling at Tara as she yanked a canvas bag from under the table and pulled out a pair of knitting needles with a long fray of blue yarn attached. A baby blanket, obviously.

"For my son and his wife. They're having a baby. A boy, in case you couldn't guess," she snorted. "As if I wanted the surprise ruined for me. They had one of those ultra thingamajigs, you know."

"Ultrasound," Andy filled in the blank for her.

"Right, ultrasound. Whatever the hell you want to call it, it ruined the surprise for me. In my day you took what you got and be damned if you didn't like it. The picture they sent me didn't even look like a baby, it looked like an alien, I tell you."

Tara giggled. "Well, at least it allowed you to choose the color in advance for the blanket."

Andy snickered as he poured something from the pitcher into Tara's coconut shell for her.

"It's *not* a blanket. It's a pair of booties," Mrs. DeWitt corrected as her knitting needles clacked together.

Oops.

"So, what brings a pretty girl like you to a place like this? Somebody as sharp as you should have a man waiting at home for them."

Tara sighed. She'd gotten a lot of that sort of reaction since she'd lost all of the weight. Everyone assumed she should be married by now because she was thinner. Her own mother seemed to think Prince Charming was secretly supervising her weight loss by crystal ball and when the scale's needle hit the magic mark, he'd come riding in on his white steed to whisk her away to the land fondly known as Skinny. Her dating experiences were limited and Tara kept it that way. No one wanted to date her when she was fat, so screw them now just because she wasn't. "Nope, nobody waiting anywhere for me, I'm free as a bird."

"Maybe you can have one of the leftover lover boys here."

Tara's cheeks burned. No Kelsey leftovers, damn it. "I don't need *anyone's* leftovers. I actually *like* being single," Tara said through clenched teeth and a falsely bright smile.

"Of course, you do, dear. Who wouldn't if they looked like you? Men must be lining up at your door. Andy here has no one to call his own." Mary hinted suggestively with a wink.

Jeez, she could have used Mary in the airport back on the mainland. Maybe she could have rustled that August up for her, Tara mused.

As sweet as Andy was, it wouldn't happen, not in this stratosphere, anyway. Tara wasn't on a manhunt. She was hunting Kelsey Little's...

Andy smiled at Tara over Mrs. DeWitt's head and shrugged his shoulders with a helpless gesture.

So Mrs. DeWitt was a born matchmaker and experienced in working a crowd. "And what brings *you* to the show, Mrs. DeWitt?"

Mrs. DeWitt peered at her from beneath her owl-like glasses and nodded to her plate. "The food. I live on a senior citizen's budget you know. Cat food just doesn't fill this old broad up like it used to."

Tara choked on her drink, catching the twinkle in Mrs. DeWitt's grey-blue eyes. "I know what you mean," she teased back. "I was becoming bored with cheesy liver bits myself. But a single girl has to make ends meet."

Mary DeWitt cackled. "You have a sense of humor. I like that in a girl. So, you're our foreman."

"That's me, at your service." And God willing, a master manipulator.

Jeez*, manipulator?* She was already thinking like the full-on bitch she desperately wanted to be and she hadn't even begun.

"You stole my job," Mary accused. "I wanted to be foreman of the jury," she sniffed mockingly. "But after this afternoon's little display from our bride Kelsey, I think I'm glad *you* got to be the head honcho. Is she really like that? I mean you know her, right?"

Tara fought a sneer. That was only the beginning. If Ms. Mary thought Kelsey was horrible *briefly*, just wait until she'd spent a month with her. And then Tara froze at Ms. Mary's reference to Tara and Kelsey knowing one another. "She did sound angry. Maybe she was just tired or something," Tara offered. Impartially, objectively..."and yes, I did know her briefly in high school. We only had a class or two together so there isn't much I can offer in the way of information about her other than we dated some of the same boys." *As if...*

Ms. Mary clacked her knitting needles down on the table. "Hmph. All I know is we were *all* tired, but we didn't behave like she did. She sounded like a spoiled rotten child."

Tara didn't agree or disagree, but Andy chimed in with, "Maybe these guys better think twice before marrying her, huh?"

Ms. Mary gave him a wink. "I know I wouldn't marry a shrew like that. I'm sorry, Tara. I spoke before I remembered you were friends in high school. I hope I didn't offend you if you were close friends."

HAH! Offend-schmend. "No, Ms. Mary, I'm not offended at all. Everyone has a right to their opinion and like I said we only knew each other briefly."

Andy nodded his agreement.

"So what was our big-mouthed, ill-tempered bride like in high school?" Ms. Mary asked, her eyes looming large behind her glasses.

Tara leaned back in her chair and hoped the dim lighting worked in her favor, because her face was on fire again. God, she hated lying. "Kelsey was very popular. A cheerleader and homecoming queen. We moved in different circles for the most part." Brief, to the point, not exactly a lie. All of these "not really a lie" lies were going to turn her stomach into a pit of acid.

Ms. Mary seemed to lose interest and said absently, "Well, that's nice, dear."

Oy. Tara sank back in her chair.

"Sure wish they'd had a show like this when I was your age. I was a looker," Ms. Mary said, resuming her knitting.

"I've no doubt about that," Tara said with a grin.

"Oh, the damage I could have done back then. But then I met Josiah and the rest is history."

"How does Josiah feel about you being here?" Tara wondered aloud

"He's dead," Mary answered flatly.

Shit. Way to score points with the jury members, Tara.

"It's all right, Tara. From one pretty girl to another, it's only natural for you to assume that I'm married too. Josiah was a good man, God rest his soul. I'm sure he'd never approve of me doing this." She clucked her tongue.

"Mrs. DeWitt is from Indiana." Andy changed the subject, rolling his eyes at Tara over Mary's head.

"Gary, to be precise," Mary said.

"Yep and Diana is from Massachusetts, Walter is from North Dakota and Gianni is from California." Andy pointed each juror out to her as his gaze briefly lingered on Diana.

"She's pretty," Tara commented to him with a whisper.

Andy blushed. "Yeah, she is. But I think she's engaged or something."

"Don't let that stop you, Andy," Mary cut in. "You're a fine looking fellow." Leaning across Tara, she straightened the lapel on Andy's suit jacket. "Girl like that would be lucky to have a nice young man like you."

Andy groaned his embarrassment.

Tara patted his thigh to console him. "So when do we get to see the foo...er, men we have to work with?"

"I don't know, but I hope it's soon. I've been waiting a long time to get a gander at all of this prime male flesh." Mary set down her knitting and rubbed her hands together.

Tara took her napkin and mocked a swab on the corner of Mary's mouth.

Mary waved her away with a chuckle. "I'm drooling, right? It's been a *long* time for this old girl."

Tara winced as if her own mother had just told her she and her father actually had sex and then laughed at Mary's eager attitude. "I think the festivities begin tomorrow. So we'll just have to wait until then to see what we have to work with."

The band struck up a conga line and Mary's shoulders began to bounce to the rhythm. "I just love to dance. C'mon,

Andy it's time to liiimbo!" Andy shuffled off behind her, leaving Tara to watch the spectacle that was Mary shimmy over to the band.

This was going to be a very interesting month. Mary wasn't going to be easy to sway.

Tara made a point of threading through the crowd, getting to know each juror.

Time was of the essence.

Glancing at her watch, Tara noted the late hour and smothered a yawn. All of this time change and deceit were killing her, not to mention running into hot guys with names like August. She shivered. Tara hadn't had this much excitement in one jam-packed day in her entire lifetime.

Maybe she'd walk along the beach before bed.

Plot Kelsey's demise or something...and frig the damn guilt.

Chapter Six

Everybody's goin' surfin'...

August was pissed off. After the plane ride from hell with a bunch of jocks who couldn't read the airbag instructions if they had pictures on them, a ride with some native guy whose name he couldn't pronounce and he just knew was having a good laugh at his expense, then yet another plane ride, he'd had enough.

He should have never listened to Greg. This was about the dumbest idea he'd ever had. What was he thinking when he decided to do this? He *wasn't* thinking, that much was clear.

But think of Kelsey. All tight assed and perky breasted. She could be mine. She could be all mine, along with a bundle of cash. His scorned high school counterpart revved its lusty engine.

But what if she didn't look like she did in high school? He sure as hell didn't.

Running a hand through his shaggy hair, August focused on the opposition as they sat at a long table, eating the "getting to know the competition" dinner. Platters of food, heaping with island specialties sat before them, but he wasn't very hungry. The competition was undoubtedly stiff. There wasn't an ounce of extra flesh to be found as he assessed each contestant. Plenty of easy monthly installment plans for the gym would be found in these parts.

All told, there were twenty contestants. The first elimination round would ditch ten of them. Damn, he sure hoped they'd get rid of the guy whose teeth were so white against his bronzed skin it hurt August's eyes to look at him.

Shit. These guys were nothing short of perfection. Chiseled and lean, they epitomized the word "beefcake." He couldn't be this perfect if he spent his entire life in a plastic surgeons office.

"Hey, dude." Mr. Bulging Biceps leaned over him and whispered. "What's that look for?"

Dude. Did anyone still use that word? *Dude...* "Er, I was just thinking that the competition's rather stiff and I'm still sorta reeling from being thrown on a plane to Hawaii in two seconds flat."

"Yeah, that it is and it was kinda freaky, but it wouldn't be reality TV if they didn't do something to rock your world, would it? I'm Aaron Caldwell, nice to meet ya." Aaron licked his finger free of pineapple juice and stuck out a slender hand for him to shake.

August squinted to get a better look at him. Lean, very tan and bleached blond. He was not the kind of guy who spent his time in an office.

"August--August Guthrie, nice to meet you too. Where do you call home?" *No, wait lemme guess, pretty boy... Blond, tan, the lame usage of the word dude... California!*

Aaron smiled brightly, revealing dimples which deeply grooved either side of his perfect mouth. "California."

Go figure.

Play nice. He'd only just arrived and already he was making crude assumptions.

Well, he *was* from California... *August* ... his mental etiquette police warned.

Oh, all right. He'd play nice. Jamming a finger in his ear, he shook it to shut up the advisory counsel in his head. "I'm from Colorado."

"Very cool, mountains and shit right?"

August nodded affirmatively. *Yeah, mountains and shit.*

"So what made you decide to try out for the show?" Aaron asked.

Kelsey Little's ass and a bet from my stupid friend..."I went to school with Kelsey." August assumed that information was okay to pass on. Henry Abernathy actually encouraged it in the acceptance letter he'd gotten in the parking lot.

Aaron slapped him on the back with enthusiasm. "Oh, dude, the whole unrequited love thing?"

Big word there, pretty boy. *Unrequited...* Um, love. No. Lust, oh yeah. "Nah, not love, but I liked her."

"Well, you're one up on the rest of us, knowing her and all. So what was she like?" Aaron's eyes were big and wide with interest now.

August shrugged his shoulders. What was she like? Did he actually know anything about Kelsey's personality? Her likes and dislikes? Her *eye* color? He'd never looked at her eyes, just her ass.

God, that was shallow.

August hung his head. Yep, it was shallow all right, truthful, but shallow. He was hoping if he had the chance to get to know her, she'd be the woman he'd created in his mind. Warm, sensitive, loving ... able to do the wild thing at a moment's notice...

When he took the compatibility test they'd given him just before the oral audition with Henry, he'd been a good match--at least that's what the test guy said. Taking the test was another hurdle he'd passed with flying colors in order to get on this show. So he and Kelsey must have *something* in common.

"She was ... nice, very *nice.*"

Aaron cocked his head inquisitively. "Nice? That's it? I mean we all know she's hot cuz we saw her picture. There was no way I was signing up for something like this unless I knew what the chick looked like, but *nice*? Don't you know *anything* else about her?"

Shame on me... Now, how would he answer that? Tugging his earlobe, August tried to squelch his yakking conscience. Always right on time, reminding him this hadn't been the best laid plan. Or the best plan to get laid. No, he didn't know much more about Kelsey than the shape of her booty. It was lust, pure and simple. Lust and a dare... *Oh, you're going to burn in Hell for this, August Guthrie.*

Damn his second thoughts. *Shaddup, would ya?* "We didn't exactly move in the same social circles," August offered carefully.

Aaron's grin widened. "Oh, I get it. You were hot for her, but she didn't know you existed. You were a dweeb or something, right?" Aaron chuckled and slapped him on the back.

August could feel sweat trickle between his shoulder blades as he used his thumb to push his imaginary glasses further up his nose, forgetting he had his contacts in. Jesus H, it was hot here, even at night. A cameraman swooped in on August and Aaron's conversation, poking the lens closer to their faces. August fought an on-camera grimace. Henry said they should pretend they didn't see the camera, which would be fine, but it didn't have to be up his ass did it? "A dweeb? Well, something like that. Let's just say, I was one of many who Kelsey didn't know existed."

August Guthrie was no damn geek and he wouldn't have footage of him saying so. Not anymore and this time she'd have to recognize that whether she liked it or not.

The cameraman moved away, off to find another victim as Aaron thumped his shoulder, obviously excited over August's geek/not such a geek anymore, status. "Dude, if you were a geek, this chick's in for a *major* surprise."

August shook off the nerd in him that lingered far longer than he'd liked. Yes, Kelsey was in for a surprise of grandiose proportions.

"So, why are *you* here, Aaron?" Hah! Answer that, surfer dude and get off my back about the geek crap.

"The cool trip, man. There are some serious waves to be had here in Hawaii."

Honesty is a good thing. Hawaii and the waves are *certainly* a reason to get married.

Like Kelsey's hot ass was a better one? August twitched. "Just the trip? This is serious stuff, Aaron. Getting married isn't something you should do because you wanna hang ten in Hawaii."

Oh, nice lecture. And he wanted to what? Discuss Tolstoy with her? One shouldn't throw stones at glass houses when the only thought that crossed his mind was beating Greg at his own game and getting laid.

Aaron was young. He was doing him a favor by teaching him caution.

Do yourself a favor and think about your own motives for being here, Mr. Libido. Don't preach to the choir, Auggie boy, he heard his grandmother's favorite adage zing through his head.

"I know," Aaron gave August a sheepish grin. "I'm also here to meet the chick who can hang ten with me--for life." Aaron smiled again before he tore into some cantaloupe. "Who are you bunking with?"

August managed a smile at that. The show carefully placed them in rooms with contestants who best suited one another. He'd ended up with a guy from Duluth, who was a combo pack of Dolph Lundgren and Pee Wee Herman. Nice enough, just a shade shy in the Crayola rainbow pack, but still nice.

August pointed to the end of the table. "Gordon's my roomie. You?"

"I got Rico Suave, er ... Vinny. He's okay, just a little heavy on the testosterone, ya know?"

Indeed, August did know. Vincenzo Lambati, from Brooklyn, New York in da house. Dark, slicked back hair shortly cropped to just above his ears and long on top. Olive skin, further enhanced by a tanning salon payment that August was sure came close to equaling his mortgage, a few gold chains and a tattoo that read, "Who's your daddy?" on his bulging bicep. August met him on the plane, a real stallion Vincenzo was.

Vinny must have noticed them eyeballing him. He waved his turkey leg in the air in a salute from the other end of the table.

"Do you think Kelsey would pick someone like *him*?" Aaron sounded almost frightened by the prospect. Vinny *was* scary and a macho, macho man in every knuckle-dragging sense of the word.

August fought back a snort and sipped whatever the hell was in the coconut shell with the pretty pink umbrella. "You never know, Aaron. Look at last season's show. Did you really think she'd pick Bryan?"

Aaron laughed. “I was rooting for Leo, myself. No, I never thought she’d pick Bryan, he was a long shot.”

“So, you just never can tell, now can you?”

“No, I guess you can’t. We’ll have to see who floats her boat, I guess.”

August was still wondering if *she* would float *his* boat. In order to win the cash, you had to agree to be married on the spot and stay married for a year. But how well could you *know* a person after a month of the occasional date on national television? Well enough to marry them?

Shoulda thought of that before his pistol of passion sucked up all the oxygen to his brain ... *nitwit.*

August pushed his food around on his plate while the contestants got to know each other. The show’s host--Preston Weichert--was supposed to make an appearance and everyone was supposed to stick around for his illustrious manifestation. Otherwise, August would be history. He was tired and hot and overwhelmed by all of the banter.

A rumble in the crowd yanked him out of his misery. Kelsey’s name was circulating, whispered in hushed tones. Like the Second Coming had finally happened.

Ah, she’d arrived. Now was as good a time as any to find out if he and Kelsey had a shot at happily ever after.

Or at the very least a good boink.

August, ya need to shut up.

Chapter Seven

Have we met?

August was disappointed to find that it wasn't Kelsey who'd caused the stir. It was Henry Abernathy and crew. Henry spent a good hour filling them in on what to do and what not to do. Where they could go and where they couldn't for what seemed like the hundredth time. Now that they were on the island, they couldn't go home unless they were dead or a family member was. No backing out, even if they didn't marry Kelsey in the end. More damn restrictions than August wanted to contemplate and death as the only option to relieve him. Shooting began tomorrow, bright and early. They were due back at the pool at eight a.m. sharp for the formal introductions and then, the game began.

Cameras twenty four-seven. He'd had but a taste of that tonight and he wasn't sure he liked it. While some of the guys were real hams, August was what the crew called "camera shy". He wondered if they might not shy away from a camera if it was shoved up their nostrils.

After going back to his hut and changing, he decided to take a run. Falling into a light jog, August headed up the long strand of beach and set free the battle that waged in his brain over his stupidity.

Fuck, he shouldn't have done this. Attention was something he liked best focused on someone else.

And marriage? Shit, he should have given this more thought and listened to his nether friend much less.

Well, movie star, it's a little late for that now, don't you think? He'd have a camera up his ass for the next friggin' month.

The conversation in his head was obviously not going to take a vacay either. I'll go through with it, he consoled himself. I have a purpose here. Kelsey's probably not going to pick me anyway.

He didn't know that for sure. She might fall madly in love with him. He might fall madly in love with her...

It could go either way, he conceded.

And then he could get married, live happily ever after and all that mushy stuff.

Marriage... The word loomed ominously, clanging around in his head. Was he ready for marriage?

Might I remind you, you should have thought about that before you got here, stupid. Look, you've had your say, August reminded his conscience. I know this was an impulsive move on my part, he defended himself, but I'm here now and I can't leave unless I *die*.

Impulsive? Um, yeah. He just wanted to show Kelsey what she missed in high school, make her think he was hot shit and then shove Greg's dare up his ass. Now, look...

August stopped short as he came upon a little cove, covered with the local greenery, situated far from the crowds of people gathered at the dining area. A place to find some peace and quiet. August pushed his way through the lush vegetation and big red flowers and poked his head around the corner.

"Oh!" A feminine voice yelped. August jumped. Nothing was sacred apparently.

So much for peace and quiet.

* ~ *

Tara yanked her shoe off and held it high in the air as she scrambled to a standing position.

That's the way, Tara. Shoe 'em whose boss... Death by stiletto.

Her heart raced as the tall, bulky intruder's shadow entered the cove. Didn't they have security here? She shouldn't have wandered so far from base camp. Maybe he was a part of the crew.

Or, maybe he's the island serial killer. Gilligan gone mad...

"Who are you?" Tara squealed, trying not to let fear keep her from giving him a good whack in the head if need be.

"I'm August Guthrie. I think you can put that thing away. I promise not to ask to borrow them. I'm just looking for a little downtime."

Hearing the chuckle in his tone, she lowered her shoe and slid it back onto her foot. Okay, so he probably *wasn't* a serial killer and his name was August... The moon cast a dim glow over him, catching a blond glimmer of his shaggy hair. Tara squinted to adjust her eyes, trying to make out his features. His bulky frame was a blur. The only thing she could determine was that he was big, *really big.*

August? Oh, crap! Wasn't that the name of the guy she'd met at the water fountain before her interview? The same guy from the airport? August took a step closer with his hands in the air, to show he had nothing in them. He had big hands too. Big, big hands...

Oh, good gravy it *was* the same August. Damn, damn, damn! Was he part of the crew? Tara shivered. "Are you from the show?"

"Yeah. You?"

"Yeah, I am too." Tara answered hesitantly, better to be honest. "I don't think we're supposed to talk to each other and I was here first. Unless you're part of the crew, that is." *Nice cologne...* As the breeze picked up, the scent found its way to her nose.

"Nope, I'm not one of the crew," his husky voice was indecent, meant for a 1-900-Wanna-Fuck hotline.

Oh, Hell's bells. He was one of the babes. Tara just knew it. Strictly a no-no. "Um, one of the contestants?"

August took another step.

Tara experienced an odd ripple of awareness as she breathed in his scent. Whew, he was of the masculine flavor all right and in a very good way. Chemistry *was* her deal, after all. Her nostrils flared in response to his nearness. Musky and fresh all rolled into one.

"Yup," August of the heady scent and the minimal words answered.

"We can't talk to each other, you know." *Of course, he knows, Tara. What are you, beefcake patrol?*

Shut up, he's making my stomach do the jig. I'm happy, why can't you be? her inner slut demanded.

"I know," he answered her.

Oh, that voice. All scratchy and ... and sinful. "I was here first," Tara reminded him. So, nah, nah, nah, nah, nah.

Mature...

It was hot, she was tired and she wanted to be left in peace with her diabolical plan and uber mountains of guilt, thank you. Tara was feeling anything but mature, and absolutely not interested in making friends, she mentally reminded her overactive libido.

"Yep, you were." August's broad chest was coming dangerously close to the top of her head.

Tara's hands felt their way along the sharp rocks as she backed up. The cool press of stone touched the tender spot behind her knees. She plopped down before she lost her balance. "Then you have to go or we'll get into trouble and be kicked off the island. Article twelve-section sixteen, paragraph three, very clearly states that if jurors and contestants are found in any compromising..."

"--settings, they will under no circumstances be allowed to remain in the game of 'Whose Bride Is She Anyway?'," he finished for her.

"Right, so *you* have to go."

"I won't tell if you won't tell. I can't tell. I don't even know your name and I can't see you very well." August's big body found its way to the rock beside her.

Tara shivered again, despite the muggy air. She literally felt his presence, strong and a bit overwhelming. "My name is, Tara and I'm telling you, we'll get into trouble if we get caught," she hissed at him.

Folding his arms across his chest, his biceps came into better view.

Oh, wow.

"Look, uh, Tara," August's voice took on a tone meant to appease. "I just want a little peace away from the crowd. Get some perspective here before the madness begins. I won't tell anyone I met you here and you keep a lid on it too. Let's just not talk about the show."

Looking around nervously, Tara half expected to find a camera hidden in one of the tropical bushes.

Oh, Tara, just sit nicely and talk to Brutus. Relax, he's cute. Tara's inner slut, ever insightful, offered a solution.

Yeah, he was a cute contestant. A hunky contestant looking to get married.

Trust your deepest desires. That would be me, piping up here. I can smell a hottie from twenty paces. Now make nice with the hunk and forget who he's here for.

Tara's gaze wandered to his thighs. Wow again. There wasn't much to August that didn't wow her.

Yeah, wow indeed. Thick and muscled, bet he has something nice between them too. I ain't your slut thermometer for nothin', ya know.

Tara's cheeks were glowing in the dark, she was sure of it. Where the hell had that thought come from?

Her long lost libido, that's where.

Well, check it at the door, Tara wordlessly scolded herself. No libidos allowed. Yummylicious August Guthrie is strictly off limits.

August leaned back and sighed, obviously content with their current predicament. The light of the moon rested directly on his abdomen.

Tara gulped. Damn, he was sculpted.

"How are you affiliated with the show?" August asked, intruding on Tara's physical checklist of him.

"Shh, would you be quiet? I thought we weren't going to talk about the show?"

August's chuckle drifted to her ears on the breeze. "Sorry, how about we start over? I'm August Guthrie, from Colorado." His fingers grazed her arm, trying to find her hand, sending a path of heat right to the tips of her French manicure.

Where were her manners? *Shake the man's hand, Tara. It shows good breeding, refinement.*

Sticking her hand out, she let August's envelop it. Warm skin seared hers, leaving behind a tingle. "Tara Douglas, I'm from Colorado too."

"Really, where in Colorado?"

"A town..."

Laughter rumbled again, deep and rich like Häagen-Dazs® double chocolate fudge.

Oh, my hell.

"That was vague," August mumbled. "Okay, no personal information, I get the drift."

Tara finally smiled too, relaxing a bit. "Good. The less we know about each other the better off we'll be." With that settled, she leaned back on her elbows and let the fragrant breeze caress her flushed cheeks. The silence they shared was somehow comforting, though filled with his presence.

"Guess that just about screws this conversation, huh?"

Now, it was her turn to laugh. Her giggle sounded all giddy and breathy to her ears, making her cheeks hotter still.

Jeez, how much more girlie could she get? This was so unlike the exterior Tara she presented to the world. Cool as a cucumber was her motto, and now she was what? Flirting with a potential man for Kelsey, behaving rather like she'd watched Kelsey behave in high school, fighting off her libido in her head and just begging for trouble.

"Yeah, it kinda does screw it," Tara agreed. If you couldn't talk about anything personal, which was primarily what *would* happen day in, day out on the show, then what was left? "It's hot here," Tara said lamely.

Brilliant topic... The weather always lends to exciting conversation. *Thank you, Al Roker.* Ugh, she sucked at small talk.

"It's supposed to be. It's Hawaii..."

God, she was so *not* good at this. She would always be a geek when it came to small talk with men, especially men of August Guthrie's caliber. "It's a beautiful island, don't you think?"

August reached his arms upward and stretched. Clasping his fingers together, he cracked his knuckles. "Yep."

"So, do you want to just sit here together and say *nothing*? I mean, there is no clause in the contract for us just sitting together. I don't think, anyway. I read the contract pretty carefully, too. Used a fine-tooth-comb, and sitting could hardly be called compromising. Right? I just wouldn't want anyone to think I was biase--d--or--anything." Her words came out in a rush, tripping over each other and stumbling on the word biased.

God, she was like a brook. Babbling away like an idiot all while giving her jury status up.

Smooth move, Ms. Covert. Shit, shit, shit. Shutting her yap now would be what someone with her SAT scores might consider smart.

"You're a jury member..." August's voice trailed off. "Never mind, don't answer that. I think quiet would be the best thing we can be together, for now."

"Quiet, right. Okay, I can do quiet."

"Can you?" August sounded doubtful.

Sighing loudly, Tara sat back up. "I can be so quiet you won't even know I'm here." Tara rose to her feet. "August Guthrie, it was nice *never* meeting you." Turning on her heel, she fought her way through the flora and fauna and scurried her way back down the beach.

* ~ *

August ran a hand over his face, realizing with the time difference, he had a serious case of stubble. Shoot, Tara

Douglas had a really nice ass. The moonlight followed said ass, as Tara beat feet back down the beach.

And what an ass it was, it looked even better than it had at the fountain or the airport. The high curves rounded and firm, were further accented by the clingy dress she wore. More long dark curly hair than any one woman needed and a full mouth, meant for devouring, licking...

Ahem August, this is your conscience calling again *and quite frankly, I'm beat ... have we forgotten all about perky breasted Kelsey?*

No.

Then what was this all about? He was here in paradise because of Kelsey, not because he should be picking up stray chicks at a secluded cove, especially a jury member. This was not Fantasy Island. August heard the warning bells in his head. But *listening* to them was the key.

Nope, August was going to opt to ignore them right now. Tara was gorgeous and there was nothing wrong with a red-blooded man appreciating that.

Yep, he knew a hot ass when he saw one, by a water fountain or accented by moonlight. Hot was hot.

That wasn't the point. Tara had a big fat no-no written all over her and that in and of itself was what should make him quit ogling anyone else from here on out.

He'd better back off the broad and focus on his mission. Get the girl. *The girl you came here to get, not the one who's off limits.* There was the cash too...

No, he was here for Kelsey, not the cash. He'd try to remind Auggie junior of that when he thought of Tara.

August ran a hand through his hair. But shit, Tara's breasts ... they were all round and firm and thrusting upward when she leaned back...

Kelsey had breasts too. He'd called them perky... All right already! Kelsey, Kelsey, Kelsey. Kelsey of the perky breasts.

Sitting up August decided that was a much better attitude. He needed to prepare for tomorrow. Question being, was he ready for tomorrow?

Sorta.

What kind of answer was that? August shook his head. He'd damn well better hang onto his hat if he wanted to be in top form in order to win Kelsey. There was a boatload of studs just lining up for her.

Worse still, he knew that.

Oh for Christ's sake, he wasn't the August Guthrie of twelve years ago. He could hold his own with a woman. He just wasn't sure he wanted to hold it with Kelsey after finding Tara so physically appealing.

Shit, he'd been so damn determined to get on this show to prove his point and now he was teetering on the brink of meeting the girl of his high school wet dreams and he knew next to nothing about her.

Maybe Kelsey will be a fantastic conversationalist. Maybe he'd fall head over heels in *love* with her. August fought the accompanying cringe the "L" word brought with it.

He just might fall head over heels, but it was more likely it would be as a result of tripping and falling.

On that note, August rose and decided to get a good night's rest so he could beat the snot out of all those boy toys in the morning and he wasn't going to waste another minute thinking about that Tara.

Peeling back the bushes, August stomped over what he couldn't physically part with his hands while he thought about Tara Douglas just one last time.

Well fuck, wasn't that peachy? He was having lustful thoughts about a woman he'd met all of two seconds ago, *officially* anyway, while fighting to remember what Kelsey looked like in that picture the show had given him.

He was tired, that's all. Tomorrow everything would look better. Tomorrow he'd see Kelsey Little for the first time in more than twelve years and all would be right with the world. She'd be smokin' hot and tootin' his horny toads.

Trudging back up the beach August let that thought carry him back to his hut. As he slid between the cool sheets, letting his eyes drift slowly closed, the image of Tara Douglas' silhouette against the moon came unbidden, yet oddly welcome.

Shit, she sure had a nice ass ... was August's last thought before everything faded to black.

Chapter Eight

Lights, camera, action!

Tara shifted in her folding chair as makeup people swarmed around the jury members, combing and powder puffing them to gleaming. As if it wasn't hot enough, huge lights sat behind them, adding to the intense heat.

For crap's sake, could they get the show on the road? She'd been up since five in this damn bikini that was giving her the wedgie of the millennium, her thick hair, normally curly, was beginning to go south and the heavy makeup felt like mud. Jesus, this was a lot of work. The producers of the show thought she'd make great ratings for them wearing a bikini.

Tara snorted when she'd been brought the request. "Oh, Ms. Douglas, you have a gorgeous figure" Chad or Brad or some guy with a soap opera name drawled, long and slow. "Trust me when I tell you, you are faaabuulooouuus."

A bikini? In front of Kelsey Little? Miss Babe-o-licious?

Fine, not a problem. She didn't feel the least bit insecure about showing off the ass that made her infamous in high school. Not one stinkin' bit. It wasn't the same ass anymore. Tara looked A-okay in a bikini, thank you. Chad--or was it Brad--said so. Tara just hoped that were true because while she might have felt fine about the bikini earlier, two hours later she had pause for thought.

So here she was in a bikini, feeling totally insecure and hating it. So much for all her *in your face, Kelsey* bravado. It was sticking uncomfortably to her and she felt certain if that sneaky cameraman did a close up on her thighs the planet Earth as a whole would cringe in unison.

"That Henry looks like a chicken with his head cut off doesn't he? You'd think he was preparing for the Oscars," Ms. Mary commented.

Tara tugged self consciously at the thin strips of material holding the girls in place and ground her teeth to keep from screaming. "I'm sure he's as nervous as we are, Ms. Mary," Tara cut in. "There's a lot of money invested in this."

Henry Abernathy was busy running around, shouting directions to the prop people and in general behaving like this was a remake of Gone with the Wind.

"Jury members!" he called, clapping his hands as he made his way around the kidney shaped pool. "Listen up! The men have arrived and we're waiting for Kelsey. Now, all I need from you is your silence. If you can manage that, we'll be on the right path. We don't want the viewing audience to see your reactions to the contestants, or your reaction to Kelsey's reaction to them."

Mary DeWitt leaned over and gave Tara a quizzical look with a snort. "What the hell did he just say? I didn't like him much on that interview I had with him. He's gay. I'd bet my son on it."

Tara snorted back. "Just keep a blank expression on your face and don't give away how you feel about the contestants.

That means no drooling over the hunks, Ms. Mary, because then Kelsey might know who you favor."

"Oh hell, okay. And what's *this* for again?" Mary held up the large cardboard scorecard each jury member was given in order to rate each contestant. They were to note their initial reactions to each piece of beefcake by giving them a score of one to five--five being exceptional. The cards were kept for future reference in their decisions.

Tara giggled. "Do you have your hearing aid in, Ms. Mary?"

"Don't be fresh, young lady. Of course I do, I'm just so tired from all that limbo-ing last night. I'm not the spring chicken I used to be. I didn't hear what he was saying."

"I just want to be sure you hear *everything*. I don't want you to miss something important." *Like helping me pick the biggest jerk this side of Forgotten island for Kelsey.*

Tara explained the scorecard, listening with half an ear to Henry Abernathy drone on about how once the cameras were on, they wouldn't go off until the show was over.

Blah, blah, blah. As if she hadn't heard this two bazillion times?

Preston Weichert, the show's host, sat parallel to the jurors in the host's chair, sipping a bottle of water. He seemed as friendly as he appeared to Tara on camera. Cool and calm, he was the epitome of collected.

Tara's stomach, on the other hand, was engaging in the electric slide, shifting and sloshing its way to a jumbled mess as she fought off the heat and her anxiety over walloping Kelsey Little. She just wasn't cut out for all of this undercover crap. Pretending she was something she wasn't. Tara Douglas was not, nor ever would be Kelsey's friend. Not in high school and not now. She was on the edge of doing something dreadful.

Covering her mouth, Tara struggled with the bile that rose in her throat.

"Hey, you all right there, missy?" Ms. Mary asked. "You look a little green."

Tara breathed deeply. Green with envy? Green around the gills? Oy. "I'm okay, just a bit nervous is all."

Ms. Mary patted her hand and Andy cracked his knuckles. "Once everything begins to happen you won't even know the camera is rolling," Andy assured her.

After last night's run-in with August Guthrie, Tara was a bundle of nerves. She should just get up right now and leave. Go home, make something up, lie, cuz God knew she was getting better and better at that.

"Hey, Tara," Diana called to her from the end of their row of jurors. Tara shaded her eyes and looked in Diana's direction. "You ready to rumble?" Diana wiggled her eyebrows and giggled.

Rumble? Like cause trouble rumble? Oh, God save her from herself and her guilty conscience...

Tara sat up and winked at Diana like she knew what she meant. "Ready when you are!"

What if someone discovered her reason for being here? What if someone went digging for something dirty on the jury members and found out about that damn video tape of her? Oh, Hells bells, Tara could just see the headlines now. *Geek plots revenge against reality show bride.*

Now wait a minute, that was just silly, Tara thought. No one knew what she wanted to do to Kelsey. They couldn't read her mind. Ah, but she could hear the questions now as microphones were shoved in her face; "Tell us Ms. Douglas, why would you want help Kelsey find a husband if she shoved you bare-ass-naked out into a hallway full of basketball players?" And how would she answer that? Forgive and forget? No hard feelings?

And then of course there was the added element of August Guthrie to really make things complicated...

"I think they're linin' 'em up, Tara," Walter yelled over the crew member's noisy last-minute preparations.

Tara's head shot up and she gulped as the muscles in her stomach tightened, but she rubbed her hands together for Walter's benefit. "I'm ready as I'll ever be!" she yelled back cheerfully.

She was going to see August again...

What if someone found out Tara Douglas thought August Guthrie, "Whose Bride Is She Anyway?" beefcake, was hot?

Did she just admit that?

Oh, she did not think he was hot.

Did too...

She did not. How could she possibly think he was hot?

How quickly we forget the water fountain and the airport, long before you even knew August was a contestant.

Oh, fine. She'd seen enough to know he was hot.

And what had she been thinking about just before she fell asleep last night? Hmmm... June... July... August! Why, yes, it was August Guthrie doing the dance of lust in Tara Douglas' dreams.

So he *might* be cute. Big deal. All of the contestants were cute, for crap's sake. It's a pre-req to be on the show.

But would they elicit the amazing physical response she'd had over someone she hardly knew? Tara would bet her bippy not. It was pretty rare a man turned her on like August did, especially *because* of the fact that she'd been consistently hot since their initial meeting. He smelled soooooo good and now he had her nostril hairs all in a twist.

Andy pulled a handkerchief from his Hawaiian shirt pocket and wiped his brow. “It’s getting hotter by the minute even under this canopy. I wish they’d start.”

Hot? Did Andy say *hot*? Tara sighed and twirled a long strand of her hair absently. It was true. She’d been thinking about the *hot* August and their encounter last night.

It didn’t matter, she had to focus on her mission and it didn’t include her hanging all over August Guthrie gushing and being stupidly girlie.

It involved making Kelsey pay and it was time for one last refresher course in payback.

Okay, so, here’s the plan... *Find a jerk for Kelsey*, enjoy your first vacation in five years, *find a jerk for Kelsey*, relax and have a good time, *find a jerk for Kelsey*, get a tan, *find a jerk for Kelsey...*

In that order, please. If she didn’t have a nervous breakdown first. The twist of Tara’s gut reminded her she was a complete amateur at this conniving stuff.

“Tara!” Ms. Mary said. “I think they’re going to start. Sit up. You’re going to look so pretty on camera.”

Oh, shit, shit, shit! She was making a huge mistake. Was what she was planning really worth it? Was making Kelsey Little squirm in front of millions of people on national television going to make her complete? Fill up her account of revenge in the bank of Tara? How exactly did she plan to make her squirm anyhow? Tara wasn’t terribly confrontational, it wasn’t like she was going to jump up while the cameras rolled and start yelling, “Kelsey Little is a low-down dirty slut. Wanna see why, my fellow Americans?” It was more about getting some personal satisfaction. It was about reading in the tabloids over her morning coffee and seeing in print just how miserable Kelsey was and how she’d had to give up the money because she couldn’t stay married to a slimeball. Tara wanted

Kelsey Little to look her in the eye and *know* who she was. Know that it was Tara Douglas who was in charge now.

Gripping the arms of her chair, Tara rolled her head from side-to-side, trying to calm her nerves.

No one said she had to go through with it. Not a soul knew about it but her.

Taking a deep, cleansing breath, Tara consoled herself with that very thought as more chaos erupted.

Commotion reigned as the men began lining up in front of the jurors and more importantly, the queen of mean had arrived.

Diana catcalled and whistled, "Woo hoo! Bring on the pretty boys!"

Tara hid a smile as she caught sight of where Kelsey would be.

She sat in a chair shrouded with gauzy material, waiting to view her potential husbands. Her haughty outline was just visible. The humid air was thick with excitement and rife with testosterone.

Tara's nostrils responded to the scent of suntan lotion *and* August Guthrie ... standing but ten feet from her in his bathing suit and nothing else. She'd know that body anywhere. Oh, my...

Hookay, so he *was* hot. Great... Tara groaned. He looked even better than he had the other day. So good, he was making her nipples tighten and her legs quiver.

I told you, her libido sing-songed.

Holy fanfreakintastic...

She must always listen to her libido and it was saying, yippee skippee.

Omigod.

Chapter Nine

Kelsey, Kelsey, Kelsey

When had the ozone layer eroded so much that the hot sun beating down on his head felt like molten lava? August ran a hand over his slippery chest. Jesus, he was greased like a pig. The makeup people made a big deal out of sliming them up for the cameras with suntan lotion and it was just plain gross. It showed up well on camera, according to Chaz or whatever the costume guy's name was. His nose filled with the scent of coconut-banana. Rolling his head from side-to-side, relaxing his tense muscles, August looked up to see what the jury was all about.

Holy hell.

August rocked from foot to foot nervously as he saw Tara in the full light of day.

Smile, August ... look who the foreman *of the jury is.* Wow, that was a really big sign they gave her. It read: Tara Douglas, Jury Foreman, in big bold letters. Right behind her pretty head. The girl from the water fountain was part of the jury and to top all of this wonderful reality show insanity off, she was the *foreman* and she was just as good looking as she'd been, if not better than when he'd first laid eyes on her.

Jesus.

Tara *Douglas*...August rolled her name around his brain again. Didn't the jury foreman have to be a friend from Kelsey's past? It was bad enough to lust for her, but to lust for a friend of Kelsey's was just ugly and wrong. August adjusted his sunglasses to make sure his eyes were covered and he wasn't caught ogling Tara.

What to do about the fact that his cock was ogling Tara too...

August shifted his stance, spreading his legs. Had she seen him too? And did she give a shit if she had? He hadn't exactly been a fountain of sparkling conversation last night.

Tara had reminded him quite plainly last night that chatter was out. Besides, who needed Tara Douglas and her hot ass? He was here for *Kelsey*.

Yep, that's right. Kelsey, Kelsey, Kelsey.

Now if he could just tell that to the big hello he was waving to Tara from his drawers.

Henry Abernathy had already given them the "on camera" speech, they were just waiting for the sound crew to finish and they'd be ready to go.

Let's do this already, August thought, tapping his toe in the stupid sandals the show provided. Looking down, August pursed his lips at them. They were kind of girlie.

Looking up, he saw that Tara Douglas had some really great legs. Long and slender with plenty of thigh to wrap around your waist while you--

August! he scolded himself, *cut that out, now!*

He groaned. His conscience would just happen to show up *now*. Go figure.

No. He would ignore the newest battle in his head and savor this last moment of lust for Tara before Kelsey came along and zapped him with her uber amounts of sex appeal. Just this once he was going to win the war in his head and get it out of his system--with whatever he could come up with to assuage his guilt over thinking about Tara.

Now, a man's gotta do what a man's gotta do and that included giving Tara Douglas the once over in *peace,* without any further interruption from his morality meter. So, August challenged his ethics, *lemme finish, would ya?*

Now, where was he? Ah yes ... her hips...

The soft curve of her hip was a perfect place to hold on to when thrusting--

Danger Will Robinson, danger! No thrusting, absolutely none.

August scoffed, he could thrust all he wanted in his imagination if he chose to. No one had to know.

Au contraire ... he could be stopped when his imagination did *that.*

August looked down at his crotch.

Oh... Yeah, that was noticeable, huh?

Not unless someone's eyes were traveling south.

August grimaced and folded his hands in front of his crotch, continuing his journey into the mind candy that was Tara.

She had great breasts too. Full and round and he'd bet her nipples--

Whoa, since when did he call them *breasts*? Wasn't the word "hooter", used on more than one occasion when referring to that particular part of the female anatomy?

Somehow, it just seemed more appropriate for a woman like Tara to have her hooters referred to as breasts, was all. He was just doing some harmless looking...

He'd need eye surgery if he continued to "look" the way he had been.

Tara repositioned herself in her chair, licking her raspberry-tinted lips. Full and pouting, they called his name. Hair, black as midnight, with chocolate highlights fell to just below the curve of her breasts.

August groaned. The tip of her pink tongue was making him nuts as it ran over her bottom lip.

That bikini was awfully small... Looking around he saw that the rest of the pretty boys had noticed Tara too.

She was attractive. One would expect that others would see that as well. August rolled his shoulders. It was cool.

Just then, Vinny, the Italian Stallion waved to Tara from two guys down the line.

That's it! They'd better back the fuck off. They were here to win Kelsey, *not* Tara.

And he was here to do what? Win the big stuffed panda bear?

Okay, it was pissing him off that these jerks were covertly observing Tara behind sunglasses that hid nothing but lust! Beach boy tilted his sunglasses upward and nodded at Tara casually. How *observant* did they have to be? Weren't they here to win Kelsey?

Reality check here, August. That's why he was here too. This thing with Tara was just a mere physical reaction, it would pass.

It better, cuz it was show time and he had a hard on... And it wasn't for Kelsey.

Crap. Kelsey was thirty or so feet from him on the other end of the pool. They'd kept her secluded with a big, filmy tent around her. This was stupid. They already knew what she looked like.

Ah, but Kelsey didn't know what the contestants looked like. *Duh.*

Henry Abernathy ran toward them, his face flush with the heat and obvious excitement. "Okay, boys, its show time. Take your places, please and do as you were instructed by the stage managers."

August only vaguely heard Henry as he tried to focus on seeing Kelsey for the first time in twelve years. Shit, what was the instruction?

When they call your name, make an entrance.

Aaron leaned forward and grinned his oral wet dream of a smile. "Ready, man?"

August nodded. Was he ready? Hell no.

All at once, the pool area took on a serene calm, everyone remained still and then, Preston Weichert entered the picture. His dulcet tones invited the viewing audience to join them for a new edition of, "Whose Bride Is She Anyway? Where marriage means money." Preston spoke as though he were intimately sharing a personal conversation with each and every audience member.

A blur of silent movement had the men shuffling toward their assigned spots as each contestant's name rang out in the humid air.

August's legs moved like lead, his girlie sandals flip-flopped noisily as he clunked down the long walk to Kelsey. Twelve long years of waiting was now, officially over. *Do you hear that?* August scolded his hard on for Tara. *It's all about Kelsey now, buddy.* So just forget Tara Douglas because it's show time...

* ~ *

As each contestant made their way to the end of the pool, where Kelsey would eventually reveal herself, the jurors busily rated them. Tara could hear Ms. Mary snicker softly.

Tara tried to keep her face impassive as each hunk sauntered by. A dark haired, beef of a babe strolled nonchalantly past her chair and winked arrogantly at her.

Oooh, he's hot as the day is long!

Be quiet, Tara hushed her libido... *I'm thinking.*

His name was Vinny. Vinny, Vinny, Vinny. Hmmmm... He needed a rating.

Three, Tara decided. He was be-a-utiful ... but he had a tattoo that said "Who's your daddy"...

So?

So, Tara didn't like tattoos.

But, maybe Kelsey did. Hahah!

Good, then she couldn't have him, now, could she? Vinny gets a three and that's final.

When August's name was finally announced a thrill of excitement shot up her spine. Tara sat up, keeping her back erect and her legs tightly crossed, refusing to make eye contact with him. Instead, she busied herself, staring at his crotch. Her cheeks flushed.

Tara scribbled the number two on her piece of cardboard.

Two, two, two!

A two? A two? Her conscience screamed its rebellion in disbelief. *Now, you're not being honest are you? August is much more worthy of at the very least, a four, and you know it.*

She'd written two. *Two, two, two...* Tara darkened the number with her pen for emphasis. Hah!

Now what was she accomplishing by lying about August's rating but possibly keeping Kelsey from him?

Keeping Kesley from him...

Oh, God what had she been thinking? This was wrong, just ugly and mean and ... well ... on the other hand, kinda empowering.

Squirming in her chair, Tara made a heart around August's rating. It remained a two. So there, she mentally stuck her tongue out at him.

August looked rather uncomfortable under the hot sun. His bronzed skin glistened in the shimmering heat, oiled and slick from too much suntan lotion.

Holy guacamole, he was a big boy ... and his shaggy blond hair, in complete disarray, was thick and shiny. She didn't normally favor blond men, so that does that. August just didn't do it for her. Not a lot anyway...

"You gave him a two?" a voice squawked in her ear with disbelief. "A two? Wanna borrow my glasses, missy?" Ms. Mary nudged her hard.

Tara shrugged her shoulders. "He's not *that* cute."

Ms. Mary cackled, "Oh, riiiigghht. All that blond hair, just imagine what it would be like to run your fingers through those rumpled strands. Especially after a good bout in the old sack..."

"Ms. Mary, we're supposed to be judging them by what we feel best suits Kelsey. Not just by how hot we think they are. Looks aren't everything."

Ms. Mary crossed her eyes at Tara. "Well, aren't you the uptight one? Chill out, would ya? Have some fun, enjoy the eye candy. If I could give him a ten, I would."

Tara bristled. "I'm here to pick a *husband* for Kelsey," she whispered fiercely under her breath. "Not choose Mr. America."

"Look, she's going to marry a guy she's known for less than a month, the least he can be is cute. I say we're helping the poor gal out." Mary muttered from under the brim of her hat.

Poor gal? Please. "Let's just focus on rating them *overall*, shall we?" Now, lay off August, you old coot, Tara thought.

She was behaving like a cranky, spoiled child. Tara Douglas was ... *jealous.* Tara winced at that thought, then straightened. She was *not*.

Yes, yes she was.

Crap.

Several of the on-camera staff began to gather by Kelsey's gauze covered chair. Preston Weichert introduced her to the world at large in muted tones, creating the much anticipated drama the viewing audience would expect when they watched from their arm chairs at home.

All cameras pointed to Kelsey.

Tara's stomach lurched violently. It was now or never.

Chapter Ten

Chemistry-schmemisitry

As the gauze fell away, revealing a chubbier Kelsey than Tara remembered, the crowd of contestants went wild. Clapping and wolf whistles drowned out everything else as Kelsey made her big entrance.

Tara's gaze narrowed in on August. He remained stoic compared to the other men. He calmly viewed Kelsey as she jumped up from her chair and pranced in front of them in her thong bikini.

Man, her ass had some newly formed cottage cheese Tara didn't remember when Kelsey stood arrogantly atop the pyramid as captain of the cheerleading team.

Kelsey smiled at the camera, turning toward the men, assessing each one from head to toe. Her eyes lingered just a bit too long on August Guthrie.

Tramp. Slut. Man-eater.

Tara clamped a hand over her mouth as though her thoughts were spoken out loud. She should care that Kelsey was all of the above, why? August was clearly off limits and he quite obviously enjoyed a tramp now and again.

This is strictly payback, no emotional attachments to a man she'd merely *smelled.*

Tara watched carefully as each juror wrote his or her initial reaction based on Kelsey's. Deciding whom they felt Kelsey might have chemistry with, by her facial expressions and long lingering looks.

Really *long* lingering looks.

Bitch.

Ms. Mary's pen bobbed furiously as she scribbled on her cardboard as she cast an all-knowing sidelong look at Tara. "Well, if you don't like August, Kelsey sure as heck does."

Tara narrowed her eyes and reiterated her previous thought. Kelsey was a slut, of course she liked August. All sluts would.

Did that make her a slut too? No, she didn't really *like-like* August. Tara *liked* ice cream and French fries. That was *like-like.* August wasn't quite as high on a list of good dairy products, so she wasn't a slut after all.

Whew.

Preston gave his arm to Kelsey and escorted her to the jury members. Kelsey's stride was confident as she landed precisely on her mark. Presenting her to the jury, Preston asked her to tell the nice folks at home about herself.

Kelsey cocked her head to the side and smiled sweetly. Flaxen curls, lush and full flowed over her shoulders, blowing softly in the humid breeze.

Tara took a closer look at Kelsey from behind her sunglasses. *Betcha Clairol had something to do with all those flaxen curls.*

Kelsey pursed her full, red lips--lips that matched her thong perfectly and gave her long overdue Miss. America speech.

"My name is Kelsey Little, and I'm from Colorado Springs, Colorado. I love the great outdoors, gardening, cooking and reading. I work at..."

--pulling the wings off moths, frightening innocent children and sleeping with anything that walks. Oh, and naturally, world peace. Tara struggled to keep her mouth firmly clamped shut. Kelsey sounded like a walking endorsement for wannabe wife of the year.

Did she say *read*? Puuleease. Kelsey Little read? She was lucky if she could sound out Dr. Seuss without stumbling and if Tara remembered correctly, Kelsey failed Home Ec because she burned the salad... Or something like that.

"--as an administrative assistant at a well-known advertising agency," Kelsey continued. Pretty as a picture, she spoke with poise and grace, turning once more to wink at the camera.

Tara was going to gag. Would gagging be inappropriate on national television? Oddly, the presence of the cameras was Tara's least concern now that her nemesis was but mere feet away.

Preston asked her a series of questions ending with, "How about you tell the nice folks what qualities you'd like in a potential husband, Kelsey?"

Oh, yes, please do. It was like placing your husband order at a fast food joint.

Kelsey paused a moment in thought. "Someone who's honest and forthright, a man who knows what he wants and isn't afraid to say so. Kind, considerate, a sense of humor is especially important, and if he's good looking, I won't be unhappy." She flashed another smile, white and perfect.

Can I have fries with my new husband, please? How many brain cells did Kelsey lose, rehearsing that load of shit? Takes time to perfect such bullshit.

Probably as much time as Tara had spent convincing herself, and anyone else who would listen to her, what her motives for being here were.

Guilty as charged, your Honor.

"Now, Kelsey, meet the jurors who will help you choose the man of your dreams. First up, Mary DeWitt..."

Tara held her breath as Preston got around to her introduction. She bit her lip and fought not to scream as Kelsey stood before her, smiling and posing for the jury. A fake, a liar... Tara could barely focus on Kelsey for fear that she'd reveal Tara for who she once was.

A fat, unpopular, dateless ex-dork.

Accused unfairly of sleeping with everybody's favorite, Evanston High sweetheart's boyfriend, taunted endlessly for her nude scene debut in the locker room hallway for months on end.

Tara lifted her chin, even as her cheeks burned over remembering Kelsey's harassment. Tara refused to show any signs that Kelsey had torn her world to shreds in one horrifying act of cruelty. As she sat in her jury chair, facing the now woman who'd made her life a living Hell, her pride refused to allow Kelsey the satisfaction of seeing her squirm. Tara felt fat and awkward all over again, even if she really wasn't, but she would *never* let Kelsey know it. Her nemesis was now her prey ... and if Tara could only keep that clear in her mind, that she had leveled the playing field and she and Kelsey were equals in the bod department, she'd be okay.

"Kelsey Little, meet your jury foreman, Tara Douglas. Tara hails from your very own home state of, Colorado. You may remember her from high school. She was the president of the trigonometry club and all round four point O student. Currently, Tara's a chemist in a perfume factory and aspires to create her own line of perfume one day."

Tara watched Kelsey's eyes flash something unidentifiable, waiting to see if she'd tell the world at large they didn't really know-know each other. Tara smiled and waved with attitude, while still holding her breath until she felt like she might have to begin to breathe out of her ass.

Kelsey waved back, "Hi, Tara, how have you been?" Very cool, very calm, very blissfully unaware. Either that or she'd honed those acting skills to a razor sharp point.

Tara let loose a long, slow exhale of relief. Then, Kelsey dismissed her promptly, setting her sights on Andy, batting her eyelashes and smiling. God she was so obvious. What a tart.

Kelsey didn't appear, outwardly anyway, to have a clue who Tara was. Tara wasn't sure if she should be pissed or tickled pink that her mission was semi-accomplished. How could she possibly forget what she'd done to Tara? It was despicable, unthinkable--totally going to work in her favor.

Well, Tara thought, if Kelsey didn't know who she was now, she sure would...

~

"No."

"What do you mean *no*?"

"I just don't think he's right for Kelsey."

"Are you kidding me? He has the kind of body that's lickable from head to toe!" Ms. Mary squawked.

Tara sighed and tried to behave reasonably. So much for manipulating the jury. "I'm only trying to suggest that August didn't seem to share much chemistry with Kelsey. Isn't chemistry a part of the 'marriage' package? Lickable doesn't seem to be a quality that's a requirement." She was a chemist, she knew these things.

Mary swatted at Tara with her now, men's size twelve, knitted baby bootie. "They had so much chemistry you could set a house on fire with the fumes alone. What's your beef with August?"

Tara calmly sipped her pineapple juice and measured her words carefully. "I have no beef with August, Ms. Mary. I don't even know him, for goodness sake. I just didn't see it the way you did." Tara watched the faces of her fellow jurors carefully, especially Ms. Mary's. Everyone seemed convinced but her.

"Then you need glasses, girlie," Mary chided.

Tara clenched her teeth. As they sat around the table in the jury room, lollygagging over the "right" choice for Kelsey, Tara twiddled her thumbs. How hard could this be? It wasn't exactly brain surgery...

"How about we set aside August for a minute and focus on the other nine contestants that we need to choose?" Andy interjected.

What a load of shit this was. Ms. Mary was determined to give August to Kelsey on a silver platter.

This troubled her, why?

Tara shook her head. It didn't trouble her.

Um, yeah, it did.

Tara sighed again. Okay, so maybe it did, but only a *little* and only because Kelsey-Fabulous-Little got whatever she wanted, whenever she wanted it even when Tara was so damned determined to see to it she didn't!

Fine, just freakin' fine. She'd let Kelsey have August... This round, anyway. A noble gesture on her part indeed.

Tara stood up and waved the final voting sheet. "How does everyone feel about August going to the next round? All in favor say 'aye'."

Every damned one of them confirmed the "aye".

Well, hell.

"Okay, so August, Vinny, the Italian Stallion..." Tara cringed thinking about Vinny's tattoo, he was just ... well, just ... icky was the word that came to mind. But, he might make a nice little partner in life for Kelsey.

Who's your daddy?

* ~ *

The evening was officially a free-for-all. Each contestant, member of the jury and Kelsey were invited to a barbeque, monitored of course, by the crew so no funny stuff went on. Henry had made that clear. The jury could watch Kelsey in a relaxed atmosphere and see how she interacted with all of the contestants together and for the contestants to strut their stuff for the jury. It was probably more like an opportunity for the camera crew to get some embarrassing footage of contestants doing stupid stuff as they chugalugged a Tiki Tornado.

Tara sat on her chair at the bar, watching from a short distance as Kelsey pawed August Guthrie. Flirting and cooing her ass off.

Well, not totally *off,* that would be like turning water into wine. Tara snickered. It wasn't a nice thought, but it was the truth. Tara never thought the day would come when she could say her ass was in better shape than Kelsey's. She couldn't get over how much Kelsey had changed and how completely unaware she seemed to be of that fact. Even more surprising, Kelsey didn't even remember who Tara was. Tara had suspected she wouldn't, but it took a great deal of the fulfillment factor out of the game for her. She was just another victim in a long line of Kelsey's antics, but the ugliness of the act should have at least rendered a glimpse of recognition, left some kind of impression on Kelsey. Of course, that would require mental retention on Kelsey's part and that was probably stretching the bounds of her teensy-weensy perimeters.

"Hey, Tara!" Diana smiled as she floated past her with a plate full of barbecued chicken. "Today was really something, huh?"

Tara smiled and nodded wearily. "It was and I don't know about you, but I'm beat." *And feeling more than a little relieved that I haven't been caught yet.*

Diana laughed and shook her head. "Nah, I'm a night owl and all off schedule from jet lag. You gonna join us?" Diana pointed to the table two rows away.

"Maybe in a bit. I think I need to catch my breath."

"Okay, well if you change your mind, you know where we are."

Tara smiled and waved Diana off just as she caught a glimpse of Kelsey's pink nails when they flashed under the tiki torches, making yet another pass over August's forearm.

Tara gritted her teeth and folded her hands together. Wasn't that special? Kelsey might look different, but her tactics were ever predictable when it came to a manhunt.

August leaned back a bit against the bar and smiled with what *looked* like a polite response to the tramp's roaming hands.

Or was that just wishful thinking? His profile under the light of the torches seemed rather stoic, as if he wasn't at all interested in Kelsey. That just wasn't possible, was it? Everyone wanted Kelsey Little, including August Guthrie. Tara wondered what August's story was. Auggie needed some cash and a little rumble between the sheets.

Andy came up behind Tara's chair, making her jump and startling her. Tara tilted her head back and smiled up at him. "Hey you, how's it going?"

Andy grinned. "You looked so serious, whatcha thinkin'?"

"I was just wondering why men like Aug--um, like these men, who look like they do, need a reality show to win a wife?

I mean they don't look like the kind of guys who lack female attention."

Andy shrugged and said, "I hear August was hot for Kelsey in high school and I can tell ya, from this guys perspective, the money is a pretty good gig."

Tara didn't hear the last part of Andy's answer because her ears were still glued to August was hot for Kelsey in *high school*.

Who the hell was August Guthrie and how did he know Kelsey Little? Had he really been in her graduating class? It was a big class, but no, Tara would have remembered a name like *August*, no matter how large her class was. Even when she'd met him at the water fountain his unusual name didn't ring a bell. Maybe he was younger than she was? Oh, God she didn't need this now ... what if August knew what had happened to her with Kelsey? He wanted to win her and if he wanted to win badly enough, maybe he'd rat Tara out.

Shit, her head screamed, while her mouth said to Andy, "Money? I don't know Andy, that's a pretty serious commitment, no matter how much money's involved."

Andy chuckled, "Yep, it sure is, but it's only a year and she's okay looking. I guess after a year you can get yourself a Hollywood divorce."

Tara patted Andy's hand and shook her head at his very male take on marriage. "If you go into marriage that way, you may as well not bother."

"Well, it *is* a million bucks," he said as he moved from behind her, his eyes obviously drawn to Diana, who waved to him from the table. "Come join us, Tara."

"I will in just a bit. You go ahead."

Andy headed straight for Diana and Tara smiled. If Andy had his way, Diana wouldn't be engaged for long.

August captured her attention as he leaned over the bar and shook hands with the bartender, taking the beer he offered.

Those hands... Lean and long fingered, but as wide as the Grand Canyon.

This was just lame. Tara's heart was jumping and her pulse was racing over August Guthrie for no good reason. They'd had a conversation that lasted all of ten minutes, he probably didn't even last that long in bed.

Bed ... now there was a place Tara could envision him.

Hellooooo... Since when did she become stimulated by just a man's looks? Tara needed conversation, IQ scores, job stats. Lust never entered the picture in her small, but organized dating world. She'd been judged far too long on how she looked and now she was using the same discriminatory tactics she so despised. The road obviously went both ways, fat or skinny.

A high-pitched giggle intruded on her thoughts, bringing Tara's head back up. Kelsey was suddenly whisked away by Gordon. He pulled her to the dance floor and began to do something Tara wouldn't venture to qualify as an Arthur Murray certified dance step.

August turned his head toward Tara's table and their eyes met. Or clashed, or something like that. Locked on one another was a suitable term. He was doing that eye contact thing again and it was driving her insane, making her squirm and the dilemma of all dilemmas ... it made her nipples so tight she could crack open bottle tops with them.

August lifted one corner of his mouth.

Was that a smile? Tara lifted her chin and gave him her right profile. *Take that, you lust evoker!* She sensed movement from her peripheral vision, then the scent of big-hunky man assaulted her nostrils.

"Hey."

Oy. Hey, hot-stuff, wanna do it 'til we collapse? Gawd, this was shameful and wrong, just *wrong.* Tara looked around to see if the crew cared that she and August were communicating. The rules stated they couldn't fraternize unless supervised. Well, they were supervised, if you counted George the cameraman slumped over the bar, pink umbrella drink in hand.

While it wasn't likely they'd do the hump-backed beast here in this group setting, Tara didn't need any suspicion cast her way. No one seemed to care much, so she guessed it was okay. Hell, Ms. Mary was pinching booty left and right and no one made a peep.

August placed a big hand on her arm momentarily, giving her a slight nudge. A pinprick of heat spiraled outward into a house on fire all along her arm and right to her shoulder, making her snatch her arm back.

"Hey, August, right?" Tara answered, as non-welcoming as possible. Pretending she didn't even remember his name seemed cool and distant. He'd never guess all she'd thought about since she met him was *doing him,* and now she had the added worry that he was a former classmate.

August pulled a chair out beside her, the metal legs scraping on the pool patio. He didn't seem concerned at all that she'd pretended she didn't know his name. "Yep, that's me. Did you have a good day?"

Oh, yes, August! She wanted to scream at him. It was tres fantastique. How could it have been anything but good when it meant that Kelsey Little was going to get what she wanted yet again? "Yeah, it was okay. Hot, but okay. How about you?"

"It *is* hot here."

Tell me about it... Here ... there ... anywhere in your general vicinity, Tara thought, as she blew out a breath. "It's nothing like Colorado, that's for sure."

August's laughter rumbled and her head began to swirl. "No, it's not like home, but it's a nice diversion from the same old-same-old."

Oh, for sure, Tara thought. There was nothing same or old about going on a reality show to pursue your old high school hottie, now was there? "It's beautiful though. I love the beaches."

August nodded, "Yep, me too. So, do you like living in Colorado?"

Tara nodded curtly. Keep it neutral, she reminded herself, people from the show's staff might be watching. "I like the mountains and it's where I was raised. What's not to like?"

He ran a hand over his jaw, his fingertips scraping the stubble from a long, hard day. Leaning near her he sighed. "I didn't say you couldn't like it. I was just asking."

Then ask yourself this, August. Why the hell is it making me nuts just sitting near you? "I know," Tara said defensively, twisting her upper body away from his big Leaning-Tower-of-Pisa one.

"Did you eat?"

Did it look like she'd eaten? Were her thighs flapping in the breeze? Was August calling her fat? Was he *mocking* her? She never should have worn that stupid bikini because now he thought she was fat and if he thought she was fat, it was going to trigger his memory from high school and then he'd know who she was. Oh, God! Tara didn't know how much more pressure she could take.

Whoa, now that was conclusion jumping, rather hasty. Good gravy, she was a bundle of nerves and taking it out on August. How could he be blamed for being babe-o-licious? It wasn't his fault he made her drool buckets and if he remembered who she was, he certainly was good at hiding it.

Closing her eyes, Tara took a slow inhalation of air, and smiling serenely, she responded, “Yes, I did eat, thank you.”

He put his hand on her arm again. “Are you okay?”

If he would quit touching her arm, thereby turning her into a horny, salivating freak show--she would be just frickin’ glorious. “Don’t I look okay?”

August removed his hand. “Yeah.”

Good. “Well, I am, fine that is.”

August grinned. “Me too.”

Oh, God. Why wouldn’t he just go away? The heat from his body was slamming into hers and rivulets of sweat were making a puddle in the space between her breasts. Was he trying to impress her? So she’d pick him for Kelsey? Grabbing her drink she took a long sip, then rubbed the cool of the glass over her forehead. “Good. It’s important that you’re fine. You need to be strong and mentally healthy for the competition ahead of you. So you should go to bed and get a good night’s rest now.” *Shoo-shoo. Go away and leave horny Tara alone.*

Leaning into her further, August whispered close to her ear, “I’m not tired. It must be jet lag or something. I’m wide awake and rarin’ to go.” Tara found herself inching toward the heat of his breath and thinking about his tongue jammed in her ear while he was *rarin’ to go*. Her nipples tightened ... this must end. *Now.*

“Not me, “Tara faked a big yawn. “I’m still tired. Must be all that sunshine. I’d better go off to bed now. Sweet dreams.” With that, Tara slid off her chair and slipped away as fast as her tingling toes could carry her.

Crossing over the dance floor, she headed for the nearest palm tree and clung to it to steady her breathing.

Why, why, why did Kelsey Little always win? Why, why, why did she want a man who wanted someone else and was willing to make an ass of himself on national television to get it? And why, why, *why* couldn't she have met August Guthrie back home?

Because that just would have been too damn easy.

She had to get some sleep. Tomorrow marked the first round of competition and she'd be so involved in torturing Kelsey, Tara would forget all about August Guthrie.

Chapter Eleven

Love your outfit, darling

Tara rubbed some SPF on Ms. Mary's very pink shoulders as they prepared for the first round of competition to begin poolside. And it involved nothing but the jurors and a big screen television. It was set up at the far side of the bar and cushioned lounge chairs sat around it. Tara was fuzzy on what was expected of them today, she'd spent another restless night either panicked over being outed by August or hot and bothered over August.

"Ow!" Ms. Mary yelped and winced. "That hurts," she said as she perused her tender sunburned flesh.

"I'm sorry, Ms. Mary. I'm trying to prevent further damage. You spent far too much time in the sun yesterday and you can't afford to get any more on those shoulders or you'll be far worse off than you are. Now be nice to me, sit still and let me finish."

Ms. Mary sighed, "I know, but there was so much to see. I mean have you ever seen such a beautiful landscape of men?

Never mind, that was a silly question. Of course you have. All the hunks in your neighborhood must just line up to date you."

Tara snorted at Ms. Mary in disbelief. "Yeah, the line was so big all the guys in the 'hood had to part like the Red Sea when I stepped outside of my apartment." Please. Most people in her complex didn't even know who she was. Who could get to know her when all she did was use the damn place to sleep? Tara loved her work and by far it took precedence over dating and her sadly lacking social life. "I hate to disappoint you, Ms. Mary, but there's no line of anything, unless you count the line to use the laundry room. I work a lot."

Ms. Mary's eyes searched Tara's. "Well then, girlie I think you've done yourself and the male population at large a grave injustice. You're young and beautiful, why wouldn't you want to share that with someone?"

Tara smiled at Ms. Mary and waved her hand, dismissing her comment. "Pretty is as pretty does. I just haven't found anyone that I find interesting enough to date much is all." If you discounted August that is. And he was definitely being discounted. No August. Not on the island, not in her imagination, not in her dreams, not in a car, near or far, not here, not there, not *anywhere.*

"If I were you I'd get out more, Miss non-sociable. I had a grand social life before I met Josiah. It's how I knew he was the one for me. I tested all water available *first.*" Ms. Mary's smile was wistful.

Tara repositioned the umbrella over Ms. Mary's head and sat down next to her. "You were lucky, Ms. Mary, there's no denying that. I'm sure if the time is ever right, Mr. Wonderful will drag me off into the sunset." *Or to a secluded cove...* Ugh. Tara shook her head. No coves, no August Guthrie.

Mary chuckled, "I have a feeling it won't be long now."

Tara appeased her with, “I’m sure you’re right. So what’s on tap for today? I see the TV is set up. What do these poor men have to do to win a date with Kelsey?”

Ms. Mary scanned her list of activities. “Today is ‘Shop ‘Til You Drop’. This ought to be oodles of fun. Each contestant has been filmed shopping as they pick out an ensemble for Kelsey, something they’d like most to see her in and guessing the closest to her correct size. Then Kelsey looks them over, chooses the one she likes best, but she won’t know who bought what. The outfit that Kelsey chooses will determine her date for the evening. She also has to wear the item chosen on the date. All we have to do is vote on the contestant we feel took the most care in finding her an outfit. We have *ten* videotapes to watch”

Tara began to laugh, squealing in a fit of giggles. “I can’t wait to see how this turns out. I actually feel sorry for these poor guys. Men don’t know anything about a woman’s size or what she really likes.” She wondered what August would like to see Kelsey in.

Most probably--*nothing.*

Okay, enough with the August crap. Let Kelsey have him for all she cared. One mustn’t lust for what one couldn’t have. It was like a reality show commandment or something.

Videotape. She’d focus on videotape and then vote on the prettiest clothes for the Queen of Mean to wear. Tara jumped up, grabbing one of the videotapes and turned to the jury already assembled in their lounge chairs, drinks in hand. “Ready guys?”

Everyone nodded their heads. “Okay, first up is...” Tara looked at the label on the tape, “Aaron Caldwell...”

Ten videotapes and ten shopping spree’s later, Gianni was snoozing in his chair, Walter looked dazed and Ms. Mary had chugalugged one too many drinks with the pretty pink umbrellas.

Ms. Mary's head bobbed on her neck as she waved her empty glass around and said, "That is the ugliest dress I've ever seen in my entire life and believe me, my life ain't been of the short variety."

Diana began to laugh, holding her stomach and wiping tears from her eyes with her shoulder. "I--I..." she held up her hand and took a long breath to stifle her fit of laughter. "I'm sorry, but what would make August choose--ch--ch--oooose," she snorted again, "thaaaat?"

Andy rolled his eyes, prepared to defend his own species. "It's not *that* bad, Diana. Give the guy a break."

Diana stuck her tongue out at Andy, still giggling. "Oh, yes it is, Andy. I wouldn't be caught dead in something that frightful!" Her laughter turned to a high pitched squeal as she tried to explain the horror of the dress to Andy. "It's a purple and orange muuuuu--muuuu..." Diana managed to squeak out before she doubled over.

While everyone laughed, Tara slowed the tape down to stop the frame on the dress August held up against him. He looked awkward and uncomfortable as he explained why he chose this particular dress for Kelsey to the camera.

My hell, it was the most God-awful disaster on a hanger she could ever remember in all of creation. Tara had to agree with Diana, the big purple flowers splotched randomly over the orange background really did make quite a statement. Not one Mr. Blackwell might agree with, but a statement nonetheless. When asked why August chose that particular dress for Kelsey, August claimed he thought the purple flowers would compliment her coloring.

If Kelsey were a couch maybe...

Tara was tired of watching video tapes and tired of rehashing the outfits the contestants had chosen for Kelsey. For the most part they were just flat out mismatched, something her grandmother might wear, or ugly. August's being the ugliest, grand prize winner. It was time to get this over with, she decided. "Um, so I'm going to go out on a limb here and assume we don't think August put as much care into choosing something for Kelsey as say, Vinny or Aaron?"

Ms. Mary rocked back in her chair. "Well, I wouldn't say August didn't choose what he *thought* was best, but that Vinny could give Calvin Klein a run for his money. Loooove the purse he chose with those shoes. Perfect, if you want an honest opinion."

"But you have to admit, the dress looked sorta small for Kelsey. Seemed more like wishful thinking on Vinny's part if you ask me." Giovanni joined in, rubbing his eyes free of sleep. "I just want to get this over with. That was the most boring two hours of my life, but Vinny looked like he had the time of his."

Yeah, Vinny did seem to take great pleasure in sorting through racks of clothes and running his hands in appreciation over the surfaces of shoes. Maybe he has a foot fetish? Nevertheless it looked like Vinny was on top of the heap for this round and Tara was feeling just a smidge of satisfaction because of it. August couldn't possibly be chosen for this round, because if Kelsey chose his outfit and wore it, her eyeballs would burn for days after, even if Tara didn't really care whether August was picked or not. And she didn't either... "Let's take a vote then, shall we?"

Giovanni groaned his agreement, "Please, let's vote and get it over with. I can't look at another tape. It hurts my head..."

Tara tallied the votes and let the crew know they'd made a decision. One of the staff went to get Kelsey.

Kelsey flounced out onto the pool deck and glanced at the dresses.

The jury watched carefully as Kelsey perused the outfits she had to work with. Each of the contestants were lined up on the far side of the pool, waiting for her to make her final selection. Kelsey absently twirled a strand of blonde hair as she tried to decipher which dress she'd choose. Looking across the pool, Kelsey looked at August, but he was watching Tara.

Tara caught August's stare in her direction and turned her head in feigned disinterest.

Kelsey turned and ignored the men as she picked up the purple and orange dress August had chosen. Her face distorted a bit as she held it up and then she smiled as she saw the camera zoom in on her, covering her obvious distaste. When Kelsey came upon the dress and shoes Vinny chose, she grinned. Preston Weichert hovered close by with his stupid microphone and whispered, commenting on what Kelsey might do next.

Tara fidgeted as she waited for Kelsey to make a choice.

Picking up the slim fitting gold dress, Kelsey fingered it, biting her bottom lip as she did. It really was fabulous, Tara thought, and the shoes were stunning. Kelsey ran her fingers over the gold dress. Smiling, she turned to Preston who asked, "Have you made your decision, Kelsey?"

"I think I have, Preston," she paused and rested her fingers lightly on Preston's arm. "Though all of the outfits were just lovely, I think this best suits my coloring." Kelsey put the dress in front of her, plastering it to her bikini-clad front.

"Do you think it'll fit, Kelsey? You have to wear it tonight for the winner."

Gianni stifled a snicker at Preston's question and Diana chuckled softly. Tara had to wonder if Kelsey *would* fit in the dress. It looked pretty tiny.

Kelsey looked at the tag and frowned briefly, her eyes narrowing. "Well, of course it will. It's too beautiful not to!"

It was a size four if Tara remembered correctly. Uh-oh. Tara wasn't even a four... Kelsey could forget getting her chubby ass into that dress without a crowbar.

Ahh, life was good.

Chapter Twelve

Some enchanted evening...

Tara spied Kelsey walking slowly toward the carriage that would take her and Vinny on their date. The jury was supposed to meet here, according to the crew's instructions, but no one else was around. Tara glanced at her watch. Well, she was a bit early.

Kelsey looked awfully uncomfortable in her dress, Tara noted. She added a sweater to the ensemble, which was ridiculous considering it was a hundred degrees out.

Kelsey kept looking at her breasts, as well she should. They were seeping out of the top of the square neckline. Tara slid behind a big palm tree to remain unnoticed. A little unhindered observation of the "bride" couldn't hurt. Especially if the potential bride didn't have a camera trained on her.

Kelsey kept tugging at her clothes. It seemed no matter what Kelsey tried, she couldn't keep all of her flesh from flowing out of one opening or another. Kelsey tightened the sweater around her, revealing the gap in the back of her dress.

Tara chuckled softly. Kelsey couldn't zip that dress up if she had a pair of needle nose pliers and a zipper buddy. It was just too damn small.

Poor Vinny ... he was dreaming if he thought Kelsey was a size four. How could he think Kelsey was a four? Tara would bet she was an eight. Well, ten/twelve if she wore something made in China. There was no shame in it. Why didn't she just tell everyone it didn't fit? Because Kelsey Little couldn't bear the idea that she was a chubby ex-cheerleader... Being shorter, Kelsey couldn't handle the extra weight and it showed. So much for her size-one glory days in high school, Tara mused.

Heading straight for the nearest palm tree, Kelsey clung to it, pressing her back against it and watching while the camera crew assembled by the cobbled driveway. Squishing up against the tree Kelsey smiled as serenely as possible, while attempting oxygen intake.

"Hey Kelsey, did you know you're zipper's down?" One of the makeup crew shouted from across the paved walkway as he hurried to help her.

Kelsey's hand flew to her back as he yanked her sweater down over the gaping zipper.

"Here, I'll help you," he offered. "Why didn't you give me a buzz at the trailer? I'd have been happy to help. It's tough to get these sometimes."

Kelsey inched further into the tree. "No, thanks, I got it. I'm okay."

"No, darling you are not okay if you're not zipped in snug as a bug in a rug. C'mon," he motioned his hands for her to give him her back, "Turn around for Chad and I'll make it all better."

"No!" she barked at him. "Er, I mean thanks, I'm fine," she said, softening her tone.

Chad lifted her sweater before she had the chance to stop him. "Um, sweetums ... this is *not* fine. You can't go on a date with Vinny if you're falling out of your dress."

"Look, I've had enough friendly advice from the queer eye for the straight guy for one night," Kelsey hissed in exasperation. "Listen, you manly-man, I said I don't need your help and I *meant* I don't need your help. Go the fuck away, okay?"

Chad tsk-tskd her with a cluck of his tongue, "I was just trying to help. You don't have to call names. It's blatantly obvious it doesn't fit. Maybe I could have sewn in an extension or something."

Kelsey looked stunned as though Chad's choosing to share this information with her now was a huge revelation.

Tara saw Kelsey's face turn ugly beneath the moonlight. She'd seen Kelsey behave like this before. Chad was in for a lickin', cuz Kelsey was bent. "I don't need your help, but if and when I do, I can assure you I'll give you a call, butt boy."

Tara slapped a hand over her mouth to cover her intake of breath.

Chad gasped sharply too, giving Kelsey the evil eye before he stomped off and went to whisper to the other crew members about what a bitch Kelsey was.

"Prissy," Kelsey taunted into the dark night.

Tara heard the rustle of feet and noted that the jury was making its way down the path to gather for whatever was next. Tara had a funny feeling they were going on this dinner date with Vinny and Kelsey. Tara shushed them with a finger over her mouth and they hovered behind the tree with her so they could all watch Kelsey.

Heaving one last breath, Kelsey prepared to make her entrance as the carriage pulled up and Vinny sat in it, smiling like the poor, misguided fool he was. As carefully as she could,

Kelsey leisurely strolled sort of sideways to the carriage, keeping her sweater from flapping in the breeze that stirred the humid air. The cameras zoomed in on her and she kept her best side to them.

Vinny held out his hand to her from inside the carriage. “Evening, Kelsey. You look,” he squinted, cocking his head as he eyed her closer, “Um, nice. Very nice.”

Tara and the rest of the jury caught the look of confusion that flashed across Vinny’s face.

“Thank you, Vinny. You do too,” Kelsey replied. “I love a man in a tux.” Placing her hand in Vinny’s she let him pull her into the carriage. Just as she pushed off with her foot to step up, a loud ripping noise carried on the breeze of the fragrant evening. Ms. Mary and Andy wedged their way forward behind the palm tree to see what happened, knocking shoulders with Tara.

“What the hell was that?” Vinny yelled.

“That pretty dress--ruined is what that was,” Ms. Mary said in a whisper.

“Shh, Ms. Mary,” Diana cautioned.

Kelsey shoved her way into the carriage and plopped down, taking Vinny with her and whispering something to him. She snuggled closer to a bewildered Vinny, tucking her arm into his. “C’mon ,Vinny tell the driver to get going. I can’t wait to spend some alone time with you.” Kelsey smiled prettily and cocked her head, commanding his attention.

Vinny inched over a bit and whistled obnoxiously to the driver, “Hey! Move it, bud.”

As the carriage pulled away carrying them off, another followed behind them with Henry Abernathy in it. He jumped out and headed for the jury. “It’s a surprise group date! All of the jury members get to *share* this date with Kelsey and Vinny. Jury, you’re going to observe Kelsey and Vinny in an intimate setting and your foreman, Tara will take notes." Henry handed Tara a small notepad.

Tara sighed as she headed for the carriage. Kelsey was just gonna love this... The jury piled into the carriage and took a different path than Vinny and Kelsey had, allowing them to arrive before the couple. Scrambling out of the carriage, the jury quickly took seats at small tables in the outdoor dining area and sat quietly as Henry explained the rules. The jury could listen to everything Kelsey and Vinny said, but they couldn't interrupt in any way.

A crew member with a walkie-talkie quieted the group and told them to prepare for Kelsey and Vinny's arrival. As the clop of the horses hooves neared, everyone hunkered down in their seats, preparing to yell surprise.

Kelsey was still plastered to Vinny when the carriage pulled up right beside the jury's table. She rose and looked into the dark, frowning. A giggle from Diana stopped Kelsey in her tracks. Someone flipped on the lanterns that surrounded the tables, illuminating them.

The jury waved to her. "Surprise, group date!" Gianni yelled excitedly. Everyone began to laugh.

Vinny ran around to help Kelsey, chuckling. "So I guess being alone isn't on tap for us tonight, huh?"

Kelsey took his hand and threw her shoulders back. "I'm sorry, Vinny. We should have known they'd throw us a curve ball," Kelsey scanned the group and zeroed in on Tara, sitting in the dimly lit corner at the head of the small table with Mary. Kelsey turned her nose up at her.

"Is it me? Or is this broad just a snot?" Ms. Mary wondered aloud.

Tara snickered. "She was caught off guard, let's give her a chance."

Tara saw Kelsey struggle to keep from pitching a fit over this new turn of events. Tara knew that look only too well. It was the one Kelsey wore when she was fixin' to freak out. One of the crew members held a finger over his mouth to hush the jury.

Kelsey strolled into the center of the dining area on Vinny's arm and said hello to everyone, feigning joy over being joined by the jury.

"Hey, Kelsey, hope you don't mind us butting in," Walter teased. "You guys go right ahead and have a nice time. Don't mind us."

George, the cameraman hissed at Walter to pipe down.

Kelsey yawned as she and Vinny sat at a table situated right near the jury, complete with candlelight, fine wine, and a fabulous dinner. Tara figured Kelsey would have to struggle not to inhale her meal because she was eyeing her lamb chops up like they were smothered in chocolate sauce. If Kelsey hoped to keep that dress on, she'd better not dig too far in. Tara drew her small notepad out and began to make observations for the jury's records.

Vinny chatted easily with Kelsey. He went on and on about, of all things, his mother. His thick New York accent clung to the balmy air. Tara noted Kelsey twitching a time or two. "Hey," Andy said to Tara. "Vinny sure loves his mother."

Tara smiled at Andy. "That's a good thing don't you agree? It means he's sensitive..."

Ms. Mary looked down at Tara's notepad and tapped it. "It means he's a mama's boy. Put that down in your notes."

Vinny proved his point by poking a finger at Kelsey's dress and saying, "My mother just *loves* the color gold. It's what made me choose it for you, ya know?"

"Really? That's nice, Vinny. You talk *a lot* about your mother. I guess she's an inspiration in your life," Kelsey fluttered her big green eyes.

Vinny snorted as he swirled the wine in his glass. "Yeah, I love my ma. There's no one like her. And no one, I mean *no one* makes pasta like her. Do you cook, Kelsey?"

Oh, Kelsey was in deep shit now. Tara remembered Home Ec and cooking wasn't Kelsey's thing--unless you counted Kentucky Fried Chicken as cooking. Then Kelsey was a real Emeril.

Crossing her arms in front of her to cover her seepage, Kelsey smiled at Vinny. "Sorry, I don't cook much," Kelsey replied out of the corner of her mouth.

Vinny frowned and put his wine down, sloshing the burgundy liquid onto the tablecloth. "You don't cook?" he said in disbelief.

No, no and no again. Tara giggled as she scribbled a big *no* to cooking in her notes.

Kelsey shook her head no and Vinny frowned.

Ms. Mary pulled her knitting needles out of her bag, clicking her tongue in disgust and whispered under her breath, "What kind of woman doesn't know how to cook?"

"Not everyone enjoys cooking, Ms. Mary," Tara said in hushed tones. God, what had the world come to? She was defending Kelsey's right to not cook.

"Shh, guys," Gianni said. "I want to hear what Vinny says to this. If he's a good Italian boy he's not going to like it." And Gianni was right.

"Are ya sure?" Vinny sounded astonished. "No stuffed shells, lasagna? Not even a plate of Bolognese?"

Maybe Chef Boyardee, Tara thought. Poor Vinny.

Kelsey sat up straight. "Nope. I just don't really enjoy it. Do you cook, Vinny?"

Throwing his napkin on the table Vinny snorted, "Are ya kidding? No way. I eat at my ma's every night."

"I knew it," Diana whispered to Andy.

Kelsey seemed at a loss for words. As the date wore on and the jury members leaned in to hear Kelsey and Vinny's conversation, Kelsey looked more and more like she was growing perturbed.

"Well, what else do you like to do?" Kelsey asked Vinny. "Other than go to your mother's for meals?" She smiled sweetly and turned her profile to the camera.

"I like the track. You like the horses?" Vinny asked as his big black eyes gleamed in the candlelight.

"Like horse racing? I've never been. I'm sure it's fun, though," Kelsey cooed.

"Aw, man, Kelsey you should try it. Once you're there, it's like you can't ever get enough. There's nothing like slapping down a hundred bucks and walking away with two grand!"

Oh, if Vinny only knew Kelsey like Tara did... This date was on a fast train to Nowheres-ville. Kelsey didn't like to cook or clean or do anything remotely motherly. They were batting a thousand on the commonality scale. Tara made a note of that.

Kelsey shivered, but Vinny paid no attention. He was too busy studying her shoes. "Those are great, don't you think? I love the feel of real leather, the smell too. They look kinda tight on ya, though."

Kelsey smiled absently. "Oh no, Vinny, they're just perfect. I *love* Prada."

"Good, cuz I was thinkin' they're my ma's size if you don't want 'em when we're done." He looked a bit sheepish. "Like a souvenir from the show, ya know?"

Fat chance, bucko, Tara thought. Kelsey wouldn't give up the Prada until "ma" was a made-for-TV special, featuring how to raise a mafia buffoon. That was it for Walter. Apparently he couldn't hide his laughter over the date anymore. He began to laugh, leaning back in his chair and wiping his eyes with a napkin.

Kelsey narrowed her eyes at the jury. She'd tried to ignore them for most of the evening, that much was obvious, but she was beginning to fail dismally.

Kelsey yawned openly and finally, it seemed, Vinny took note of it. "Oh, excuse me, Vinny it's not the company. It's been a long day..." Kelsey purred.

"Yeah, no shit. C'mon, let's go back." Vinny got up without even glancing at her and headed toward the carriage, now parked right beside the jury's table.

The jury stayed in their seats as Kelsey rose slowly, looking down at her pumps. Her feet were oozing out of the shoes and swelling like sausages cooking in a frying pan. Stumbling toward the carriage, she tried to appear as graceful as she could. It had to be hard to saunter with a sway to her hips when every step she took looked like sheer agony.

Vinny was busy fidgeting in the carriage with nothing, waiting for Kelsey.

"Could you help me up, Vinny?" Kelsey called to him.

"Oh, yeah. Sorry, what was I thinkin'?"

Vinny yanked Kelsey into the carriage with a hard tug. She fell on top of him as a breast finally gave in to the pressure of suffocation and fell out of her dress.

The jury gasped. Ms. Mary's clacking knitting needles thunked to the ground. Tara shifted in her chair and her mouth fell open. Oh, boy...

Kelsey twisted to sit up as the sound of ripping material tore through the night.

Reacting quickly, Kelsey grabbed Vinny's lapel and planted one on him.

Long and hard.

Vinny seemed to resist a bit at first and then he let his lips go slack as Kelsey tried to manipulate them. From the jury's vantage point he didn't look like he was enjoying it much. He turned his head just a little, so it looked as though he were just taking a breather. "Um, Kelsey?"

Kelsey rolled her eyes. "What?"

Kelsey was kissing Vinny, for Christ sake. Shouldn't he be in a facsimile of Prada heaven? He didn't look too pleased to Tara.

"Maybe we shouldn't do this so soon, ya know?" Vinny said out of the corner of his mouth, avoiding closer contact by tilting his head back and away from her.

"Are you serious?" Kelsey hissed, knowing full well the jury was watching.

"Yeah, I mean we might give everyone the wrong impression."

"What harm's a kiss going to do?" Kelsey whispered fiercely.

"Might make everyone think I'm a stud. Well, I am, but it *is* just our first date."

"Stud?"

"Yeah, like *stud mare*? All suave and debonair, might make you look like a slut kissing me first and all."

Tara let her head drop to her chest at Vinny's comment. A stud mare, eh?

"Don't you like kissing me, Vinny?" Kesley whined sharply.

Vinny's face was solemn. "Su--sure. Yeah," he said with more confidence than he was obviously feeling. "It's fine."

"Then get busy."

Vinny looked down between them and whispered to her again. "I think you better fix your dress first."

A scream of laughter built in the back of Tara's throat, boiling just below the surface of her last shred of composure.

Now Kelsey was pissed. Vinny could stick his pasta, Prada's, and his ma up his Italian Mafioso ass from the look Kelsey was giving him.

Diana let a snort loose, then firmly clamped her hand over her mouth as Walter bit his finger.

Sticking her fingers in her mouth, Kelsey did a Vinny and whistled sharply to the driver. "Hey!" she yelled, "move it, bud!"

Date over.

Chapter Thirteen

A kiss is still a kiss...

Tara and the others unloaded from their carriages and scattered in all directions. Tara had gone back to her hut to get a book and a blanket to spread on the ground, and now she was reading under the dim glow of hanging lanterns as she wound down from the day's events. Kelsey arrived back from her date with Vinny flustered and obviously angry as she stalked off down the path toward the huts. If the date with Vinny was any indication of what the rest of the contestants were in for, Tara almost felt sorry for them.

Thankfully, she'd found a fairly secluded spot and now all she wanted to do was rest.

Flipping the pages of her book, which she just couldn't seem to get into, Tara gave some thought to Kelsey's date with Vinny. What would it be like to date someone who had "Who's your daddy?" tattooed on their arm?

At least the date hadn't been with August.

Tara shifted positions, straightening the blanket. This was just not okay. August was bad ju-ju's. *No August.*

"Tara?"

Hookay, she acknowledged as a chill skittered up her spine, maybe just a little August, but only a smidge. Tara looked up to find the hunk-o-rama himself staring down at her, his big body looming ever closer to her own traitorous one.

"Hello, August." Tara smiled, cool as a cucumber.

"Can I sit?" he asked with an awkward smile.

Can you fuck while you sit? Oh, my. Tara's cheeks flushed with shame. This must stop and to prove to herself that she could keep from lusting openly for his body, she patted the blanket for him to grab a seat. Albeit she patted the edge of the blanket, but what was a little proximity in the scheme of things? "Sure, but only for a minute, you know, the rules and all. Have a seat. What's up?"

"I just wasn't tired. Thought I'd come and see what was going on. Not much, I guess. It's pretty quiet. Wonder how Kelsey's date with Vinny went?"

Tara would bet August did wonder. Was August jealous that Vinny won the first date with Kelsey? It didn't matter because Tara couldn't ask. Jury info was top-secret. "Oh, I wouldn't know. I'm going to hope she had a wonderful time and Vinny did too." Liar, liar, pants on like *inferno...*

"Okay, I get the picture. No talking about Kelsey and Vinny."

As the breeze picked up, Tara got a whiff of August's cologne and felt the familiar itch he incited whenever he was near her. Damn... "Right. No talking about much of anything. Sorry, August, but those are the rules." Very authoritarian. She sounded just like any good jury foreman should. Yeah, like she'd followed those rules so religiously. But the rules didn't say she couldn't secretly lust for a contestant--just not openly. So she hadn't broken anything yet. Only the rules in her mind.

"I know the rules, Tara." his tone held some irritation.

"Good," she shot back in her best teacher's voice, "then I won't have to remind you again."

"So, are we going to do the quiet thing again?"

Well, yeah. Now if her libido would just consent to the quiet place she'd be in like Flynn. "Yes, quiet is best I think."

"Okay, then I'm just going to lie down if that's all right." August smiled sheepishly and stretched out on the edge of the blanket, facing her with his chin in his hand. His long body, solid and firm made her mouth water and her eyeballs glaze. "Whatcha readin'?"

How to hornswoggle a man into sleeping with you when you're on a reality TV show and the lead contestant wants someone else? Tara shook her head. God, she was losing focus here. "Just a book."

"I see that, but *what* book?" August smiled again at her. The flash of his teeth set hers on edge.

A book is a book is a book. What difference does it make when you're laying here in front of me making my estrogen levels do the jig? Tara looked at the cover, 'Chemistry and You'. See? It says it right on the cover." She pointed to it like he was a two-year-old.

"You are touchy. Is chemistry stressful? I mean it seems pretty solitary."

Your chemistry is stressful, Tara wanted to scream, but refrained and said, "Sometimes it's a lot of work under pressure. Trying to get all the kinks worked out before a perfume is due for production. I think I put more pressure on myself than anyone else does. I like perfection to show in my work even if no one will ever know I was responsible for it."

August rolled to his back and reached upward. Tara gulped. His abs rippled under his shirt and his thigh muscles flexed beneath the gold of his skin. "Ah. Who would have guessed? So, do you have any brothers or sisters? Does your family live in Colorado?"

His arm brushed her calf and Tara scooted back, plastering herself to the tree. She could do this... "Yes and yes." *Succinct, Tara.*

August sat up then, moving quickly and raising his legs to rest his elbows on his knees. "Don't you think you're taking this quiet thing a little too far? We can talk about stuff in general, you know."

Yeah, sure I can be general ... can you tell me how many inches you're packing? Is that general enough for ya? "I really don't think that's a good idea, August. Cameras are everywhere and I have to go anyway. It was nice talking to you."

"Or *not* talking to me." August held out his hand to help her up, but Tara ignored it. He ignored her right back and grabbed it anyway, pulling her up swiftly. Dropping her book, Tara bent to retrieve it, as did August. Their heads bumped and they both looked up.

August's eyes pierced hers, his gaze intense and searching, almost as if he was asking permission. Tara was lost for a moment in the deep blue of them, allowing herself a lap or two in their depths. His lips were but a breath away and her nipples knew it because they were tight and rubbing against her bikini top. August leaned forward slightly and kissed her with light lips, testing to see if she'd respond.

Holy, hell ... the firm pressure brought with it a tidal wave of simmering heat, sharp and swift. August slipped his tongue into her mouth inch by agonizing inch, caressing hers with firm strokes. Tara's heart pounded in her chest as she savored the taste she'd only imagined, but somehow managed to be better than she could have ever conjured up. The silky surface slid over her lips in light licks and her groin clenched with need. Tara swayed with the gentle pressure, reaching out a hand to hold onto his forearm, she clutched it. He dragged her against him, pulling her tightly to his rock-hard chest as she clung to him. The kiss became longer, deeper and more dangerous with each pass of tongues. Tara wanted to rip his clothes off and have him in front of all who cared to witness it.

August's moan and the hard ridge pressing against her thigh brought reality with it. Pulling away, she tore her lips from his, instantly feeling the cool air that replaced the warmth. Taking quick, short breaths she said, "August, stop! Stop now before this goes any further. We could get into a great deal of trouble!" Yes indeedy, trouble was the word. Wasn't stopping her though, Tara's hands were still glued to his arms and she was flatter than a pancake against his chest.

"I don't think I want to stop, Tara and I don't think you want to either."

"Yes ... yes, I do too want to stop," said her lips as her neck arched into his hot tongue.

"Why?"

Had any man ever asked her why she wanted to *stop* kissing him? What possible response could she have to something like that? Maybe she could just tell him the truth? "Well, August see it's like this. If we don't stop now I'm going to strip you naked and ride you like a wild stallion."

No, that would never do. Instead Tara said, "Because it's unethical and we've just broken a huge rule! That's why! We have to stop. You're here for Kelsey and so am I, in a roundabout way. Now, stop," she said as her fingers worked their way along each bicep, kneading the flesh with fevered fingers.

August molded his hands to her ass. “I think I made a mistake coming here,” his whisper floated past her ears and along her jaw as he nipped at it.

Hysteria over getting caught made Tara grip August’s arms and push him back as she rose to her feet on shaky legs. “Well, now is a fine time to figure that out and you’re not going to do it at my expense. I’m not part of the package.” Even if she wanted his package. “What were you thinking? That you could get a little while you wait for Kelsey? Not in this lifetime! I’m not some slut that can be manipulated into a reality show fling, so that someone can find out with their secret spy-cam and plaster it all over those TV shows. You’d better just watch yourself or I’ll go to ... to...” she trailed off as her train of thought was lost to August, who was on his feet now and hovering over her all blond and yummy.

“Look, you can tell whoever you want. I don’t have some stupid spy-cam. Wanna pat me down to see?” He grinned at her teasingly.

Did she want to pat him down ... shit yeah, and then some. “No. I just want you to go away before we invite trouble.”

“But I don’t want to go away. I sorta like you.”

“You don’t even know me. How can you sorta like me?”

August shrugged his big shoulders. “I don’t know. I just do ... sorta”

“Well, guess what hot stuff? I don’t even sorta like you!”

“Yeah? That’s not what those lips of yours were saying just a minute ago.”

Oh, of all the conceited, arrogant, pompous jerks! Just what she’d expect from a jock strap carrying boy-toy. “That is so not true. I just didn’t want to be rude.”

“And what, not swallow my tongue?”

Oh, all right, we were going to play like that were we? "Kinda hard not to swallow something that's jammed down your throat!" *Take that, you--you, sex God!*

August started to laugh. Was he mocking her yet again? "Okay, I give. Let's just chalk this up to nerves and forget it. Howzat?"

Forget it? Forget the best friggin' kiss she'd ever had in this hemisphere? He could just forget it? Oh, fine. Sure. Let's just forget it.

Forgotten. Over. History. Finito.

Tara grabbed her book and pushed August's chest, standing up and stepping around him "Consider it forgotten."

"Well, wait. I didn't mean..."

Tara held a hand up and stopped him from saying anything else that would leave her girl power completely crushed. "Goodnight."

Tara slithered off into the night, refusing to look back and heading straight for her hut.

Forget it? Forget that kiss? Forget you...

Chapter Fourteen

The luck of the Irish...er, August

Ya know, August thought, he hadn't had this much luck since ... well, since *ever.* August scratched his head and pondered how he'd managed to win a date with Kelsey, without even trying when all he could think of was Tara Douglas. And her lips. Her lips, her ass, her *attitude...*

It was because Tara was watching and he wanted to show off. August never turned down a good bout of competition if it meant he could prove he was a winner. Lame maybe, but true nonetheless. He showed Tara Douglas a thing or two about smarts and his desire to win Kelsey. So there.

Back atcha, Tara Douglas!

However, there was a downside to all of this.

Now he was going to have to cook dinner for Kelsey. It just wasn't fair. How could he, the master of all things macaroni and cheese possibly cook dinner for Kelsey?

Because he had the IQ of Einstein and he'd won the trivia contest. So he was good at memorizing facts, did it mean he should have utilized those skills at that particular moment in time? Oh, but of course, how could he help himself? Tara was watching and he'd banged on that stupid buzzer like his hand was a sledge hammer in a bell ringing contest at the county fair.

So now he had the pleasure of cooking whatever Kelsey deemed her favorite meal. August hoped it included a box and some cans, cuz he didn't know how to cook much else, but what came in the box and cans.

August rolled over on his bed and stared up at the fan, listening to the whir of it in the quiet of the afternoon. He didn't want to play anymore. Maybe it was time to take his toys and go the hell home. Screw the triple dare from Greg. He was beginning to worry that Kelsey didn't do it for him like Tara did. All he had to do was look at Tara across a room, across anywhere and it was enough to make his cock erect and his brain mush. Tara obviously didn't share his very lusty attitude. She'd made that clear as the day was long, no hanky-panky. But she'd kissed him back...

Well, fine. Chicks like her never wanted to go out with geeks like him and whatever had compelled him to go for it last night, was slapping him in the head today. Women of Tara's caliber wanted men like Aaron and Vinny, even if Vinny was slow on the uptake and had a bizarre attachment to his mother. He was still what August called a pretty boy, something August would never be. No matter how much he worked out, no matter what he did, August wasn't good at the charm school crap.

Still a geek after all these years and not the slightest bit interested in sticking around to have that reinforced by Tara or Kelsey who genuinely didn't have a clue who the hell he was. Which should disappoint in him ways he couldn't fathom, but *didn't* in ways he couldn't fathom. Kelsey pretended she did, though. When Preston did the introductions and revealed they went to high school together, she'd smiled as if they'd always smiled like that at one another throughout high school.

Bullshit! He was Kelsey's easy grade in high school and nothing more and he saw that more clearly than he ever had, but now he wanted her to notice him despite his waning attraction to her. To know he was the August Guthrie from Evanston High whom she would thank vaguely for letting her cheat. August Guthrie didn't have to let her copy off of his English papers anymore. He was going to cook this *meal* for Kelsey and *make* her remember him. Maybe she'd be so fucking fantastic he'd forget he ever even considered Tara Douglas worthy of him.

The sharp ring of the phone intruded on his plan to wow Kelsey. "Hello?"

"August? It's Gabe, down in production. Look, it seems as though Kelsey has come down with some sort of migraine and can't be disturbed. Something about laying in the dark and ice on her head. Anyway, she has to cancel tonight's date, buddy."

*Aw, too bad so sad...*Whoa, where had that come from? Instead of disappointment, he felt relieved and this troubled him. "Oh, well okay. Do we have to reschedule it?"

"Well, you did win the date..."

"But I get the feeling you can't fit it into the production schedule, because it's tight and on a budget."

"Henry said he'll give you a gift certificate for some fancy restaurant to make it up to you, if you'd like."

August smiled. "That's okay. No problem. I totally understand. Thanks for calling, Gabe." August hung up and jumped up off the bed.

Hoo Rah! No cooking!

But was it just the cooking he was relieved he didn't have to do? Oh, man, screw this torn between two women stuff. He was going to go for a run, maybe hit the cove and not think once about screwing Tara Douglas.

No, no screwing Tara. August sighed and tried to wipe the memory of her lips beneath his out of the visual in his head.

Not gonna happen.

~

August beat a hasty path to the cove, hoping to catch a moment's reflection over his rejection by Tara. This time he brought a flashlight with him.

"Hey August! Wait up," someone called to him from behind.

Shit. Shit. Shit. He just wanted some quiet.

The stomp of feet catching up with him made August turn to find Vinny, smiling and amicable. "Hey, Vinny, what's up?"

"Nuthin'. Wanna grab a beer or somethin'? I'm bored as hell here when there's no action going on. What happened to your date, man?"

August shook his head in the negative. "I was just going to go for a run. Kelsey had a headache or something. I think I need some 'me time' ya know?" he said, hoping Vinny would take the hint.

Vinny slapped August on the back and nodded. "Yeah all these camera's kinda get on your nerves. I understand. You go ahead," he said over his shoulder heading back toward the huts. "I'm gonna go find Aaron."

August heaved a sigh of relief as Vinny's hulking form grew distant.

August took up a light jog and thought about tomorrow. That's when he'd know if he was selected to go onto the next round. It meant another shot at a date with Kelsey. He was trying to get even a little woody over that. August looked down at his crotch.

Nuthin'. Not a single twitch.

Whatsamatter little buddy? Don't you like, Kelsey?

Silence.

His tallywhacker was on strike.

Well, shit. After waiting over twelve years to see Kelsey again, it turned out to be pretty anticlimactic. She looked okay, a bit something *more* that he couldn't pinpoint, but not nearly as hot as his mind's eye recalled.

But, all those luscious blonde curls.

It was fake.

Who doesn't need a little salon help every now and then? He pondered, shooting for fair.

Kelsey had *a lot* of help.

He might as well just think it. Kelsey just wasn't Tara. The less Tara paid attention to him at the barbeque and under the tree, the more determined he was to get it. Tara Douglas was making his underwear wad up.

Oh, shit...he was screwed.

No, no, he wasn't. He just hadn't had the chance to talk much to Kelsey alone. If that happened, he'd bet she'd be *far* more appealing.

Right. Like his attraction to Kelsey was ever based on conversation. It was based on high school lust.

August sat down on the edge of a smooth rock and watched the tide roll in. Maybe he should just leave. Walk away, forget the whole damn thing. It was dishonest to stay in the game if he wanted the jury foreman more than he wanted the bride to be. But leaving just wasn't an option. The contract said so. August could almost hear the evil music play when he thought about what he'd signed.

The bushes stirred behind him and August froze. What the hell...

Shaaa-wing, his drawers responded. It was Tara, in that skimpy damn skirt thing that made him go sit with her at the barbeque the other night in the first place. Her hands were on her hips and her eyes flashing accusations.

"You're here again. You know, I was here first the *last* time," Tara fired at him, all breathless and irritated...and really, really smokin'.

"Well, I'm here first, *this* time," August shot back, irritated that she made him horny just by simply being. August wanted to kiss her again and that made him even touchier, because she'd made it pretty clear she didn't want to kiss him. Fine, just fine.

"You have to go away."

He crossed his arms over his chest. "You know, you really need to get a new line and say's who I have to go away?"

"Who what?"

"Who says I can't be here too?" August demanded.

"The contract for the show says *who*." Her neck bobbed in a circular motion as she spoke.

"What do you want, scheduled cove visitation?" August's tone took on a sarcastic edge. He was just a little tired of having this contract shoved in his face.

"You have *no* visitation rights. I was here first. We don't share joint cove custody," Tara retorted back.

August began to laugh, because she was so damn cute, all angry and fired up, her breasts heaving and her eyes narrowed. "Okay, okay. I can leave if you want, but wouldn't it be nice just to sit here and hang out? Away from the cameras? It seems like this is the one place on the whole damn island the crew didn't find."

Tara seemed to consider that, but then a frown crossed her face. "If we get caught, we can get into some serious trouble. I don't think so."

August slid over on the rock, just a little closer to her and grabbed Tara's hand, pulling her to sit beside him and because he wanted to feel her skin beneath his. "Live dangerously."

Tara's shoulders sagged as she reluctantly allowed herself to be coerced into sitting with him. Her posture was stiff when she finally arranged herself next to August and pulled her hand from his. "Okay, but we absolutely *cannot* talk about the show."

August nodded solemnly and inched closer to her, sucking up the heat her body sent in waves of unconscious sexuality. "Deal." Whoa, she smelled good, all flowery and fresh. She'd tied her hair up in a knot on top of her head; tendrils of curls fell around her face. Tara's bare thigh pressed lightly against his. August's cock pressed roughly against his shorts.

Shit.

*August...*he warned himself.

"So, you work as a chemist? That's interesting."

"That's not what you said the other night, but I can see now you await explanation with bated breath," she teased and let go a little tinkle of laughter that did something--August was sure wasn't very male--to his stomach.

"Okay, so it's not really all *that* interesting," August admitted honestly. Besides who cared what she did for a living when he couldn't think about anything else but tackling her in the sand and hollering "touch down"!

Tara laughed, her breasts rose and fell with each chuckle.

So did August's shaft of love. The old manroot was lookin' for some lovin' and after the kiss they'd shared the other night he wanted more.

"At least you're honest, August. It may seem rather uninteresting, but it's a living, you know?" Twisting a strand of her dark hair around her finger, her eyes flashed under the light of the moon, dark and sultry. "You're a graphic artist, right?"

"Yep." August answered. He was fighting to focus on her words and not the glossy lips they came from. Glossy lips that he'd tasted and now wanted more of.

"Is this the 'less said the better,' conversation we had the other night?" Tara countered.

"I think so. You did say we couldn't talk about anything that had to do with the show and almost everything that has to do with me has to do with the show. I'm an open book being on TV and all."

Turning to August, Tara smiled and as a result, his pulse thundered in his ears. "Okay, so we can talk about what's already been said, like your occupation...Stuff like that, because I know all of that from the show and the other night. We *can't* talk about your feelings for Kelsey. Period," Tara added firmly.

How about we talk positioned horizontally and forget Kelsey? He couldn't say that. It was crass and forward and...*true.* Whatever she was wearing, the scent was making him nuts. Fruity and subtle. Did she smell like that all over?

August smothered a groan. No matter how you sliced it, Tara was tipping the Richter scale of his testosterone levels.

"Sounds good," August agreed, clearing his throat of the knot that had formed in it. "So, what made you decide to try out for the show and how do you know Kelsey? The jury foreman is supposed to know the bride, right?"

Tara looked uncomfortable with the question. Letting her head fall back on her shoulders, revealing the smooth column of her throat, she answered, "We went to high school together..."

Shifting positions, Tara brushed against his thigh again. August's muscles tensed in response to the pressure of her bare leg, while he thought about the arch of that neck under his lips and the leg he was sure was smooth and soft...August's fingertips tingled.

"*You* went to Evanston?" August managed without squeaking like a girl. That's right. Preston said she was the trig club captain in her introduction. He'd forgotten that. Now, why didn't he remember her? Seemed unlikely he'd forget lips like Tara's, even with his perpetual hard-on for Kelsey back then.

Tara made a face he caught only a glimpse of in the moonlight. "I looked a lot different in high school. How do *you* know the name of my high school?"

"I went to Evanston too." She didn't seem to remember *him* either, not that August was very memorable as a teenager.

Tara's hand brushed his leg and came to rest alongside of it, creating heat waves that shot straight to his "other half". Hoookay, this had to stop, or his cock was going to inflate to new and unseemly proportions, thereby causing mass hysteria and even worse, *massive* embarrassment.

"Small world, huh?" she commented about their attending the same high school as she leaned a bit closer to him.

But not a small hard-on. "Sure enough." Too small apparently, because Tara began to stand up, obviously ready to leave, but she lost her footing and fell backwards, landing in his already aroused lap. Tara lay draped across him sideways with her legs dangling off his thighs. August gripped her shoulder with one hand and caught her around her waist to steady her with the other. If she didn't quit squirming...

"I'm sorry, I slip--ped..." Her breath fanned his face, minty and clean. When she licked her lips quickly, it was all over for August but the cryin'.

He lunged for her, crushing those raspberry lips to his and dragging her body against his. His cock pressed painfully against his shorts, seeking the warmth of her round ass. August's tongue found hers and tangled with it, the recesses of her mouth hot and sweet. Tara's arms went up around his neck, her fingers skating through is hair, clinging to him. Her breasts lay flush against his chest, driving him to fight to keep his hands to himself.

He groaned, low and guttural, into her mouth, digging his fingers into her hips. Tara's ass sank further into his aching crotch.

Ding, ding, ding ding, ding! The old siren of lust sounded in his head. *August! You must stop this instant! You gonna get in some real trouble here...*

Think co-n-t-r-a-c-t.

Nuh-uh. August ignored the warning bells clanging in his head and kissed Tara harder. She arched toward him, running her hands along his arms, gripping his biceps.

His cock was on fire, his hands itched to yank off her dress and his lips ached to taste her erect nipples. Jesus H. he had to stop this before it went too far...

Good idea.

August's hands brushed her shoulders as he tried to remove them from her body. Her skin was soft and silky ... and ... he didn't wanna stop.

August Guthrie!

Tearing his lips from Tara's August spoke harshly, taking ragged breaths between words. "Do you want me to stop? Because I'm not sure I can, but I will if you want me to, because what we're doing is completely and totally against all those rules you keep spewing for the sh..."

She didn't answer him. Instead, she pulled his mouth back to hers and licked at his lower lip.

See, she didn't want to stop either...

Oh, August...

August overruled his conscience and stuck with his cock, which by now, was screaming Tara's name like no others before her. He hauled her to her feet, fastened his hands to the underside of her ass and lifted her. Tara's legs automatically straddled his waist. The heat between her legs seared his cock through the material of his shorts.

August stumbled toward the small patch of sand he'd seen earlier and they sank to the ground. Wrapped tightly together, under the shelter of a palm tree, their lips continued a fevered exploration.

Now he couldn't control himself as his hand cupped the underside of her breast, thumbing her nipple. Tara responded by wrapping her fingers around his wrist and curving into his body. His fingers skimmed the skin exposed at the top of her bikini and she moaned in response. He kissed his way down the smooth column of her neck, nibbling at the hollow. Tugging at her bikini top, he unclasped the metal hook between her breasts.

The moonlight wove its way between the palm fronds, shedding enough of a glow to give him his first look at her full, round breasts. Her nipples were small, dark, and erect, stiffened from the warm breeze.

"Christ, you're beautiful," he ground out. Tara hid her head in his shoulder, but her hands found the outline of his shaft.

The heel of her hand rubbed him lightly as she located his zipper and slid it down. Freeing him, Tara wrapped two soft hands around his cock and caressed him lightly. Hand over hand she grasped him, touching every last sensitive nerve in his body.

Heat, hard and like white lightning shot to his groin. All sanity left behind, August arched into her as his lips found a nipple, skimming it with the warmth of his breath and the wisp of a lick. As the tip of his tongue tasted her lightly for the first time, his senses exploded. Blood rushed to his ears, pounding out a rhythm of lust.

Tara cupped his balls, gently massaging them. His cock thrust forward into her soft hand, letting the warm tunnel envelope him.

He nipped the swell of her breast and quickly wrapped his lips around the pebbly surface of her nipple. She straddled his thigh, rocking against him. Finding the top of her bikini bottoms, he let his fingers linger there, tracing a small pattern on her smooth abdomen. Dying to touch the heat of her, yet loving the anticipation of discovery, he suckled her nipple. Licking and kissing as he fought to keep his hand from tearing her bottoms off and driving his fingers between the wet lips of her pussy.

She gasped sharply when he tugged at her breast, her legs squeezed his thigh tightly. Wedging his hand between them, he ran a tentative finger inside her bikini bottom, tracing the crease where her thigh joined her pelvis.

Smooth, she was smooth, soft and wet. With forefinger and thumb, August spread her folds and grazed her clit. Tara shuddered under him, groaning as she held fast to his cock, milking it with her hands, fondling his balls until he wanted to explode from the building pressure.

Pulling his lips from her breast, he continued to drag his fingers through her warmth. Her head fell back on her shoulders, and her chest rose and fell with rapid intakes of air.

August wanted her to come, from the touch of his fingers, the rasp of his tongue. He found her ear, sucking the lobe and whispered, “I want you to come, Tara.

Tara’s response was to hike her body upward, sliding her bikini bottoms over and pressing her pussy to his erection. The smooth lips of her wet warmth enveloped his hard cock, gliding along the hard surface, leaving a trail of moist desire. His hand was caught up in the friction of her wet cunt against his cock. Aching fingers grazed her swollen clit, over and over, eliciting small moans of delight from her throat. His mouth, open and hot, surrounded a nipple again, rolling his tongue over it.

They rocked together, locked in an embrace of heat. August felt his own orgasm build, steam-rolling over his body, clutching his balls and pulling them tightly. Tara's body jerked and rolled, undulating against him. He reveled in the small sigh she let go as she came.

The first spasm of release hit him like a freight train and he pulled back to keep from exposing her to his climax. His cock jerked, yet Tara didn't take her hands away, she milked his response, as her hips fell from his and he spent himself in the sand.

Tara looked up at him and focused on his gaze for the first time. She had that "what the fuck have we just done" look and she was looking like he was the only one who'd done it.

Uh oh.

Well, this is a fine mess you're in, literally and figuratively. Look what you've done. You've left your mark in the sand. Nice ... he chided himself silently.

Ms. Douglas was back on terra firma and looking just a bit bent out of shape. Or was she just freaked out? Tara pushed her skirt down and tried to sit up, but August pulled her to him and refused to let go, because she wanted him to.

"I know what you're thinking. I'm not going to let you run away, Tara. Now, look at me." She didn't struggle, but held herself tense and unyielding.

August smoothed a hand down her spine and kissed her lips softly. "We probably shouldn't have done that..."

"Probably? Probably? Um, yeah, I think that's the understatement of the millennium," she squawked, cutting him off.

"Hey, we *did*, now, we can choose to forget it, or we can acknowledge it and move on. I don't feel an ounce of regret. It only solidifies what I was feeling anyway."

"Move on to what, getting kicked off the show? Humiliated in front of the entire nation? Do you remember what happened to the guy who fooled around with one of the staff members a season or so ago? They threw him out and told the entire world..."

August kissed her again, silencing her as her body leaned into his. Tara put her hands on his chest and tweaked his nipple, hard. "Ouch," he complained against her lips. "That hurt. No one has to know what happened between us, Tara, but this isn't the end, Tara, not by a long shot." He damn well meant it too, screw Kelsey, and screw the show. It was a dumb idea, brought on by a decade-old adolescent crush that was now, officially over. Kelsey held little appeal for the adult August. He realized that in a rush of clarity. The guilt he felt over it dissipated and replaced itself with having Tara. He would just flub a competition or something and get booted out by the jury. Easy as the proverbial pie.

Tara lay on top of him, making his cock hungry for more *and* making him forget everything else but her. "Why aren't you on your date with Kelsey? We're going to get in so much trouble. They'll sue us, you nymphomaniac!"

"No name calling," August scolded, licking at her neck. "And my date with Kelsey was canceled. She had some migraine or something and what can they sue me for? They can't sue me for what they don't know about."

"Arghhhh!" Tara yelped. "You never know what's going on when you're not looking. Not only did the jury pick *you* to go on to the next round of elimination, but your contract states clearly you aren't supposed to be fraternizing with me! Besides which, the jury thinks you have the most chemistry with

Kelsey and all this time you've been hovering around me is bound to be noted. I can feel it, August, they'll find out about what just happened. Or someone will claim to have seen us. How can I explain *this*," she waved her hand at their tightly locked bodies, "to the jury?"

The jury, he'd forgotten all about them. If they kept voting for him he'd never get the hell off this island without having to say no to Kelsey and marriage publicly.

Oh, fuck.

"Okay, so the jury doesn't need to know."

"I'm so glad you agree. For a minute there I felt compelled to rush in and scream my joy poolside to them. Just as a heads up that I've been toying with the contestants and breaking every rule this damn reality show has."

"You've toyed with the others like *this*?" August mocked.

Tara snorted, "Sure, of course I did. I rolled around on a beach with every last one of them. I just want to be sure Kelsey's getting a prime cut of man. Only way I can do that is if I stick my hand in the hunk jar, right?" she rolled her eyes at him.

"Well, she ain't getting this cut of man."

"August?"

"What?"

"I don't want to hear anymore."

"Hear anymore what?"

"You're breaking another rule. I'm not supposed to know how you feel about Kelsey. So shut up!" Tara put her fingers in her ears to block out his words.

He pulled them out. "I will not. I don't like Kelsey."

"I can't heeeaarr you."

"Can so."

"Cannot."

"Can."

"Not."

"Can."

"Arghhhhhhhhhh! August we're in a lot of trouble. Stop it and take this seriously!"

"I am and I don't--like--Kelsey--Little!" Accent on *don't*.

"August?"

"What?"

"We're screwed. We violated the contract *big time*."

He sighed. So they were immoral, unethical, contract breaking pieces of white trash.

But holy orgasm, baby...

Chapter Fifteen

I'll get you, my pretty, and your Barbie dream house too!

Tara panicked, yanking away from August and paced in the sand. Her heart slammed against her ribs and her throat was clogged.

Omigod, omigod! What had she done?

She'd had a wonderful orgasm, courtesy of a guy who's named after a month. That's what she'd done. Who'da thunk?

She'd slept (sorta) with Kelsey's (sorta) man ... realization hit her like a freight train.

I slept with Kelsey's man! I slept with Kelsey's man! Tara wanted to sing! Take that you, cheerleading/baton twirling/blonde Barbie-like/skinny/stuck up/tramp!

Oh, she'd sunk so low ... so very, very low. She was a wicked girl.

Yes, this *was* bad. Very un-Tara like. Tara didn't even feel badly that in a small, as of yet, unrecognized way, she'd beaten Kelsey without even trying. But they were going to find out and sue the snot out of her for breaking every rule in the show's damn contract.

Had she said this was bad yet? This was soooo bad, so very bad. Tara was going to Hell in a handbasket and so were her plans to ruin Kelsey. Oh, God what had she done?

Yes, that's it, Tara told herself, remorse. Remorse is good. It validates me, your conscience. She just didn't do things like this! Tara Douglas always followed the rules.

Always.

August caught her by her arms and pulled her to him.

Tara flattened her palms against his chest and pushed away from him, but he wasn't letting go so easily. He circled her wrist and held her with a firm grip.

"Would you calm down? Okay, so the jury picked me ... did *you* pick me?"

Tara snorted, "I thought we weren't going to talk about the show?"

"Don't you think that's irrelevant now?"

Yeah, after all, she was just half-naked and clinging to him for all she was worth. This was definitely what one would call irrelevant.

Oy.

What part of no fraternization with the contestants had she been remiss in remembering? Could it be the part where you're not supposed to be alone with them? Or was it the part about no 'familiar relationships' with the jury or contestants that wasn't spelled out clearly enough for her hormones?

Tara brushed sand from her legs. "You can't be caught with me, August. You can't. Kelsey likes you and you haven't even given her a chance to get to know you ... and your contract says you shouldn't be screwing around with me or they'll sue us." Tara wanted to scream over that. Just throw herself on the ground and howl in a fit of temper. Damn Kelsey Little.

"Well, I *don't* like her. I spent a little time with her the other night at the pool and she wasn't doin' it for me like you were. I tried to figure it out, but you kept popping up. So, too damn bad, because I *do* like you."

"That's only because you copped a feel off me. You haven't even had a chance to get to know Kelsey, much less cop a feel."

August chuckled, his big, goofy shoulders shaking. "I copped a lot more than a feel..."

Tara's face burned with fury and humiliation. "Oh, just throw it in my face! I wasn't the one popping out of my pants, bucko. You started this." She shoved a finger under his nose.

He nipped it and smiled, "Yep."

Damn him and his stupid, sexy grin. He sent a wave of pure lust spiraling through her body. He left her breathless and giddy. She felt no shame in thrusting her trampy body right up against his like she'd been doing it forever. "Don't yep, me, man of the infamous sentence in one word or less. We're in *big* shit here."

August tangled his hands in her hair and nipped at her neck. "Yep."

Oh, my... Her nipples began that tingle. "August, please, we have to figure this out."

"Can't we figure it out later? I have other, far *bigger* shit, we can get into together." He wiggled his eyebrows.

Tara giggled, unable to help herself. Her eyes sought his, and cupping his chin, she kissed him just one more time. He was like a potato chip, you couldn't have just one, and they were bad for your thighs... Especially if you spread them wider than the great state of Montana for a man who was marked for someone else!

Tracing the outline of his lips with her tongue, Tara found she just couldn't resist. But she had to. Who was this woman, wanton and wild? Doing some guy she'd known less than a week? Where was the Tara of old who didn't sleep with men who were contractually obligated to someone else?

August interrupted her thoughts with, "I thought we were gonna talk?"

Talk, yes... "Look, you can't be caught with me. You have to go through with this because the contract is clear. You stay till you're voted out. We would be massacred in the press if they found out what we just--just--did," she tripped over her words as she thought about the tabloid headlines she'd seen on previous contestants who'd done far less than she had. "And I hate to be the center of attention. Can you imagine what the press would do if they found out? Besides, you've been voted for by every last jury member *and* you were just talking with me at the barbeque. What if someone saw us under that tree? People might get suspicious. And I'm going to reiterate here, the *entire* jury voted for you to stay. You have no choice. This isn't like the 'Bachelor' where you can just leave and take your toys with you when you choose to go."

August's arms were around her waist, squeezing her gently, his fingers splaying over her hips. "I know I can't. I know the rules. They all voted for me? Even you?"

Tara shook her head. "I can't tell you that. I *won't* tell you that, because I've already broken enough rules to satisfy a litigation attorney for a lifetime! But I will tell you, you *have* to show up tomorrow and smile nice for the cameras and ignore me. Don't even look my way, or we are dead meat! Hear me? And, by the way, did we graduate together? Class of nineteen-ninety-two? I don't remember you." Tara's brow furrowed into a frown at hearing the question out loud, but she *had* to know.

"Only if you promise to meet me back here, tomorrow night and yes, I think we did graduate together."

"I can't, tomorrow is another competition, remember? You have to show up and win, win, win." Tara paused for a moment. "Why don't I remember you? Seems to me your name is so unusual, I'd remember it. When I heard that guy calling you at the water fountain the name August didn't ring any bells." *Had he been on the football team?*

August smiled. "I have no intention of win, win, winning the stupid date. If I don't win, I can't go on a date now can I? Then we can meet here and I don't think I remember you either, but I won't forget you now."

"I can't control who wins the date. Besides, the jury likes you. They could vote you right into the 'last man standing round' even if you don't win the dates, unless you like really make Kelsey hate you and it shows on camera. Our voting is based on our impressions of you, not necessarily whether you win a date or not." Tara frowned again. "I can't believe we graduated in the same class and I don't remember you."

"Then I'm going to screw up the next competition no matter what it is and I wasn't very memorable."

Tara laid her head against his broad chest. "No, you can't screw it up, everyone knows how physically deft you are and brainy to boot--so stop being macho man because we--we--well, you know. You've been playing this game like a champ so far, except for that dress you chose... Please don't stir up suspicion. For me? Besides, we hardly know each other. Give Kelsey a chance."

Ugh, the very idea made Tara ill. Not to mention the fact that she wanted to rip Kelsey's hair out, follicle by follicle for having a shot at a man Tara wasn't allowed to have. This was ridiculous, she'd just met August and she was jealous.

Green with envy even. Wasn't that part of the problem she'd had with Kelsey to begin with? She was jealous of her ... and now she'd done something that would leave Kelsey curled up in the fetal position and she couldn't even share it proudly. Damn. What a waste of a good taunting.

August's voice was tense, "I honestly think they make you sign that contract on the off-chance you just might turn the bride down. I almost think the producers would like that better, ya know? It would really stir the ratings up wouldn't it? On almost all of the other reality shows you can hit the road if you find you aren't attracted to the other person. So now I have to get voted out. It's nuts." August sighed. "Look, what if I told you I don't like Kelsey *quite* the way I like you? And *we* were working on getting to know each other, if you would have talked to me at the barbeque."

I'd tell you, good answer. He liked her better than Kelsey? Well, shut up. Not in a million light years would she have believed this. August was also right. What kind of reality show made you stay until they kicked you out? Maybe it was because the contestants could opt not to propose in the end.

Tara closed her eyes and said, "I'd tell you, you don't know Kelsey any better than you know me." Her stomach clenched into a tight knot. *Nice answer, very PC.* Shit. She was backpedaling and doing a piss-poor job of it. She couldn't force August to do something he didn't want to do. He could lose a competition if he wanted to and she couldn't stop him. It was even tickling her ego--just a little, mind you--okay, more than she was willing to admit--that he might go to such great lengths to get out of this stupid show because he was interested in her.

August sighed. "Fine, but I'll only agree to play nice if you agree to meet me here tomorrow night."

"Okay," Tara gave in, even if it left her feeling edgier than she already was. "I'll meet you here tomorrow night, after date night is over. Then we can do all that getting to know one another." She couldn't believe she was agreeing to break more rules. But her body didn't seem to care as much as her conscience did when it was pressed up against August's. He was competitive. Tara had witnessed it when he'd won his first canceled date with Kelsey in the trivia contest. If she humored him, maybe that competitive spirit would kick in and he'd forget all about what happened between them.

Which would be the story of her life. Once he got a moment or two that was almost completely alone with Kelsey, he wouldn't want any part of Tara again.

Damn Kelsey Little and her charm to hell.

Tara gave him one last lingering kiss before they parted because it could well be the last. Her heart clenched tightly as she realized the best almost schtupp of her life was officially over once Kelsey got her hands on August.

They were in major trouble if they were caught. The tabloids would have a blast if they knew the jury foreman had her hand in the cookie jar labeled "hunk". After Tara was kicked off the island for burning her contract in effigy--that Henry guy would exploit the hell out of what she'd done, because that made for good promotion. Then, the press would dig and dig into her life and they'd find out why she was here. Or someone from high school would remind them of the "moo incident".

On the other hand ... *what an orgasm, baby...*

~

Tara tugged on her shorts and crossed her legs as the phenom, otherwise known as Kelsey, trotted up and down the length of the pool. A restless night last night led to a cranky Tara this morning, as the next elimination round began.

It was another day in paradise. Balmy breezes, hot sun and enough testosterone to make a woman tear up. Each jury member was again lined up and at the ready to observe Kelsey as they sat under the large canopy by the pool.

Kelsey's job was to take the list of men chosen by the jury and present them with a key to her hut, thus signifying they'd made it to round two. A key to Kelsey's hut meant you had a shot at getting inside with it. If your key opened her hut door, you won the door prize.

A date with Kelsey.

Of course, Tara and August hadn't known that last night. Tara figured the date would have to do with a physical effort, not just plain luck of the draw.

Tara couldn't summon up much interest in it anyway. She was too busy thinking about August, his biceps, his lips, and his ... well... his *skills* and how that was all over if he won this date with Kelsey. He'd finally have the woman of his dreams and his roll in the sand with her would be history. All his talk of liking her better than Kelsey would be forgotten.

"Hey, Tara," Diana snapped her fingers at Tara to get her attention. "How much more of a show do you think Kelsey could put on?"

Tara blinked and caught the look of disgust on Diana's face. Kelsey wasn't making a real hit with the jury which was exactly what she wanted, wasn't it? "She *is* good with the camera, huh?" Tara kept her comment nonchalant and objective.

Diana scoffed, "I'll say she's good. Or at least her boobs are." A ripple of laughter skittered down their row of chairs around the pool.

Kelsey teetered on her heels toward August, unaware that the jury was having a good laugh at her expense.

Tara gazed at August, shoving Kelsey out of her thoughts. Why couldn't she get a clear image of him from high school? Was he a part of the popular crowd? If they'd graduated together, surely he knew what Kelsey had done to her and that made Tara cringe. He'd learn her motives for being here and then it would be all over between them.

There was nothing to be over, Tara reminded herself.

August's gaze kept locking with hers from across the pool, making her flush with guilt, no doubt. She didn't need this. Screw him.

Tara averted her eyes to keep from hurling pool toys at Kelsey and whacking her in her big, fat, blonde, curly head. She clenched the arms of her chair, digging her nails into the wood and sinking further into the puffy cushions.

Walter nudged her. "So who do you think will get lucky tonight?"

Walter knew ... no, no he didn't. Now Tara's tendency to see shadows where there were none was on overkill. Tara leaned over and smiled casually at Walter. "It's anybody's game tonight, I think."

This was so not good. All night long, guilt plagued her, keeping her tossing and turning. She was *not* here to sample the beefcake, yet she'd clung to August like he was the last granola bar on Survivor. Behaved like a tart and she wasn't even into the second week. This was *not* something Tara did on a regular basis. She'd never felt an attraction this strong to any man, and even if she had, she certainly wouldn't have behaved the way she did last night.

Well, wait a second--she didn't know that because she'd just said it herself, she'd never felt something like *this*. And, it was sooo good.

Good it was, powerful and explosive and *forbidden...*

She didn't have to go through with this. She could simply stop right now. Choose a man for Kelsey, a decent one and walk away, sans national humiliation. If she could keep it that way she might leave without an ulcer. No one knew her real motives for being here except Tara and her conscience. That was one thing the cameras couldn't have.

Tara heard August's deep laughter rumble as he and Vinny joked about something from across the pool. "That August sure is cute, huh, Tara?" Ms. Mary said. "I sure as hell hope he's up to taking on Kelsey. She's a real viper."

Tara giggled. She couldn't help it. "August seems like he's man enough to take Kelsey on, don't you think? Maybe we've just been catching her at the wrong times. This show can be very stressful, Mary. All the cameras and stuff."

Ms. Mary wrinkled her nose. "Well then, Kelsey sure is stressed *a lot*. I hope August gets to see that side of her too, seeing as we can't actually *tell him*."

Tara understood Mary's frustration in ways she couldn't imagine. "Eyes open and mouths shut, Ms. Mary. It's the jury's motto. We have to remain objective."

"Then I'm just going to hope August finds out about Kelsey on his own while I'm being so *objective*," Ms. Mary said with a fierceness Tara didn't quite understand.

Tara had her own worries about what August might find out.

What if August found out about her too? Found out that she was a spiteful, vengeful, dried up old loser from the graduating class of nineteen-ninety-two.

A geek with a grudge.

But ... but, what about the shitty stuff Kelsey did to me? Tara asked herself, outraged at her thoughts. *Kelsey humiliated me. Made me the laughing stock of my entire senior class. Should I just let that go? Leave the beast to rape and pillage yet another of my villages?*

That was rather dramatic, she admitted. She couldn't change what had happened. But she could change how she handled it *now.*

Tara also couldn't change what had happened between them last night at the cove. She wasn't all that sure she wanted to anyway. If this was some island fling, then so be it. It was uncharacteristic of her, but who said you had to have character when the sex was that hot?

August adjusted his dark glasses and peered out over them at Tara. She narrowed her eyes at him and she knew he got her drift because he raised one eyebrow and shoved his sunglasses back over his nose.

Kelsey strode toward August, her perky, bikini clad breasts bouncing up and down. Tara wondered if she stuck a pin in one of those silicone bad-boys, would they deflate? Handing August the key, Kelsey smiled and kissed him full on the mouth. As she pulled away, August shuffled from foot to foot and pushed his thumb along the bridge of his nose as he glanced Tara's way.

There better not have been any tongues involved... The bitch needed to *die*.

"See, I told you Kelsey liked him," Ms. Mary reminded her, setting Tara's teeth on edge.

If Ms. Mary only knew about all the men Kelsey had zapped with her *like* radar.

August caught her eye one last time. Tara couldn't quite make out the emotion in his gaze from so far away, but he sorta had the deer in the headlight thing going on from this distance. Which meant what? He was happy Kelsey kissed him?

Jerk.

The nervous tension grew, hanging thick in the humid air as Kelsey made a big production out of giving the final contestant a key. The losers exited stage left, heads hanging low.

Now, all that they had left to do was find out which man Kelsey would go out on a date with tonight. August just better hope he had a bum key...

Chapter Sixteen

Kiss me once, kiss me twice...

Well, fuck. August looked at his copper key, bewildered. Where the hell was all this luck when he'd been in the tenth grade, lusting for Kelsey?

Now, he couldn't get rid of it if he tried. As the cameras rolled and each contestant tried their key, he thought surely he was safe until he was almost the last man up at bat.

Well, think again. Second-to-last at trying the lock, August's key, (miracle of all miracles), opened Kelsey's hut. Squeals of delight clung to his ears as Kelsey bounced excitedly up and down and hugged him. All at once, everyone was slapping him on the back and congratulating him.

Crap, crap, crap.

"Oh, August, we'll have so much fun," Kelsey cooed, running her fingertips along his arm.

Not a single response, not one shiver, not even a tingle. August smiled warily, ever aware that the cameras were on him. "Yeah, it'll be fun."

Preston Weichert babbled into the camera about when and where they would meet for this *date.* Some famous dried up lava pit.

"So, August, how do you feel about winning the date with Kelsey?" George the cameraman asked as he zoomed in on August's face.

August tempered his tongue before replying, "I guess we'll see if Kelsey and I have anything in common for sure now. Gotta go get ready!" August smiled cheerfully and ducked past George.

Damn, damn, damn. He didn't want to go on a date with Kelsey. He wanted to meet Tara in the cove. Stomping off to his hut to shower, he went to prepare for his *date.*

Stop being a baby, his conscience berated him as he prepared himself mentally for a rendezvous he didn't want to go on. Why couldn't the competition for the date be something he could totally blunder? No, it was the luck of the draw and if he got any luckier he'd be a rabbit's foot.

His roommate Gordon poked his head into the bathroom. "You pumped or what, buddy?"

August slapped a grin on his face. "Yep, like a hot air balloon."

Gordon shook his head. "Sure wish it was me going on that date."

August nodded with real sympathy. "Me too, Gordon." *Me too*

"I'm outta here. Going to slug back some brews with the rest of the guys and ease my pain. Catch ya later."

August slapped on some cologne and wondered absently if Tara would like it.

Shouldn't he wonder if Kelsey would?

He didn't care.

You know, you have no way of knowing whether you'll enjoy Kelsey's company or not. Can't you just give this a chance? Isn't that what Tara had said?

Damn woman, she wasn't just explosively hot, she was *right.*

Reluctantly, August agreed that giving this a chance was the only way to prove to himself that he really meant his high school hard-on for Kelsey was over. His choices were few, and if he gave it a chance, then there would be no doubt. He only hoped Tara realized he was doing this for her, not because he wanted to. Their encounter last night had been volatile, to say the least. Physical attraction was important and his body definitely had some of that goin' on for Tara. There was more too, he sensed it intuitively. If he'd met Tara anywhere but here, he would have dragged her off by her hair to his hut and had his way with her for the rest of the night. Circumstances wouldn't allow that, neither would his air-tight contract, but as soon as it was remotely possible, he would find a way to be with her and ditch this show. This TV thing was a stupid idea, hatched from adolescent angst, and nothing more than a distant memory. Kelsey no longer interested him, but Tara did.

* ~ *

Okay, "giving this a chance" time was officially up. August wanted out.

O-u-t.

He was having trouble focusing on the words Kelsey was spouting, because well, she really wasn't all that interesting and Tara was waiting.

"Oh, August, who would have ever thought you'd turn out to be so darn cute?" Kelsey was gushing for the cameras again and turning him right toward them. They were sipping champagne from fancy glasses and eating strawberries with whipped cream.

"Well, my mom *always* thought I was cute." August smirked and winked at the camera that was about an eighth of an inch from his face, while popping a plump strawberry in his mouth. August knew he was supposed to pretend it wasn't peering into his soul, but what the heck.

He was getting much better at this. Very movie star-ish.

Kelsey ran a pink-tipped nail down the front of his shirt. "Of course, she did. I did too, you know." She gave him a knowing smile.

Oh, she did not either, his bullshit thermometer warned. He would not fall for this mountain of crap and it was pissing him off that he'd never realized before now what a liar she was. Just went to show you that a man's head was definitely ruled by his winky.

August tugged his earlobe to stop his thoughts from driving him insane. He wasn't stupid anymore. Now he was just playing the game...and getting better at it by the second.

It would seem someone tipped Kelsey off about August and she'd finally recognized him. A blast from the past. So, exactly what did Kelsey remember about August Guthrie? It was time to find out and do it so the camera crew had it all on tape, because the crap she was feeding him so far was all just that--crap.

"Yeah?" August challenged her. "*When* did you notice I was cute?" Atta way to toy with Kelsey's gray matter, he congratulated himself. *Answer that why don't you? Was it before or after I helped you ace English?*

Kelsey tilted her head and widened her big green eyes in feigned interest. "It must have been in chemistry class."

"Did we have chemistry class together? I had Mr. Gambino, I don't remember you being there." August leaned back in the lounger, casually placing his arm around her shoulders, waiting for an answer, knowing full well there was no answer, nor any chemistry class. Speaking of which, wasn't it funny that before he'd had all these muscles, Kelsey never looked twice at him?

The low hum of the camera echoed in the silence of the quiet evening. One of the crew snickered. Probably George. He loved a good laugh.

Kelsey placed a hand on his thigh as she wiggled into a more comfortable position. A position obviously best suited for lying. "No, I didn't have Mr. Gambino," she flashed a mind-blowing smile at him and shrugged. "Oh, well it doesn't matter. I still thought you were cute." Kelsey cuddled closer to his side and August let her. First, because nothing short of a crowbar was going to unglue her from him and second, all this false I-thought-you-were-cute-in-high-school crap deserved some looking into. Because if Kelsey thought he was anything more than an easy A in English he'd never been aware of it, but he was aware that she'd used him and maybe back in high school he'd talked himself out of it, but not anymore. If there was one thing that pissed him off it was a liar and she was lying. Making nice for the cameras and America, so they wouldn't see who she really was--a stuck up, using liar.

"Which did you think was cuter, my bifocals or my buck teeth?" Raising an inquiring eyebrow August patted himself on the back again. *Beautifully executed.*

"Oh, August..." Kelsey sighed as her eyes became shifty. "Let's not talk about high school. Let's get to know each other in the here and now."

"Here and now" kind of sucked. There wasn't a single thing he found interesting about her. They'd spent two hours up on this damn lava pit, swinging on a lounger, eating rabbit food and he was bored to tears. Kelsey didn't remember him, but she'd let all of the free world watching think she did.

Not gonna happen. August was having way too much fun proving she didn't, which also made it easier for him to pursue Tara. Now the shoe was on the other foot and he was feeling omnipotent. If Kelsey had just been honest at the outset of this date--if she'd just been truthful about not really remembering him ... but then that would make her look *shallow.* If America knew what August looked like in high school, and then they found out Kelsey Little never paid attention to him unless she was sucking up for a test to copy, she'd have to admit she was superficial at best. That would look really bad for America's newest bride.

August decided to take this game to another level and play it up for all it was worth to the cameras. For every test she'd copied off of him, for every night August had spent thinking this one test would be the one that made Kelsey notice him--he was going to screw with her. Just a little before he left this dumb fantasy behind for good.

Catching Kelsey's hand with his, August tugged her onto his lap and fought not to groan out loud. Damn, she was heavier than she looked. "Okay, what do you want to talk about?" *The theory of evolution?*

"You're a graphic artist, right?"

"Yep."

"That's sooo interesting."

August fought back a yawn, remaining silent. *How interesting?*

Kelsey leaned in next to him, hiding her mouth with her hand from the cameras and whispered into his ear, "Don't you want to kiss me?"

August pulled back, aligning his face with hers. To the viewing audience it looked like they were sharing a romantic moment. “Not really, I hardly know you,” he whispered back.

“But, isn’t this how we get to know each other?” Kelsey let her bottom lip fall into a pretty pout.

“With our lips?”

“We only have a month.”

“A month to what?”

“Get to know each other, silly.”

“But, this is only our first date.”

“Do you have any idea how many men...”she stopped short, “--how many *times* I thought of kissing you?”

“In high school? You didn’t even know me.”

“Yes, I *did*,” she hissed.

“You did not, not the real August Guthrie. You only knew his IQ.”

“Does it really matter now? You must have wanted to be on the show for a reason. They told me that we went to school together and you knew that before you tried out for the show. So that reason was *me,*” she hissed.

“Yeah, that’s true,” he conceded, albeit begrudgingly and a stupid triple-dog dare .

“Then why won’t you kiss me?” Kelsey was beginning to sound like a petulant child, whiny and sniveling.

August tilted his head and pecked the corner of her mouth. “There, how’s that?”

“Like the kind of kiss you’d give your grandmother,” she said dryly.

“Grams never minded. Sorry, maybe we just weren’t meant for each other.” August was doing his best to worm his way out of this. When the jury saw the video tape, he was sure they would see that he and Kelsey had very little in common and zilch in the chemistry department. He'd be voted out and then he could chase some Tara tail back home.

"How can you know that? We haven't had a chance to get to know one another."

"I already said that, but *you* wanted to kiss me anyway."

"And you didn't want to kiss me?"

August sighed, "I already told you, *not yet*." What did she want from him, a lung?

She wasn't used to being turned down, that much was obvious. "Well, that's fine."

"Good, so is this over?" August began to rise, pulling away from Kelsey's clutches. *Let's get the hell outta dodge,* was all he could think.

Kelsey wasn't letting go so easily. She tugged his arm, pulling him back down on the lounger. August tripped over his feet and landed on top of her. Kelsey giggled.

August was trying to get a glimpse of his watch over all of her blonde hair. He spit spidery strands of it--coated with hairspray--out of his mouth. Shit, it was getting late and he wanted to spend some more time with Tara. As gracefully as possible, he untangled himself from Kelsey's octopus like limbs and held out his hand gallantly. "Let me walk you to your hut."

Taking his hand, she used it as leverage to hurl herself at August. Throwing her arms around his neck, she tried to kiss him full on his mouth. As Kelsey hung from his neck, it was all August could do not to fall backward.

August gasped and coughed loudly. Dayum, she had big bones.

"Thanks for a wonderful time, August." Kelsey batted her eyelashes, giving him a dreamy look.

"Um, you're welcome," he grabbed her by the wrists and set her down as gently, but firmly as possible. He looked at the camera crew, “I think we’re done.” August departed as quickly as possible, leaving a fuming, angry Kelsey and a stunned camera crew behind.

Chapter Seventeen

Stupid head...

Tara paced the length of her hut in her underwear. This was just wonderful. August had won the date with Kelsey. It figured, now he wouldn't give a rat's fuzzy ass about her anymore. He'd be too busy being bedazzled by Kelsey.

Stupid head...

She should have known. Tara Douglas was no match for Kelsey Little and she never would be. No matter how much weight she lost, no matter what kind of makeover she had, Kelsey was light years ahead of her in the snagging-a-man department. Hell, August auditioned for the show just because Kelsey was on it, so why would she think he'd end up any other place but with her. At least that's what the gossip was in the jury pool, confirmed by Andy, that August Guthrie was hot for Kelsey in high school and he'd carried a torch ever since then. That was a long time to carry anything, let alone a torch. Tara couldn't figure why this information had all of a sudden become a bone of contention for her. She'd known he was hot for Kelsey early on in the competition. So was he bullshitting her by telling her he liked her better? Just screwing around with her to occupy himself?

Tara had auditioned for some of the same reasons August had, albeit she'd done it for slightly less than altruistic motives and it had nothing to do with a piece of ass.

Her phone rang and Tara ran to grab it, knowing it wasn't August because he had no access to her hut number, but she went for it assholes and elbows anyway. "Hello?"

"Tara? It's Mary. I'm just checking to be sure you're okay."

Well why wouldn't she be okay? Tara cringed and cleared her throat. "Of course, I'm fine Ms. Mary. Why would you think I wasn't?"

"It's the mother in me, what can I say? I noticed you didn't eat at dinner and it worries me. Hunk picking is hard work. You need your strength."

Tara's heart clenched with warmth and guilt and then warmth again. Shit. Right now she really missed her mother. "I think it's just the heat, Ms. Mary. I'm not used to it being from Colorado and all." And the guilt over this mess she'd gotten herself into. Let's not forget what that does to a girl's appetite.

"Well, have a little fruit or something for me, okay?" Mary prodded.

"I will. Promise," Tara assured her. "Thanks for checking on me. G'night Ms. Mary."

"Night, dear."

As Tara hung up she realized this was killing her or going to if she wasn't careful. Why couldn't she just slam Kelsey and smile while she did it? Because now I've changed my mind, Tara thought, and screwing Kelsey doesn't seem like as much fun anymore. However, it obviously did seem like fun to August. The screwing part anyway.

Tara sank to the bed, defeated. She had no right to August in the first place, so she shouldn't complain. Her behavior last night was outlandish at best, so she'd just take her lumps and move on.

Unethical was the word that came to mind, but nothing that couldn't be forgotten now that August had the chance to meet Kelsey, he sure wasn't going to tell anyone what they'd done because he risked being sued by the show. He'd forget all about her and skip off to Kelsey Little wonderland. Jealousy ate at Tara's innards and a small tear nearly escaped her eye. She wanted August and was so close to having him she could taste it. Now that he'd spent some one-on-one time with Kelsey, Tara was convinced he wouldn't give her a backward glance. Why would she want someone like that anyway? A hunky player with brains...

Jerk.

A scraping noise roused her from her pity party. Now what? Another stupid voting session? A secret meeting for the members of the jury? If she recalled prior episodes correctly, that wasn't an unlikely possibility. Grabbing her robe, she threw it on and moved closer to the scraping, it was coming from the sliding glass doors. If it was one of those big, icky island critters they'd warned them about she'd scream.

Moving the curtain back slowly, she found August on the other side of the glass, grinning at her.

Unlatching the door, Tara slid it open. "Are you insane?" she hissed at him. Not only because he was taking such a risk, but because he was wearing a smile. A smile Kelsey must have left on his face.

Stupid head. Had he only come to do the "right" thing and let her down gently?

August pushed his way in and closed the slider firmly behind him. "Maybe, but you didn't show up at the cove. I do believe I've been, what's better known as 'stood up'." He grinned again, this time clearly revealing his dimples.

Tara narrowed her eyes at him. "You should be on a date with Kelsey, not here in *my* hut." She couldn't help the sarcasm in her tone.

"Date's over." His rich voice rumbled, thick like chocolate sauce over a sundae.

Tara tightened the belt on her bathrobe. "So soon? Gee whiz, that was a wham-bam-thank-you ma'am."

He grabbed her around the waist and dragged her to him. "Do I hear bitterness in your tone, miss?" Carrying her over to the bed, he dropped her on it.

Tara harrumphed, "Look, you shouldn't be here and you know it. We're going to get caught."

He shrugged his big shoulders and flopped down next to her. "I did what you asked and now, I'm *done*."

Tara scrambled to her knees, "What do you mean you're done?"

"I mean, I went out with Kelsey and it's over."

"It's not over until the jury votes you out."

"You can vote for me as many times as you'd like in or out, but the end result will still be the same. I won't like her anymore than I did tonight. She's just not for me. I didn't know enough about her in high school and what I learned tonight left me cold," August said, his face set in a hard line, his tone inflexible.

Really? Tara wanted to scream and shout, jump up and down. Hahahahaha, Kelsey loses. Round one goes to the geek!

Coolly, she replied, "Oh."

"So, now is it okay if I really screw a competition for a date up?" August moved closer to her, his breath fanning her face. An index finger trailed over her exposed collarbone.

"No, it's not okay and we both know that. We're doing something that's really wrong. Let's just wait and see what happens with the jury after they see the tape of your date. Maybe they'll realize you don't share anything with Kelsey and you can leave the right way, instead of leaving me here to possibly deal with gossip."

His lips found the hollow of her neck, "Kiss me first and I'll think about it."

Tara rolled her head on her neck with a groan. "I will not bribe you, August Guthrie."

He clasped her shoulders, "Well that's just plain unfair. There's nothing like a good bribe. How about *I* bribe *you*?" His lips moved down to the swell of her breast. Swiping at it with his tongue, he dipped beneath the lacy covering of her bra.

She pushed at the solid wall of chest, protesting with a squeak. "I cannot be," *Oh*... "bribed..." Well, okay, maybe just a little bribe, she mused as August laid his mouth over her covered nipple. It rose to meet his mouth, tight and needy. "We shouldn't be doing this. It goes against every rule the show has." As if that mattered now, after last night. Nag, nag, nag. The rules, the contract. No, August we can't... We have to stop, August...

She was beginning to sound like an old fish wife to even her own ears.

Long fingers untied the belt to her robe, parting it with ease. "I already told you I wanted to forfeit a date last night, but you wouldn't let me. Today's date had nothing to do with skill. Only luck of the draw, and giving it some thought I decided--if I keep winning dates it means I can stay here with *you*." Pulling her tightly to him, August buried his face between her breasts, kneading the flesh of her ass. Tara's hands found the thick thatch of his hair. She clenched the silky strands for support as he nudged her bra out of the way. He seemed to know exactly what to say and Tara couldn't figure if she should be alarmed or thrilled. "You'd better be very careful about how you do that. Sometimes I think the producers make controversy when there isn't any just to get good ratings. If we cause even the slightest bit of suspicion it could be very bad for us..."

But, this--*this* was *anything* but bad.

"I could stop, you know. You just have to say the word."

His hands lifted the lacy scrap of material. "We hardly know each other," she protested ... sort of.

"If you'd be quiet, we could get to know each other."

Tara laughed, "I don't mean in the biblical sense."

He licked an exposed nipple, drawing it deeply into his mouth and suckling. Thrills of heat shot to Tara's pussy, stabbing at the tender flesh, leaving her moist and aching for more.

"Tell me to stop and I will." He gathered the two creamy swells of her breasts, bringing them to his lips and alternately began licking them.

Let's not be hasty... Her hands cupped his jaw as her head fell back on her shoulders and her knees shook. Sliding her fingers beneath his, she cupped her breasts, offering them to his hot tongue. The rasp of wet, hot flesh against her strained nipple gave way to the seductive sound of his low, throaty groans. A sultry, carnal desire swept over her; she allowed the liberated and wild Tara, yet untapped, free to explore this intense attraction to August. They could find themselves in a heap of trouble if they were caught, but this all-consuming need to have him ran deeper than anything she'd ever experienced sexually.

Tugging at her panties, he pushed them down to her knees. August's hands found the mound of flesh between her legs and with his palms, he lightly caressed her, running them around the lower half of her body, yet skirting the wet lips of her cunt.

Tara let her fingers roam free as well, over the arms that held her, tracing the thick contours of muscle. She kneaded them, reveling in the feel of his hot skin beneath her touch. Pulling at his shirt, she lifted it over his head and threw it to the floor. Pushing at him, he lay on the bed and for the first time, Tara was able to admire him in the dim glow of the bedside table. His skin was bronze with a hint of gold. A white band of flesh, left untouched by the sun, was just visible above the waistband of his shorts. Thick thighs, sprinkled with golden hair, clenched as her hands whispered over them. A tapered waist led to the firm bulge between his legs, and using thumb and forefinger she outlined it. August sucked in a deep breath and held it, arching upward.

Sliding her panties and bathrobe off, Tara quickly straddled him, letting the heat of his flesh seep into hers. Bracing herself on his chest, she clutched his pecs, kneading them. Tara bent forward and licked the flat disc of his nipple, and to her satisfaction it beaded beneath her lips.

August's hands threaded through her hair, and he groaned when she popped open the button of his shorts and unzipped the fly. He kicked at the restraints of his clothing, until his legs were free. Tara licked the ridges of his abdomen, sliding her fingers into the crisp thatch of hair at the top of his cock. She savored the salty taste of his skin on her tongue.

Rigid and lightly veined, his cock lay against his stomach. When she brushed it lightly with her lips, he jumped and muttered something she couldn't quite hear. Grasping him with both hands, she slowly enveloped him within her mouth. Inch by painstaking inch, she laved his thick shaft.

His knees rose and he bracketed her body. Cupping his balls, she kneaded them and slowly licked the smooth surface of his cock. Long laps of her tongue and hands made him moan, as he twisted his body upward to meet her strokes. His hands wrapped around hers, following her up and down motion, gripping them as he ground his hips at her. Pressing her tongue flush with the sensitive area below the head of his cock, she nipped him lightly with her teeth. A bead of pre-cum, thick and salty lingered on her taste buds.

His hips rocked in a slow circular pattern as he thrust into her sucking. His breathing was ragged and shallow. Tara slid her hands beneath his ass and clutched the muscular globes tightly, pushing him into her mouth, taking his long length in as far as she could. He rose on his heels, frantically jabbing at her as she washed him with her tongue.

Suddenly, he pulled away, out of the warm cavern of her mouth. Gripping her shoulders, he dragged her upward. Her breasts scraped his chest and arrows of heat pricked at her when he slid his tongue over her teeth. Parting her lips, he crushed his mouth to hers and his hand cupped her breast, thumbing her nipple to rigid desperation. Tara groaned, breathy and low as he left her lips to trail a path of wet kisses over her breasts and down the plane of her belly. Strong hands found her waist, thrusting her upward until his hot breath caressed her bare pussy. His tongue snaked out to explore the crease in her thigh, her legs fell open, welcoming the slick invasion, but instead he traced the outer lips of her cunt. In slow, tantalizing licks, August explored her. Her clit throbbed, aching and swollen as she held her breath, waiting ... he drew a finger between the slick folds of flesh, back and forth, kissing the vulnerable skin, but not entering it.

Tara's heart pounded wildly in her chest as she squirmed beneath him. When he took the first pass over her clit with his tongue, flames shot through her veins, and she fought to keep from screaming. Her hands clutched wildly at the comforter as her ass slid forward to meet his mouth. He began to suckle her clit, swirling over it while his hair grazed her inner thighs. Tara grabbed wildly for him, cradling his head against her belly as he moved expertly inside her cunt.

Callused fingers slipped inside her and her world tipped on its axis. This time she heard her own squeal ring loudly in her ears. Tara bit her lip and arched into the glide of his fingers. The wet suction of his tongue and hands drove her over the edge. She came hard, slamming into him, crushing his head to her and rocking on his finger. Her thighs gripped him tightly as she came again in wave after wave of shudders. Tara's head swam and colored lights flashed behind her closed eyes.

He slithered up her body, his thick cock dragging through her wet pussy. Heaving chests clashed and her nipples strained against him. Bracing his hands on the bed, he lingered, rolling his hips. "We don't have a condom, Tara, we have to stop." The agonized tone in his voice made her heart clench. It sounded genuine and sincere.

Tara wrapped her arms around his neck and met his thrusts. "I have some, in the nightstand."

August chuckled, his husky laugh sent chills along her spine, "Pretty presumptuous of you."

Kissing him soundly she laughed too. "I didn't bring them with me, and I didn't go buy them at the nearest island pharmacy, Mr. Confident. They were in the nightstand drawer," she said as she reached between them and grasped his cock.

"Then let's get it, dammit." His eyes were dark and stormy.

Curling her fingers into his hair, she kissed him again, sliding her tongue against his, tasting herself on him. She pulled away and leaned over the side of the bed to find the condom.

He licked her nipples as she tore the foil wrapper off and slipped it on his cock.

"Lay on your stomach," he demanded.

She rolled over with anticipation, lying on her belly. August put his arm under her waist and tugged her to him. Her knees scraped the carpet and her ass pressed firmly against his thighs. He lay over her back, moving her hair aside, rimming her ear with his tongue. "Are you afraid, Tara? I won't hurt you, I promise. If you want me to stop, say the word."

A strong sure voice returned his answer, "Fuck me, August. Now."

His hand drifted to her cunt again, fondling her from behind as he said, "I won't fuck you, Tara. I'll make love to you tonight. We'll fuck another time... When I can show you the difference and you'll know it still has as much meaning."

She shivered and responded by lifting her ass high and pushing against him, encouraging him to enter. He moaned in her ear, "Christ, Tara I want you," he grated as he slipped slowly inside her.

Tara took gulps of air as he filled her, stretching her to accommodate his thick girth. August pulled back gently and she found herself pleading with him, "Please, August, harder ... give me more."

Her words sent him thrusting into her with more force, hard and hot. "Like that, Tara? Is that how you want it?" He twisted his hips to emphasize his words, "Tell me," he demanded.

"Yessss," she fairly screamed when he thumbed her clit as he rose behind her again and plunged once more. "August..." she said his name on a breathy sigh.

He stilled again, cupping her pussy, "You're tight, baby, tight and wet and I want to ram my cock into you. You were all I could think of when I was on that damn date." He gasped again, as she reached behind her and put her arm around his neck, digging her fingers into his scalp.

"Then do it," she commanded, arching against him, straining to pull him in deeper.

August complied, plunging into her balls-deep, the friction of wet and heat making her pussy clench in response. Milking his cock as he rode her, Tara felt his teeth nip her shoulder, his ragged breathing rasping in her ear.

Their rhythm increased its tempo and his hands ran over her ass. "God, Tara, don't move like that or I'll explode."

Lifting herself high against him, she ignored his request, rolling her hips, gyrating with the beat of each forceful thrust.

His cock twitched and his body tensed, "Stop," he said between clenched teeth, "stop or I'll come. I want you to come with me..."

Her skin was damp and clinging to his, the brush of his thighs and hands was driving her mad. "Then make me come with you..." she taunted him. He loomed behind her, large and bulky, his chin pressing into her shoulder. Turning her head to reach for his lips, she pulled his mouth to hers and drove her tongue into it.

Teeth and tongues gnashed as August drove into her, tweaking her nipples as his other hand spread her flesh, weaving through the folds of her pussy. The force of his thrusts took her breath away, slamming her against the edge of the bed. His cock, hot and silken, slid with the ease of her moisture.

She came with the force of a tidal wave rushing over her, swarming every nerve ending with sensation. The slap of skin against skin, callused fingers in her cunt and his lips against her own was electrifying. Blood rushed to her ears and her heart throbbed painfully against her ribs. She tore her mouth from his and buried it in the bed, biting the comforter. The orgasm clung to her, overtook all sanity, leaving her wracked with small tremors. Tara heard nothing but the sound of her own heartbeat and August's frantic words in her ears as he, too, found release.

He collapsed on her, panting for breath. Her eyes stung with unshed tears. She'd never experienced something so all consuming, so utterly uninhibited and wild.

His hands smoothed over her skin, soothing her shattered nerves, whispering across her flesh. Pulling out of her, August turned her and gathered her in his arms holding her close, tucking her into his lap.

As her breathing slowed, Tara snuggled her head against his chest, listening to the steady, sure beat of his heart.

Chapter Eighteen

There's got to be a morning after...

Tara pried her eyes open. They were glued shut from sleep. Bright sun filtered through the gauze curtains of her hut. Another day in paradise...

A finger traced a pattern between her breasts slowly.

"Hmm..." she snuggled deeper into the warmth of the body next to her.

Body?

Oh, Hells bell's, she snuck a peek at the clock. Seven, whew, she had time to languish.

Um, hellloooo ... the body, Tara's overworked brain called to her.

Yes, the body... Warm and muscular, pressed firmly against her ass and moving its fingers over her, teasing her nipples.

I repeat, the body.

Tara twisted her head, looking over her shoulder. August's white teeth flashed her that big grin. "Morning."

She groaned, "We are fucked, August." Oh, Jesus, she was such a tramp. Driven by lust and ruled by her libido.

Rebel, she scorned herself silently.

"No, Tara, but we did fuck and I think I wanna do it again." He wrapped her arm around his neck and drew circles on the underside of her arm.

"We cannot do it again. What do you mean, *you think*? If we get caught..."

"We'll be in sooo much trouble," he mimicked her words. "And when I said 'I think', it's because you haven't exactly given me a warm welcome this morning."

"We're going to get in trouble! How can you *think* about anything else but the trouble we'll be in if you get caught with me?"

"Because I don't care who knows, so let them catch me."

"Look Neanderthal man, it means *I'll* be caught too and that means I could quite possibly be sued, plus get a good dose of national humiliation when they boot my ass outta here, on top of the fact that they will undoubtedly have grounds for a lawsuit! Remember the fraternization rule?"

"Shit."

"Yeah, like I said, *big* shit."

"So, we'll just keep this a secret."

Tara snickered openly, "How the hell can we do that when it's broad daylight and there's nowhere for you to hide?"

"I'll find a way to get past the camera men. They don't hang out as much with the jury, unless you're in a session." This, August offered as he kissed his way down her waist and over her hip.

Her hands automatically found his thick hair. She clutched it and bit her lip. God, he was fabulous, she mused, as her body arched into the tongue that now swept over her thighs.
"August, please ... we have to stop. You have to get out of here

and I have to get dressed." Tara was beginning to sound like a bad romance novel--even to herself. "No, please stop, August--wait, please..." Good hell.

August's lips were brushing the globes of her ass and his voice was muffled from beneath the blankets.

"We have plenty of time," he said as his finger slipped inside her and his thumb found her clit. Kissing his way back up her body, he pulled her tightly to him with his other arm and lifted her leg to rest over his hip. Tara melted into his chest and focused on the hypnotic rhythm his finger created as he slid in and out of her.

His cock, hot and hard as steel, slipped between her open thighs, caressing the slick warmth of her pussy. Her clit throbbed and swelled with each slow thrust he made.

"Still want to get dressed?" August questioned on a ragged breath.

"Maybe we can wait."

She felt his smile on her shoulder, "Maybe?"

Tara gasped and moaned her disappointment, when he pulled his finger from her. She reached between her legs to caress his cock and found him condom clad. "You're pretty bold, Mr. Guthrie. Already have that condom on and everything, huh?"

His response was to ease his way into her. She stiffened a bit, still tender from last night. "Did I hurt you last night? I couldn't seem to control..."

Tara closed her eyes and snuggled closer to his chest. "It's all right, neither could I. I'm okay, just a bit sore."

Wrapping his arms around her waist, August began to withdraw.

She pushed against him, pulling his hands to her breasts and gripping his wrists. "Are you backing out on me now? Don't stop..."

Cupping her breasts, he lay still. “But you’re sore. I don’t want to hurt you. Rest today and we’ll make up for it tomorrow.”

“If you move, August Guthrie, there will be no tomorrow... So show me what a stud you are and put that love gun of yours to good use, okay?”

He circled her nipples with his index fingers, “Well, if you insist. But, I gotta warn you, when my cock is in you like this, I can’t seem to think straight and I don’t want to get carried away. You’re incredible,” he said, as he pulled back, inch by agonizing inch. The sensuous glide of his cock and his words in her ear made her smile smugly.

To have this kind of power over a man as big and strong and sexy as August was foreign to her. She’d had very few relationships, only two that were sexual, but this, this chemistry with August, this need to have him inside her, his hands on her, sore or not was insatiable. That he felt it too, at least the physical aspect of whatever was happening here, was empowering. Men said all sorts of things to get in a girl’s drawers, there was no doubt about that, but Tara sensed a genuineness in August that was rare indeed. For now, she would accept this at face value and let it happen.

She was having the sexual experience of a lifetime and letting any inhibitions she harbored go. Words that she might never have uttered before didn’t seem so inhibiting anymore. “I think I’d have to agree on the incredible thing. This,” she reached around to press him tightly to her, “is incredible.”

The rhythm of his strokes increased slightly as he suckled the hollow of her neck. Tara pressed her ass against his abdomen, rocking with him. “And you have the most amazing ass I’ve ever seen.” He emphasized his point by splaying a hand across her waist, holding her firmly to him and moving his other to cup her backside.

"My ass, huh? That's it? Just my ass?" she wiggled against him, meeting his thrusts.

"Well, there *are* other things, like this..." he said as he reached under her and slid his fingers between the folds of her pussy, massaging the wet flesh as he stroked into her with his cock.

Tara's hand covered his, following the path his fingers made. Exploring with him was new and exciting. Her clit throbbed as he fingered it, and Tara sighed. "I don't think I've ever experienced anything quite like this, August." She arched against him as the low hum of orgasm began to vibrate through her. Her muscles clenched him tightly and he groaned as he kept his pace steady.

"Slow down, Tara, you're already sore. But, if you keep this up, I'm going to have a hard time holding back."

She couldn't slow down if she wanted to and she didn't want to. As his cock filled her, she rode it with slow fierceness. Her world narrowed to the glide of his hard shaft and his hands taking her to heights she'd never reached. "I can't slow down, so shut up and make me come."

August chuckled, the rumble of his chest against her back making her nipples tighten almost painfully. "I think I can manage that," he ground out as he began to move his fingers more rapidly and his hips crashed with hers.

His hot breath grazed her shoulders as he tensed behind her. Tara felt it too, the tug of orgasm, from the tips of her toes as it began to sweep over her. Beginning as a tingle and raging to a molten hot fire, assaulting her pussy, racing through her until she couldn't hold a scream back. It tore out of her throat and echoed in the quiet of the room.

August came too, with a grunt and a twist of his hips, his teeth grazing her shoulder as he drove into her one final time.

Tara couldn't catch her breath, and gasped as August fought for his own.

Pulling out of her, he turned her around, hauling her across his chest. He kissed the top of her head. "Damn, woman," he muttered.

She rested her head against the bulge of his pec and giggled.

August cupped her jaw, raising it so her eyes met his. "Can't we just stay here today?"

"No, we can't and you know it. If I don't hurry, I won't have time to shower, so let me go, you Neanderthal."

He went to kiss her lips, but she ducked him.

"Morning breath," she muttered.

"Gimme a kiss or I'm not letting you up."

She pecked the corner of his mouth. "Now let me up."

"Nope, I want a real kiss."

Tara twisted her head to look at the clock. "August Guthrie let me up now! I'm going to be late."

"Kiss me and I will."

Tara laughed and pressed her lips to his, lingering for a moment longer than she should. Oh, those lips, firm and pliant, they did wicked things to her body. His tongue slithered into her mouth, hot and hungry.

"You're right," he said against her lips. "You *do* have morning breath."

She cackled, "Get off of me, you brute."

He let her go and she slid out of the bed, not even thinking about the fact she was completely naked in front of him. August followed behind her. "You gonna invite me to take a shower with you?" His eyes twinkled with amusement.

"I am not. What will happen if I do that?" She tugged at his cock, still cloaked in the condom. "We'll end up latching onto each other all soapy and slick and then we won't be able to keep our hands off of one another and you know what happens next." His cock twitched in her hand, *it* obviously knew what happened next.

"I promise to be good. " He held up his hands in the air. "I won't even offer to wash your back."

Tara giggled again. She was doing that a lot lately. "Well then, Mr. Guthrie," she said over her shoulder, "I suppose if you promise to keep your hands to yourself you can shower with me. But, you better not ask to borrow my shower gel."

He followed her into the bathroom, picking up the purple bottle of gel and sniffed it. "I think you can take me on my word that I don't want to smell 'raspberry morning fresh'."

Tara stood in front of the mirror and began to brush the tangled mess of her hair. August took the brush from her and stroked her long curls. The sight of his bronzed body, thick and muscled, behind her lighter one, made her legs weak. She felt small and vulnerable in the shelter of his wide chest.

Small, vulnerable ... and *naked.*

Oh, God, she was *naked.* This was a new experience. Even the few sexual encounters she'd had, she's never let anyone see her completely nude. Tara Douglas and naked had a long, sorry history together. Tara gripped the edge of the sink to keep from yanking a towel off the rack to cover herself.

By some miracle, he didn't know about what happened twelve years ago between her and Kelsey, so there was no reason to behave as if she didn't do this naked gig all the time.

Well, not *all the time* because that would just be slutty. A confident appearance in front of August might be a better way to go about this. Sorta like she did this occasionally, just enough to warrant ease with her body. God, she was such a fraud...

Tara's pulse raced as she thought about August finding out about her and Kelsey and their little run-in at Evanston.

Followed shortly by those damn tingles only he had the power to evoke, thus making her forget Kelsey. Tara's nipples tightened as he brushed strand after strand. "We need to get in the shower and you need to get the heck outta here. Won't your roommate wonder where you were last night?"

He laid the brush on the sink and circled her waist with his arms. "Yeah, yeah., I know--the rules, August!" he mimicked her. "Gordon was sound asleep when I left after I changed from my date."

Tara turned around and wrapped her arms around his neck. "I'm sorry. I know I talk about the rules all the time and that stupid contract, but I've never, ever done anything this--this sneaky, you know? I try not to make a habit out of being deceitful." Tara hid her face in his shoulder. Hah! She really hoped that whoever was making her room in hell right now would take into consideration that she'd never meant for any of this to happen with August.

"Let's look at this logically. If you pretend to forfeit a competition and anyone finds out about us, not only will you be sued, but you'll have to leave the island and they won't let you come back, then we can't see each other for almost three weeks. If you stay, and you win the elimination rounds, we can still see each other, as completely unethical and totally wrong as that is. I'll understand completely if you want to go because it would be the right thing to do. I'm just not sure forfeiting a competition is the way to do it honestly. *Honestly* leaving would mean you'd play the game like a champ and if you're picked by the jury and Kelsey, you'd just turn her down when it came time to propose."

And now, Tara Douglas, meet your conscience... Tara felt like she was dragging August into this deception with her, when her intent had only been to one-up Kelsey. This was growing far too complicated for a novice-revenge-seeker like herself.

She nipped his earlobe and forgot about the nagging little problem Kelsey presented. “So what’s it going to be, stud? Stay here with me and we schtupp our brains out, or,” she paused for effect and cocked her head, “you can be a big, fat wimp and chicken out, which would also mean we might both be sued if you leave, because you know they like to stir up trouble *after* the fact and the schtupping part of this deal is *over*.”

“So, you’ll let me come boink you if I keep competing?”

It was always about the boink, wasn’t it?

Tara burst out laughing. “It’s totally against the rules and completely unethical, but, yeah, you can have hut visitation. As long as you promise to be careful,” she warned.

Careful was an understatement.

~

Piercing screams filled the air as Tara made her way to the makeup trailer. She threw open the door to find Kelsey waving her arms wildly and screaming at the makeup people. “Look at my face! Oh, my God, I can’t go on national television like this!” Kelsey slapped the hands that tried to help her and screeched, “Get the hell away from me, you idiots! Can’t you see I need a doctor?”

Tara came up behind Ms. Mary who was in the opposite chair, waiting for her turn. Her knitting needles clacked furiously. “What happened?” she whispered to Mary.

“She has a rash.”

“What? What kind of a rash?”

“I dunno, but it’s pretty ugly and red, wouldn’t you agree?”

On closer inspection, Tara noted the angry red blotches over Kelsey’s cheekbones and forehead.

Oh, yuk.

Oooh, this wasn't pretty. "Did she have an allergic reaction to something?"

Mary shrugged her shoulders and yawned. "She must have eaten something that didn't agree with her."

Tara really should take a look at it. She was a chemist. She had some limited knowledge about allergic reactions due to her perfume making, what types of chemicals caused them, but her focus hadn't been on medicine, so it was fuzzy at best.

And then again, she was no doctor. They had one on the set. It was just a rash, for heaven's sake.

Guilt overruled her satisfaction over how truly awful Kelsey looked. Sighing in exasperation, Tara tapped Kelsey on the shoulder. "Let me take a look, Kelsey. Maybe I can help."

Kelsey sneered at her, "I don't think so, *Tina*. What could an idiot on a jury do to help *this?*" She pointed at her face.

Tina? Well, well... Kelsey really might not know who she was. Damn her self-absorbed, cellulite-riddled ass!

Tara laid her hand on Kelsey's shoulder and gripped it tightly, swinging her makeup chair around to face her. "I'm not just a juror, I'm a chemist. You know, Kelsey, like 'I don't just play a juror on TV'?"

Tara heard Ms. Mary snicker over her shoulder and she turned, shooting her a warning look to pipe down. Mary stuck her tongue out at her in rebellion and crossed her eyes.

Kelsey shoved Tara out of the way. "Get away from me! I don't want anyone to touch me, especially some stupid jury member!"

Kelsey began shoving her way past the makeup people and out of the trailer, yelling obscenities the entire way. Tara struggled to maintain her composure and not burst into gales of laughter. Whatever brought that rash on it was God-awful. Bet those men wouldn't be drooling all over the scabs on her face.

God, Kelsey was such a bitch, she deserved a rash. She had men lining up for her and she couldn't even appreciate the fact that a bunch of hunks were vying for her. Nothing was ever enough for Kelsey.

"Hey, Ella?" Tara called to the back of the head makeup artist who was on her way out the trailer door and shaking her head. "Are you okay?"

"Oh, sure, but thanks for asking. You don't think Kelsey is the first diva we've had on this show, do you? Girls like her are a dime a dozen. They think the world should only continue to rotate if they give us the head's up."

She gave Ella a sympathetic smile. No one knew better the affect a tirade of Kelsey's could have on a soul better than Tara. "If you only knew how well I understand that, Ella. Maybe you can go and take a nap in a hammock under the nearest palm tree."

Ella gave her a wave over her shoulder. "I think I just might. See ya later."

"You know, Tara my girl," Mary said. "You're a patient lady. I'd have slapped that bitch Kelsey senseless if I were you."

Well, it wasn't like she didn't want to ... but it wouldn't be proper jury foreman etiquette, now would it? She had to continue to appear sympathetic to Kelsey. "It's okay, Mary. She's cranky is all. Who wouldn't be with that mess all over their face? And between you and me, you're right," Tara whispered, "she is a bitch sometimes, but I'm going to chalk it up to the stressful environment. C'mon, let's go ogle men." Offering Ms. Mary her arm, Tara helped her down the steps of the makeup trailer and off to the pool.

As a result of Kelsey's mishap, shooting was delayed for two hours. Two hours she and August could have spent with one another, she pondered as she settled into a lounge chair by the pool. Diana and Andy were huddled in a corner, having a rather intense conversation about deodorant jingles. Gianni opted to take his leave and make a monitored phone call home. Walter was at the beach body surfing and Ms. Mary snored softly beside her, napping.

Tara smoothed suntan lotion over her arms and tried to relax, wondering what August was doing right now. Kelsey's rash was going to take a couple of days to heal, but the producers decided to forge ahead anyway. Time was of the essence and they could shoot around Kelsey. She was off now, getting some kind of cream to ease the itching.

Tara picked at her plate of fruit and cheese absently when Henry Abernathy came buzzing by. "Hey Tara, have you seen August?"

Why would Henry ask *her* that? Did he know? Oh, crap. And why was he looking for August? Tara tugged at her bikini and faked a yawn of indifference. "No, I haven't. We've just been hanging out here while Kelsey gets her rash cleared up. I mean, the *jurors* and I have been hanging around the pool." Absolutely no contestants. None. *See Henry? I would never touch a contestant.* Tara squirmed under Henry's gaze.

Henry smirked. "I think it may be awhile longer before Kelsey can shoot. The rash seems to be spreading."

Tara gave him a sympathetic smile. "I'm sorry to hear that. Please tell Kelsey I hope she feels better soon."

Henry wiggled his fingers at her and said, "Will do. Gotta go find August."

Tara sat back in her chair and breathed again.

August, August, August... Tara shivered. He was so incredibly sexy in a rough, brash way. She fought a war of excitement and fear in her head. He harped on her for reminding him that they were inviting trouble, but that was nothing short of the truth. Lawsuits and litigation flashed before her closed eyes.

Your Honor, I just couldn't help myself. He's just so ... sexy. It isn't often a girl meets a guy who can do things to her body that no man has done before. Would you deny me the rapture of orgasmic bliss just because we were playing a stupid game on national television?

Somehow, she doubted that that particular argument would go over well. Yet, at moments she didn't give a hoot. She was having the sexual enlightenment of the millennium. It pissed her off that Kelsey was even remotely keeping her from enjoying it to the degree one should enjoy a good boinking. Kelsey seemed to haunt her wherever she went, even if she didn't know that she was doing it this time.

But Kelsey knew what she was doing her senior year...

Yes, she'd known what she was doing and she'd made a laughingstock out of Tara. August *must* remember that. The entire school laughed for days over it. Damn, she should have brought her yearbook with her, then she could read up on August.

"Tara?" George the cameraman called her from across the pool. "You're due for an 'Impressions Session'." He tapped his watch impatiently.

Glancing at her watch, she realized that she was due for her 'Impressions Session'. Tara gave George the thumbs up. "I'll be right there, George."

As foreman of the jury, she would sit in a sequestered room and give the overall "impressions" the jury was getting on Kelsey and the contestants to a camera. The videotape would be aired later in the competition, keeping the viewing audience apprised of which contestant was in the lead and who was on their way out. Each contestant made one too. She wondered when August would do his, or if he already had.

It probably wouldn't be good if she shared her newly found feelings about August. She could just picture their reaction when she told them she thought he was hot and she knew that for a fact because she'd sampled his wares. *Just trying to be sure he's fit for Kelsey's consumption, fellow jurors.*

Um, that wouldn't be a good idea.

Tara sighed and rose to go meet the staff member who would take her to the videotape booth, shading Ms. Mary with the umbrella on her way.

Passing the contestants pool, she caught sight of August, off to the right, sitting with Aaron. Her heart skipped a beat at his red bathing suit. Their eyes met when he looked up and he gave her a quick wink.

Fighting off the thrill that shot up her spine, she continued on to the tiki bar, where she was whisked away for her taping.

Settling into the booth, Tara scanned the list of questions as she prepared to turn the video recorder on. How do you feel about your role in choosing a husband for Kelsey Little? Who do you think the jury finds best suited to her? Which contestant is your personal favorite? Who do you think Kelsey likes so far?

Kelsey, Kelsey Kelsey ... *yark.*

The small room was soundproof and darkly paneled. A small stool was provided for her to sit on, facing the camera. Tara smoothed her hair and sat up straight, clicking the recorder on.

"Um, well, let's see. I feel very confident that the jury will come to a satisfactory choice for Kelsey. Although, I have to admit, it's pretty scary when you're choosing a husband for someone. I mean, I haven't even chosen one for myself and now I'm responsible for someone else's. It certainly has its pressures. I mean, how can you ever be sure of your own feelings, let alone someone else's? Marriage is a big step and if we don't make the right choice, then Kelsey will join the statistics of divorce and I'd hate to see that happen. Divorce is ugly and..."

Tara caught herself mid-babble and reminded herself to shut up already. *Less is more.*

Tara cracked her knuckles and continued. "We like *all* of the contestants, it's not a matter of like or dislike. It's the matter of who's best suited to Kelsey. For right now, we've focused our attention on narrowing the field of contestants."

Very general ... better, much better.

What was the next question? Tara looked back down at the paper.

Which contestant is your personal favorite? "Well, I'm trying to remain neutral, but, if I'm honest I'd have to say I like Vinny. He's funny in a ... a quirky sort of way."

Scratching oneself in unseemly places in public is quirky? Or was it the way he drinks from a straw in his nose? She was lying again...

No, really, Tara thought--he'd be perfect for Kelsey. He could help her scratch her rash.

"Oh, and I think Kelsey likes him too." Tara winked at the camera. "I saw her at the bar with him and they were laughing over something."

Okay, so Kelsey wasn't really laughing *with* Vinny, Tara recalled. Kelsey had her mouth open because she couldn't believe he could drink from a straw in his nose. It was shock, not laughter.

Same damn difference.

Impressions Session officially over.

Besides she had a competition to judge. Save The Damsel In Distress, if she remembered correctly from her schedule. That certainly had to involve something physically required by the contestants from the sounds of it .Hopefully, Kelsey's rash would survive it. Hopefully, August would do what he said he intended to do and *lose*.

Chapter Nineteen

My Hero

August was tired. After a night with Tara, all he wanted to do was go back to the hut and climb in bed with her. So did his nether friend.

He definitely didn't want to play, "Save the Damsel in Distress", but it seemed Kelsey's rash was on a quicker mend than the crew had anticipated.

What a sport, that Kelsey.

Again, with the luck of a blue-haired lady loose in Atlantic City with a cupful of quarters, August's name was chosen at random to compete for another date with Kelsey. Five of the eight remaining contestants had to complete a series of obstacles and save Kelsey from the castle.

The contestant with the best time after crossing the moat of mud wins.

Yippee Skippee.

As of now, the time to beat would be Aaron's, who'd hauled Kelsey over the finish line with apparent ease.

The jury members sat in a row on the lush green lawn at the end of the obstacle course overlooking the ocean. August's eyes scanned the course. It seemed simple enough. Jump a hurdle or ten, swing across some vile smelly stuff, climb a wall, swim the length of a pool, get Kelsey from the fake Styrofoam rock and drag her ass through the moat to the finish line.

If he took his time, he could easily let someone else win. Then he'd be free to spend the evening with Tara, who was sitting, pretty as a picture, at the end of this stupid He-man event.

"Hey, August," Aaron called to him as he jogged over to where August was standing.

"Hey Aaron, nice time you made there." August slapped him on the back.

Aaron smiled, looking as refreshed as if he'd just stepped out of the shower and certainly not like he'd just lugged Kelsey's butt over the finish line. "Well, yeah. I ran track all through high school. I'm not normally one to brag, but I'd dare *anyone t*o beat my time," Aaron said smugly.

Oh, really ... a dare, you say? Was that cocky August heard in Aaron's tone? August cracked his knuckles. "Well, I didn't run track in high school, but I was a late bloomer."

Aaron smiled with an odd look on his face. "Cool, dude. Good luck."

Are you saying I need luck, dude? August sucked his gut in and slapped his belly as his competitive streak flared. He could run faster than a stupid kid who came to a reality show to find a bride to "hang ten" with him.

Watch this, Bruce Jenner...

August lunged, stretching his legs and absently thought about the jury. He hoped Tara was watching. August resigned himself to the coming rant his guilt was going to plague him with.

Okay, it was time to give it up, it was supposed to be Kelsey he hoped was watching, not Tara. August knew that, but his conscience wouldn't quit reminding him of it--it was fast approaching a rather sore point. He'd already decided he was going to forfeit this round of competition no matter what, because he didn't want to go out with Kelsey and so he could go on boinking the fabulous Tara.

And the hell with this damn show.

Well, thank God he'd gotten that straightened out.

August rolled his shoulders and took his place at the starting line. The time to beat was "beach boy's." Aaron was quick and spry. If he paced himself, he could come in a couple of seconds off and walk away the *real* victor.

Preston Weichert blew the whistle and August was off and running.

August easily cleared the first ten hurdles, without breaking a sweat. All of the jury members were whistling and yelling his name but Tara. Well, what the hell was that about? She sure thought Vinny was all that and a bag of chips when he'd swung over that pile of gunk. August pumped his legs harder, straining his muscles to out-perform Vinny.

He grabbed the rope, nearly losing his grip and swung in a wide sweep over the slime. When his feet touched the ground, he slipped in some of it, but regained his footing and charged toward the wall.

Up and over.

Easy cheesy, Japanesie.

Diving gracefully into the pool in a smooth arc of flesh and a fearsome desire to strut his stuff, he pounded the water. Clearing the pool and popping out the other side with a quick jump.

The roar of the jury fed the flames of victory for August. He could taste it on his tongue, hear it in his head. He forgot all about losing as he charged toward Kelsey, perched high atop a fake rock, squishing all the way.

August ran over the rough terrain in his soggy sneakers as though it were nothing more than a walk in the park.

When he reached Kelsey, she smiled broadly. "I knew you could do it!"

August ignored her and the red crap all over her face. Grabbing her around her waist, he threw her over his shoulder and began to make his way back down the slope of rock.

He grunted as she slapped against his back. Jesus H. she was heavy. Sweat began to drip from his brow as the hot sun made pretty, brightly flecked rays of light appear before his eyes. He gripped her tighter, just below the knees, running for all he was worth. Kelsey yelped as she bounced violently, but he could barely hear her for the roar of competitive muses screaming in his ear.

August, August, August!

Diving into the mud moat, he almost forgot Kelsey was on his back, but for the pounding, she was doing with her hands against his ass and the sag in his now aching shoulder. He schlepped his way through the thick mud, half-dragging, half pulling her big butt, digging his fingers into her flesh to keep from losing his grip on her before he made it to the finish line.

Just a few more feet and he would greet victory with a rebel yell. Every muscle in his body screamed its protest as he tripped and stumbled through the last leg of the race.

He victoriously threw Kelsey over his shoulder with a howl of agony and dropped her just over the chalk line finish. The jury went wild, clapping and chanting his name. Everyone but Tara, who he could just make out through the clumps of mud in his eyes. She clapped politely and sat back down in her chair, tight lipped.

Kelsey lay on the ground, mud spattered and red faced. Her blonde hair streaked with dirt, lying limply around her face.

"Four-point-two!" someone yelled from the crowd.

Huh?

Four-point-two? Yep, that was his time, now who was the real Bruce Jenner? He'd beaten Aaron by two tenths of a second.

August hobbled over to the grassy area by the jury and sank to the ground, letting his head hang between his legs and remembered what he'd won as a result of his amazing physical display.

Please, not *another* date.

Well, he was a real Superman, now wasn't he? So much like Superman, he'd won the contest for the date with Kelsey. Crap. He should have thought of that before he went screaming through this contest like George of the Jungle.

August groaned long and loud. It was the geek in him, always trying to prove he was superior. It made him competitive and ornery and determined to win at all costs.

Oh, he won all right. Aaron was smacking him on the back to confirm it.

It must have been the confusion on his face that prompted Aaron to ask, "Know what the prize is tonight, champ? A dinner date with the lovely Kelsey, poolside."

August gasped for breath, "Tonight?"

"Yep."

Hell.

~

August straightened his tie as he crossed the path leading toward the pool. Soft, twinkling lights glowed in the trees and lanterns were scattered on the tables surrounding the pool.

He guessed the table with the red tablecloth and candles was the place to be. What a production for a little pineapple and booze. A bottle of champagne sat in an ice bucket with two fluted glasses nearby. He hated champagne.

The camera crew sat around drinking coffee, awaiting Kelsey's arrival.

"Hey, guys. How's it going?"

"Nice job today, August. That was the best time I've seen yet," Gary, the soundman commented.

He couldn't help a smug smile. "Thanks."

And look what he'd ended up with for all of his efforts. *You Olympiad, you.*

Chairs shuffled as Kelsey fluttered to the table in a black dress and heels. And the camera crew readied themselves. George barked orders in an unusually short tone to the rest of the crew set to tape the date.

Hookay, let's get the show on the road so I can get the hell out of here was all August was thinking. A piece of pineapple, some booze to wash it down with, and he was gone.

"August, don't you look handsome?" Kelsey said as she made her way directly for him.

August accepted her embrace, giving her a quick peck somewhere around her ear.

"Do you like my dress?" Her breasts pressed against his chest.

August pushed her back at arms length, hoping to avoid too much contact with her. "It's very nice." Could you catch whatever that gunk was on her face? August felt the cold chill of a shudder zip up his spine over the very prospect of it.

Kelsey smiled sweetly. "Thank you." She wasn't letting go.

"Why don't we sit down?" August untangled himself and pulled out a chair for her.

"Oooh, champagne. I love champagne, don't you?"

A beer would be far more satisfying. "I'm not much of a drinker."

"Pour some and we'll have a toast."

August dutifully sloshed some of the champagne in the glasses and handed Kelsey one.

She raised hers and did the sultry, seductive thing with her eyes. "To us and tonight."

Yeah, yeah. Whatever. "To tonight," he agreed. There will be *no* us. The sound system designed especially for the pool was playing something slow and romantic.

"Oh, music! C'mon August, let's dance." Kelsey held out her hand to him.

"Um, I'm not much of a dancer." He whispered low, hoping the cameras wouldn't catch it.

"I'll show you how. C'mon," she coaxed.

August took her hand reluctantly and she clung to it, pulling him flush to her. "There, see it's easy." Her hips fashioned themselves to his and she draped her arms around his neck. "Oh, August," she whispered in his ear, "Is that a pencil in your pocket, or are you happy to see me?"

August's hand went immediately to his pocket. Nope, not a pencil... A pen. "It's a pen," he answered honestly.

Kelsey let her head fall back on her shoulders. "I think you're just teasing me," she giggled at him. Her laughter tinkled in the air, grating on his nerves. "You were really great out there today, August. You fought hard for me."

Not on purpose. "I've always liked a good competition."

"Especially when the prize is me?"

"Yeah..."

Kelsey pulled his face down to hers. “So, I guess you’re ready to kiss me then?”

Christ, were we back to the kissing thing again? She was like a dog with a bone. August sneezed in her face--her perfume was killing him. It clung to his nostrils and invaded his sinuses like Custer at the Battle of Little Big Horn. She didn’t smell nearly as good as Tara. “Sorry, did I spray you?” He wiped his nose with the palm of his hand. “I think we should still wait on the kiss. This is *only* our second date...”

Kelsey huffed at him, “How many dates to we have to have before you kiss me, August?”

There aren’t enough in this *lifetime.* Especially not with that crap on her face. “Why is it so important to kiss me, anyway?” August wondered aloud.

Kelsey was clinging to him as she swayed with the music, ignoring his question. Her eyes had that dreamy look about them that made August cringe.

“Hold me tighter,” she encouraged, wrapping his arms around her waist.

As she tightened her hold on him, he looked more closely at her face. Man that looked like shit, all red and scaly. “So did you find out what caused ... *that*?”

“What?”

“That crap on your face.”

Kelsey frowned. “A rash, I ate something I was allergic to, or at least that’s what the doctor said. Forget the rash and dance with me.”

It was kind of hard to focus on much else, those big angry welts looked like they might pop at any second and ooze something really gross. He shivered in distaste. Kelsey must have thought this meant he was all turned on, because the next thing he knew her tongue was in his mouth and she was dragging him around the pool.

Okay, date stops here. August tweaked her waist and she yelped, losing her footing.

It happened in slow motion, all at once and without warning.

Kelsey stumbled, her feet flying out from under her as the heel on her shoe broke. Rather than clinging to his neck, she let go with a scream, startling him, making him let go of her as she fell backwards into the pool with a mighty impressive splash. If they'd been doing cannon balls or something, she'd have scored a ten.

August stood stunned by the edge of the water, while Kelsey sputtered her way to the surface. Her hair was plastered to her head and her dress floated in a big black pool around her. One lone shoe floated past her.

One of the crewmembers yelled, "Stop ... stahhhhppp..." he gasped for breath, "roll--iiing." The "ing" in roll came out with a long squeak as he choked with hilarity. The camera man had to lay his camera down because he was having a screaming fit of laughter. His high-pitched giggle broke August's composure. He started to laugh too, then he howled while he reached blindly for a chair to hold him up. He had to stop laughing because his stomach hurt.

"Dammit, could someone help me here?" Kelsey screeched from the pool, pounding her fists on the water's surface.

August held out his hand and yanked her out with a tug as the makeup people came running with a bathrobe and towels.

He jammed his hands in his pocket and rocked back on his heels, staying in the background while everyone fussed over the sopping wet Kelsey.

Now was the time to make haste. He walked over to Kelsey's chair where she sat shivering. That was just a little dramatic it was freakin' ninety degrees. "I'm sorry, Kelsey. I hope you feel better soon. You'd better go back to your room and rest up and have them take care of that ... that stuff on your face. G'night."

He moved like lightning, away from the pool and back to his hut. It was only eight-thirty, so Tara would still be up. His heart did that stupid girlie thing in his chest over seeing her.

Gordon wasn't in the room when he got there, thankfully. August ripped off his suit jacket and pulled off his tie. The night was young ... and meant for schtupping. He grinned.

Chapter Twenty

It's a bird, it's a plane!

"Well, well, look who it is." Tara swung open the door to her room, "It's Mr. Triathlon. What brings you to this neck of the woods, Super Boy? Don't you have a poor, helpless female to rescue?"

August pushed his way past her, sliding the door shut firmly behind him. "I'm sorry, all right? I didn't mean for it to happen, it just did. And it's not a triathlon. I did like four or five events that would make it something quite different. I think it's *decathlon.*"

Tara knew she sounded petty, but after August's performance this afternoon, she was hard pressed to believe he didn't want to win this game *and* Kelsey. "Really? Gee, it sure looked like you were pretty determined to win, judging by the way you hauled Kelsey over the finish line."

August snickered, "Believe me, it wasn't easy getting her there either. My shoulder is killing me." He rubbed it vigorously for effect. "You could make it feel better, you know..."

Hah! As if that was going to happen. More likely she'd offer to dislocate it. "Why don't you see if Kelsey is available for massage therapy?"

"You're jealous..." He seemed rather pleased by this turn of events.

"I am not."

"Yep, you are. If you weren't jealous you wouldn't be angry over me winning the date with Kelsey. You would know I can be trusted."

Tara threw her hands up in the air. "Well, gee Auggie, maybe I wouldn't question your trustworthiness if you didn't seem hell-bent on winning every competition like some damn winning machine."

August frowned, "Hey, I didn't pick the winning key. It just happened."

"Oh please. Like making a time even Flo Jo couldn't beat--*without* carrying Kelsey on her back--doesn't look like you're hoping to lose! Give me a break."

He smiled at her, all sexy and sweet. "I don't have nails nearly as nice as Flo did..."

"Quit making jokes, if you want Kelsey, say the word and then go away."

Turning on her heel, Tara plopped down in the chair and crossed her legs.

August kneeled in front of her and put his hands on her knees. His eyes were doing the puppy dog thing to the best of his limited acting abilities. "But, I don't want Kelsey to massage me or anything else. I'd much rather have *you* do it. Besides, she's kind of 'all wet' right now."

"All wet?" Tara's ears perked up.

August traced the outline of her breast through the thin material of her silky bathrobe. “If you’re nice, I’ll tell you all about it.”

Tara grabbed his finger and stopped him before he got to her nipple. Already her thighs were damp with anticipation and this must stop. He had some splainin’ to do. “What constitutes nice? If I have to feel sorry for you, then forget it.”

Inch by inch he moved the short bathrobe up over her thighs. “Hey, I did it for you. Remember, you were the one who said I had to stay in the game if I wanted to be with you.” He bent his head, his tongue skirting her inner thigh. A shiver shot straight to her loins.

“I said stay in the game, not win every damn contest!” Oh, she was becoming whiny. They were already doing something totally against the rules, but actually asking him to forfeit was as unethical as it got.

He looked up from her lap, “It’s the geek in me,” he admitted. “I can’t let an opportunity pass me by to show off my manhood. It just happens.” He gave her a sheepish smile.

“You’re no geek.” He was anything but geeky and he knew it.

His hands bracketed either side of her face. “But I was in high school.”

Tara found herself softening a bit. “Really? Me too.”

“It’s kind of funny that we didn’t know one another, both of us being geeks and all. You’re not so geeky either, anymore. Now, can we forget Kelsey?” His thumb slid into her mouth, rough and callused against her tongue.

Nipping it, she smiled, “Not until you tell me why she was all wet.”

He slid his tongue over her lower lip, “Only if you take your clothes off...”

Tara wrapped her legs around his waist, pulling him to her. "I will not. Either you tell me, or you'll pay for your sins."

He let his now-hard cock brush against the heat between her legs. He teased her by rotating his hips, and her nipples hardened in response. "That would mean I can't do this?" His hand slid between her thighs and cupped her cunt. Freshly out of the shower, she had nothing on underneath her bathrobe.

Tara arched into him, letting the warmth invade her veins. Her pulse quickened and her heart began the new, yet familiar throbbing he seemed to evoke. "Well, no, not exactly ... but, you might shut me up if you tell me." Grinning slyly, she rubbed the heel of her hand over the outline of his hard shaft.

August took a deep breath and spoke in a rush of run-on sentences, "Kelsey-and-I-were-dancing,-not-that-I-wanted-to,-but-she-made-me. I-hate-to-dance. The-heel-of-her-shoe-broke-and-she-fell-in-the-pool. Date-over. Now-can-I have-you?"

Tara's eyes widened in surprise. "Whoa, slow down, champ. Her heel broke and she fell in the pool?"

"Yep," He murmured as he swept his tongue down the length of her neck.

"Oh, that sucks... Oh..." she gasped her pleasure when his tongue found her nipple. "Is she okay?"

His teeth grazed the stiffened peak, "Kelsey's fine, except for that really gross rash on her face. She just got wet. She fell in the pool, not the worst thing to happen, I suppose. Now, look, I don't want to talk about Kelsey anymore. Let's just hope the jury votes me out soon, because I don't want to *win* anymore dates with her. Can we please schtupp now?"

Appeased, Tara began to laugh, bringing his lips back up to hers. "Is that all you can think about? Shouldn't we sit together and maybe do something novel, like talk?"

He parted her robe and skimmed his hands over her breasts Heat stabbed at her pussy, making her squirm. “Sure, we can talk. How about we talk about what I’ve been thinking about all day long?”

“Winning a date with Kelsey?” Tara said snidely

But he wasn’t put off. He leaned forward and lightly licked the nipple he was thumbing. “Nope.”

“Trying out for the Olympics in the He-man event?”

Swirling his tongue over her rigid flesh, he shook his head. “Uh-uh.”

Sighing with pleasure, Tara pressed her breast to his lips. “Well, I can’t think of what else we can talk about.”

“How about we talk about your nipples?” He offered around an already ripe, rigid one.

His words excited her, making her pussy clench and her heart slam against her ribs. “Is there something *wrong* with them?” Her tone was husky and low in her ears.

Lapping at each one alternately, he moved his tongue back and forth between them. “There’s nothing wrong with them, except they weren’t anywhere near my mouth all day long.”

Groaning, she pulled him tighter, letting his words wash over her. “And why is that a problem?”

“Because I thought about them all day,” he replied, his voice hoarse and tight.

Hooking her ankles behind his waist, she rubbed against his still-clothed body. “You only think about my body parts?” Tara taunted him, pressing her hips upward, rubbing her clit on the material of his shorts. The delicious friction made her shudder.

“Well, yeah...” whispering over her belly, he removed his lips from her breast and licked his way back to her mouth. His fingers went south, trailing a path to her swollen clit. “When you’re dressed like this. Is that a problem?”

"I guess it depends on what you're thinking about them." Tara suckled his lower lip, and worked the zipper down on his shorts. Slipping inside them, she used both hands to envelope his cock, now rigid and pulsing beneath her touch.

August groaned against her mouth. "Do you want to know what I was thinking?"

Bold and wanton were words that briefly flitted through her haze of desire. Words she'd never used before were now easy and seductive. "Only if you want to tell me."

Sliding her lower body down the seat of the chair, so her hips lifted upward, he devoured her mouth. Spreading the wet flesh of her pussy, he opened her with his thumbs, yet left her exposed. Cool air washed her heated flesh. She squirmed, thrusting her tongue into his mouth, their tongues tangled for a moment, but he pulled away.

"I want to taste you, run my tongue along your cunt, slide my fingers into your tight pussy."

Her hands cupped his balls, heavy and soft. "Then what are you waiting for?" She arched into his hand, her pussy screaming for him to touch her.

Still, he didn't move, "I'm waiting for you to tell me you want that too..."

"I want that too, August," she almost whimpered, biting her lip to keep from demanding he do it.

"Say it." His demand was crisp and sure.

Shoving his pants down over his ass, she massaged the firm flesh, kneading it, freeing his cock to rub at her open pussy. "Lick me, August, lick my pussy. Put your fingers in me, fuck me with them." A flush of heat swept over her cheeks, but she was beyond caring about being embarrassed. If he wanted to hear the words, she was more than happy to supply them. They made her feel seductive and desired.

He pulled away from her briefly, removing his shorts and shirt. She gazed at the body that was so much like a piece of art through half-closed eyes. His cock was stiff and thick. He held a hand out to her, "Come with me." His gaze was dark and mirrored her own desire.

A shudder of anticipation coursed through her as she complied, taking his hand and following him to the bathroom, letting her bathrobe fall as she went. August spread a bath sheet on the long marble vanity, then lifted her to sit on it. The top of his thighs just toughed the edge of the counter.

Licking each nipple, then caressing her clit quickly, he said, "Don't move, I'll be right back." She heard him dig through the drawer by the bed, he returned with matches and condoms.

He lit the candles that sat on the bathtub, they gave off a soft glow, just enough to see one another. August stood between her legs. He lifted the heavy curtain of her hair, sprinkling kisses over her shoulders. Tara wrapped her arms around his neck as fire burned in her veins. If he didn't make love to her soon, she would explode.

"Lay down, Tara," his tone was thick with arousal.

She swung her legs around and lay down, resting her back against the smooth surface. He stood over her, tracing soft patterns over her nipples. "Look at me." Her eyes fastened on his, hypnotized by his stare. "See the mirror?" She looked to her left and nodded. "I want you to watch when I lick you. I want you to see my tongue buried in you. I want you to come with my head between your legs, while you see my mouth fuck you."

Tara's breathing quickened to short pants at his erotic request. August leaned forward, letting his lips hover near hers. Her pussy wept, slick and needy, aching for him. Snaking his tongue across her mouth she whimpered in response. "Please, August..."

"Please, what?" he whispered as he slipped a finger inside her, forcefully enough for her to revel in the entry, hard and fast, catching her by surprise.

Gasping, Tara struggled to find her voice, as her hands clutched at his shoulders. "Lick me, do it now, I want to watch as you fuck me with your tongue." This time he groaned at her words as he slipped his finger back out.

August wasted no time parting her legs. He draped one over his shoulder as he twisted his body to stand between them. "Open your eyes, Tara, watch..."

She did as he demanded, turning to the left, seeing the side of his head poised between her legs. Blond hair, thick and shaggy brushed her inner thighs. Lifting her hips, she offered herself to him. "Don't make me wait anymore, August, please..."

Brushing kisses along the outer lips of her pussy, his hot breath tormented her. "Open yourself for me, Tara, help me lick you."

Fighting back a scream, she let her hands drift between her legs, parting the smooth flesh, she so carefully shaved for him.

And he licked. A single, long, hot stroke.

The wet, moist contact made her hips jolt forward, pushing his tongue against her clit. White, hot bolts of electricity shot through her as he swirled his tongue over the swollen nub. Her fingers slid inside his mouth as he pleasured her, and the rasp of his tongue was slick with her juice.

Her eyes were glued to the mirror as she watched her own hands move in time with his head. Looking up at her, his lips moist with her arousal, he demanded more. "Touch yourself, Tara, let me see you slide your fingers through your cunt."

Mesmerized by his words, she fingered her clit and August slipped his tongue back into her. She caressed the wet surface, turned on by their combined touch.

Feverishly, he suckled her, pulling her fingers toward her tight entrance. It seemed natural to let two fingers slip inside her warmth and this time, she did scream as he lapped at her and she moved within herself. Her nipples beaded tightly, as she slid in and out of her pussy and August licked every exposed surface. Tara's pussy clenched her fingers, riding them as his mouth strayed to her entrance. He joined her fingers, stabbing his tongue inside her, fingering her clit. Soft hair brushed her arms. His head moved to a rhythm all its own as he wedged his tongue into her.

Strong hands clutched at her ass, gripping the flesh tightly, tugging her to fit his mouth. Moving back to her clit, he buried his lips in her, licking, sucking and the tight tension, building to an almost painful need for release, snapped, snaking outward, lashing at her pussy.

Tara rocked against him as she drew her fingers in and out, watching her body tense in the mirror. Her mouth was open, her body arched toward August's head, her arm hidden between her legs. Using her other hand, she tugged a nipple, seeing her own surprised look as she prepared to explode.

Heat engulfed her, tearing at her flesh as she came, with August tonguing her clit and her fingers plunging deeply within her. There was no fighting the scream that ripped from her lips, as she shuddered, jamming her hips down on the hard surface.

She gasped for air as her body quivered with the aftershock of the most incredible sexual experience she'd ever had. Slowly it began to mellow, leaving behind a fine hum.

August withdrew her fingers gently, licking each one with a sly grin. Tugging him to her, she kissed him deep and long, gripping thick handfuls of his hair. His cock strained against her skin, hot, hard.

Two could play at the game he had so skillfully created. Letting his head go, she lightly skimmed his cock as he thrust forward. "Look at me." His eyes found hers. "Tell me what you want."

Chuckling hoarsely, he answered, "Payback?"

"Do you want me to put you in my mouth, August and lick you?"

"Yesss," he hissed into her mouth.

Covering his cock with her hand, she pumped slowly. "Then, tell me what you want." Hearing the command in her voice, she shivered at the power she now held.

His hard shaft jumped at her demand, "I want you to lick my cock, suck me." The words echoed around the bathroom, heavy and needy.

"I want you to come to *me*, August, put your cock in my mouth. Do you want that too?"

He bit her neck softly, "Yes, Tara..." he said through clenched teeth.

Smiling against his hair, she pumped his shaft with more vigor. "I want you to watch, August. I want you to watch in the mirror as I suck your cock, lick it ... fuck you with my mouth."

August tensed, his body rigid against her. Was she driving him as insane as he'd driven her? "Stand up, August, put your cock in my mouth." Tugging the hard shaft, he stood at her request, as she turned slightly to her side, still reclining on the vanity. She drew him to her lips, letting her breath graze the heated flesh, but not opening her mouth. "Are you watching?" Her question was teasing.

Digging his hands into her hair, he cradled her head to him, "Yes," he said, stiffly, as if his control were slipping. "Tara..." his tone was pleading.

In one fell swoop, she swallowed him, taking his entire length into the warmth of her mouth, then stilled, resting her tongue on the silken surface. August sucked in a sharp breath when her tongue danced slowly upward, pausing at the sensitive area just below the head of his cock. Laving it, she suckled with her lips, suctioning him as she cupped his balls. He groaned as she jammed his length into her mouth. She peeked upward to see his eyes trained on the mirror. His hands clutched her head when she took him as deeply as she could.

Her cheek grazed his belly, the crisp hair above his shaft scraping against her skin. He cupped her jaw with his hands as she pulled away from him, swung her legs around, slipped off the vanity and knelt before him on the bath mat. Making sure he was still facing the mirror, she reached upward to trace the hard lines of his abdomen. He wrapped his arms around her shoulders as she spoke. "Was that what you wanted?" She whispered between long, swift strokes of her tongue, "To be licked like this?"

His thighs trembled against her, and he thrust his cock at her lips, "Lick me, Tara," he commanded.

Spreading his legs a bit, she swept her tongue over his balls, pushing them gently upward, laying them flush to his cock. Running her open mouth over him, she teased him from the bottom of his balls to the tip of his cock, darting her tongue in and out over his flesh. "Help me August, help me to please you ... give me your hand."

His hand touched hers and she wrapped it firmly around his cock, closing her own over it. She suckled his fingers, weaving between them, grazing his knuckles as she helped him pump his cock. Enveloping him once more, she followed his hand, sucking him deep into her mouth. August gripped the top of her head, the heel of his hand against her forehead, directing her, thrusting into her. His moans increased as he feverishly moved his hips.

"Stop," he nearly yelled, dragging his cock away from her and yanking her roughly upward against his hard length.

Tara circled his waist with her arms, pressing her aching nipples into his chest. She buried her head in his neck when he said, "Trying to beat me at my own game?"

She felt no shame in admitting she needed him to want her as much as she wanted him.

"Does that mean I win?" Leaning forward, she licked the flat disc of his nipple.

Walking her backwards, he turned her around to face the mirror again, cupping a breast and slipping his other hand between her thighs. Her arms went up around his neck and his cock burned against her spine. Arching against him, she sank backward into the solid wall of his chest. August's hands were everywhere, skimming her thighs, fondling her clit; he licked a finger and rubbed it over her nipple. The need to have his hard cock buried inside her burned her pussy. She leaned forward on the counter, bracing herself on her elbows, watching his reflection in the mirror.

"Do I win yet?" She taunted him, raising her ass high in the air, pressing it against his muscled thighs, daring him to thrust into her. Spreading her legs, she exposed the soaking wet flesh that awaited him.

He reached for a condom on the vanity, ripped open the package and slid it on. "What do you want to win, Tara?" Leaning forward over her body, he ran his hands over the outside of her ass, kneading it, massaging it. "Do you want my cock in you?" he whispered over her shoulder.

"Yesss," she echoed his response from earlier.

"Tell me, tell me what you want," he insisted as he pressed closer to her entrance, letting the tip of his cock hover there.

Boldly, she narrowed her eyes and stared into his. “I want your cock in me *now*, August. Fuck me hard. Don’t waste any time, just--fuck--me.”

Without hesitation, he thrust upward with force. Hard and thick, he slammed into her, stretching her until she was full with the heat of him. She jolted forward from the impact, inhaling sharply. Widening her stance, she braced her feet on the floor and straightened as her head fell back on his shoulder and her nipples tightened into stiff peaks. His body hunched to accommodate their height difference and she reached behind her, wrapping her arms around his waist. “Is that what you want, Tara?” He cradled her close, running his fingers along her arched neck, one hand holding her steady around her waist, flush against the wall of his chest. Plunging upward again, he asked once more, “Is this what you want, Tara?”

Meeting his hips with hers, she answered his question with a question. “Is it what *you* want, August?”

He slowed the pace of his thrusts, sliding in and out of her easily. “I want to fuck you until I can’t fuck anymore. I want to bury my cock so far in your cunt, you’ll never want another again. You’re so wet and tight, like no one I’ve ever experienced. I want to lick you until you beg me to stop, watch your luscious lips on my cock and drag my fingers through the sweet juice of your pussy.” His gaze pierced hers, smoldering, on fire.

Those words, crudely honest, utterly carnal, were her undoing.

Gulping for air, she grabbed his wrist at her throat and eyed his reflection, big and intimidating behind her, “Oh, August...” she gasped as her heart tightened in her chest. “Don’t make me wait then, do it, do it now. Fuck me until I scream, until you come hard and fast, buried between my legs, take me with you.”

And it was over, he lost control, ramming into her as she rolled her body into his. His hand, no longer around her waist, thrust between her thighs, stroking her aching, swollen clit. The distant slap of flesh excited her as they crashed together.

Her eyes, half closed, took in the sight before her. August's darker skin, a dark contrast against hers; their bodies joined, tightly woven in a dance of lust. She was more fulfilled than she'd ever been before. His cock inside of her brought her a sense of completion, the slick slide of him was *right.*

With that thought, she let go of his waist and cupped her breasts, circling her nipples. Burning with the need for release, she arched into him for the last time, coming with a fierce howl. He pumped hard into her, keeping his hand between her legs as his big body shuddered. He nearly lifted her off her feet with the impact as he finished stroking, and she clenched him tightly with her inner walls.

Tara heard his struggle for breath, the rasping intake of his gulps for air. She shook from head to toe and leaned forward to rest against the vanity.

Withdrawing from her, he discarded the condom and quickly washed up at the sink.

Tara wobbled, breathless, speechless. He scooped her up and carried her to the bed, setting her down gently. Keeping her close, he kissed her eyelids, her nose, lingering on her lips.

"Oh, August ... I ... I've never..."

He climbed in beside her, pulling the covers up over them and snuggling her to him. "Me either," he mumbled into her hair.

"You have very little to say for yourself, Mr. Guthrie," she chided, smiling against his chest. "Especially for a man who had *so much* to say in there."

The deep rumble of laughter vibrated against her cheek. "You taunted me, teased me, made me do *unspeakable* things, Ms. Douglas." He mocked the indignity of it all.

"I made you?" Tara rolled her eyes. "Oh, that's rich."

"You did, I never talk dirty like that. I'm a small town boy."

Resting her chin on her hands, she giggled. "Well, I'm a small town girl, August Guthrie and where I come from, we don't talk like that."

Kissing her forehead, he guffawed, "Sure could have fooled me, potty mouth."

"Like you should talk? You of the one-word sentences, all loose lipped and free."

"Yep."

"August?"

"Yep?"

"What are we going to do? It's just not right for you to keep competing, but we don't have a choice. Not only could we get in serious trouble, but we could end up hurting Kelsey in the process." That shouldn't matter to her, but the outlandish part of Tara who wanted to see Kelsey hurt for the torture she'd put her through had to stop living in the past. She'd made lemonade out of lemons, Tara was better for the cruelties she'd suffered in high school, she was in shape and happier because of it. Kelsey was still small, self centered and selfish. Nothing much had changed about Kelsey and pointing that out to her on national television was only going to make Tara just like her.

Whoa ... well, wasn't that the revelation of the millennium? It happened with rapid-fire discovery, and maybe a little because she was feeling generous now that she'd found August. In a way, that was enough justice unto itself.

For the first time since she'd begun this stupid vendetta against Kelsey, she was thinking clearly and it replaced the jumbled, freaked-out mess her head had been in since she started this journey. Not to mention her stomach.

But then there was August...

Ick. If August didn't like Kelsey's behavior, how would he feel about her own? It mirrored Kelsey's to a degree that now made Tara squirm with distaste. She had to tell August...

August snorted, "I don't think Kelsey *can* be hurt. She's a mean, pushy diva. Did you hear the way she screamed at the doctor and the makeup people?"

Tara nodded, casting her eyes downward. "The jury was all abuzz about it and Ms. Mary and I had a little taste of it. Look, I know firsthand what a bitch she can be, but what we're doing isn't much better."

August tilted her chin upward. "I'd like to hear about this *firsthand* thing sometime when you're ready. I get the feeling it was really cruel and one of the reasons you're on the show to begin with."

Tara cringed. *If he only knew...* How could he *not* know? Tara shrugged and chose to bite the bullet. "Where the hell were you all of your senior year? We did graduate from the same class, didn't we?"

Entwining his fingers with Tara's, he stroked her hand with his thumb. "I graduated early. I finished up what was left of my credits and left in March. Told ya I was a geek."

That explained it. August had graduated *before* the locker room incident. Tara wasn't sure if this was a good thing or a bad one. Opting for the glass-half-full theory, she shut up. She wasn't ready to tell him yet, not when she'd only just begun to accept what happened as something she could never change, no matter how much humiliation she heaped on Kelsey. "Still, what we're doing is wrong."

August sighed. "We didn't expect to meet each other, and if it wasn't for the fact that you were here, looking the way you do, I'd have forfeited the dates week one, but I just couldn't stay away. Winning some of those dates was strictly to impress you with my He-man abilities. I have a hard time turning down a challenge. I really think Kelsey's interests will change once she has a date with someone other than me."

Tara's heart skipped a beat. "You still have to be voted out if we're going to keep suspicion off of us."

He sighed again. "That's true and I won't deny I hope it's not until much later in the game. I don't want to leave the island and miss all this dirty talk." Tara's face flushed. "But that also means I have to try and stick around, which *is* cheating."

There was a smaller solution to this bigger problem. "Will you hate my guts if I stop voting for you? I won't say a word to the others, but I warn you, they really like you with Kelsey. They probably will even if you *do* lose a competition." Tara hated that. The jury members thought August was better than sliced bread and every session they had to vote she wanted to scream, *He's mine, damn you! Keep that slut away from him!* But she couldn't and now she was in deeper than she ever dreamed she'd be. She was omitting information about her history with Kelsey, not just to the jury and the people on the show, but to August too. Now she regretted ever doing this stupid show. She was going to have to come clean. No one really had to know her motives for being here, but *she* knew, in her head. It was more guilt than she could take and August deserved to know she'd come here hell-bent on revenge and now, she just wanted to forget it ever happened. Showing Kelsey Little the new Tara Douglas wasn't as important as what she hoped to create with August.

However, August was pretty competitive and if he won just one more date with that tramp...

"I think I've made myself pretty clear here, Tara. I don't want to be with Kelsey."

"Oh, yeah... Judging from the video tape we saw of your little lava pit rendezvous, I'd certainly say it didn't look like you were too terribly upset about it." Well, now she was pouting, it was unattractive and silly and even worse, it made her look jealous, but she didn't give a crap, because she *was*.

"Listen, girlie, let me tell you a little something about the magic of television. First, I'd lay bets they edit it before you guys ever see it. It is one of the camera crew that hands you the tape isn't it?" Tara nodded. "They encouraged us to sit together and Kelsey kept pushing to lay one on me. I kept saying no, and she kept asking anyway."

Tara felt smug momentarily. "You said no?"

August twirled a strand of her hair around his finger. "Well, yeah. I told her it was only our first date and I don't do *that* on the first date."

Tara really began to giggle now, "Good thing she doesn't know what you *really* do on your first date with slutty girls from small towns, huh?"

Shrugging his shoulders, he grinned at her. "Well, that was different. You talk dirty and it kind of wasn't a date."

"Dirty my eye, you started it." Sliding over his body, she straddled him. His hands automatically cupped her breasts and his cock began to rise underneath her. "Oh, no, Mr. Guthrie, you have to go." Leaning over him, she kissed his lips. "I don't want to take a chance that you might get caught. Your roommate is probably wondering why the heck you don't sleep in your room."

He slipped a nipple into his mouth, rolling his tongue over it. "Can't I just stay here and sneak back out again in the morning?"

Tara groaned at his request and pressed his flaxen head to her breast. “You are insatiable. No, August, please let’s not take any chances. I kinda like you being here on the island.” Swinging her legs off him, she jumped off the bed and gathered his clothes, holding them out to him.

She crooked her finger at him. “C’mon, handsome, you have to get dressed.”

His big shoulders slumped and he hung his head. “Okay, I’ll go, but I won’t like it. Somehow I think sleeping with Gordon just won’t be the same.”

Hooking her arm around his neck, she snuggled against him. “Promise me something, August?”

“Well, I’m thinkin’ you can pretty much have whatever you want right now.”

Tugging at his cock, she smiled, “No dirty talk for Gordon, okay? It’ll make me insanely jealous.”

Chapter Twenty One

Hoo Rah

"She what?" Ms. Mary squawked.

"She fell in the pool," Diana confirmed, nodding her head. "Can we run the tape again for Ms. Mary, Tara?"

Tara pressed play and turned away from the television. She just couldn't watch August hold Kelsey in his arms again, because she was going to pick up the damn chair and wing it at the pretty screen. Kelsey's body molded to August's enticingly. Tara's stomach rebelled against the image made larger than life by the big screen. Did the camera crew really edit these? You couldn't edit Kelsey so close to August a toothpick wouldn't fit between them...

Taking a deep breath, Tara closed her eyes and rubbed her aching brow. She admitted it *was* rather funny to see Kelsey soaking wet and her face covered in pus-filled hives. Andy played it over and over, stopping the tape each time Kelsey tipped backwards into the pool. Laughter filled the air, someone's high-pitched giggle pierced the night, and then the tape went blank.

Ms. Mary shook her head, "Well, she sure was a mess, huh? But do you see the way August looks at her?" Mary's voice turned dreamy and wistful.

Diana nodded her head again rapidly, "Yeah, he's pretty hot for her. He was something else in that race. I've never seen anyone work as hard as he did to get over that finish line. That's chemistry for sure."

Shut up, shut up, shut up! Tara was hard pressed not to scream it from the top of her lungs. Damn them all, they were going to vote for August again. She could feel it. Even if it meant August would stay around, it also meant Kelsey could quite possibly win another date with him.

It was time for an anonymous vote so she could slink off and not be stoned publicly for ignoring all this *chemistry* August supposedly had with Kelsey, because it looked that way on tape and he'd better be telling the truth about the tapes being edited to look as though they were hot for each other. Although, she had to admit, it wouldn't surprise her if they did edit them. So he might get the benefit of the doubt this time--because it beat the green-eyed monster.

"Okay, guys," Tara interrupted. "It's time to vote. This round is anonymous, so grab your pencils and head off to the voting room."

Andy raised his hand as he was wont to do when he was going to ask a question that made Tara wish she could wrap his mouth shut with duct tape. "Why does it have to be an anonymous vote, Tara? We all pretty much agree August is hot for Kelsey, so he's a keeper and we already decided on the rest of the guys."

Andy, Andy, Andy. Would you shut up?! I don't happen to agree that the barracuda has any chemistry with August and what I say goes.

Tara tugged at her shirt uncomfortably. She was wielding her big jury foreman's sword of power and that wasn't okay.

Yes, yes she was, because dammit, if she had to watch one more freakin' tape of Kelsey Little, pawing her man, she'd rip her tonsils out with her bare hands.

He's not officially your man.

No, that's true, she admitted mentally. But, if I have anything to say about it, he will be.

Way to get your man, tiger. In the meantime, she'd better chill with the possession is nine tenths of the law thing, cause everyone would catch on and then she would be *screwed*. Of course, that's all she'd done for the past few days, so maybe it wouldn't be so bad.

Hell's bells. She was going to be roped into voting for August again. "I'm sorry, Andy, I lost track. Okay, August it is. Do we have the next five finalists to be eliminated?"

Andy handed her the slip of eliminations. Why didn't everyone like Vinny the way she did? He was cute in a wise guy sorta way. So he was a bit brazen, a little rough around the old edges. Big deal. Kelsey could whip him into shape in no time flat. She'd have him filing her nails and dancing until dawn without batting an eye.

Straightening her shoulders, Tara headed toward the door. "Let's get this over with. I really hate this part of jury duty."

Gianni bobbed his head in sympathy. "I liked Gordon..."

Poor Gordon. On the other hand, August no longer had a roommate who could tell anyone he was gone late into the night.

Yeah, baby...

* ~ *

August half feared, half hoped the jury would boot his ass out. If he was eliminated it meant he couldn't see Tara for another three weeks, until the show was over. But if he stayed he might have to keep going on dates with Kelsey. Quite frankly, he'd rather have his eye teeth ripped from his mouth with a pair of rusty pliers.

Damned if you do--damned if you don't.

As the jury members made their way back to the pool, he watched Tara take her seat from behind his dark glasses. Her face was impassive, not tipping him off in either direction. She held the magic envelope with this round's eliminations.

Jesus, she was beautiful. Long and lean, lightly honed and well rounded in all the right places. Last night had been amazing to say the least. She excited him like no other woman, and far more than Kelsey Little ever had or did now--since he'd spent some time with her.

He'd been foolish to think his adolescent crush was anything more than just that. If he looked back on his high school days honestly, he saw Kelsey for what she was. Funny, how a little lust could alter the perception of reality.

August wanted the freedom to explore this thing with Tara. Beyond the explosive sex, beyond the constraints of this damn show. There was no denying their physical compatibility. His cock burned with the need to simply be inside her. But, he didn't just want to screw her brains out, he wanted to *turn* her brains inside out. Learn all of the things that made her tick. Find out why the hell they'd never run into each other, seeing as they were from the same geeky social circle.

And then, he wanted to take her out, buy her dinner, do all the normal stuff people did when they dated, and after all that, he would screw her brains out again. Trouble was, he had to keep his hands off of Tara ... all of his good intentions flew out the window when she was nearby and especially when she was nearby and naked.

"Hey, man, where are you?" Aaron interrupted his thoughts.

August blinked. "I'm just tired, I guess. This is stressful."

"Yeah it is, especially when you can't get a date with the chick." Was that envy he heard in Aaron's tone?

"Your time will come." He hoped.

"I was checking that Tara chick out from the jury, man, she's a hottie."

August's jaw twitched. *I'm sorry, did you mean my, Tara?* He wouldn't say it.

"She's pretty." August kept his comment non-committal.

Aaron nudged Vinny. "Pretty? Did you hear that, Vin, August says Tara is pretty. Are you on crack, dude? She's got a killer ass."

Vinny raised his glasses. "And those hooters! Would I like to sample that fruit."

August twitched again, clenching his teeth together and fisting his hands at his sides.

Remain calm, he told himself. He would not offer to duel Vinny at dawn over Tara's hooters. *Hold that thought*. Vinny called 'em hooters too... Oh my, God. He was officially a pig.

"Fruit?" August spit through his teeth.

"Yeah," Vinny smirked. "Ya know, like melons?"

August was this close to offering Vinny a chance to see how good he was at crushing *his* melons.

No, he had to play nice if he wanted to stay in the game. Tara would encourage that.

"Guys," he cut in, "it probably wouldn't be a good idea to get caught on camera talking about the jury foreman's hooters, ya know?"

Each man sobered instantly, glancing around surreptitiously for the cameras.

Back away from my woman slowly, you swine.

"Gentleman, are we ready to behave like adults and do what we came here to do?"

Aaron and Vinny nodded. "Sorry, August, you're right." Aaron was contrite.

"So let's play hard and fast. Scale the highest mountain, swim the deepest sea ... win the girl of our dreams." *Go team, go!*

Vinny and Aaron slapped each other on the back in the spirit of competition.

Hoo Rah.

* ~ *

"Oh, August! How did you do this?" The small table in Tara's room held silver, domed dishes. Candles were lit and a glass of white wine waited for her.

August smiled at her and pulled out the chair, motioning her to sit. "I stole it from the kitchen. I figured we'd need nourishment before we get down to business."

"Of course, you mean before we carry on an intelligent conversation, minus our body parts tangled in an embrace of passion?"

His hand reached out and caressed a nipple through her thin cotton shirt. "I like your body parts."

Waving his hands away and ignoring the wetness between her thighs she replied, "That's the trouble, we like each other's body parts far too much. So indulge me, okay?"

"Oh, all right."

Tara kissed him quickly before taking her seat. "We were supposed to go to the mixer tonight. Everyone will wonder where we are."

"Nah, I started a rumor about you. No one will wonder where you are."

Her eyebrows rose inquiringly. "Great, wanna share what that rumor might be? Just on the off chance I need to prepare my story. Like am I a transvestite or something?"

August laughed heartily. "I told them I heard you were lovesick for your boyfriend and you wanted some 'alone time'." He swiped his fingers in the air, making imaginary quotation marks.

She giggled and gave him a cocky eyebrow raise. "Oh, good, that might have worked, but Ms. Mary already knows I don't have a boyfriend."

August smirked at her, his blue eyes with that devilish gleam in them. "Ms. Mary said she just knew you were full of crap."

Tara tipped an imaginary hat at him. "Touché."

He spooned rice onto her plate, followed by tender, white slices of chicken. "So was that the truth? Do you have one of those?"

"One of what?"

"A boyfriend."

Munching on her chicken happily, Tara swallowed before answering. "Nope."

August's face relaxed, "Good."

Tara's heart beat faster. "Do *you* have one of those?"

His smile was flirty. "A boyfriend?"

Wiping her mouth with her napkin, she giggled again. "Yeah, a boyfriend."

"Nope."

Sighing loudly, she nibbled a cucumber from her salad. "A girlfriend, August. Was there anyone you left behind? Someone I should know about, or better still, someone *Kelsey* should know about."

He frowned, his lower lip sticking out. "I'm hurt."

"Why?"

"That you would think I'm capable of such deception."

"So, no girlfriend?"

"Nope," he said, winking at her.

She relaxed in her chair, letting the day's events slip from her mind. Forgetting that August was the forbidden and good girl Tara just didn't do this kind of stuff. Forgetting that she needed to come clean with him about why she came on this stupid show. He was the easiest man to be with. Even in silence, he brought about a comforting calm.

"Tell me why we didn't know each other in high school? I just can't place your name. What clubs did you belong to?"

Damn high school. Tara would bet if she told August she was part of the decorating committee for a prom she never went to because of that video, he'd remember her. Surely that rumor had spread beyond Evanston's walls. She still couldn't believe he didn't know what happened between her and Kelsey. "I was captain of the trig club."

"You really *were* a geek, huh?"

Tara gently tapped his shin with her foot and smiled "Don't make fun of me. So what was your gig in high school?"

"I was in band."

"Well, there's the problem, I traveled in far more *interesting* geek circles."

"Hey, the tuba is interesting."

Stabbing her tomato, she brought it to her lips, licking the slice free of salad dressing.

"Stop doing that."

"What?"

"Licking your lips," he growled.

"Do you want me to just rip my clothes off now and we can dispense with the learning about each other phase of this relationship?"

"Now you're talkin'."

"August," she warned, "it's only for a little while, then, I promise to get naked, lie on the bed and let you have your wicked way with me if we can just talk."

"Pinky swear?"

Chuckling, she held up her pinky. "Pinky swear. So after high school you graduated from college, and..."

"I started my own web-site design company."

"I know next to nothing about computer graphics. What kind of web sites do you design?"

"I specialize in custom sites for commercial companies, like cars and food products."

"It sounds much more interesting than being a chemist."

August took a long draw from his beer. "I think chemistry is cool."

She bristled over that word. "That's just what everyone keeps saying you have oodles of with Kelsey."

"That's because they can't hear me telling her to keep that tongue of hers in her own mouth."

Tramp, slut, whore.

"Thank God Vinny won the date tonight." He genuinely seemed relieved by that.

And August didn't even have to cheat for it to happen. Vinny won the poker game fair and square. Brooklyn in da house. "Yeah, it means we can talk while everyone else is off doing their own thing," Tara reminded him. Tonight, after the mixer was a free night and most everyone opted to go back to their huts and relax.

"Are we done doing that yet? Because I remember hearing someone say they'd get naked..."

His insatiable lust shifted her heart into overdrive, and there was nothing she wanted more than to throw herself at him and shout "*do me like a sow in heat.*" But she also wanted to know about August and he was making it very difficult.

"Not just yet. Where are your parents? Do they still live in Colorado?"

"Mom raised me, with Gram. My father left when I was a kid."

A tear stung her eyes. "Oh, August, I'm sorry."

Shrugging he grinned at her, the dimples on either side of his mouth deepened. "Don't be. Nobody could whack a baseball like Gram. What about your parents?"

"They live in Colorado too, still married, still nuts about each other. One brother, two sisters. All married with too many kids to count. Do you have any siblings?"

"Nope, it was just me. I think I was more than enough."

"I can't begin to imagine why you'd think that. You're so *not* demanding." Tara mocked teasingly, lacing her tone with sarcasm.

Throwing his napkin on the table, he pushed his chair away and rose. "C'mere, wench. Let's get more comfortable."

"You mean naked comfortable, don't you?"

"Well, I don't want to be *too* demanding..."

Unbuttoning her shirt, she gave him a sassy smile. "Is it time for you to have your wicked way with me?"

August slid out of his pants, revealing his boxer-briefs. They hugged his thighs and molded to his already thickening cock. Yum, he was delicious in every way, so she gave up trying to learn anything about him until they were done getting naked. Maybe he didn't want to get to know her?

Well then fine. She'd never had a ride quite like this and she wasn't ready to get off the train just yet. "Past time."

Hiking up her skirt, she pushed it off. Standing in her panties and bra, she pushed at his now naked chest. “Lay down, big boy.”

“I like those panties.”

“Do you? Want me to leave them on?”

He stretched out on the bed, his eyes beginning to darken as he stretched out. “What do you think?”

Tara slipped out of them, tossing them at him. He caught them and threw them in a corner. Straddling him, she slithered up along his solid length and reached over him, digging for a condom on the nightstand. He took the opportunity to capture a nipple, already swollen,.

“Oh, August, that feels so good...” she sighed, inhaling at the tingle shivering up her spine. Having him beneath her afforded her the control she wanted tonight. She needed to slake this fevered desire quickly. No fuss, no muss. Pulling away, she sat up and tore open the condom wrapper, slipping it over his cock with fluid ease.

“Don’t move. Let me do the work.” Lifting her hips, she slid slowly onto his solid shaft, sinking on top of him, letting the thick invasion take over.

He muttered something incoherent when she settled on him. His fingers parted her slick flesh and found her clit. Rocking forward, she ground her ass into him, feeling the crisp pubic hair above his cock scrape her swollen nub.

Moving his fingers in a circular pattern, he fondled her, sending waves of electricity straight to her pussy. Tara braced herself with her hands on his belly, rock hard and rigid with muscle. She ran her fingernails lightly over him, burying them in the thatch of hair surrounding his cock.

He moved in her, slow and easy, precise thrusts of hard flesh, making her pussy clench him tightly, tightening and contracting with each jab.

Each hand covered a breast. Pulling them to his mouth, he suckled her nipples, then took long, hot swipes at them. Her hand found her clit of its own accord, fingering it to a frenzy of white-hot need.

She reared up, and let her head fall onto her shoulders, circling the heat of his cock with her pussy. He placed his hands at her waist and offered her full control, allowing her to set the pace.

This slow, gentle side to August tugged at her heart, she could ride his cock to madness given the opportunity. It was that good, that real, that rich in texture and clarity. Rolling her body into each thrust, her clit brushed his belly and her nipples tightened, sharply. A bolt of white heat licked at her, wending its way to her pussy, slicing through her and robbing her of anything but the feel of him inside her.

August tensed beneath her, she felt her own orgasm swell too, rising up and taking her breath away. She came on a sigh, with August sharply grinding out her name.

“Jesus, woman. You’re going to kill me.”

“Well, wasn’t it you who said you wanted to have your wicked way with me?”

“Looks more like you had yours with me.” He nipped at her shoulder.

Tara chuckled, leaned forward and kissing the firm line of his lips. “I did at that, Mr. Guthrie.”

Cupping the back of her neck, he looked at her solemnly. “You are amazing.”

“I guess I’m not so amazing at conversation, cuz look where that got us.”

“I think this conversation went very well, Ms. Douglas. Let’s do it again, real soon.” Pulling her toward him for a kiss, he slipped his tongue between her lips.

Tara ran her hands over his shoulders, gripping the thick muscle and tight skin. “We can do it as often as you like, Mr. Guthrie, as long as you realize I’m not just some sex toy to be dabbled with.” Tara said it lightly, but her heart wrenched at the thought. Men like August--geek back when or not--didn’t want women like her forever. They wanted them as long as they could have them and then they moved on to other women because once they were free from their geek limits they knew no bounds. Surely August knew he could have any woman at the drop of a hat?

He laughed at her, enveloping her in the warmth of his embrace. “Just because I don’t like to talk doesn’t mean I think you’re my sex toy. Though I won’t mind if you call me yours.”

The impulse to ask him what this all meant couldn’t be repressed. “Where are we going with this, August? I mean, there’s going to come a time when you’ll be pushed to make a choice. Leave or stay and quite possibly be chosen to marry Kelsey, if you’re not voted out. I can’t seem to convince anyone you’re not right for Kelsey. So then what?”

“Well, I’m *not* marrying Kelsey, but the longer I stay in the game, the longer I can be with you. I began to see your point ... about staying.”

“What about the money, who couldn’t use a million bucks?”

He pulled out of her and walked toward the bathroom. “I don’t need or want the money. I thought coming on this show would mean I might get to know Kelsey and we’d fall in love as a result, or something misguided like that. At the very least, I thought I’d like her, even a little, but I don’t. I’m not the kid I once was.”

Oh, that was like a shot through a familiar place in her heart. “And now?” Tara refused to sound anything other than matter of fact. If they were going nowhere with this, but simply getting this attraction out of the way, boinking it out of their systems, then she wasn't asking to be hurt and she didn't have to tell him anything. Not her motivation for being on the island and not what had happened between her and Kelsey. Okay, so that was a cop-out, but whatever.

August poked his head around the corner, "And *now,* that's not the case. I thought I'd made myself clear about it."

Her heart beat a bit faster, "What *is* the case?" she asked, sitting at the edge of the bed.

Strolling over, he plopped down beside her. "Well, now, I met this really hot chick and she's making me crazy. Kelsey isn't who I made up in my head and I'm stuck in the middle of a competition that I don't want to be in, but I don't want to leave because I'm hot for this chick. Plus I sorta came here on a bet."

"A bet?"

August gave her a sheepish look. "Yeah ... my best friend Greg, who never really left high school, bet me I wouldn't come on the show. In fact, he triple dared me. He knew I was hot for Kelsey in high school and he knows I hate to be *triple* dared. It actually sounded like a good idea at the time. A way for me to show Kelsey what she missed. Sorta like a backsie. Now, I just feel like an ass."

Tara began to laugh. "Forget Greg. This chick ... tell me about her."

He nudged her shoulder. "Well, she's got this killer ass and she's smart, she's a chemist, you know? The only problem is, she's quite a potty mouth and I can't seem to keep her hands off me..."

Lying back on the bed, she pulled him on top of her, savoring the heavy bulk of him. If she didn't keep this light she'd likely bawl. If August was just using her to get laid, he was good at lying about it and she didn't want to acknowledge that possibility just yet. Her tendency to overanalyze everything could be damned for now. There just was no science when it came to the art of attraction.

"A potty mouth and a tramp, huh? Well, I think you should break up with her. I mean, if she's a potty mouth you can't bring her home to your mother. What would Gram say?" Wrapping her legs around his waist, Tara thrust her hips at him.

August settled between them and thumbed her nipple. "But she's really cute and her hands are okay, I guess."

Tara slid one of those very hands between them and grabbed his cock again, hard. "So tell me, what are your plans for the very hand-happy, potty-mouthed, hot chick?"

"I was thinking maybe, if she's trainable, I'd keep her around for a little while."

Cupping his balls, Tara felt them tighten in her hand, and massaged them slowly. "Trainable?"

August ran his tongue along the length of her neck. She arched into the heat and groaned when he stopped at her nipple. He blew on it. "Well, yeah, I mean I can't have her pawing me all the time and take the chance she might do that in public. Could be embarrassing."

Tara cupped her breast and offered it to his lips. Savoring the wet swirl of tongue, she bit the inside of her cheek. "What if you can train her, then what?"

He tugged sharply on the tight bud, then released it and continued to lick. "Then, when we get the hell off this stupid island, I'm going to take her back to my place and screw her brains out."

Tunneling her hands in his hair, she rolled into his tongue. "Ohhh..." Heat, sharp and sweet pulsed in her pussy. "Does she get a meal before she goes back to your place? Like a real date?"

He slipped a finger in her, hooking it upward, and moved slowly within her. "I guess if I have to feed her ... maybe we should just order a pizza in. That way I can make sure she doesn't embarrass me by pawing me at a restaurant."

Raising her arms above her head, she rode his finger. Her legs fell away from his waist and she lifted upward, pushing at him. "Will this sort of thing be included in the deal, be ... because... Oh..." he slid down her body and tongued her clit, "because, I think it could work."

He licked the nub again, "You mean that?"

Tara squirmed beneath his mouth. "Yesss ... I mean *that*."

"I think *that* can be arranged, depends on how cooperative she is." Without further ado, he latched onto the swollen nub, nibbling, sucking, licking.

Tara came again, squirming against his mouth and pushing onto his finger. He rode her shudders, lapping slowly at her until she let her hips rest back on the bed.

He kissed his way back over her belly to her lips. "Hey, you're pretty cooperative."

Kissing him long and full, she felt that stupid tug on her heart again. He tasted of her, musky and seductive. "I aim to please."

August wiggled his eyebrows. "And *I'm* pleased. Seriously, I want to get to know you. I know I didn't let you talk tonight, but I really do want to see you when we leave this island. Yet, I don't want to leave the island without you. We're kind of stuck between a rock and a hard place."

She tugged his cock, "I'd agree about the hard place, and all of the getting-to-know-each-other we do is in the middle of sex."

Moaning against her lips, he said, "This thing between us is explosive. I've never experienced anything like it. So it seems right to get to know one another in the middle of it."

Tara's heart skipped another beat. Damn his logic. "Stuff like that fades, August, just the way your little fantasy for Kelsey faded."

"This," he thrust his cock into her hand, "is not fading."

Sighing with exasperation, Tara pinched his ass with her other hand. "August! You know what I mean." She didn't just want to be someone he'd slept with on an island because she was convenient. Now wasn't that a kicker? It disturbed her that he might only want her because of how *she looked*. There'd been a time when Tara might have settled for that, even while hating Kelsey for having the same opportunity.

Sex was sex, but developing a relationship that had more than that involved something other than illicit nights spent making love. Jesus, she was a jumbled mess of mixed up ... *everything.*

Kissing her forehead, August whispered, "Are you forgetting I was a geek too? I think I understand exactly what you're feeling right now. You think I just want to sleep with you because you're hot."

Tara didn't confirm or deny, but waited for him to answer his own question.

"Well, I won't deny you're hot, but that's all just the outside stuff and I think we've both had our lesson in what that means from high school. I could be wrong, but I sense we both know what it's like to be judged by how we look, back in high school and now. Kelsey Little didn't think twice about me in high school and now all of a sudden she wants to kiss me? We relate to each other because of our pasts, Tara. I don't think this is going to fade and I can only tell you that my fantasy about Kelsey didn't mesh with the reality. You, on the other hand, are feeling pretty real to me right now."

Tara ignored the thump in her heart and the butterflies in her belly. She wasn't ready to be serious with August before she thought this through. It's what she always did. So she continued the light banter they'd established. "So are you saying I'm not much of a fantasy?"

He groaned, "Woman, would you shut up? You're every man's fantasy and more and if this were my last act on earth, I'd die a happy man."

She squirmed out from beneath him, laughing. "I guess I'll just have to settle for that. C'mon stud, let's take a shower and you can see if I have any potential as 'trainable'."

Grabbing her hand, he trailed behind her, laughing. "Well, alrighty then, you're already showing signs of trainability. Compliance is *always* a good sign."

Her giggles echoed throughout the bathroom.

Chapter Twenty Two

Can we talk?

Week three was in full swing and August couldn't get thrown off the island if he paid someone to do it. Five eliminations rounds later and he was still going strong. Though he lost a date or two by now, he couldn't seem to get the jury to hate him, or even dislike him just a little bit. He was going to have to have to go through with it because of the contract. There was no two ways about it. August sure as hell wasn't going marry Kelsey; he'd rather be tied buck naked to a tree and flogged within an inch of his life than marry her, but he was going to have to say no in front of a bunch of people.

Sorry, Kelsey. You just ain't doin' it for me. I thought you were a hottie, but you're a low down, lying bitch. It's been nice. See ya.

This was undoubtedly a dilemma of monumental proportions. If he ended up as one of the last guys and Kelsey picked him, she was in for a surprise.

But he didn't wanna keep playing this stupid game either.

Don't be such a girl.

It was only a week until the end of the competition.

But would he rather wait to see Tara or have to say no to marrying Kelsey in front of a live audience?

Oh, yuck. The answer was clear here. No way in hell would he marry Kelsey, but he sure as crap didn't want to have to make a spectacle by saying no to her in front of a bunch of strangers.

"Auggie! You look intense, buddy, what'cha doin'?" Aaron asked as he sucked down a beer and smiled happily.

August cringed because he just wanted some quiet time. "Just thinking. It's been a long three weeks, ya know?"

Aaron nodded. "Dude, tell me about it. I don't want to disturb you. Just came to see if you want to get a game of volleyball going on the beach?"

"If you don't mind I think I'll skip today, bud. I gotta take a break."

Aaron winked at him. "Gotcha. Check you later." Aaron sauntered off in his relaxed, beach boy way. August watched him and found himself hoping Aaron would be picked for the final round.

August knew he was in deep, way deep, but he planned to get the fuck out of this ASAP.

Deep ... yeah, he was that too, with Tara. He smiled. This might be the real thing with her. Like the "L" word, followed shortly thereafter by the "M" word, then a house and a picket fence and babies and stuff.

August grinned to himself.

Well, wasn't life grand? Mom was really going to do the happy dance over this.

But, you've only known her for less than a month. August could hear Gram's words in his head before she spoke them. The words she would speak if she were alive.

So? He'd tell gram. Love was love no matter the length of time.

So that's a short amount of time, Auggie boy, to make a life altering decision like this, she'd say. Not unlike the one he'd thought he would make on this stupid show.

He'd better slow the frig down. He wasn't going to marry Tara tomorrow and he knew he wouldn't marry Kelsey.

Though he probably would marry her tomorrow if he knew Tara would say yes. If things kept going the way they were going, he wanted Tara with him all the time. And not with anyone else. Period.

Hold on, Neanderthal man ... what if Tara didn't feel the same way? What if he *was* just her boy-toy?

They'd spent almost every night together since they'd met. At this stage of his life, he hoped he'd sense something like that. Of course his experience with women was only short-term relationships and nothing as intense as it was with Tara. Most of their time here on the island had been spent in bed pawing each other like two teenagers.

August grinned again. His friend in his drawers agreed that was a cool perk. But that didn't mean Tara wanted to take their relationship to another level--they did spend more time in bed than out of it.

How could she want to spend the rest of her life with someone who had his tongue down her throat, and was too busy enticing her into doing the horizontal mambo than learning about her?

Made for difficult conversation.

He couldn't expect her to consider anything long-term with him if he never gave her a chance to have meaningful dialogue.

Tonight he promised himself.

Tonight he'd sit down with Tara and they'd talk about life. He'd make a point of learning all about her, what kind of food she liked, the movies she wanted to go see, her family...

All the shit that was important to her.

All the shit...

* ~ *

"Hey, beautiful." August pecked Tara on the cheek and slid past her into the cool of her hut.

"What kind of hello was that?" she asked, hands on hips. Her long, dark hair hung just past her nipples, covering her naked breasts. She was naked, completely naked.

He gulped, then groaned, turning his head he pretended to look at the view from the slider. "What was wrong with that hello?"

Tara came up behind him, slid her hands around his waist and pressed her body against him. Her hand drifted to his cock, ready, willing and able, as it always was whenever she was around. She slid her hands slowly over the erection tenting his shorts. "Well, it certainly isn't the greeting I've become accustomed to."

Unbuckling his belt, she tugged on the button of his shorts and unzipped them partially. August jammed his hands in the pockets to keep from pulling her around his body and throwing her on the bed. No, they were going to *talk*.

Talk, talk, talk. "I just thought you might want to hang out for a little while first."

Kneeling, she slipped between his thighs to sit in front of him. Looking up, her eyes gleamed, wicked and glazed with mischief. "We can *hang* out, August," she said as she freed his now burning hot cock. Pulling his shorts and underwear over his hips, she slid his sandals off and lifted his feet out of his shorts.

Yes, hang out. He was definitely doing that. He was hanging out a lot whenever he was with Tara. A sure sign he had to stop her now. *Remember the conversation thing?*

Her hot breath grazed his cock as she circled it, letting her lips brush it lightly. A jab of electricity shot to his balls, making him rock back a little on his feet. Her hands slid upward over his abdomen as she hovered near his needy shaft. "What kind of hanging out would you like to do?"

Jesus, how was he supposed to stop her when she was at his feet looking like this? Her lush lips prepared to wrap around his cock, her tongue ready to lick him until he wanted to scream. The soft swell of her ass, round and full, was making him fucking nuts.

It was torture, it was ... it was ... stupid to turn her down, but he was going to anyway so he could prove to her that his intentions were for the long haul.

Gripping her upper arms lightly, he pulled her up to look at him. "The kind of hanging out where we *talk*," he said as he smiled.

Tara rolled her eyes, probably in disbelief and said, "Oh, well, all right, let's *talk*." Pushing at his broad chest, she directed him to the edge of the bed. Sitting between his thighs, she tucked her hair up on the top of her head, tying it in a knot.

Shit, he loved when she did that. Draping her arms around his neck, she tilted her head and waited. August sat on his hands so he wouldn't touch her nipples; they looked too downright lickable. Damn, his fingers twitched. "So..."

She kissed the side of his mouth, tracing his lower lip with her tongue, pressing her breasts to his still shirt-clad chest. Her hand found his cock, circling it she slid up and over it with ease. "So? Tell me what you want to talk about? I'm all ears." Giggling, she kissed her way down his neck, nipping his earlobe.

His cock twitched against her hand. Closing his eyes he tried to focus, but his hips rose to meet the thrust of her hand, soft and supple. Christ! “Let’s talk about *you.*”

Good, that was good. He gave himself a silent pat on the back. It showed intent.

She was kneeling between his thighs again, hovering by his shaft. “What about me?” Her tongue snaked out to swiftly lick him.

Holy Hell... “I... tell me ... tell me what kind of ... of movies ... damn,” he gasped as she took him in her mouth, “you like...”

Sliding back up his shaft, she cupped his balls and answered him, “I like all kinds of movies, action/adventure, comedy, documentaries. Next question,” she said as she lapped at the area just below the head of his cock.

His thighs tensed when she kneaded them and his cock throbbed painfully. He couldn’t keep his hands still. He gripped her head, directing her movement as she suckled with long slow passes. God, the silk of her tongue made him insane. “I like action/adven ... tuuuure,” he fairly screamed, keeping his teeth clenched as he spoke.

Letting him go with a pop, she replied, “Good. Think we can rent a movie here on Gilligan’s Island when I’m done?”

Disappointment flashed through his cock when she released him. “I don’t know. Do you like to rent or see it at the movie theater?”

Resuming her position, she ran her tongue over his balls lightly. They tightened, pulling against his body. Spreading his thighs further apart, she ran her nails over his thatch of pubic hair. “I like to stay at home. The movies are so expensive. Besides, if I were in a movie theater, say right now, I couldn’t do this...” Falling on him with her mouth, she took his rock-hard cock all the way into the heated cavern, then slid back up with a rasp of tongue and lips.

Okay, he was really trying here and she just wasn't playing fair. How was a guy supposed to learn stuff about a chick if she was doing this? How could he string coherent thoughts together when his balls were on fire and his cock could rival a two-by-four? Maybe he really was just a good lay... "I'm beginning to feel like this conversation is going nowhere," he threw out as casually as he could without sounding like a girl.

Nipping him lightly, Tara looked up from his lap. "Really? Why is that? I thought we were doing just fine." Rising, she straddled his lap, letting the heat of her pussy settle near his screaming cock. She arched her body backward, lifting her breasts to just below his lips.

Oh, she so did not play fair.

"We can't talk when you're doing *that*," he complained as his cock slipped between the folds of her pussy, sliding along the wet flesh.

Up and down, up and down.

"What am I doing?" She cupped her breast and thumbed her nipple, offering it to his lips.

August didn't know how to stop himself. He licked at the tight bud, savoring the rippled surface, letting it roll over his tongue.

Christ, he *was* just a boy-toy.

"I don't know what *I'm* doing, but I like what you're doing. Do some more..." she encouraged, holding his head close to her chest.

August slid his hand between them and found the swollen bud of her clit. He loved the slick feel of her on his fingers. "I feel so used, Tara..." he said around the sweet taste of nipple. He was shooting for nonchalant, teasing.

Gasping when he slid a finger into her wet warmth, she circled his hand. "Used, why? How could you even think such a thing? Do you think all I want to do is have my wicked way with you, then discard you, moving stealthily on to the next prey?"

There'd better not be anymore prey... He sighed, long and suffering for the effect he knew it would evoke. "I'm starting to wonder if it's just my body you want and not my mind."

Pressing his cock between the folds of her cunt, Tara held it there, moving against it as his finger impaled her. August refused to be deterred, no matter how much he wanted to ram his cock into her and fuck her silly.

Purring at him, she said. "Well, I do like your body ... it's very," he stroked her breast, "ahhh," she moaned, "it's very nice."

Nice? Nice? "Nice, it's just nice?" He kept sliding into her with more force in his thrusts.

"I said *very* nice, didn't I? Now, can you shut up so we can fuck like rabid animals and talk later?"

He stopped moving in her. "No. I want to talk *now*," he replied with as much petulance as he could muster.

Tara swung her legs off him and went to the table by the bed, taking the foil wrapped condom and ripping it open. She lay down and smiled, "So, talk to me."

Well now, how was he supposed to do that, when she looked like this? August snatched the condom from her and slipped it over his cock. She was lying on the bed all sexy and wanton. Her breasts tipped upward enticingly, and the taper of her waist led to the soft swell of her hips. Hips he loved to clutch tightly when he came. Smoothly shaven, her pussy was sweet and wet, he loved to bury his face in her, make her come with his lips and tongue. He loved hearing the gasp of breath she took just before she sighed his name.

Her eyebrows rose, as she trailed a finger over her nipple, wandering over her belly and pausing at the smooth mound of flesh between her legs. "So, talk to me August..."

She slipped her hand between her thighs, licking her lips, letting her eyes slide closed as she arched into her hand.

Oh man. August's cock was shrieking as his eyes watched her pleasure herself. She let her legs fall apart as she fingered her clit and tugged at her nipples. Lifting her head, her eyes half-open she repeated, "Let's *talk...*"

Talk, schmalk... August was between her legs with his tongue buried in her pussy as far as it would go in two seconds flat. Lapping at the wet, musky flesh, he listened for the gasp she would make when he made contact with her swollen clit.

"Ahhh, August..." Her hands clutched his head as she pressed his tongue flush to her clit. Bringing her to a swift orgasm, he suckled her hard, keeping her tight to his mouth, rolling his tongue over the now hard bud.

Bucking beneath him, she tore at his hair and jammed her heels into the bed. Her belly rose and fell rapidly beneath his head as she wrapped her legs around his shoulders.

Gripping his shoulders, she pulled him up on top of her. Her slender body pressed tightly to his as she wrapped her arms around his neck and her legs around his waist. She slipped her fingers between his lips and he nipped the tips of them.

His cock, ramrod stiff and flush with heat lay at the tight opening of her pussy. "Can we talk now?" She teased him, lifting her hips to encourage his cock's entrance.

With a shift of his hips, he plunged into her and let out a growl of satisfaction as her muscles clenched him. "Woman, I tried to talk to you, but you wouldn't listen, you just can't keep your hands off me."

Raising her hips, she jerked beneath him, buried her head in his neck and giggled "Whaddaya say we talk later, fuck *now*?"

He stroked her slowly, gliding easily from the wet, tight entrance, only to plunge into her once more. There would never be enough of this woman for him. August would never tire of lying between her legs, feeling her smooth skin beneath his as she whispered his name in his ear. His heart clenched tightly in his chest when her breath quickened and his cock began to pulse with heat.

She thrashed beneath him, straining against him, dropping her heels to the bed and rising up on her elbows. He felt her body tighten as her head fell back. He kissed the smooth hollow of her neck, pumping into her, rocking against her hard as she came, yelping his name.

August let go as hot, thick spurts of come coursed through his cock. Tara collapsed back on the bed and closed her eyes.

Kissing each of her eyelids, he stayed inside her, savoring the tight canal.

"Oh, Mr. Guthrie, it would seem what you lack in conversational skills, you more than make up for orally."

He nipped her nose, "I tried, you wouldn't let me ... you kept doing that thing with your lips and tongue, ya know?" He pretended indignation.

Tara laughed and snuggled under him. "Well, now you know how I feel. You completely ignore me when I try to talk to you, then distract me with this..." She tugged the base of his cock, "this weapon of love. How can a girl think when you're waving this thing around?"

"So, it's true. You're just using me and then you'll discard me when you're through with me. I *am* a boy-toy." He wasn't sure how he felt about that. There'd been a time when that would have been just fine and dandy, but Tara was different. He didn't mind the boy-toy part, so long as the long term part came with it.

"The best damn one I've ever had too. Besides, if I recall, you said you wouldn't mind being my sex toy." She grinned up at him.

"Okay, wench, listen up. From now on, we are going to engage in conversation for at least a half an hour before we get anywhere near each other. Otherwise, you can't keep your hands off me and then I'll end up feeling used and abused. Cheap maybe." He was joking away his concerns, but he was in for a fall if Tara really was just using him and that was territory he didn't want to venture into.

Running her hands over his back, she kneaded his flesh. "I can't keep my hands off you? Hah! Who's the one who can't get through a meal without pulling my clothes off? I figured I'd fight fire with fire."

Well yeah, that was true. August felt a bit better. She was using his own weapon against him and loving it. "Point taken. I promise to let you eat first, then rip your clothes off."

"Well all right then. So how is Vinny feeling about winning another date with Kelsey? I heard she's sick again, or something equally as gross as that rash."

Rolling off her, August went to the bathroom to clean up. "Yeah, she's got the runs or something. One of the guys said he could hear her yelping all the way over by the pool."

"She's been having a lot of trouble here. It's been one thing after the other."

He slid back between the sheets and hauled her next to him. "Yep, but it saved me from another possible date with her."

"We're getting closer to the end of the competition. What's going to happen if you end up one of the last two standing? The way the jury's going, I'd say you're a shoo-in."

"I wanted to talk to you about that. Here's my plan. If I'm not voted out before the last man standing round and *if* Kelsey chooses me, I'm going to have no choice but to go on camera and tell Kelsey 'no can do'. Finishing the competition is in my contract. I'd leave if I could, believe me. I don't know what that will mean in the aftermath. It's not exactly lying if I tell the press that I don't really want Kelsey, because I don't. I just can't tell them I want *you* instead. The contract doesn't have a "I don't want to play anymore' clause. It's nobody's fault but the show's if I won't marry her. It's not like I can get out of this even though I want to. However, I think that may cause controversy anyway because no one has ever turned down the million bucks. I didn't stay for the free trip and I don't care about the money. I can't help my competitive streak, winning the dates was just the Neanderthal in me screaming to prove I'm a bad-ass. It's stupid and macho, but that's the truth. Plus, my roundabout way of cheating meant I could stay here with *you*." August tilted her chin up with a finger. "Do you get what I'm saying?"

Tara nodded and smiled at him, returning his gaze.

"I might be voted out between now and then and that's fine by me. There's one more date competition. That's when the jury has to vote out man number three, and then Kelsey chooses between the two contestants left, correct?" He hoped he would be voted out. It would save a lot of unwanted attention from the press.

Tara nodded again. Now was the time to show her he was as serious as ever about pursuing this thing between them, *after* they got off the island. "Then I'm going to forfeit a date or trip and fall flat on my ass in the next date competition. *Whatever* it takes to be voted out before the Last Man Standing round. This way you won't have to be dishonest about *not* voting for me and the jury *can't* vote for me if I really screw up a competition for a date *and* I won't end up in the final two no matter what happens." There it was. August wanted her to know that he meant business and when he decided to cheat in order to stay in the game, it was all about not wanting to leave *her*. He didn't give a shit about the million bucks that was up for grabs and he wasn't going to marry Kelsey, no matter what. Now he had to do the "L" thing... Telling Tara he loved her was on the tip of his tongue, but it was stuck like it always was when something important needed to be said.

"August, the jury could still vote for you anyway and you'll have to leave if you fudge a competition and the jury gets smart enough to realize you're not the man for Kelsey. I know it's only for a few days, but I don't think I like that," she groaned, straddling his thigh.

Tightening his arms around her, he hoped that meant she wanted this thing between them too. "Will you miss your boy-toy if I get ditched?"

Laughing Tara smiled up at him. "Well, duh? Who's going to keep me warm at night?"

"Damn well better not be anyone in here keeping you anything at night, while I'm gone."

"You're pretty territorial aren't you?"

"Yep."

"What are you going to do to screw up the chance to win a date?"

"I have no clue what the competition for the date will be tomorrow, but I'll focus on losing at all costs. I promise. That will leave only three days before the show is over. How about I meet you back at the mainland, can you take the extra time off?"

Tracing his nipple, she asked, "If I do take more time off, what will you do with me back on the mainland?"

Sliding down her body, August suckled her nipples in slow easy strokes, running his hands over her back and legs as he nibbled. "What do you think?"

Bracing her hands on his shoulders, Tara giggled, that sweet laugh that made his insides turn over and his cock thicken again. "August, "she moaned as she filled his mouth with her breast, “I think I’m the toy here. Will you feed me on the mainland *before* the activities?”

He pressed his hands between her thighs, running one underneath her and over her ass, as the other fondled the swell of her pussy. “If I promise to feed you, will you promise to shut up for now?”

“A meal or no deal, August Guthrie,” she bargained.

Latching himself once more to her clit, August sighed as he nuzzled it. Her scent made him wild, made his cock burn with need all over again. “I promise to feed you...” he said between long strokes of his tongue.

“Then I think I can shut up now... Oh, August...” She shivered against him. He smiled at the familiar call of his name on her lips. It wasn’t going to be easy to leave her for three days, but he would do it if it meant in the end she’d be with him.

He immersed himself in the taste and texture of her body, forgetting everything else but the call of his cock.

Chapter Twenty Three

Dead Man Walking

Tara stared aghast, as did everyone else on the jury while August pretended not to know how to put the oversized puzzle pieces together. Aaron and Vinny ran around the big square, slapping puzzle pieces together while August yawned and feigned confusion.

"What's the matter with August?" Diana asked. "He's usually like a house on fire and today he can't even put a simple puzzle together?"

Andy frowned. "I don't get it either. He's pretty smart. He won that trivia contest hands down and now he's standing around acting like he can't put one foot in front of the other."

Oh God, he was really flubbing this. It was a little too obvious that he was faking this competition for a date. The jury knew how smart he was, for crap's sake and they weren't going to fall for him not getting something as simple as putting together a puzzle. Tara sent August as many signals as she could to get his ass in gear, but he was ignoring them. "Maybe he's just tired. I think this whole ordeal is getting to everyone." Tara hoped that would help cover his sad attempts at losing, cuz he was pretty unconvincing as far as she was concerned.

"Yeah, he does look tired and who wouldn't be after all this emotional upheaval," Diana offered.

Ms. Mary yawned loudly and rubbed her eyes. "Can't say as I blame the guy. These late nights are killing this old woman."

Tara heaved a sigh of relief. August continued to gaze with a blank stare at the puzzle when Aaron began jumping up and down.

Ah, a winner...

The jury clapped dutifully as Aaron was proclaimed the winner and the jury was sent off to do the final voting. Tara shot one last glimpse at August, his big body tan and glistening in the hot sun. Her heart did its typical nosedive as he lifted the corner of his mouth in a sort of smile at her. Tara had to believe he'd done this for her. Now she could only hope the jury would vote him out and they'd see one another on the mainland in a couple of days.

Tara shivered. Then, she had some 'splaining to do...

~

"So August is out, guys? I mean, he was one of the stiffest contenders." Tara kept her voice light and breezy, but was a mess of nerves on the inside.

Walter nodded his agreement. "Look at how he behaved today. He's been tired before, Tara, and it sure as hell didn't stop him from beating the pants off of everyone before. I'm reading it as a sign."

Diana cocked her head. "A what?"

Andy jumped in with his two cents. "I think what Walter means is this is August's way of telling us he's fried. It's subtle and hard to pick out, but I'd like to think I know my species well enough to know when a guy wants out."

Tara rolled her eyes. Thank God for Andy and his species observations.

The jury, after much deliberation decided August couldn't possibly want Kelsey as much as he seemed to if being tired was his only excuse for screwing up the puzzle. He'd excelled in everything else, fought like a champ and now he was appearing disinterested to them. It was a good thing no one seemed to think that was odd. They talked about it and decided if you had to vote on intent alone, then Aaron and Vinny were the most consistent winners thus far. They went over all of the video tapes from the Impressions Sessions too and while August competed well physically, mentally the jury decided he wasn't very good at expressing himself and that's what would make the best overall mate for Kelsey.

Tara almost snorted when Walter brought that up. If Walter only knew *how* August expressed himself to *her*...

Tara scooped up the voting box and placed it in the voting room, returning to give her final edict for the jury. "Okay guys, you know what to do. Fill out your votes and I'll tally them up."

As Tara took her turn and wrote out her vote she didn't feel a single scrap of guilt when she chose Aaron instead of August as one of the final two. Poor Aaron, he had no idea what he was getting into, but, it didn't matter who she chose. Tonight August would be eliminated entirely by the looks of the final votes and he would leave the island.

She'd held her breath and for the most part, her tongue, while the jury did exactly what she wanted them to do without even breaking a sweat.

August just might have managed to do it, Tara thought. He'd probably be voted out. Tara returned to the jury room where everyone was chatting softly.

Mary sighed long and loud. "Damn, I feel sorry for August. I hope what Andy says is true about him wanting out."

Tara bit her lip. So did she. "It's been a long road, huh, Ms. Mary? You look worn out."

"Yep. I am, dear. It's been fun and a nice break from real life, but I'm ready to call it a day."

Tara hugged Mary's shoulders. "Me too."

Soon she and August would be free to pursue a relationship away from the show. Aaron was nice enough, maybe he and Kelsey really would fall in love. Tara almost knew that was wishful thinking. Kelsey probably couldn't love anyone but herself. But maybe if the right man came along that would change. Aaron was gentle and kind and unassuming.

God love him. If he only knew what he was competing for.

At least Kelsey wouldn't have August.

"Only three more days," Gianni commented. "And then it's back to the land of the living. I gotta tell you, I'm almost glad to have to go back to work. I have to think less there."

Andy chuckled. "I know what you mean. This easy living isn't so easy after awhile."

Three days... Tara's heart throbbed painfully in her chest at the thought of August leaving the island. It was only three days, but already she was too far gone to even consider it. It was for the best. They only had three more nights until the end of the competition and the promise of something more to come when this stupid show was over.

Smiling to herself, she let the warm fuzzies have their moment. Tara Douglas was falling in love and she knew it.

"What are you smiling about, Tara? Diana asked.

Tara tilted her head. "I was just thinking that I wish I could take all of you back to Colorado with me. I've enjoyed getting to know all of you."

Mary chucked her under the chin. "You're a nice girl, Tara Douglas. If my son weren't already married, I just know he could fall in love with you."

Love... Did August feel the same way? They'd only known one another for a little over three weeks. Maybe she was just a fling and he wouldn't stick around on the mainland to wait for her.

That would suck royally.

Tara fingered the note in her pocket that he'd left for her this morning. *Let's continue this conversation on the Mainland... See you in three days, August.* Surely he wouldn't make promises he didn't intend to keep. What would be the point of leaving her a note, if he was just going to boink her and go back home?

"It's funny," Diana said. "My reasons for coming here were to get a free vacation. Now I just want to go home so I can not have to think about picking a husband for someone. It's such an important decision to leave in the hands of virtual strangers."

A free vacation ... if only that was why Tara had come in the first place.

She had to tell August *why* she'd come to the show. If she wasn't honest, completely honest, then there was no point to this. He would find out sooner or later anyway. When they got back home, he'd look her up in the yearbook and then he'd know who the infamous Tara Douglas from the class of nineteen-ninety-two was. Someone from school would have eventually cackled about it even if he had graduated early.

Well, Tara reasoned with herself, she didn't have to tell him but, she *had* to tell him. She didn't go through with her diabolical plan anyway, so it didn't make a difference.

But it's the thought that counts...

Yeah, yeah, she knew that. Nonetheless, she had to tell August, there just wasn't any putting it off anymore. If he thought she was a flaming bitch because she could be so devious and hold a grudge for so long, then so be it. She was human and like him, she'd wanted to show Kelsey a thing or two about the new Tara. It was wrong, she could admit that. Now she was just going to hope that this thing she and August had would turn into something more than just the screwing of the millennium and he'd understand her motivation for wanting Kelsey to suffer. Though, the screwing gig had its merits... No one affected her quite the way he did, she felt not a single inhibition with him and that had to mean something, because it wasn't the case with the few men she'd encountered. Sexually this was the most freeing experience of her life and now she wanted more than just the sex. Her heart told her it was right to pursue this, to take this path and find out where it led as long as she was truthful with August from here on out.

Tara wanted the whole shebang.

"Okay guys, we all done?"

They jury each nodded their tired heads and Tara sighed. This was it.

As she headed back to the voting room to tally the votes she felt a measure of relief. Turning back to the voting box, she sealed it and handed it over to one of the staff. Soon this would all be over and she could go back to her life, hopefully that would include the very sexy, insatiable, wickedly hot, August Guthrie.

* ~ *

What the hell?

August groaned as he watched Aaron pack. *Oh, this sucked big-time.*

"Dude, I wish you luck, cuz if anyone deserves Kelsey, it's you. You competed like a real pro. I know you were just tired today, otherwise my ass would have been toast." Aaron jammed his hand under August's nose; August shook it and slapped him on the back.

"Man, I'm really sorry. I hope everything is okay back home." Aaron's brother had been in a serious surfing accident. A freak occurrence was the word around the island that came down just after the jury picked Aaron for the last man standing round.

"I just can't believe he was so stupid, ya know? He knows better than to surf without a buddy. The doctors say he's pretty shaky right now. I don't know what I'd do if I lost him, ya know? I just want to go home and see him in case--well, in--case..." Aaron threw his duffle bag over his shoulder and headed toward the door, unable to finish the thought.

August nodded his understanding. "Good luck, Aaron. Keep in touch." As the door closed behind him, August ran a hand over his face. Damn, poor Aaron. August sat silently, holding a good thought for Aaron's brother.

Now what the fuck was he going to do? Aaron's leaving meant that he and Vinny were the last men standing. He'd gotten just what he didn't want.

A *win* by *default.*

Shit, how could he even think such a thing when Aaron's brother might be dying? It didn't change anything anyway.

This meant Vinny won the kewpie doll ... cuz August didn't want it.

August ran over the contract in his mind and cringed. He had no choice but to stick this out because the contract clearly stated if someone was to default by injury or unfair play, the next man in the running won the coveted second spot and must complete the competition. Aaron's brother's accident was enough to allow him to leave the island, but it also locked August into staying.

Fuck, fuck, fuck.

August ran a hand over his chin. It changed nothing; he was still saying no to Kelsey. It just meant he couldn't slink off unnoticed. Now he'd have to publicly tell Kelsey he wasn't marrying her if she chose him. No big deal. Well, except he really hated the public thing. It would be a much easier transition if he and Tara could just fade to black. Now if Kelsey chose him as her groom, he'd have some explaining to do to the press--who'd want to know why he'd ditched a million bucks for the first time in the show's history. Maybe Kelsey would pick Vinny. Lord, *please* let her pick Vinny. He didn't care anymore what the press might do to him. Aaron's brother's life hung precariously in the balance and that was more important than the controversy the press would create when August told her no. So August would do what he had to. He wasn't marrying Kelsey, but he'd fight off the press and hope Aaron's brother was okay.

He exhaled slowly and grabbed the handle of the door. A beefy hand caught him by the shoulder as he was leaving the room. "August, could we talk for a minute?"

"Yeah, Vin, what's up?"

Vinny led him back into the room, pulled out two chairs and motioned for August to sit down.

His head hung low as he folded his arms over his knees. "Stinks about Aaron's brother."

"Yeah, it does stink. I feel pretty shitty for the kid."

Vinny agreed, "Me too. I heard you have to stay now. Look, I gotta talk to you about that. Man to man and all."

Well, for crap's sake, now what? "Yeah, Kelsey and I, we're just not right for each other and I was kinda glad when the jury voted me out. Shoot, Vin, tell me what's on your mind."

"With Aaron gone, well, this kind of bites."

If he only knew just how much it bit. Vinny should be doing the happy dance and soon he'd do the dance of victory, because Kelsey would be all his--lock, stock and pus-filled rash. "Yeah, it does bite for Aaron, he really dug Kelsey."

"It bites for me too." Vinny sighed and gazed intently at August.

Okay, now he was confused. How could this possibly suck for Vinny? "Why does it bite, Vin? You'll win Kelsey and if she chooses you and accepts your proposal, a million bucks." August watched the tattoo on Vinny's arm ripple as he shifted positions.

"Cuz I'm *gay*, August."

Oh, Hell, that *did* bite. Who's *your* daddy?

August remained silent, he didn't know what to say or think or do. The repercussions of this were monumental. Now there was *no one* to marry Kelsey.

"I know what you're thinking, August, but, I did it for the money and now I realize I just can't go through with it. I thought the jury would pick you and Aaron, so I'd be in the clear and just look like the guy from Brooklyn who was ditched. But now, with Aaron gone, it's just you and me. I was pretty sure Kelsey would pick you and then everything would be all right. But what if she doesn't? I'm fucked. If I go to the producers and tell them I'm gay, it's over for me. I signed a friggin' contract that looked pretty heterosexual to these eyes. If the producers hassle me, they'll dig shit up that's better left buried. I can't afford to have the press get wind of the fact that I'm gay."

"Jesus H, Vinny! Why the hell would you even consider something like this? Are you fucking crazy?"

Vinny shrugged and gave him a sheepish look. "Gambling debts, man. I got plenty and coming here was a safe place to hide from the assholes who want to break my legs. It looked like easy money and the freaks that want me dead wouldn't risk being caught by the press trying to knock me off. It seemed safe, but we have to be married for a year for me to get my hands on that money and I don't think I can do that. I hate to say it and I know you were hot for her in high school, but she's just gross, ya feel me? I thought I could do it, but I can't. Not after that date..." Vinny visibly shuddered and squeezed his eyes shut briefly.

Now that feeling August could identify with entirely. "Well you should have thought about that a long time ago, Vin."

Look who's talking...

"Yeah, you're right. But if she picks me, I have to tell the world I won't marry Kelsey and people will start digging and they'll find out I'm gay anyway. If you say no, they'll just think big deal and eventually go the hell away. Shit, even if I *do* marry Kelsey, they'll find out I'm gay and my fucking parents will kill me. So, please somehow ya gotta find a way to get to Kelsey and tell her *you're* her man."

August had to laugh as he snorted derisively, "Bud, people want to kill you and you're worried about your parents finding out you're gay? Have you lost your mind?"

Vinny's black eyes narrowed, "You don't know my family. The people that want me dead may as well kill me if my folks found out. So I'm here begging you, man. Find Kelsey and convince her to *pick you*. Somebody has to be picked and it ain't gonna be me. It's only a year and then you can have the cash too. Or even if you don't marry her--just convince her to pick you and say no when she does. It'll piss her off, but she'll get over it. I can't take the chance Kelsey will pick me. I can't and *I won't.*"

There it was. Vinny dropped the words like a cherry bomb. They were on the floor spinning out of control, just waiting to go off, shooting in all directions.

August's radar went into overdrive. "Nope, can't do that, my man. It wouldn't be right. I'm not going to go to bat for you because you did something stupid." *As a matter of fact, I'd rather be gay*, he thought.

Vinny leaned in close and whispered, "Would you do it for *Tara*?"

August clenched his fists at his side. He'd fucking kill Vinny. "What are you talking about?"

Vinny cocked his head and eyed August. "You *know* what I mean, August. I know where you go every night. Some fuck-fest you got goin' on there, bud. I'll tell everyone what you've been doing with your evenings and the show will sue Tara for breaching her contract and you right along with her. The press will be so busy stalking you two they won't have time for Vinny Lambatti and I'll do it *before* the Last Man Standing round."

Yep, August would kill him. "You fucking scumbag. I'll tell the producers you're gay, you shithead."

Vinny's look became deadly calm, his face a mask of eerie determination. "You can't prove that, but I *can* prove you've been screwing Tara. Would you like me to show you?"

He knocked his chair back and grabbed Vinny by his shirt so quickly the other man yelped, struggling to maintain his tough guy image. "You rat-bastard, chicken-shit, weasel," August hissed in his face, tightening his grip on Vinny's shirt. "What happened to gay pride? What are you afraid of? I swear to Christ if you fuck with Tara, I'll kill you..."

Vinny thrust his jaw at him defiantly. "I'm not the one who has to worry about *fucking* with Tara, now am I?"

He threw Vinny flat against the wall and jammed his face in his, "If you don't give me what you have or anything that remotely involves Tara, I'll fuck you up."

Vinny's head jerked up, "You can't be any worse than the goons who want me dead. Bring it on Auggie," he sneered August's name as if he were speaking to the anti-Christ live and in person.

All at once August felt sorry for him, his steam lost in how pitiful this all was. Vinny had gone out of his way to prove what a man he was because he didn't want anyone to know he was gay. So he was willing to squelch his sexual identity to come on a reality TV show just to win some money? Now that was the gamble of a lifetime, or the debt of a lifetime. The fear in his eyes wasn't for August, or even quite possibly being killed by a bookie, it was over *who* Vinny was and someone finding out about it.

August loosened his grip on Vinny's shirt, shoving him on the bed with a hard jerk. "Pay attention. We're going to work this out. It might not help your financial troubles, but we're going to do this my way and if the thought of fucking with Tara ever crosses your mind again, you won't have any gambling debts to worry about--because I'll kill you long before some bookie gets his shot at you."

"Cool," Vinny looked up at him. His face was impassive and his eyes once again narrowed. "So, Auggie, let's make a deal..."

Chapter Twenty Four

Holy not so heterosexual, Batman...

Tara waited for August at the cove impatiently. What the hell was going on? He should be well on his way to the mainland, but she'd found a note under her door from him when she'd come back from the final jury selection.

Pacing the small stretch of sand between the rocks, Tara pinched the bridge of her nose. Deep in thought, she didn't hear him rustle through the bushes.

"Tara, are you okay?" He tapped her on the shoulder.

"What the hell is going on? You should be off the island. What are you doing here?"

August gathered her in his arms and kissed the top of her head. "We got trouble."

Her stomach flip-flopped. She wrapped her arms around his waist and shivered. "What's going on?"

"It's Vinny and Aaron."

Gazing up, she shot him a confused look. "What's wrong with Vinny and Aaron?"

He kissed her eyelids, "Aaron had to withdraw from the game. His brother was in a serious surfing accident."

Tara shook her head. "Oh my, God. I'm so sorry to hear that." She paused for a moment, "But wait, that leaves you and Vinny as the last men standing. Oh, shit!"

"Vinny is gay."

"What?!" She clapped a hand over her mouth, hoping the breeze didn't carry her voice.

August pulled her down to sit beside him on the sand. "He's *gay*."

"Then why the hell did he audition for 'Whose Bride Is She Anyway?' Can't he read? It's bride, not *groom*!"

"Listen to me baby, that's not all of it..."

Tara cringed, her mind raced to piece it all together. Aaron was gone, Vinny was gay and August was left holding the bag. What a freakin' disaster. "What else is there?" She was almost afraid to ask the question, yet, inevitably, she knew it was going to get worse.

August leaned back against the rocks, pulling her into his lap. He sighed and ran a hand over his chin, "Vinny knows about us, Tara. He told me everything. He has pictures of me going to your room. He sure is good at this shit."

Oh--my--Hell.

A heavy weight sank to the pit of Tara's belly. They were screwed. "Okay," she said slowly, "So he knows about us. It's not the worst thing that could happen, so I still don't get it."

"He doesn't want to marry Kelsey, and he knows I don't want to either. He told me if I didn't stay in the game and convince Kelsey to pick me, he'd tell the producers about us."

"That goddamn jerk! How could he? He's here under false pretenses too!" Tara cried.

August brushed the hair from her face, "Yeah, he is, babe because he's got gambling debts out the wazoo. It's why he came on the show in the first place, and he told me he's afraid Kelsey might pick him. If I don't convince Kelsey to pick me, she might pick Vinny and all of the television exposure if he turns Kelsey down will lead to someone finding out about his lack of interest in the opposite sex. He said he'd rather be dead than have his family know his sexual preferences. The press might haunt me if I turn Kelsey down, but I'm not gay. All I have to do is just say I didn't want to marry her. Even if he did win and he does marry Kelsey, he runs the risk of the press finding out. His reasons for being here were as bad as mine are for staying the moment I knew I didn't want to marry Kelsey. I should have lost a contest right about the time I knew I wanted you. But I can't prove Vinny's gay. He *can* prove we've been fooling around. He has the pictures. If I stay in the game and Kelsey picks me, and I turn her down publicly, Vinny can slink back off to the rock he crawled out from under as the scorned contestant. It wouldn't be nearly as bad as if he was picked by Kelsey and wouldn't marry her. I'm not gay... The press would eat him alive over it and he could be sued for signing on under false pretenses."

Tara searched his eyes. "So why is it okay for him to put your head on the chopping block? He has no way of knowing *for sure* that Kelsey *won't* pick you." That was as ludicrous to her ears as it was when she thought it in her head. Of course Kelsey would pick August, but there was no way she could convince Vinny of that. He was too far gone in his own paranoia. "Never mind, that was a stupid thought. Of course, she's going to pick you. Who wouldn't? I mean Vinny is a total goombatz, a real dork. Who drinks from straws in their nose unless they're still in kindergarten?"

August shook his head. "But we don't *know* that, Tara. We don't know anything for sure and now I've got to find a way to get to wherever the hell they're keeping Kelsey sequestered and convince her to choose me, which really sucks because I'm going to have to turn her down on national television and I hate attention focused on me. But I won't let Vinny slander you. I'm not going to take that chance. I do know I got myself into this and I'll get myself out. I knew what I was doing when I signed the contract."

Suddenly, she just didn't care anymore. Fuck all of this. Forget revenge. Forget the slander and inappropriate behavior the show would sue her for. Forget it *all*. She was sick and tired of Kelsey Little coming out on top no matter what she did to people and she'd be damned if she'd let Vinny have the best of her.

"You know what? I don't give a damn, August. Let Vinny do whatever he wants, the pig! I don't care if they sue me for tampering with a contestant. Let them. I mean what's the worst that can happen? I'll be broke and labeled a slut, right? It's not like the contestant tampering police are going to put me in jail. There are worse things, I suppose. I'm sick to death of Kelsey and this show and sneaking around."

August held up his hand. "Calm down, please. Listen to me, we'll figure this out, I promise you. I won't let them hurt you. It pisses me off that if Kelsey chooses me we're going to have to lay really low from the press. If she chose Vinny and we were caught hooking up *after* the show was over, the world would probably cheer. But that won't be the case if I say no to her and we get caught on the mainland or even back home in Colorado for a while. I'll be the first contestant in the history of the show to turn a bride down and the press is going to want to know *why*. If they catch us together they'll make mincemeat of you and I won't let that happen." August rubbed his hand over her stiff back in soothing, circular motions.

She twisted in his lap, "Make mincemeat of me? I'm not worried about *me,* August. Forget me! What about you? I won't let Vinny force you into scorning Kelsey publicly to save his own ass. I say let the chips fall where they may. Why should you have to beg Kelsey to save me? It's not fair to put you in the position where you have to say no to her publicly and beg her to let you do it too, just because Vinny is a chicken shit. He's offering you up for scrutiny because he doesn't want to take a gamble on paying the piper. I'll turn myself in. I'll tell them I'm in love with you and I have to withdraw from the jury."

Silence fell between them. Good gravy. Had she just admitted that?

August broke the silence first, his voice low and husky, "In love with me?"

Oh, for Christmas sake. Open mouth, insert anything big enough to shut her the hell up. Tara fiddled with the straps on her bikini.

August nudged her shoulder, "Hey, I'm talking to you."

Tara looked down at her lap, "Funny... You're *talking* to me now."

He laughed, "So, what's up with the love thing?"

Her cheeks flushed in irritation. "Shut up, August, it's not the time to talk about this."

He swung her around, laid her flat on her back and covered her upper body with his own. He made her look at him by tilting her jaw upward. "I think it's the perfect time. Now, give."

Tara avoided his eyes and pushed at his chest. "I will not. We have some really serious stuff to worry about right now."

August pressed his lips to hers briefly. "I'd say this is just as serious, now put your arms around me and woo me right, woman."

Giggling, she wrapped her arms around his neck. "I do not woo, Mr. Guthrie. I am to be the woo-ee, not the woo-er."

His tongue slipped between her lips and his big hand cupped her breast through the bikini top. Her nipple swelled in response, immediately straining to feel his touch. "You said it first," he accused.

Tara shivered as he lifted her bikini and stroked her nipple with his tongue. The cool breeze and the heat of his breath made her shiver. "August, we're doing it again. We're having a conversation while we paw each other."

Nipping the underside of her breast, he said, "You're right, and if you don't tell me what you meant, I'm going to ignore you and keep right on doing what I'm doing."

And this would be bad, how?

No, no, no, she thought. It was time for the two of them to behave like adults. His lips wrapped around her nipple and suckled. Oh, oh, oh... Giving him a shove, she detached him from her breast and bracketed his head with her hands. "August Guthrie, stop that right now. No more sex until we straighten this out!"

"Then say it," he demanded.

Grinning at him, she kissed him full on his firm, sensuous lips. "I think I'm falling in love with you."

Cocking his head he replied, "You *think*?"

"Yes, I *think,*" she answered smugly.

"So does that mean you don't *know*?"

"Maybe..."

"C'mere woman." He kissed her once again, hard. "Now there is no maybe about it. You love me, I can tell."

"Do I?" she asked innocently, delirious from the kiss and praying he'd say it back.

"Yep." Nuzzling her neck, he let his hand drift back to her breast.

"Argghhh, get off me, you beast!" She pushed at his big body to no avail.

"Oh, all right. I *think* I love you too, Tara Douglas. How's that?"

He rolled over a bit as she pinched his sides, and she used that to her advantage, scooting out from under him. Jumping to her feet she brushed at the sand stuck to her butt. Pointing her finger at him, she shook it. "Now pay attention, Mr.-I-think-I-love-you, we can't be rolling around in the sand when we have some real trouble. So get up and let's try to figure this thing out."

August sighed, long and suffering. "Can't we roll in the sand first, then figure this out?"

She rolled her eyes at him. "No, we can't. Now, if you promise to behave and help me work this out, I'll let you cop a feel. Okay?" Holding out her hand, she offered to help him up.

August jumped to his feet and took her hand, "Okay, but remember, you *promised*."

Turning from him, she wiggled her hips and pulled him up behind her. "C'mon, good looking, we need to get crackin'."

"Ooh," August snickered, "do you have a whip to go with that crack?"

Tara's laughter rang through the air, "Come with me, Mr. Guthrie and I'll introduce you to the dark side."

As they made their way out of the cove a big camera loomed, large and black in the moonlit night.

Oh, fuck.

Thankfully Tara was ahead of August by just a bit and he ducked down into the bushes.

"Hey, Tara," the cameraman crowed, "Wanna tell us why you came on 'Whose Bride Is She Anyway'? We heard a rumor about you and Kelsey in high school and we'd like to know if you want to confirm it..."

Yep. *Fucked* would be the appropriate terminology.

Chapter Twenty Five

Let's get ready to rumble

Oh, Jesus. Oh, God.

Noooooooooo. No, no, no.

Tara took a gulp of air, sucking in the salty breeze. Her heart clamored in her chest and her stomach rolled like the swelling waves in the ocean.

Oh, my holy hell.

Tara could literally feel August's ears perk up without ever seeing him from his hunched position beneath the bushes.

Cringing, Tara heard the cameraman repeat himself. It was George... "Is it true that you slept with Kelsey Little's boyfriend in high school?"

Jesus Christ in a mini skirt. He knew about the locker room incident at Evanston High...

Tara fought the sudden swell of tears, clenching her jaw and fisting her hands, she struggled to remain calm. "No," she answered on a shaky breath. "That's absolutely *not* true."

The camera zoomed in on her face, but if she turned away, she would look guilty. Tara gritted her teeth and stared at it head on, waiting.

"We also heard a rumor about a locker room incident. Wanna share?" The voice from behind the camera taunted. Which camera guy was this anyway?

Tendrils of fury gripped her intestines, ripping at her gut. Tara wasn't going to budge no matter what they asked. "I have nothing to share," she said calmly.

"That's not what we hear," George said.

Christ, was there a clause in the contract that had to do with revenge? Because if there was and she'd missed it, she was screwed. But that wasn't what really mattered to Tara now. What really mattered was August was hearing this from someone else and not her. Who the hell was behind this camera?

"We hear you slept with Kelsey's boyfriend and the two of you had a fight. You ended up outside of the girl's locker room--*naked*. That's why you're here--for *revenge*." The word hung in the air for what seemed like hours, clinging to the heat of the night, ugly and oppressive.

A small sob escaped Tara's lips pressed tightly together.

Oh-my-God. They *knew*.

A growl from the bushes sent Tara stumbling forward as August thrashed his way from behind his hiding place and charged the cameraman, knocking his camera to the ground with a heavy thud and tackling him in the sand.

Tara scrambled to get her footing and pounced on August's back, yanking at his shirt to pull him off of the unsuspecting cameraman. His hands were firmly planted around George's throat, shaking him while George clawed at his hands. "I'll fucking kill you, George! You leave her alone or I'll kill you.

Do you hear me?" August roared over the rush of tide and wind, his jaw clenched and his face a mask of fury.

"August! Stop it! Get off of him!" Tara yelled and tugged harder on his hands, forcing him to release George.

George rolled away and stood, backing as far from August as he could, rubbing his neck. "What the fuck is wrong with you, August?" he yelped hoarsely, rubbing his throat. "I'm just doing my job..." and then, George's eyes narrowed, glittering in the moonlight. "And what are *you* doing in the bushes with the jury foreman?"

August stalked after George, his face a mask of uncontained fury. "Shut up George or I'll flatten you. I swear to God I'll ram my fist down your throat!"

George straightened his back and made a wide circle around August to get his camera. He lugged the heavy machine back into place with a grunt. "Not before I ram this tape down yours, buddy. You're fucked because the sound was still on," George retorted.

Tara gripped August's arm to keep him from going after George again.

He pulled away from Tara roughly and swung around to face her. His mouth was compressed in a thin line and his jaw was hard. "So, Ms. Jury Foreman--is that why you're here? To get some revenge on Kelsey? Maybe steal her groom?"

Tara wrapped her arms around her waist. What could she say? It was almost exactly the reason she was on the island. "No--August. Wait--let me explain. I..."

"You *what*, Tara? If you aren't Kelsey's friend from high school, which I pretty much figured out all on my own with my little pea brain, then what are you? I figured Kelsey had done something pretty bad to you, but that doesn't give you the right to fuck with *me!*"

Tara's legs shook and her stomach rolled with wave after wave of fear. She had to explain to him, but she didn't know how. How did you explain away something that looked desperately obvious, only wasn't? "If you'll just calm down and listen to me I'll explain."

His big body visibly tensed. "How do you explain screwing me to get back at Kelsey?"

Tara sobbed, skipping pride and aiming right for a direct bull's eye on remorse. "Nooooooo, August. That wasn't my intention. I swear to you, I never meant to get involved with you!"

He shook his head in disbelief and snorted, "Oh, yeah? And how did you plan *not* to get involved with me with your tongue down my throat?"

That was just it. Tara was fried emotionally and physically and she'd be damned if she'd take the fall for wanting to hurt Kelsey like Kelsey had hurt her by way of toying with someone else's life. Namely August's. Gathering her self-esteem and some of her integrity Tara spat, "Excuse me, but as I recall you couldn't stay away from *me.* I kept telling you to go away and you kept coming back for more!"

August nodded knowingly, crossing his arms over his chest. "It was your vixen-like plan all along, wasn't it? How's a guy supposed to resist you when you kept pretending to be hard to get?"

"Oh! I did not!" Tara hollered, sticking her face in his. "No matter how attracted I was to you I knew you were off limits. That wasn't the plan, you nitwit. I planned to vote for the freakiest guy I could find to be Kelsey's husband and while I was at all this cloak and dagger shit, I was going to convince those stubborn jurors to do the same God--damn--thing! You know what? I can't convince you of anything and I'm sick and tired of trying. Believe what you want," Tara said, defeated. "I only have one more thing to say to you, August Guthrie. If you think I'm capable of using you--anyone--to hurt someone else, then I can't be the girl for you because you don't know jack shit about Tara Douglas!"

So there, Sherlock Holmes. August thought he had her all figured out, well she'd just set Mr. Know-It-All straight.

"What the hell else am I supposed to think? You came to this island to get back at Kelsey for whatever reason. I'm the perfect payback." His face was harsh and unforgiving.

Tara sucked in her cheeks and narrowed her eyes as she confronted him with a quiet calm that belied the fury simmering deep in her belly. It wound its way toward boiling right out. "Yeah, you're the perfect payback. So perfect I'd risk being sued, screwed, blue and tattooed just to make Kelsey squirm by stealing her potential man! Makes perfect sense for someone like me--a fucking genius--with an IQ to rival Einstein--to do something *that* obvious."

August stared at her, his eyes hard and his mouth set in a thin line.

Ah, well now, guess you can't beat that logic.

"Look, Tara..." August began, but she cut him off.

"No! You look. I've had it up to my eyeballs with Kelsey Little and this whole goddamned mess. Go to hell, August!"

Fuck all of this.

Fuck August Guthrie, Kelsey Little and Whose Bride Is She Anyway?. She wasn't going to stick around for any more accusations. Her position on the island had motives that were far from pure, but she'd never, ever drag someone else's heart into it.

Tara Douglas was taking her toys and going home.

And that's just what she'd done in one big huff of pissed off and a cloud of sand. Gone back to her hut as she'd flipped George the bird and stomped past a bewildered, angry, August

Guthrie. Her body trembled violently as she assumed what August must be thinking right now. Tara ran a hand over her tired eyes and squeezed her eyes shut.

August thought she'd used him to exact revenge on Kelsey.

Tara was screwed and she knew it, but she didn't care anymore. Nothing could have hurt more than to think he didn't believe her. She didn't even care if the show sued her and turned her name to mud in the tabloids. All that mattered now was that he hadn't believed her. Tara flew down the long stretch of beach and kept flying until she got to her hut, head down and heart in her cute new sandals.

Nothing could be worse than this. Nothing.

Tara jammed her key into her hut door and froze when she heard a voice over her shoulder.

"Well, well. If it isn't our little jury foreman," a snide voice said.

Okay, it *could* be worse.

Chapter Twenty Six

I'll get you, my pretty, and your little dog too...

"I know *exactly* who you are, you bitch and I'm going to ruin you. How long did you think you could get away with this?" Kelsey's smug tone made Tara's skin crawl. She pushed her way into the hut and quickly wiped the unshed tears from her eyes as she turned to face her long-time nemesis.

Kelsey's expression was assured, arrogant, superior and if Tara'd had the energy left, she'd of slapped it off her face.

She hovered in the hut door way, blonde as ever, cruel as ever, and shook her red-tipped finger under Tara's nose. "It was you who gave me that rash, wasn't it?"

Tara crossed her arms over her chest, ready to take on Kelsey because really, how much worse could it get? "No, it wasn't me. But, I wish I'd thought of it. Nobody deserves a rash more than you. How did you get out of seclusion? I didn't know they'd let the beast out of her cage until the wedding ceremony." Tara said each word, hanging on by a thread, keeping her voice as calm as she possibly could.

Kelsey sneered at her. "Please, you really don't think it's not possible for me to wrap anyone on this island around my little finger, do you? I can do whatever I want, you little bitch. Bet you didn't think I'd find out what you've done, did you?"

Okay, Tara was going to hedge her bets here. More than likely Kelsey knew nothing about what had just taken place on the beach, but Tara would bet she'd had a hand in setting George in motion. "I didn't do anything to you, Kelsey. Tell me, do you really remember me from high school? I mean, it has to be hard to think with all of that silicone in your boobs and man on the brain."

Kelsey pushed her way into the room and strutted across the floor. "Funny. Why would I remember someone like *you*? You're *insignificant,"* she spat.

Tara ground her teeth together. "That's a mighty big word for someone with a grade point average the size of her proposed daily caloric intake."

Wow, look at me, Tara Douglas, fighting back! *She shoots, she scooooores!*

"What do you remember, Kelsey?" Tara continued, "Do you remember how you humiliated me in front of the entire senior class? Or was that as insignificant to you as sleeping with nearly half of the male population in said class?"

Her green eyes, once brilliant, but now lightly lined with age, narrowed. "You were as stupid then as you are now."

Clenching her hands at her sides, Tara gathered steam. So, she *did* remember. This wasn't exactly the moment she'd hoped for, but it was as close as she was going to get to closure after all these years. "I guess I'm not *so* stupid, Kelsey. I managed to get on the show, didn't I? I'm kind of in charge of your destiny. Not a bad place to be in, I'd say."

The bitch actually snorted. "You don't really think I care *who* you picked, do you? This is my ticket to stardom, it doesn't matter *who* I marry and dispose of on the way."

Hearing Kelsey say money was her motivation out loud validated how right Tara had always been about her. She was beginning to regret that she hadn't gone through with her plan to humiliate the living snot out of Kelsey. "Do *movie stars* have as much cellulite on their asses as you do? Could make for a very unattractive close-up."

Oooh, me-ow, that was wickedly mean, she congratulated herself. Now it was time to tell the bitch what's what for the final time. This might be the only time Tara would ever feel as though she was on equal footing with her nemesis.

Kelsey flipped her hair over her shoulder as two bright red spots appeared on her cheeks. "Listen you nobody, I'm going to have it all and you can't stop me. But not before I share with the world what you've been doing to me. The rash was really original."

Okay, what the hell was going on? Hadn't Kelsey been the one to tattle to George on her? It must have been an outside source... Maybe not.

It made no sense when Tara looked at it logically. Kelsey wouldn't risk the very bomb Tara might drop about her role in the locker room incident. She'd look petty even if she lied about what happened twelve years ago. So it was time to call Kelsey's bluff...

Tara squared her shoulders and walked right up to her, eyeballing her with venom. "I haven't done a single thing to you. I don't know what you're talking about. But you did do something to me a long time ago. I don't suppose the nice folks in Middle America would take too kindly to their newest prime time 'sweetheart' being exposed for the spiteful bitch she is."

"You wouldn't..."

Tara laughed disdainfully, "Why wouldn't I? Payback and all ... you deserve nothing less."

"Is that why you're here, Tara? To get your revenge?"

She smirked at Kelsey, who now walked in the shoes Tara had finally shed. "Oh, I thought about it," she admitted, "and then I decided it wasn't worth it, I figured you'd screw yourself because you're too stupid not to. Worried?"

Kelsey pursed her lips, "You've changed. Lost some weight, done something with that hair... Is this going to be like a bad episode of 'when geeks attack?'."

Tara was immediately back in high school again, remembering every insecurity she'd ever had, reliving the moment Kelsey had turned her world upside down. *A mercy fuck* ... that's what Kelsey had accused Jordon of having with her.

Her cheeks burned to this day when she remembered what happened next.

Squaring her shoulders, Tara seethed with the memory. "I'm not an overweight geek anymore. As a matter of fact I've heard more than one comment about *your* fat ass from the contestants."

Kelsey reacted quickly. "At least it isn't naked and recorded on tape," she shot back.

Oh, what a fucking bitch.

"Have you taken a peek at some of the recent video footage of *your* ass, Kelsey? It may be covered, but that doesn't stop the jury from cringing every time it jiggles its way onto that wide screen. They find it distracting and hard to ignore."

"You little bitch..."

"A bitch yes," Tara acknowledged, "but I'm not such a geek anymore, huh?"

"Don't fuck with me Tara Douglas, or I'll make hell look like Disneyland," Kelsey threatened. "If you think I won't tell the producers of this rinky-dink show what you did to sabotage me, you've got another *think* coming."

Sabotage?

"Grow up. Do you really think I'd stoop to your level? I don't know what you're talking about. I had much bigger plans, but decided it wasn't worth it. You'd screw up all on your own, no matter who you ended up with. You didn't really care who you suckered into this deal because you're a cold hearted bitch with a need for some cash."

Kelsey's eyebrows rose, "August doesn't seem to think I'm so cold. You've seen the videotape yourself. He can't keep his hands off me."

Blood rushed to Tara's ears in a wave of fury, she clamped her jaw shut for a moment, measuring her words. It wouldn't help August to let the green-eyed monster attack Kelsey now when they had so much to lose. "Yeah, he's really into you," Tara let the words roll off her tongue and drip with sarcasm. "But he'll find out soon enough what kind of person you are." Tara strode toward the door and opened it. "Don't you have a wedding to prepare for? I suggest you leave before this geek *does* attack."

Kelsey swept past her in a swirl of heavy perfume and bouncing flaxen curls. "Remember what I said. I'll get you if you mess with me once more before this stupid show is over." She slammed the door on her way out.

Yeah and my little dog too...

Tara sat at the edge of her bed and shook as she replayed the events of the evening. It was over. She was cooked; well done, in fact, and she didn't have a clue how or *who* had snitched on her. Obviously, it hadn't been Kelsey. George was sent on a mission to search and destroy. He'd asked questions about her deepest, darkest secrets while he poked her in the face with the lens of a camera and he'd found out about it from some unknown source. Tara was dizzy from the endless list of possibilities about who would tell the show about her.

Did it matter? What could she do about it anyway? Start a whole new campaign of revenge against someone else? No, Tara needed to get this over with and go home.

Pack! She had to pack and get the hell out of here.

No, wait. She couldn't just up and leave. How was she going to do that? Swim to the mainland, for craps sake?

George would soon spill the beans about why Tara was here and Kelsey would very sweetly help him without even trying, because she was just too stupid not to realize it would also mean she herself would look like an ass.

Tara Douglas's name would become synonymous with the words geek and revenge in the media.

Good.

Great in fact.

She'd be all over the cover of rag mags everywhere and chased after to do interviews with those Hollywood reporter shows. They'd interview Kelsey and she'd smile her pretty smile, flaxen curls bobbing enticingly as she told them about how Tara Douglas, ex-nerd, tried to ruin her reality show experience.

Oh, God.

Tara shook as she got up and dragged her suitcase from the closet, heaving it to the bed. Unzipping the front of it she began to gather her things as a way to stave off her frantic thoughts. Taking action was what she was good at. She'd "think" her way through this ... rationally, calmly. It did no good. She was running through the hut now, grabbing things at random.

So, genius, think.

What was there to think about? August was kaput. He believed she was guilty of using him for her own gain. Her heart constricted again as she remembered the look on August's face.

It would go with Tara to her grave.

That look of utter surprise, followed by disappointment and then, anger and accusation.

Tara Douglas had fallen in love and managed to botch it up because she wanted to strike back at Kelsey for something she'd done over twelve years ago.

Pathetic. Tara Douglas, you are pathetic.

As a result of your pathetic-ness, you lost a man who makes your heart do the Riverdance and your panties sing an aria. A man who not only equaled your intelligence, but made your brain cells literally flutter.

Tara stopped rooting through the drawer of the dresser for a moment and let herself feel that loss, for all it was worth, so she could remind herself what real pain was in the future when she had nothing better to do than pick at her scabs for amusement.

It clawed at her heart, tore at her insides, screamed through her head.

Tara clamped her hand over her mouth to fight back a sob that ripped from her throat. It washed over her in waves of agonizing shame and despair and she had to grip the edge of the dresser for support.

She'd take it all back if she could.

All of it.

There was nothing to do now but face Henry and company, take her licks and go home.

Life would eventually return to normal, she soothed herself and then, she could go back.

Back to her dull life as a chemist.

Back to her apartment and her fern.

Back to the life she'd created before this reality show nightmare.

Back to the life she had before she was an ex-geek seeking revenge.

It would all be fine.

Fine, just fine.

Chapter Twenty Seven

Two heads are better than one

A sharp knock on her hut door made Tara jump out of her skin, swiping tears from her eyes.

Oh, God. Had they come to make her atone so soon?

It was Henry.

It had to be. George, or maybe even Kelsey, had ratted her out and he was beating her door down with both contract guns loaded. Tara tried to sort her muddled thoughts with rapid speed so she could find a way to keep August out of this.

She'd make it up as she went along. She'd do whatever it took to protect August. Tara gulped and squared her shoulders, refusing to back down from what would be her media death. Her legs shook as she made her way to the door and pulled it open.

August stood in the moonlight, his expression weary, defeated. Tara shoved the door shut, but he propped a shoulder against it and said, "Tara! Listen to me. We have to talk."

She was all talked out. What could they possibly say? How to save their lame hides from a media blitz of accountability? "August, go away," she said, her voice deflated, exhausted. "I'll take the blame. I'll tell them you caught me in the cove and confronted me about Kelsey. We went to high school together. They'll buy it."

"You can't do that. George has me on tape with my hands wrapped around his scrawny neck. Remember?"

Frustration welled in the pit of Tara's belly. "Fine," she hissed. "I'll think of something, just go away and let me do that," she said as she rested her head against the door. It pounded with the endless list of loose ends she had to tie up. If she could just get her act together, she'd figure it out. Tara wasn't a Mensa member for nothin'

"Tara," August's tone was demanding and insistent and right now, Tara didn't want to deal with any of it. "Open this damn door, woman! I'm not here so you can cover for me."

She let the door go with a suddenness that had August stumbling into her hut. Pivoting on her heel, she ignored him and fought to remain calm as she continued to pack her things.

"What are you doing?" he demanded harshly.

"Packing for my dream vacation. You know? The one where they haul me into paparazzi central and grill me for my devious revenge motives?"

He grabbed her arm to stop her. "Tara! Stop packing and listen to me."

She turned and stared up at him blankly. "Listen to you? Listen to you? Why would I listen to *you*, August? You didn't listen to me, did you?"

His look was sheepish as he clamped down on her arm. "I'm sorry, I really am. Ya gotta admit that it did look bad from my perspective."

She wasn't willing to accept his apology just yet. For all the grief this had caused her, she'd needed him to be on her side and he'd not even given her the benefit of the doubt. She yanked her arm out of his grip. "Yes, I do admit that, but you sure as hell weren't giving me an opportunity to tell you what really happened, were you?"

August reached for her hand and tried to pull her to him, but she brushed him off. He ran a hand through his hair. "Look. I'm sorry. I jumped. I have a hot temper sometimes and it gets the best of me, not to mention the fact that we're both strung out from this bullshit game. We're almost at the end. Don't give up now. We'll think of something to get out of this *together*."

A kernel of hope made her ask, "So you believe me?"

He held out his hand to her, "Yeah, I believe you. Of course I believe you. You don't have it in you to trash everyone around you. Your motives weren't pure for coming on the show, but whatever happened between you and Kelsey must have been pretty bad. I'm not saying it was right, I didn't exactly do the right things either, but I know just from watching you with Ms. Mary that you wouldn't strike out without reason."

Tara softened a little. Just a little. "I didn't intend to become involved with you. Yeah, I wanted to sway the jury to pick a freak for Kelsey, but I didn't come here with the intention of swaying the contestants. I swear that's not something I would dream of doing."

"Know what?" August asked as he reached for her hand.

She tugged back reluctantly. "What?"

He laughed at her stubbornness and the thick air of tension dissipated like a puff of smoke. "I think I'm glad as hell you didn't think *I* was a freak of nature."

Tara held on just a bit more. "Nobody said I didn't and don't you even try to make light of this now, August Guthrie. I'm still mad at you and I don't much like being labeled a user or a player, thank you. I was unethical enough just by coming here because Kelsey and I were *never* friends. I sure as hell wasn't going to make it worse by sleeping with you! I was already a walking ad for an antacid commercial. I didn't need the added guilt you brought, you caveman!"

He grabbed her waist and pulled her into his embrace with a chuckle. "I think we just had our first classic misunderstanding. They're rampant in romance novels, or so my mom tells me. Highly overrated, don't you agree you, vixen?"

Tara put her hands on August's shoulders and looked him in the eye. "I have a lot to explain to you, and it's not something I'm looking forward to. I was going to anyway, once we got to the mainland. I came here for a purpose and found another one instead. I would never use you. I'm not that revenge crazy, but I do want to explain my reasons for coming on the show if you'll listen."

"'Course I'll listen, but first, we have a lot to deal with because we are officially screwed. George has a tape of us together and me defending your honor."

Tara laid her head on his broad chest and tweaked it. "You big ox. If you had just stayed hidden..."

"I could what? Let George rip you to shreds? Nope, not on my watch, girlie."

Tara snuggled against him, warmed by the idea that he'd revealed himself to George for her despite what it would cost him. She sagged in relief against his bulk "I'm sorry. I hate that I dragged you into this."

"Well, I wasn't exactly screaming no, now was I? I'm sorry I jumped to conclusions, but George made some pretty serious accusations. I guess you didn't sleep with Jordon, did you?"

Tara looked up at August, her eyes serious. "No, I didn't. I tutored him, but Kelsey needed to find something to make my life hell and believe me, she did."

August ran his thumb down her nose. "So it would seem. For what it's worth, I wouldn't blame you if you did after what George said about Kelsey. I still don't get the naked part..."

Tara sighed, "I was really overweight in high school and--it was ug..."she tripped over the word, "ugly to say the least."

"I see. Kelsey really is a bitch, huh? Look, let's go find somewhere we can figure this out and hope we don't get caught while we do it. You can tell me everything, but only if you want to."

Tara threw her arms around is neck and hugged him hard as her eyeballs began to float again. "Okay, let's try and do that."

He kissed the tip of her nose. "C'mon woman, we've got some thinking to do. Two geeks are better than one."

Tara chuckled.

They spent the next hours figuring out what to do about what was going to happen to them. So far, they'd come up with nothing but to tell the truth.

She told August everything that had happened between her and Kelsey and he wanted her anyway. He was even willing to take the heat for their hanky panky on the island right along with her.

If August didn't care about the press and the lawsuits then screw it, neither did she.

Chapter Twenty Eight

Isn't she lovely?

The scent of gardenias filled the humid air, cloying and thick. Huge bouquets of flowers stood in white vases at the entrance to the mock chapel. Each pew sported a bow made of tulle and lace. Jesus H. How many flowers did a girl need to get married?

August fought back a sneeze. He tugged at his bowtie as he took his place at the altar beside Vinny. They stood before a thick, red curtain, obviously hiding the minister. Candles glowed everywhere, lining the aisle, casting a mood of intended romanticism.

Kelsey would make her choice tonight and all the world would watch as she and what she thought would be August--strolled toward matrimonial bliss.

Snort.

His stomach lurched in denial, but he held his ground. Vinny stood beside him, cocksure and ready to bolt when the festivities were over.

August would have liked to shove his fist down the Italian Stallion's throat for looking so damn glib. The cameras pointed down the flowered aisle, at the door where Kelsey would make her big bridal entrance. She would have already donned a bridal gown, specially made for her big moment. When she made her final choice and the chosen man consented--a ring and a minister would magically appear to marry the bride and groom.

'Til death do us part ... and all that jazz.

Not before he committed hari kari.

The jury sat to the far right, all in a row, dressed for just this occasion. August snuck a glimpse at Tara. She was, of course, beautiful and solemn as she waited for Kelsey to arrive. Her dark hair, swept high on her head with loose tendrils falling around her face, made his heart clench. They'd spent last night talking about Tara's real motives for being here, the grudge she was finally able to resolve and Kelsey's accusation of sabotage. He loved her all the more for admitting her quest for revenge, even if he couldn't remember the locker room thing. It pissed him off and made him more sure than ever of what he was about to do. August confessed his motivations too and told Tara all about his high school lust for Kelsey. It made him that much more certain Kelsey would get her due.

A rash and the runs were the least of Kelsey's worries now.

Thank God she'd rid herself of that gross rash. It was nothing more than patches of dry skin here and there. He hoped her runs had disappeared too, because she was going to need to have all of her faculties tonight. Christ, August felt like puking. The cameras trained on him and Vinny were enough to make him want to smash every last one of them. Now all he had to do was say no to Kelsey in front of them, poking in his face ... prying into his soul.

August tried to block out the crowd of people sitting in the pews and focus on exactly how he would say no. It was an easy word...

No, Kelsey. I wouldn't marry you even if it meant the world would stop turning if I didn't. No, Kelsey I wouldn't marry you for all the beer and a lifetime supply of season tickets to the Super Bowl for the next millennium.

That might not be the way to say no to marriage and Kelsey Little.

August tugged on his collar again and took some deep breaths. He was going to say no, no matter what. If he continued to cling to that notion, he could get through this.

Vinny slapped August on the back and offered his hand to him. "August, I wish you luck with Tara, you're a good man."

"If only the *man* thing could be said about you," August shot back, accepting Vinny's hand as if they were doing the "may the best man win" shake for the crowd of onlookers and cameras.

Vinny gripped his hand tighter. "You makin' fun of my manliness?"

"Not because you're gay, Vinny. Because you're a chicken shit asshole, who didn't have the balls to back out when he should have," August gave Vinny a "smile for the camera" grin, gripping his hand right back.

Vinny snorted, "Look who's talking..."

"At least I like *women*, Vinny. I didn't come to pay off a debt and if I were you, I'd shut up now before *all bets* are off."

Vinny blanched and pursed his lips.

Okay, August thought--just say no. He could do this, he could do this, he could do this. He'd *better* do this...

August turned abruptly to the sound of hooves outside the mock chapel. Kelsey would arrive in a horse drawn carriage.

Here comes the bride...

* ~ *

Tara watched nervously as the preparation for Kelsey's arrival finished up. The press sat in the pews, their nametags stating their assigned publications.

Tara gulped. Her worst fear was about to become a realization if the press had their greedy way. Each had signed a confidentiality agreement to keep the results a secret until it aired, but what difference did it make if they screwed her and August now or *later*?

George, (damn freak) was aiming his camera at August and narrowing his eyes at him. George glanced at Tara and winked.

Pig. He was going to show that damn tape of her and August and then this charade, this utter farce of a wedding would be over. Tara gave George a dirty look back. He smiled and winked again.

The nerve...

There just was no mental preparation she could make at this point that would help her deal with the unknown. She was completely willing to take her licks when George played that video. She didn't know if it would be here, or after the show was over and everyone had gone home. Tara only knew that he was going to shatter her private existence in the same way Kelsey had back in high school.

Fine--so be it. She had nothing left to hide. She was ready for whatever was going to happen. It was time to leave the past behind and move on. If that meant that Kelsey would have the last word on national television--if it meant Tara would be publicly humiliated again, but on a national level--in front of millions--then bring it on, baby.

But for crap's sake, could we get it over with?

Time was ticking away--agonizingly slow. This blindly trusting August thing wasn't her strong suit. She liked knowing what lay ahead. That wasn't going to happen this time...

As the small ensemble of musicians struck up "Here Comes the Bride" Tara's back stiffened and her eyes automatically sought August. He turned to face the long aisle Kelsey would walk up and his gaze pierced hers briefly. Tara's breath caught in her throat. August didn't look worried at all. The confident look he gave her was all she needed.

As expected, Kelsey made her big entrance.

Grand and with a flourish.

Kelsey floated down the aisle to stand between the two men who'd made it to the Last Man Standing round. August was incredibly sexy in his tuxedo, his shaggy blonde hair standing out against the black of the tux.

Smug and self-assured, Kelsey strutted past Tara and the jury in her wedding finery with a smile on her face and Hollywood in her cold, dead heart.

Tara didn't know what to expect next, but August had asked her to trust him and she would. It was all she knew, she had nothing more to go on, but she'd do it because he'd asked her to. What other choice did she have? If the time came and he freaked or looked pressured to marry Kelsey, Tara was going to object--like in a big way. No way was she going to let that viper have *her* man, lawsuits or not.

If she didn't poke Kelsey in the eyes first.

Folding her hands in her lap, Tara breathed deeply, focusing on keeping her cool and looking at anyone but August.

Ms. Mary sat beside her, oddly quiet for someone who'd spent so much time rallying for August. "Psst, Ms. Mary, you okay?"

"Fine, dear, just fine. Weddings make me sentimental for my Josiah is all."

Tara took Ms. Mary's hand and held it, soothing the woman who had become her friend this past month, despite the fact that she had the judgment of a five-year-old when it came to *chemistry*.

Andy leaned over from two chairs down, "I sure hate to see this end, means I have to go home and work."

Tara smiled at him. "You're a nice man, Andy. I've enjoyed getting to know you. You too, Ms. Mary."

As Preston Weichert entered the chapel, all eyes turned to him and the envelope he held in his hand. It contained Kelsey's choice of grooms.

Tara blew out a breath of anxiety and turned toward Preston, awaiting the final chapter of "Whose Bride Is She Anyway?"

* ~ *

August stifled a yawn as Preston did the whole let's keep them in suspense thing. Asking the audience, *whose bride was Kelsey, anyway?* What shocked August even more was the fact that he was as calm as the day was long. He just didn't give a crap anymore--not even with the live audience watching him with bated breath. Kelsey took her place between August and Vinny, linking arms with the both of them.

August thought once more of that really gross rash and cringed inwardly. *C'mon already, let's do this.* Hush, he scolded himself. This was Kelsey's big moment. It wouldn't be nice to spoil it.

Yeah, yeah.

Preston opened the cream-colored envelope and dramatically unfolded the slip of paper inside that Kelsey had prepared prior to the ceremony.

He read the name of the groom with great flourish.

August rocked back on his heels as he heard his name called and wanted to stick his tongue out at Vinny.

Big surprise there.

Kelsey threw her arms around August and kissed him soundly on the mouth.

Oh, yuk!

Preston Weichert shook August's hand with a broad smile and asked him how he felt about being chosen groom number three in the third hit season of "Whose Bride Is She Anyway?"

"I'm thrilled, Preston." *Just peachy.* "But..."

Preston gave August's hand one last congratulatory shake asking him to wait a few more moments to give his answer to Kelsey and then moved discreetly to the left of the set. Curtains went up, revealing a minister with a big, shiny diamond in his hand. One of the camera men zoomed in for a close up of the ring.

Sheesh, it was like the Hope Diamond.

The nice minister handed the ring to August and Kelsey held out her greedy hand to him, awaiting the rock of Gibraltar's new residence with obvious anticipation.

It was now or never.

The muses in his head chanted, *August, August, August!*

The minister asked August to wait once again before answering Kelsey and to face the crowd as the cameras prepared to roll the video, depicting an overview of their courtship.

August's stomach turned as he held his breath and waited for *whatever* was about to happen. Kelsey's fingers dug into August's arm. She no doubt was waiting for her moment in the spotlight with spiteful glee. Leaning into him further, she whispered, "Oh, August we're going to be so happy together..."

August twitched.

Preston's low, hushed voice began a narration of August and Kelsey's first meeting.

A summation of love in bloom.

A big screen popped up behind the pews and each head in the audience turned dutifully to watch. Kelsey snuggled up to August, tucking him close to her confidently as she prepared to watch their supposed romance unfold on tape.

A rhapsody of love in G-minor, it *wasn't.*

All hell broke loose in a rush of life size bodies filling the room on the screen.

Limbs flashed, tangled and woven in unity.

Flesh, in lurid quantities, flew past each eye glued to the screen as low moans reverberated through the chapel.

Sweat glistened on bare asses.

Lewd and lascivious words struck the silence like bullets, spraying out over the gasp-filled air.

Blonde curls, flaxen and perfect--whipped to the frenzied tune in an up and down motion of lust.

Sheets crumpled and fell to the floor, their luxurious four-hundred-thread count cotton forgotten in mind-boggling passion...

And the camera man, George sat on top of them--with Kelsey riding him to victory.

Silence filled the perfumed air as each guest in attendance, all of the camera crew and the jury sat in stunned, motionless disbelief.

Seconds ticked by agonizingly, turning into long, drawn out minutes.

And then the silence turned to a deafening noise as a roar went up in the crowd. Utter chaos ruled when Kelsey fell to the floor in a puddle of white. In slow motion the crew came to life and scattered every which way. Some ran to help Kelsey off the floor, others set about putting out the candles that toppled before a fire broke out--as the press rushed to be the first to get to Kelsey. The rest of the crew did a beeline for the video tape, diving for the tape player in a huddle of bodies. Microphones in all shapes and sizes were shoved in Kelsey's face as she lay on the floor. When she proved non-responsive they headed toward August.

August couldn't move. He was rooted to the spot--his eyes wide with disbelief and his mouth hanging open. He looked over at Tara who sat on the edge of her chair with the same expression. Where the fuck had *that* come from remained unspoken.

Ms. Mary had her hand over her mouth, but her eyes crinkled at the corners. Giovanni, Diana, Andy and Walter all jumped from their seats to try and help, they just couldn't seem to figure out what to help with.

Henry Abernathy stood in a darkened corner, furiously shouting orders as flowers fell and chairs tipped over in the crush of bodies.

* ~ *

Vinny snuck off, throwing himself into the crowd and running with it to the nearest exit, chuckling the entire way. And he'd been worried? Shit, *who's your daddy*?

* ~ *

"August, I'm so sorry. I don't know *who* would do such a thing." Henry Abernathy offered his apologies to August amidst the last of the chaos. The press had been corralled to another part of the island, thankfully.

August did his best to appear devastated, still unsure as to how he and Tara had escaped certain demise at the hands of George. "Thanks, Henry. I'll be all right. I mean what's left after you decide the girl of your high school dreams isn't the love of your life after all? I thought about it long and hard for the past week now and I just couldn't marry her. To see this kind of behavior--on video tape no less ... well, I just don't know what to say, but it helped confirm my belief that Kelsey Little just wasn't the girl for me."

Henry smiled sympathetically. "So you were going to say no to marrying her?"

August nodded and continued, "I thought I'd escaped when Aaron was picked, but then his brother ... well, anyway--when I thought about it last night, I just felt in my heart there was something so wrong in marrying her. Sort of like this distance I couldn't bridge with Kelsey, you know? And now I know *who* that bridge was ... *George.* " August shuddered for effect. God, that was beautiful if he did say so himself.

Henry masked the fleeting anxious glimpse he gave August and smiled once more. His tone held understanding, "Look, August, we're going to make it up to you. I would never have guessed this would happen. We've never had *anyone* not choose to marry the girl. I know you were thrown into this by default because of Aaron's brother, but Kelsey certainly never let on that she *wasn't* interested in you. If you look at all of that video footage of the two of you on your dates she appeared rather besotted. I'm just sorry you were made to participate in it. But you know... the contract and all. Oh, to have the vision of hindsight. I only know that we will make every effort to find out who put that tape in there. It was *utterly* disgusting." Henry shook his head sadly. "How about a vacation on us? Anywhere in the world you want to go."

August sighed. Long and suffering--because he needed to play this right. "Can a vacation make up for losing the woman of my dreams--then finding out she's a--well..." August sighed again. "I think not, Henry."

Oh, August! he chided himself, you are disgraceful. This is just a bit much, don't you think? But still, it was kinda fun...

Henry nodded his head in understanding. "We'll think of something. I promise you. The whole damn season is a waste now. I don't know what we'll do. Although Kelsey's contract allows for *all disclosure...*"

August watched the slick wheels of Henry's mind turn and left it at that. "Thanks, Henry I realize you have no control over such ... such..." August cringed again for effect, "such blatant disregard for the rules of the game. I had no idea this was going on."

"None of us did. Surely, had we known, Kelsey would have been sent packing and so would George. Apparently it was all about the money."

August exhaled, long and deep, keeping his head hung low to hide the gleam in his eyes and his relief that he and Tara hadn't been caught ... yet, anyway. "Money can't buy you love ... I think I'm going to go lay down if you don't mind. I don't feel so well."

Henry's look was filled with concern. "Of course. It's been a trying day for you. Tomorrow this won't seem as awful as it does tonight. Can I get you anything before you go?"

August shook his head slowly, "No, thank you. I'd just like to go now."

Henry gave him one last thump on the back and August ducked out the back door as quickly as possible just as Henry located the elusive cameraman, George. Kelsey sat in a corner alone, tears of fury coursing down her cheeks, leaving big splotches of mascara on her bridal white lap.

Chapter Twenty Nine

Naaa-na-naaaa Naaa-na-naaaa Naaa-na-naaaa! (Work with me) Hear the Charlie's Angels theme song?

August ran a finger around the neck of his bowtie, loosening the tight knot. He tore it off and threw it on the bathroom sink.

"Mr. Guthrie, I'd like an explanation," Tara's voice, smooth as silk, pricked his ears.

"Ms. Douglas, how did you get in here?" He smiled at her reflection in the mirror.

She sauntered over to stand behind him, and the sleek sway of her hips in that black dress gave his cock reason to stand up and cheer. "As jury foreman, I believe it's my duty to console the poor, grieving groom."

Tara slipped her arms under his and kneaded his chest.

"Yes, it's such a tragedy. I don't know if I can be consoled." His mock suffering made even him laugh. Tara's fingers drifted to his swelling cock, rubbing it with the heel of her hand.

"There will be no consolation until you tell me what the hell *that* was all about back at the chapel." Turning, she unzipped her dress and shimmied out of it. "However, I think a real pity party is headed your way, courtesy of me, if you give it up."

Tara threw the dress at him and wandered naked into the bedroom.

August followed close behind, peeling his clothes off. He grabbed her by the waist and nuzzled her neck. "Well, last night, I went to talk to Vinny after I left you. I made him an offer to help pay off his gambling debts if he'd just gamble this one last time that Kelsey would pick me. So he gave me the pictures and whatever else I could wrangle out of him. Then I went to find George, who was conveniently absent." Cupping her breasts, he grazed the soft underside of them.

Tara turned in his arms and wrapped her own around his neck, kissing his jaw in soft nips. His cock brushed her belly, straining toward the silk of her skin. "An offer? What kind of an offer would you make him? He's slime, August."

August slipped his fingers into the warmth of her pussy, fondling her slowly. She purred in response. "Yeah, but he's also desperate and in order to make sure he didn't show those pictures of us to the producers, I was going to give him the money to clear up his debts."

Tara's face held disbelief as did her tone. "August Guthrie! Are you insane? How much does he owe? And ... and..." her face took on a softer look. "You would do that for me?"

August pressed his lips to hers, lingering gently on the soft surface. When he pulled away he looked her square in the eye and said, "Well, yeah, silly woman. And Vinny owes a lot too, just in case you doubted my sincerity."

Tara kissed him back, hugging him closer to her. "Thank you, but I can't let you do that. If Vinny went to the producers

I'd just deal with it. Now I guess neither of you have to worry. But I think Kelsey and George might."

"I don't have to *give* the money to Vinny, honey. He's going to come and work for me, in an office I want to open in California. He'll *earn* back the money he borrows from me. Believe me, he was more than willing to find somewhere safe to keep hiding from his bookies." He nuzzled her neck and nipped at her ear.

"Still, what does that have to do with what happened tonight?" Tara wondered aloud as she wrapped her hands over his cock and stroked him.

"I have no clue. I only know Vinny said okay to my offer and we were square. I couldn't find George and I sure as hell wasn't looking for Kelsey. As the 'wedding' drew closer I just prayed George would keep his mouth shut. I was gonna do my part and dump Kelsey at the altar and deal with the fallout later. The press usually harasses only the last two men left, but if I said no to Kelsey, Vinny was pretty much home free. The press would be too busy looking into why I said no to a million bucks. I didn't figure it would be easy, but I know what the truth is and that was all that mattered. I'd have found a place for us to be in peace somehow. I just kept telling myself that eventually a new season would start and they'd forget about us."

A sharp rap on the door had them both whipping around guiltily as Tara shot August a look of fear before scrambling as fast as she could back to the bathroom. August put his finger to his lips as he followed her, grabbing his shirt and pants he threw them on, hurrying to open the door.

"Ms. Mary?" August said, surprised and hopefully keeping the thread of guilt out of his voice. "Are you okay? Do you need something? Is everything all right with the grandbaby?"

Ms. Mary's face was unreadable as she pushed her way past August and peered inside the room.

August felt it. She *knew* ... they were still fucked.

Ms. Mary cackled a sharp laugh as she followed close behind him. Her grey eyes twinkled. "Yeah, everything's fine. That's not why I'm here. I have a little something to tell you. So tell Tara to come out from wherever she's hiding and get her butt out here too."

August waffled, shuffling his feet and scratching his head, he avoided Ms. Mary's eyes. "I have no clue what you mean. Tara isn't here. I haven't seen her since I left the chapel. Why would I see her? I mean she's a juror and that's against the rules, we could be sued for that. I can't afford to be sued. It costs a lot of money and I have a business--with employees and..."

" Tell Tara to come out here and stop dilly dallying. I have to get back before Henry has a nervous breakdown."

Tara poked her head around the corner of the closet door. She'd thrown on one of August's shirts and was looking down at her feet. "Um, Ms. Mary? First, I want to apologize and tell you that August didn't do anything wrong. I made him ... well, I didn't exactly *make* him, I--well, I just--we just sort of..."

Ms. Mary held up her hand and Tara bit her lower lip, waiting for the axe to fall.

August came to stand beside her. "Look, I'll take complete responsibility for this. Tara tried to talk me out of it, but I wouldn't quit chasing after her. So go ahead and tell whomever you like, Ms. Mary. I'm in love with Tara and I don't care who knows it."

August thrust his jaw out and wrapped his arm around Tara.

"Oh, I'm not going to tell anybody anything," Ms. Mary assured them. "That diva got what she deserved in spades. I *am* going to tell you that I'm the one who put that video tape in there and why and then I'm going to let you get back to what you two seem to do best."

"What!?" Tara and August shouted in unison.

Ms. Mary shuffled to the bedside chair and eyed them both. Folding her hands she smiled cattily. "Kelsey Little is responsible for the death of my Josiah. I can't prove it, but I sure as hell wanted to see her pay for it."

Tara went to Ms. Mary's side and held her hand with a frown. "I don't get what you mean. Kelsey hurt Josiah? How?"

Ms. Mary shook her head, a forlorn smile curling the edges of her mouth. "She didn't *physically* hurt him, she swindled him out of money at that ad agency she works for with her cute act. As a result, the stress of losing so much money killed Josiah."

Tara rubbed Ms. Mary's hand. "I don't understand. I thought Josiah worked in pharmaceuticals?"

"He did and he wanted to start a campaign to boost sales for our family-owned pharmacy. So the boys would have something when we were gone. It was a small-town place and the bigger corporations were taking over. Josiah thought it was a wise business decision. I thought he was cracked and I was right! I just wanted to retire and live in peace. Do the grandmother thing, you know? But he wouldn't let it go and then he met Kelsey..." Mary smirked and gave a snort. "We lost some of our retirement fund so she could have breast implants... Her plastic surgeon prescribes drugs from our store. When I saw her name on the prescription, I just knew where our money went. So I hooked up on the internet and did a little hacking into her accounts... And that's all I'll say. Josiah became so ill because we couldn't really prove where the money went. Josiah trusted far too easily and well, it's complicated--how Kelsey got her hands on our money, but ... it pissed me off when I figured it all out!" Ms. Mary's face turned hard. "I won't go into the details, suffice it to say, nobody messes with my Josiah. In life or death. When Kelsey tried out for the show, it was just sheer luck that I happen to be a big fan of 'Whose Bride Is She Anyway?' and saw her face plastered all over that website... So I tried out for the jury and they picked me. I was only going to let her know *who* I was and watch her squirm because I knew all of her secrets. She never even batted an eye when she heard my last name. What kind of a woman steals an old fool's money and doesn't remember his last name?"

Tara and August looked at one another with complete understanding as August put a consoling hand on Ms. Mary's shoulder. "I'm sorry, Ms. Mary. Kelsey isn't the woman I thought she would be. I should have never come on this show. But I can't regret it because I met Tara and I wouldn't change that."

Tara smiled up at him and he winked at her.

Ms. Mary cackled again. "Hah! Do you know why I came here tonight to see you two?"

They shook their heads no in unison while Tara visibly gulped.

"Because I'm a real Charlie's Angel... I'm a plant!" Mary clapped her hands and laughed loudly as she watched both Tara and August's faces. "The producers sent me in to be a spy. Guess they figured nobody would suspect an old lady. So they gave me one of those fancy little spy-cams and sent me on late-night excursions to spy on the contestants and Kelsey. I'm whooped from all the shenanigans going on around here. Can't say I was too upset over you two hooking up, either. Not one bit. Kelsey deserved what she got from you, Tara. Guess she was just as ornery back in high school, huh?"

"You know about what Kelsey did to me?" Tara asked astonished.

Mary winked. "I know everything, kiddo. I've had access to things the rest of you haven't on this island. Like the internet--all under the guise of being a plant. I found a friend or two of Kelsey's who were pretty snockered over not being picked as jury foreman. They spilled the dirt on what she did to you, Tara and I spilled it to George last night because I knew what he and Kelsey were doing and I knew he'd want to impress Henry. He's a suck up and Henry loves controversy. I also needed to buy time to put that damn tape in the machine, you know. So it would be ready for today's wedding. I knew George would never have the chance to show the tape he'd made of the two of you because I'd get it first. He's stupid enough to leave that camera lying around every night, so I snatched it. Who would suspect me anyway? I am, after all, the one who gave him the dirt on you, Tara."

Tara gripped August's hand and looked down at her feet.

Ms. Mary gave Tara a sympathetic smile. "I'm sorry I let him barge in on the two of you like that at the cove, and I'm just sorry you had to find out about what happened to Tara that way, August. It was Tara's story to tell you, but I had to keep you two out of trouble somehow."

Tara's face became slack with disbelief as it all sunk in. "You told George? You have the tape of August and me?"

Mary patted Tara's hand. "Yep. It's destroyed. It'll never see the light of day and yes, I told George about the locker room, Tara. I told you I had to find a way to get him away from that damn chapel long enough to get the tape in there. The *wrong* tape. Kelsey was only yanking George's crank anyway. She didn't care who she married. Though, I'm sure she would have preferred August over Vinny. She just wanted the money and she wanted George to help her make connections in Hollywood."

Mary smiled. "And don't you worry about George telling anyone about you and Kelsey, Tara. I think the press will have bigger plans for him now that he's been caught breaking the show's strict hands-off-the-players rule, but he's got to adhere to a strict confidentiality clause too. He's in deep enough as it is. I can't make any promises about some of those girls you went to high school with, though. You two better lay low for awhile just to be safe, though I'd sure like to see Kelsey's face when she finds out August ended up with you, my girl!"

August's mind raced as he began to put it all together while Tara didn't move a muscle, remaining motionless. He was the first to speak, and his voice was rough on its way out. "I think I speak for Tara, as well as myself when I say you go ahead and do what you have to do for the show, Ms. Mary. You can tell them all about us if they make you because of the contract. I still don't regret it." August's jaw twitched.

Ms. Mary chuckled softly. "After everything I just told you, do you really think I give a darn that Tara stole you right out from under Kelsey's stuck-up nose? I can tell you I sure as heck didn't think I'd ever catch her with George, but I got lucky and caught them red-handed! I'm not giving you two up and if George ever leaks a word of this thing between you, I'll deny I ever saw a thing and I'm just the person to do that. The girls I contacted from your old high school think I'm a reporter from a made-up paper. I've tied up all of my loose ends," she said smugly.

"But wait," Tara interjected, holding her hand up. "How can the show possibly be happy about all of this controversy? It's going to look really bad isn't it?"

Ms. Mary just smiled slyly. "Economics, kiddo. They don't have to pay out the money if no one marries Kelsey, now do they? I saw Henry acting all sympathetic with you, August, but he knew all along something was going to happen. He just didn't know *what*. Henry told me to keep it to myself and I did. I told him I had something big and that was all. Henry was as surprised as you were, even if he did know I had *something* on Kelsey."

August expelled a gust of air and smiled wryly. "So you were the one who gave Kelsey that rash weren't you? And the runs?"

Tara shook her head in disbelief. "Ms. Mary, *you* gave Kelsey that rash? I can't believe the producers would let you do something like that."

August nodded, "And the shoe incident too?"

"Hey, I'm no dummy. I took some liberties with my spy status and I'm not ashamed to say I did. The producers didn't need to know about it ... I got a hold of Kelsey's application and found out she's allergic to Niacinimide. Better known as B-3, a vitamin you can get in any *pharmacy*. I crushed it up and put it in her fruit drink. Instant rash," Mary snickered. "I would never do something to harm her forever, but I wouldn't be a good Christian woman if I didn't admit I thought about it. Good thing this ended when it did. I was going to turn her hair green next.

"Oh, my God!" Tara howled. "I'm sorry, I shouldn't be laughing, but I have to know... The runs?"

Ms. Mary shot them a look of satisfaction. "Laxatives in chocolate bars. Don't even ask about the shoe. Just remember Ms. Mary isn't such an old coot."

"But how could you possibly know Kelsey would sleep with George?" Tara questioned.

Mary snorted again, "I didn't, but my instincts told me that Kelsey was a hussy at heart and so I followed her around just like I was supposed to. It was just more luck on my part to find that Kelsey and George were doing the bump and grind."

"Oh, Ms. Mary. How did you get them on tape?" Tara was picturing Ms. Mary knee deep in palm trees, hiding behind potted plants.

"I didn't do that either, George did that all on his own, seems George likes to *watch*." Ms. Mary said smugly. "I just happened on that. Kelsey showed the world what a harlot she is and I didn't have to help her one iota."

"Henry knew?" August exclaimed again, still unable to wrap his brain around the notion.

Ms. Mary huffed. "Of course he did."

August scratched his head. He was looking forward to getting back to a simpler way of living. No more glitz.

"Okay, kiddies," Ms. Mary slapped her legs. "I have to get back and you can't breathe a word of this. Hear me? Now before I leave, what I wanna know is--what the hell were you going to do at that altar, August Guthrie?"

August made a face and figured it was best not to tell Mary about Vinny. Though, as crafty as she was proving herself to be, she probably already knew. "Turn Kelsey down, of course. I couldn't leave the game because Aaron did, but I would have left a long time ago if I could have."

Ms. Mary squeezed August's hand, "Nah, you didn't want to leave Tara and I don't blame you. I thought Josiah and I were bad when we were first married, but you two take the cake! I don't think I've ever seen so much motion in the ocean!"

Tara's cheeks stained with color. "So you aren't going to turn us in?"

"Now why the heck would I do that? You made the spying thing easy for me. I always knew where you and this hunk were. It was two less people to keep track of as far as I was concerned," she chuckled.

"What about Kelsey? Won't she sue for defamation or something? That was a pretty graphic video tape." Tara said.

"Um, no, I don't think so. That Kelsey signed her soul away to the devil when she signed onto this show. It's airtight and chock full of disclaimers if Kelsey was caught at anything unethical. I doubt they'll show the whole thing on national television, but you can be sure they'll have snippets..."

"You know Ms. Mary..." August said, before trailing off for a moment. "Why did you keep voting for me if you wanted to get back at Kelsey? I don't think I've ever done something so horrible that I deserved her."

"Didn't matter *who* I voted for, August. I had that tape of Kelsey and George day three of the show. The moment it was played at the wedding she would have been eliminated, so even if you did want to marry her, you'd have done it *without* the chance for a million bucks. Like you kids say, payback's a bitch ... she took Josiah's money, I took hers." Mary had a faraway look in her eyes as she continued, "But I also wanted to know if you'd fight for your woman, August. Tara's a good girl and she deserves a nice man who'll fight for her. A man just like you--*a hunky* man just like you." Ms. Mary wiggled her eyebrows.

She rose and hugged Tara, then August. "Pay attention to me. I want you both to keep in touch with me and keep your mouths shut. Okay?"

Tara began to tear up. "I'll miss you Ms. Mary."

"Yeah, yeah. Me too. Oh, and one more thing. That Vinny, I'm pretty sure he's gay too. He skedaddled out of that chapel like there was a ball of fire hot on his ass. You watch out for him. Bye, lovebirds." She sniffed and headed out the door.

August turned to Tara. She had the same look of shock that August was sure he wore.

Tara giggled suddenly, “Well, Mr. Guthrie, this has been quite a day, wouldn’t you say?”

“Yep and now for the consolation thing...” Wiggling his eyebrows, he threw her back on the bed and had his wicked way with her.

* ~ *

Tara smoothed the lacy negligee over her hips, pausing at how utterly ludicrous it was to even put it on. August never noticed these futile attempts at femininity. He liked her naked and, well ... naked.

Sighing, Tara rubbed the last of the cream over her arms and opened the window to their suite. She savored the rush of the tide rolling in and the clean, salty air.

“Ahem, Ms. Douglas, come and sit by me. *Now.*”

Hands on hips, she strode to the bed, where he lay completely naked. “You know, Mr. Guthrie, you are awfully demanding for a naked guy. Notice, I am *not* naked.”

“Yep.”

Tara pouted, “Don’t you have anything to say about how pretty I look?”

“Very nice. Take it *off.*”

She clucked her tongue at him as she wiggled out of the nightie. “There, happy?”

August winked at her. “Eternally. Now, c’mere.”

She swung her legs over his hips and smiled down at him. His thick cock pressed against her ass, hot and ready. “It’s beautiful here, August, don’t you think?”

He caressed the swell of her hips with his hands. “Yep.”

She leaned into him, letting the warmth seep into her skin. “Not that we’d know that, I only get glimpses of the beach from the window." Leaning back, she rested her hands on his thighs. Her breasts pushed forward enticingly. and he cupped them, thumbing her nipples to stiff peaks.

"We'll go to the beach tomorrow."

Her head fell back on her shoulders as she arched into his caress. "That's what you said three days ago."

August propped himself up on the pillows and pulled her to him. He rested his head on her upper arm and began to tease a nipple with long, hot strokes. Her hands found the familiar place in his hair that she ritualistically clung to when he did this. She ran her nails over his scalp, moving her hips with a slow roll. "Tomorrow, I promise," he whispered.

Her fingers slipped inside the cavern of his mouth, chasing his tongue as he suckled the tight bud. "Oh, August ... we will not. I'm beginning to think there was some merit to my observation that I am nothing but a sex toy to you."

Chuckling, he pressed the globes of creamy flesh together and lapped them. The sway of her hips became more rapid as heat slithered between her thighs. "Do you have objections to being my sex toy?" he asked, lifting her to place her hips flush with his mouth. Sliding down, he lay between her thighs, letting his hot breath linger over her heated flesh. The sight of his blond head between her legs never failed to make her heart pound and her nerve endings sizzle with anticipation.

Tara rocked forward, needy as always, anticipating his tongue, holding her breath for the first lick. "I guess it depends on what being a sex toy entails."

His hands ran over her ass, pulling her closer, teasing the outer lips of her pussy with light kisses. Nibbling at her, he answered, "It entails this," he swiped her swollen clit, circling it with slow precision.

She gasped, welcoming the slick slide of his tongue. "Oh," she moaned, thrusting her hips for more. "Maybe being a sex toy isn't so bad after all..." A thick finger slipped between her folds, finding the entrance to her tight passage. Her hands drifted to her pussy, one latched onto his wrist as he worked his finger in her, the other caressed the nub he laved, stroking herself as he stroked her too. His hot tongue took pass after pass, spreading her flesh, making her dizzy from the rush of electricity he created.

Panting, she rode his finger and tongue, arching into him, rolling her hips at the friction of his calloused digit and his burning mouth. Her hands found his head, crushing it to her when the first wave of orgasm crashed against her needy pussy.

August always knew what to do, thrusting into her with just the right amount of force, licking her with fevered strokes until she screamed his name, release crashing through her. And always, he rode her orgasm until it was complete, lessening his tongue's caress in small increments.

Clutching his hair, she tugged him upward, then flipped their positions. Sitting astride him again she found the firm line of his lips. Her mouth sought his, and their tongues tangled. She suckled it in simulation of things to come, wrapping her lips around it, savoring the taste of herself. Wrapping his arms around her, he pressed her tightly to him, "Not such a bad thing, this sex toy gig, huh?"

She chuckled into his mouth, taking one last taste of him. "I guess it's okay."

Cupping her ass, he squeezed the flesh, kneading it as his cock pressed urgently against it. Reaching around her, she grasped it, gliding over the hard surface. "Just okay? Where have I gone wrong?"

"I don't think gone wrong is the right phrase..." Swinging her legs off him, she turned toward his reclining body and straddled him. She brought his hands around to cup her breasts as she leaned forward and took his cock in both hands. He jerked beneath her when she made contact. Lovingly, she stroked him as his fingers worked her nipples.

Leaning forward on her elbows, she brought her lips to his thick shaft. She came up on her knees and he groaned, low and throbbing. "Tell me what you want, August..."

He shifted, lifting his hips, "You..."

Her tongue slithered over him, a mere whisper of a caress. "Nothing else?" she teased him, raising her ass high in the air, knowing he saw the lips of her pussy, still wet from his tongue.

Gripping her thighs, his words were carnal and delicious to her ears. "I want you to lick me, baby. Suck my cock ... *now*, before I explode, while I bury my face in your pussy again."

Tara yielded to his wishes, taking him all at once into the warmth of her mouth. August muttered from up above as she laved his thick cock, running her tongue in long strokes over the length of him. Working her hands in a gentle twisting motion, she sucked and pumped him at the same time. Using her legs as leverage, he scooted down toward her ass and lifted his hips toward her mouth, thrusting forcefully between her lips. He wrapped his hand around her waist and pulled her back to his mouth.

Rolling a bit to their sides, they clung to one another. August buried his face between her thighs and Tara continued to bathe his smooth cock with her tongue. He ran his tongue between the lips of her pussy. She let hers lap at the sensitive area below the head of his cock. Their rhythm was frenzied as their mouths, wet and frantic, pleasured one another. Pressed tightly together, Tara arched into August's mouth, taking his cock with her in an upward tug. Their ribs crashed together as they panted, arms tightly woven around each other's legs, Tara came again and August tensed, his body taut against hers. Her nipples scraped his skin, beading tightly in aching need.

August pulled away first, scrambling upright and dragging her with him. He positioned himself behind her, and her thighs automatically wound around his as she pressed her ass firmly into his abdomen, begging him silently to ram his cock into her.

She thought of nothing else but the instant pleasure it would bring the moment he entered her. He wasted no time, plunging with force into the tight warmth, filling her until they both gasped at the impact. His hands roamed her body freely, fevered and tantalizing. "Don't move baby," she groaned at his request, wanting nothing more than to jam her hips down on him.

He fondled her clit. "Do you feel how hard I am for you?" Rolling his hips for emphasis, he stroked in and out of her once. "Do you, Tara?"

Her arms went up around his neck and her back bowed. Pulling his lips to her ear, she thrust her breasts into the cool air of the room. "Yes, I feel it."

"Tell me what you want, baby..."

A thrill shot through her cunt whenever he asked her what she wanted. "I want you to fuck me. Fuck me hard, please, August ... this time, I don't think I can wait."

Stroking her, he licked the shell of her ear, still unmoving. "What can't you wait for?" The low rasp of his voice mesmerized her, beckoned her to play the game they shared often, but she never tired of.

She ground her hips, savoring the thick cock between her legs, lifting a bit away from him, only to press back down hard on his shaft. "I can't wait for your cock, August. I can't wait for you to slide in and out of me, make me come..."

"Christ, Tara ... you get better at this every time. Your words make me insane..."

A satisfied smile spread over her lips. "Then do it, because now, if I don't come, *I'll* explode. Fuck me, with your hand between my legs and your cock in my pussy."

He grunted and let go, burying his face in her shoulder, plunging into her hard. She clung to his neck, riding the force of his thrusts, slick and wet. His teeth grazed her skin, fingers toying with her clit. Relaxing into his thrusts, she felt his balls slap her ass, driving his cock further and further into her wet passage.

A spiral of delicious heat began low in her belly, rising to cling between her legs, forcing a howl of triumph from her lips when she tightened her muscles and came in a long shudder. Hot spurts of his seed flowed in her. He twitched with the onslaught of orgasm, jerking against her, pressing her into the bed.

Tara slowly relaxed against him, caressing the arms that held her, savoring the thick muscle and tight embrace.

"Damn, woman..."

"Is that all you have to say for yourself, August Guthrie? Damn, woman?"

His nose tickled her ear, "Well, do you think now is a good time to mention we forgot a condom?"

"Then, I do believe you'll have to make an honest woman of me, August Guthrie."

Rubbing her nipples, he huffed, "Oh, all right, I guess if I have to."

Tara brought his finger to her mouth and nipped it, "No, you don't *have* to, but I don't suppose you'd like it much if I told the tabloids about our 'love child', would you? Don't make me resort to blackmail, Mr. Guthrie."

Twisting her head around, he chuckled, kissing her. They'd been hounded for a time, shortly after the news broke about the show's fiasco. "I might have to deny those allegations, Ms. Douglas and tell them it's George's 'love child'."

"Euuueww. Not on your life, buddy. So, what day shall I circle on my calendar?"

Gently pulling out of her, he pulled her up and carried her into the bathroom, turning the shower on. "A day? I have to name a day? That's like a commitment."

Tara slapped his ass as she climbed in the shower behind him. "Yep. There will be no more nookie till you take the plunge, and you better ask nicely."

Standing under the hard spray of the water, he grinned at her, "Then I insist for the future of all our potential geeky kids, that you, Tara Douglas be my wife. Now come closer so we can talk about this getting hitched thing."

She soaped his chest, lingering on the hard lines of his abdomen. "Talk? Hah! I know what you want to *talk* about. First, you have to tell me that you love me."

He tilted her jaw up and kissed her lips, "Jeez, you want it all don't you, you demanding wench. Okay," he mocked reluctance, "Tara Douglas, I love you."

"A lot? Or only a little?"

Dropping kisses on her wet eyelids he chuckled, "A lot. More than my tuba, even."

Sighing against his lips, she replied, "Oh, that is heavy. All girls want to be cherished more than a tuba. I guess I love you too, August Guthrie and I'll consent to be your wife on one condition."

"You *guess* you love me?"

"You *know* I do." It went without saying.

He pulled her tightly to him. "Um, what's the condition?"

"That you promise we'll always have talks like these." She tugged at his hardening cock.

His hands molded her to him, “I think that just might be a promise I can keep. Now, shut up and let’s talk.”

Leaning against him, she laughed, “I like the way you talk...”

Epilogue

What comes around...

Vinny Lambati went into hiding in California shortly after the final taping of “Whose Bride Is She Anyway?”. A recent tabloid report rumored him paired with the show’s former producer, Henry Abernathy. The last Vinny/Henry sighting was at a trendy L.A. coffee shop, where it’s said that Henry now sports a tattoo on his upper arm that reads, “*I’m* the Daddy.”

Aaron Caldwell still calls California his home. His brother recuperated quite nicely from his surfing accident and the brothers can often be seen buddy surfing together. Aaron found the girl of his dreams and they are now “hanging ten” for life together in the beach house they call home, sharing it with their dog “Dude”.

Andy, Diana, Walter and Gianni banded together and formed a support group for survivors of reality television.

Mary DeWitt rang in the New Year with a beautiful new grandson, weighing in at eight pounds, six ounces. Her son says that the newborn has grown so quickly he'll soon be able to wear the booties grandma made. She staunchly denied Kelsey's allegations that she tried to poison her with homemade chocolate bars, claiming she hated to cook and would much rather be knitting.

Kelsey Little's last recorded interview found her in an isolated area of Idaho, with George the cameraman and his live-in mother, who suffers from bouts of senility. Reports claim that George's mother adores Kelsey, often calling her by pet names like, "cellulite riddled bitch" and "video vixen". George and Kelsey can often be found enjoying the splendor of the great outdoors together, as they frolic each morning, mucking out the pigpens and horse stalls.

August and Tara were married on a clear, blue, cloudless day in their hometown of Colorado, six months after the end of "Whose Bride Is She Anyway?". Rumor has it their marriage remains strong due to the amount of time they spend *talking* to one another. August proudly declares that he and the new Mrs. Guthrie are expecting their very first little geek in the spring. The happy couple maintains their motto that "Geeks Rule".

THE END

About the Author:

Dakota Cassidy, ex Jersey housewife and grocery list writer phenom turned her love of a good laugh out loud into a career just two and a half years ago. Her writing career began on a whim and continues in just that way. Dakota writes in every genre, but never without a sense of humor.

She resides in Texas where she met the man of her dreams and lives with her two boys, two dogs, two cats and just one mom--in a house she fondly calls Castle Cassidy. Dakota loves to chat with her readers. E-mail her at Dakota@dakotacassidy.com and see if that isn't the truth!

Resolutions

4 ½ Stars Top Pick - Romantic Times BookClub

A Losing Proposition - Vanessa Hart
Free Fall - Jasmine Haynes
For Sale by Owner - Leigh Wyndfield
That Scottish Spring - Dee S. Knight

More Contemporary Romances from LSB...

Love Lessons

Vanessa Hart

When solid friendship and passion collide, love is inevitable. This is the unexpected lesson for Wendy and Scott when she agrees to tutor him in the bedroom so he can try to win back his wayward wife.

Impatient Passion

Dee S. Knight

A few day off turning thirty-five and life sucks. Austin needs to make big changes. When an anonymous stranger pulls her close on the bus, she chooses to indulge. Austin isn't anonymous to Tyler though. He's waited long enough, now it's time to claim the woman he's yearned for.

Club Belle Tori

Michelle Hoppe

These two have it all, in spades. Jason Hunter has it all, in diamonds. Tori Lane has it all, in clubs. When their two best friends shuffle them together, can the millionaire and the pleasure palace owner have it all together, in hearts? Book I of the Club Belle Tori trilogy deals romance, passion, sexuality … and wild cards.

Evening Star

Rita Sable

When Lilly takes a one-night job posing as an escort at a millionaire's party, she finds out that Gabe is more than she can handle...and everything she wants in a man.

One Touch

Susie Charles

For Jake Reilly, one touch was all it took, and now he wants more, much more. Now Cassie's unrequited love for him is getting requited—real quick! When he discovers her secret, can he ever forgive her and will their growing feelings be strong enough to survive it?

Single Station

Rebecca Williams

Rory McKenna is no farm boy. He's too pretty for one thing and his approach to seduction is out of this world. Rory takes Samantha places she never knew existed. How far can a farm girl go before it's too late to come back?

Racing Hearts

Rae Monet

Cassandra's beauty is matched only by her raw driving talent and ambition. Stock car legend Justin is in financial straits. A perfect setup for a tycoon desperate to revive her cosmetics empire. Too desperate—can Justin keep Cassandra alive long enough for their passion to blossom?

Undressing Mercy

Deanna Lee

Tricked into posing for Shamus, Mercy finds both her career and her body in his very capable hands. Soon Shamus realizes that his interest is far more personal than professional, and he's breaking his own rules and discovering that there is something very different about undressing Mercy